CLAY AND THE
RIVER OF SILVER

CLAY AND THE RIVER OF SILVER

BY

PHILIP K ALLAN

Clay and the River of Silver by Philip K Allan
Copyright © 2024 Philip K Allan

All rights reserved. No part of this book may be reproduced, or stored in a retrieval system, or transmitted in any form or by any means, electronic, mechanical, photocopying, recording, or otherwise, without express written permission of the author, except for the inclusion of brief quotations in a review.

ISBN-13: 9798328188555

Cover design by Christine Horner from original art by Colin M Baxter
Edited by Richard Sheehan

Dedication

To Susie Fleming (1959 – 2024)

A dear friend taken too soon

Acknowledgements

My Alexander Clay series was born out of a passion for ships and the sea, which was first awakened when I discovered the works of C S Forester and Douglas Reeman as a child, before later graduating to the novels of Patrick O'Brian. That interest was given some academic rigor when I studied the 18th century navy under Patricia Crimmin as part of my history degree at London University.

Many years later, I decided to leave my career in the motor industry to see if I could survive as a writer. I received the unconditional support and cheerful encouragement of my darling wife and two wonderful daughters. I first test my work to see if I have hit the mark with my family, especially my wife Jan, whose input is invaluable.

One of the pleasures of my new career is the generous support and encouragement I received from my fellow writers. In theory we are in competition, but you would never know it. When I have needed help, advice and support, I have received it from Bernard Cornwell, David Donachie, Ian Drury, Helen Hollick, Marc Liebman and Jeffrey K Walker. I have received particular help from my good friends Alaric Bond, creator of the Fighting Sail series of books and Chris Durbin, author of the Carlisle & Holbrooke Naval Adventures.

The production of *Clay and the River of Siver* was the work of several hands. I would like to thank Richard Sheehan for his excellent and thoughtful editing; Christine Horner from Open Book Design for the cover and the talented marine artist Colin M Baxter for another beautiful piece of art. Readers interested in exploring Colin's work further can find his details at the back of this volume.

I will always be in debt to Michael James and the team at Penmore Press, for having enough faith in me to publish my first seven novels.

Cast of Main Characters

The Crew of the Frigate *Griffin*

Alexander Clay – Captain RN

George Taylor – First lieutenant
Edward Preston – Second lieutenant
William Russell – Third lieutenant
Thomas Macpherson – Lieutenant or Marines
Jacob Armstrong – Sailing master
Charles Faulkner – Purser

Nathaniel Hutchinson – Boatswain

Able Sedgwick – Captain's coxswain

Sean O'Malley – Able seaman
Adam Trevan – Able seaman
Samuel Evans – Seaman
Edward Pembleton – Landsman

In Lower Staverton

Lydia Clay – Wife of Alexander Clay
Francis and Elizabeth Clay – Their children
Lady Mary Ashton – Lydia's aunt and adopted mother

The Cape Expedition

Home Riggs Popham – Captain RN
David Baird – Lieutenant-general
William Beresford – Brigadier-general, his deputy
Denis Pack – Lieutenant-colonel
George Gillespie – Captain, Royal Marines

In Buenos Aires

Juan Martin de Pueyrredon – A merchant and landowner
Juan José Antonio Castelli – A lawyer and civil servant
Manuel Belgrano – A lawyer and captain of the city militia
Rafael de Sobremonte – Viceroy of the Rio de la Plata

Others

Nicholas Vansittart – A diplomat
Jan Willem Janssens - Dutch Governor of Cape Colony

Contents

Prologue

Chapter 1 Home

Chapter 2 Preparations

Chapter 3 Madeira

Chapter 4 The Skeleton Coast

Chapter 5 Invasion

Chapter 6 The Battle of Blaauwberg

Chapter 7 The *Volontaire*

Chapter 8 The Spark

Chapter 9 Buenos Aires

Chapter 10 The River of Silver

Chapter 11 New Arcadia

Chapter 12 Perdiel

Chapter 13 Death by a Thousand Cuts

Chapter 14 Barricades

Chapter 15 Assault

Chapter 16 Night

Chapter 17 Escape

Chapter 18 Dawn

Epilogue

Philip K Allan

Prologue

On a winter evening a carriage drawn by four bay horses came to a halt outside the imposing facade of White's Club in London. Two bewigged doormen emerged from the entrance, one holding an umbrella against the falling rain, while the other opened the carriage door.

'Much obliged,' said the Honourable Nicholas Vansittart as he emerged and hurried towards the welcome glow shining out from the main door. Once safely in the lobby, he shed his cloak and hat to the porter, revealing a sandy-haired man in his early forties, dressed in the very height of fashion. 'My thanks, Foster,' he said. 'Pray tell me, has Captain Popham arrived yet?'

'He is waiting for you in the library, sir,' said the porter. 'Along with a Spanish gentleman. He particularly asked for somewhere you were unlikely to be disturbed.'

'Then the library was an excellent choice,' observed Vansittart. 'I doubt if most of the members even know of its existence.' He glanced towards the club's card room, crowded with men in black evening dress or the scarlet of the army, the air thick with cigar smoke.

'Indeed sir,' said Foster. 'And I sent Jeffries there to serve you. He is most discreet.'

'Splendid. Kindly see that we are not interrupted.'

'Right you are, sir.'

The library door was heavy oak and cut off the noise

Clay and the River of Silver

from the rest of the club as Vansittart closed it behind him. The glow from the fire mixed with candlelight played across the ranks of leather-bound volumes lining the walls.

Two men rose from the wingbacked chairs grouped around the fireplace. The first was a bustling man of medium height in the blue and white of the Royal Navy. He had a prominent dimple on his chin and regarded the new arrival with pale, hooded eyes. 'Ah, there you are,' said Captain Home Riggs Popham. 'May I introduce you to Mr Juan Martin de Pueyrredon?'

The captain's companion was a tall, gaunt-looking man with a long face and dark eyes framed by thin sideburns. He gave a stiff bow towards Vansittart. 'It is an honour to meet with such an influential man, *señor*,' he said in good, if heavily accented English.

'I not sure what Captain Popham has been telling you,' said Vansittart. 'I am only a humble lawyer, but pray let us be seated, gentlemen. Jeffries, these glasses need refilling, and I'll take some of the madeira.'

'Only a lawyer, *señor*?' queried Pueyrredon, with a smile. 'I understood you to be a member of your British Parliament.'

'True. I do have the honour to represent the good people of Hastings, wearisome as the task can sometimes prove,' he conceded.

'Don't be fooled by his modesty,' snorted Popham. 'He is also an accomplished diplomat who has the ear of the cabinet and a finger in every pie.'

'I wouldn't put it quite like that,' said Vansittart, brushing at some imagined fluff on his britches. 'But tell me of yourself, *señor*. I understand you to be a Spanish merchant?'

'A merchant, yes, and also a substantial landowner. But

Philip K Allan

I am from Buenos Aires, not Spain. It is a major city on the Atlantic coast of South America. In the Viceroyalty of the Rio de la Plata.'

'Which makes you a Spanish citizen, does it not?' observed the diplomat. 'Forgive my persistence on this point, but I am obliged to establish your status. Particularly as this country is at war with Spain.'

'Then to you I am a Spanish citizen,' conceded Pueyrredon. 'But of a lesser kind, for I was born in the colony. In Madrid they name us Creoles and bar us from all the senior positions in the colonial government. It is one of many grievances we have.'

'Nature knows no fury like a colonial scorned,' commented Vansittart. 'But I interrupted you. You were speaking of your grievances, sir.'

'Like many of my fellow South Americans, I find the rule of Madrid unjust, designed only to benefit the mother country. Spain only wishes to maintain the flow of tax revenue and bullion from the New World back to the Old, rather than the sound governance and development of her possessions. Meanwhile the progress enjoyed by the rest of the world sadly passes us by. Take my own position as a man of business. Trade rules that date from the time of the discoveries mean that my ships are only permitted to trade with certain ports in Spain, and can only return with Spanish-made goods. I would dearly like to buy the products made by the excellent manufacturers to be found in your country, but the law forbids it.'

'Surely you also receive the benefits of Spanish protection?' said Vansittart.

'We did, while Spain had a navy,' said Pueyrredon. 'But your Admiral Nelson destroyed much of it at Trafalgar. And now I face ruin, because your Royal Navy controls the sea. I

Clay and the River of Silver

cannot export the produce of my land and my merchantmen can be seized as those of an enemy.'

'Which of course they are,' interjected Popham. 'And they will remain legitimate prizes while they sail under the flag of Spain.'

'But imagine what South America could be, *señores*,' urged Pueyrredon, leaning forward. 'Look at the United States, now that they have thrown off the shackles of colonial rule! See how they thrive as an independent nation.'

'Not the most favourable of comparisons to be making here in London, old chap,' said Vansittart.

'Southern America could be every bit as great as the North, if only she were free,' continued their guest. 'Buenos Aires is the second biggest city in the Americas after Philadelphia. The port of Montevideo could rival New York. Imagine the trade that could flow between our countries. The revenue that it would generate for your government, to help in your long fight with France. Napoleon has just defeated the Russians and Austrians once more, no? Do you not need all the help you can get?'

'So this conversation is really about trade, is it?' observed Vansittart. 'And you are a merchant who finds himself out of pocket? Is that what has brought me out on such a foul night?'

'I am a true patriot!' exclaimed Pueyrredon, springing to his feet, his eyes glittering in the firelight. 'One of many in my country! And I will expend every drop of blood in my body and every *centavo* of my fortune to gift my people the republic that they crave!'

Vansittart waved his visitor back towards his seat. 'I admire your zeal, Mr Pueyrredon, but I am unclear as to why you wished to meet with me. Let us speak plain, I pray. What

Philip K Allan

is it that you want?'

'Your country's support for my people to gain their independence from Spain, just as the French helped your colonists in North America.'

'Oh, is that all?' said Vansittart. 'I confess that I was only a boy at the time, but did the French not send a considerable army across the Atlantic, together with much of their navy, to aid the American rebels? I'm not sure if you have noticed, but our armed forces are a touch busy at present.'

'Nothing on that scale is required, *señor*,' said their visitor. 'The Rio de la Plata is a powder keg, ready to explode. All that is required is a spark.'

'I'm a lawyer, not a military man like Popham here, so I shall leave him to judge such matters. What concerns me more is how widely your views are shared,' said Vansittart, steepling his fingers together and calmly regarding the would-be freedom fighter.

'I cannot speak for all South America, *señor*, although I know there are many who think as I do. But I do know the Viceroyalty of the Rio de la Plata. I have with me letters of support from many of the leading families. We are ready to rise. All we need is a little help.'

'And why should we divert valuable resources at this time to aid you, pray?' continued the diplomat.

'Do you know what the Rio de la Plata means?' asked Pueyrredon. 'It is Spanish for the river of silver, and it is well named. Bullion from Upper Peru, where the richest silver mines in the world are to be found, flows down it to Buenos Aires. Three million pesos' worth, every year. And there it sits, a growing pile of treasure, unable to go any further since Trafalgar.'

'Did you say three *million*?' queried Vansittart.

Clay and the River of Silver

'In an average year,' said Pueyrredon, calmly sipping his wine.

'Did I not say it would be worth your while coming?' said Popham, a hungry look in his eye.

'What force do you suppose would be required?' asked Vansittart. 'To prompt a rising and to secure this, er, river of treasure you speak of?'

'The Spanish forces in the area are weak,' explained Pueyrredon. 'The regular army have to fight incursions from Portuguese settlers from Brazil and an Indian rising in the interior, and have little prospect of being reinforced now the Spanish coast is blockaded by your Royal Navy. A few thousand soldiers might suffice, with the support of my associates.'

'I believe I understand,' said Vansittart, rising to his feet and holding out his hand. 'Very well, I have heard sufficient for now. Kindly furnish me with your credentials, Mr Pueyrredon, and these letters of support you spoke of. In return I shall take your interesting proposal to the prime minister. But pray speak not a word about this to a soul.'

Philip K Allan

Chapter 1
Home

The shipwrights looked on anxiously as the *Lydia* slid across the calm brown water on her maiden voyage. She was a modest affair, with plain wooden sides and a single sail mounted on her lone mast. A puff of wind filled the sail, and in response the newly launched vessel toppled onto her side and began to vanish beneath the surface of the pond. Her demise produced very different reactions from her three builders.

'It's sinking, Papa!' laughed Francis Clay, jabbing a finger towards the scene of the disaster with all the relish to be expected of a six-year-old.

'Almost gone!' added his younger sister Elizabeth, clapping her hands in delight.

'So it would seem,' said Alexander Clay, rising to his feet and absentmindedly running a muddy hand through his hair. 'Not enough ballast in the hold, I fear, children. I had best wade in and recover her before we are detected. We can't have it generally known that Royal Navy captains don't know how to trim toy boats.'

'You're getting into the pond!' shrieked Elizabeth, dancing with delight.

'Gosh!' added her brother, wondering if this day could possibly get any better. 'Can I come too?'

'It will be very slimy,' cautioned their father. 'We will need to take off our stockings and shoes.'

Clay and the River of Silver

'Can I come too, Papa?' pleaded Elizabeth. 'Please!'

'Your clothes will get very wet,' observed Clay. 'But I suppose you might ride upon my shoulders,' he added, as his daughter's face began to crumple. 'And you must both promise that not a word of this ever reaches your mother.'

'What am I not to be told about, Alex?' asked Lydia Clay, appearing from around the hedge that screened the duck pond from the house. Her eyes narrowed with suspicion at the guilty way the group spun around at her approach. The three were well matched. All shared the same arresting grey eyes, and Francis's gangly frame promised that he might one day match his father in height.

'Nothing, my dear,' said Clay. 'Children, doesn't Mama look lovely in that primrose dress? Is it the fabric that my sister gave you?'

But Mama was not so easily deflected. 'Why has Master Francis removed one of his shoes?' she demanded. 'And is that your silk handkerchief I can see, Alex? Floating in the middle of the pond.'

'No, Mama, it's a sail,' corrected her son. 'For our boat. Only something was wrong with it, and it sank.'

'That is a shame. Well, there it must lie until the seas shall give up their dead ... or until the gardener's boy can recover it. You all have fifteen minutes to wash your hands and faces and change out of those muddy clothes before luncheon. Nanny is waiting for you children in the nursery with hot water and towels. Run along now.'

The prospect of food drove away all thought of boats and ponds. The children raced away towards the house, leaving their parents to follow in their scampering wake.

'You weren't truly considering jumping in the pond with our children, were you Alex?' asked Lydia.

Philip K Allan

'Er ... no. Of course not,' said Clay. 'It was but a little foolery with them.' He tried to slide an arm around his wife's waist, but she deftly evaded him.

'Have a care,' she warned, taking his hand instead. 'You may be content to look like a ditcher, Alex, but I have no desire for mud on my dress. You know you have some on your face?'

'Oh, undoubtedly,' he beamed at her. 'Getting filthy is an essential part of the attraction. I still cannot believe how much Francis and young Elizabeth have grown. And how much I have missed them.'

'As we have missed you,' said his wife, turning him towards her so she could brush his lips with a kiss. 'Let us hope that now we have beaten the enemy's fleet so soundly, you will not be required to return to sea for a while.'

'I would not be so certain,' he cautioned. 'Boney in his turn has thrashed the Austrians and Russians on land every bit as soundly. I fear this war will run for many years yet.'

'At least we have you with us for now,' she said, kissing him again. 'How was your journey to see poor Lieutenant Blake's parents?'

'They were very distressed, as you can imagine, although proud that their son fell serving his country at such a great battle as Trafalgar.'

'You chose not to share with them the particulars of his death, I assume?'

'That he perished in the storm that followed?' said Clay. 'No, I thought it better to let them form a more gratifying picture of his final moments. Drowning is such a terrible way to go. For my part, I shall miss John terribly. The *Griffin* will be a sadder place without him, although his fellow officers will at least be spared the constant smell of turpentine in the wardroom.'

Clay and the River of Silver

'He was such a talented artist,' said Lydia with a smile. 'That lovely portrait he did of me for our wedding was truly wonderful.'

'Indeed, and I will think of both him and you when I look at it on my cabin bulkhead.'

'But enough of John for now. You too must make haste and get changed. You know how my aunt dislikes waiting for her food.'

Clay was met with three beaming smiles and a scowl when he entered the dining room of Rosehill Cottage a little later. 'I trust I have not kept you waiting long?' he asked, as he took his place opposite his wife.

Lady Mary Ashton looked pointedly towards the case-clock that stood against one wall and opened her mouth to speak, but her niece was quicker.

'By no means, Alex,' said Lydia. 'Nancy, you may serve up.'

'Yes, madam.'

'Good,' declared Master Francis. 'I'm starving!'

Lady Ashton regarded the young boy with distaste, before turning to her niece. 'You know, Lydia, after you came to live with us, your uncle and I never saw the need for you to join us at table until you were much older than these two. Do children no longer take their meals in the nursery?'

'They do when we have company, but when it is just us we prefer to dine *en famille*, as the French would have it,' explained Lydia.

'My mother has no objection to the presence of her grandchildren when she visits,' said Clay. 'And I regard my time with them as precious, given how frequently duty takes me away. Indeed, I was just now remarking how they have grown since I was last at home. It was over two years ago that I left.'

Philip K Allan

'Did you see any snakes in India, Papa?' asked Francis.

'Yes. I even had one in my cabin, if you can believe it,' he began, before noticing the look of alarm on his wife's face. 'But no harm came of it, for it was despatched by Napoleon.'

'Napoleon?' queried Lady Ashton. 'What nonsense is this?'

'It is the crew's name for a mongoose they adopted while we were there,' explained Clay. 'He is inordinately good at slaying such creatures, and makes short work of rats as well. He is still on board the ship, although he doesn't find a Plymouth winter much to his liking.'

'What about oliphants, Papa?' asked Elizabeth. 'Did you see any of those?'

'Yes, I saw many, and even rode upon them on occasion, for they are exceedingly strong. They employ them in the dockyard at Bombay, where I witnessed them moving huge beams around with their trunks as if they weighed no more than feather bolsters.'

The children laughed delightedly at this, and Lady Ashton's frown grew a little deeper, but Clay's attention strayed towards the bay window.

Lydia turned in her seat and watched a horseman in mud-stained boots trotting up the drive and dismounting a respectful distance from the house. He opened a heavy leather saddlebag, pulled out a letter, and disappeared from view as he made his way towards the front door. 'That isn't the usual postboy,' she remarked. 'Besides, he has already been.' She glanced anxiously towards her husband.

'It is probably nothing of great import,' said Clay, toying with his food, as he pondered what the rider's arrival might mean.

'Do mounted messengers often bring tidings of no

Clay and the River of Silver

significance to your door then, Alexander?' asked Lady Ashton. Clay didn't answer and the children grew solemn, looking from one parent to the other with concern.

Nancy left the room as the doorbell rang, returning shortly after with a sealed envelope on a salver. 'It is addressed to you, sir,' she said, holding it towards him.

'Is it orders, Alex?' asked Lydia, her voice trembling.

'I think not, my dear,' he said with a smile of reassurance. 'The rider was not in Admiralty livery. And see? The seal is crimson rather than black and is not their fouled anchor but some sort of coat of arms.' He opened the letter and quickly scanned the contents. 'God bless my soul,' he exclaimed.

'Alex, please!' said his wife. 'What does it say?'

'Your pardon, my dear, but I am quite taken aback.' He returned to the letter. 'It says that I am commanded to attend a levee at the Court of St James, where I am to be made a Knight of the Bath.'

'Made to take a bath?' queried little Elizabeth. 'How dreadful!'

'No, my angel,' corrected Lydia, her face beaming. 'Your father is to be knighted. Isn't it marvellous? And not before time. You have a fighting record that is decidedly superior to most of the captains on the list.'

'Will you get to wear armour and have a horse to ride?' asked his son excitedly.

'Armour would be very inconvenient on a ship, Francis, especially if I should fall over the side.'

'I daresay it follows on from Trafalgar,' sniffed Lady Ashton. 'The government has run quite mad with this victory, and is handing out peerages and honours to all. What part did you play?'

Philip K Allan

'Only a small one in the battle itself,' he said. 'Frigates rarely engage in combat during fleet actions, Lady Ashton. By custom that is left to the ships of the line. My duty was chiefly to relay signals and to take in tow any ships disabled in the fighting.'

'And for this you are to be knighted? Goodness! Can every tugboat captain and postmaster expect such elevation?'

'Aunt, you do Alexander a disservice!' protested her niece. 'His role was instrumental in bringing the enemy to battle! Why, if he had not found Villeneuve and chased him to the Caribbean and back, there might have been no victory at all.'

'Well, I suppose you are to be congratulated,' conceded Lady Ashton, holding a hand out towards him. 'Sir Alexander does sound rather better than plain Captain Clay. Perhaps now I will no longer have to explain to every acquaintance why my niece saw fit to marry the penniless son of a parson.'

'I am sure that shielding you from such embarrassment was the principal reason the honour was bestowed,' said Clay, taking her hand and kissing it, while rolling his eyes in his wife's direction.

'Isn't Papa funny,' exclaimed Elizabeth.

'When is the ceremony to take place?' asked his wife, struggling not to laugh.

'Next week, and the invitation is extended to you, my dear.'

'Is it?' said Lydia. 'What fun! I haven't been to court since I was a debutante.'

*****

The Cornish fishing village of Polwith had lain at the end of its

Clay and the River of Silver

small inlet for the best part of a thousand years. It was a self-contained little community, proud and independent. A headland shielded its thatched cottages from the worst of the weather, while a stone breakwater cast a protective arm around the fishing boats in the harbour. Much of the villagers' requirements could be obtained locally. There was fish from the sea and mutton from the hillsides. Vegetables from kitchen gardens and water from the chattering stream that flowed down through the village. Anything else could be bought from visiting tinkers or local markets, while the tiny church provided nourishment for the soul. The only thing Polwith lacked was a school, but that was in the process of changing.

Ann Sedgwick looked over the temporary schoolroom she had established in an old boat shed above the beach and smiled encouragingly at her pupils. There were eight of them and all were different ages. She had arranged them like a set of organ pipes on two benches, from tallest to shortest, and they filled the space with the rasp and squeak of chalk on slate as they traced out their letters. She had done her best to counteract the smell of tar and old fishing nets that infested the place with bright hangings on the walls and flowers in a jug. But soon she would have somewhere better to teach the children, now that the parish had released a plot of land on the edge of the village. She could picture the new schoolhouse in her mind, with its swept oak floor, freshly plastered walls and sunlight streaming in through its tall windows.

Silas Penhaligon, the tallest of the organ pipes, coughed pointedly from his place at the end of the back row, bringing Ann's attention back to the gloom of the boat shed. 'All finished?' she enquired, and the children nodded and held their work out to be inspected. 'Those be nice flowers you drawn there, Katie,' she commented to a solemn little girl, barely

Philip K Allan

larger than her slate. 'Not much in the way of writing, mind.'

The girl shyly pointed to one of the flowers and Ann peered a little closer. 'Oh, beg pardon, I see now. There be a letter at the heart of each. Hmm, I do like flowers, but perhaps a touch more writing and a little less drawing tomorrow?' Katie nodded quickly in agreement and Ann moved on through the room. 'Lovely work, Betsey, specially them there Fs. Still a bit scruffy, Silas, but I see it be coming ...' Her voice trailed away as she became aware that the attention of her class had moved on. She turned to see that a large, well-built man had appeared in the open door, regarding her with dark eyes above a beaming smile. He wore the high-waisted trousers and short jacket of a sailor and held a broad tarpaulin hat which he waved towards the class in a friendly manner. 'Afternoon, nippers,' he said.

'You come to tell us about that battle of Trafalgee, Mr Sedgwick?' asked Silas.

'Are you two going to kiss?' added Katie, wide-eyed at the prospect.

'I think that will be all for today, children,' said Ann, feeling her face flush. 'Clean your slates and stack them at the front, and then you can go.'

When the last of the children had stampeded out, she stepped into her husband's embrace for a long, lingering kiss.

'Back from Plymouth, then?' she said a little later, still within the circle of his arms.

'Aye, while the old *Griffin* has her hull seen to,' he confirmed. 'The dockyard there be busier than a hive, what with all them ships as fought at Trafalgar coming in. Our barky has only now been taken into drydock. Mind, that were a caution, and no mistake! They got this new steam engine in a shed as smokes and spits like the devil himself. No sooner had we warped the barky in than it had pumped the basin dry, quick as

Clay and the River of Silver

quick!'

Ann laughed at this. 'Oh, my lover! We got a way to go afore you'll pass for a Cornishman! The tin mines hereabouts have had such engines to pump them clear of water for many a long year.'

'But they be huge buggers with beams an' the like,' said Sedgwick. 'This were proper small. Small enough to fit in a ship, I were thinking.'

'Good,' said his wife. 'Then maybe the navy will have no more call to take our menfolk for sailors. How long you back for then?'

'Captain Clay has given me two whole weeks this time.'

'Well, that be the least you deserve, what with the navy taking you away a week after we be wed for the best part of two years, chasing them Frogs half way to China and back, not to mention Trafalgar. Ain't I the lucky one!'

'You have no idea how I missed you all that time, Ann,' he growled.

'In truth, you did a passing job at telling me in all them letters you wrote, Able Sedgwick. Now let's get out of this noisome place, to where I can breathe clean air for a change.'

She took his arm, and they wandered through the village, their heads leaning close, lost in each other's company. He was thirsty for news of the village from the time he had been away, while in return he shared some of the exotic places he had visited. Eventually they reached the site of the future schoolhouse, a patch of waste ground close to the church. She pulled him from place to place, explaining what would be where, and conjuring up her plans and dreams with bold sweeps of her arms. He was quiet, content to let her enthusiasm fill the evening air. The sun dropped below the headland as she spoke and blue dusk filled the valley like water in a tank. The first few

Philip K Allan

lights appeared in the village beneath them, echoed by those on a passing ship out on the darkening sea. Ann pulled her shawl close against the coming of the night, and stepped nearer to him, resting back against his chest and enjoying his warm arms as they enfolded her.

'You ain't talked any about this Battle of Trafalgar?' she asked, after a moment of peace. 'What were it truly like? An' spare me the version you'll tell young Silas, all full of blood and glory.'

She felt his breath in her hair as he kissed the top of her head, and then he began to speak.

'It were a warm day, calm, with just enough breeze to waft our fleet down upon the enemy. By rights the sea should have been flat, but there were an odd swell. Mr Armstrong, our ship's master, reckoned it were the foretaste of heavy weather to come. Our fleet was such a sight, two lines of ships, bearing down on an enemy as filled the horizon, but all moving proper slow, as if the sea were made from molasses.'

'Sounds more like som'it in a dream,' murmured Ann, her eyes closed as she pictured the scene.

'Aye, very like,' agreed her husband. 'Then came the battle. In truth I saw aught but noise and fury for the most part. With a wind so indifferent, the smoke lay in a fog across the sea, and what with we being but a frigate, our part were to stand off and relay signals. But when the last gun fell silent, and the smoke parted, we saw that dream of yours were more of a nightmare. There were broken ships as far as the eye could see, friend and foe alike. All had masts gone, and the sea so thick with bodies and flotsam it looked firm enough to walk upon. An' coming up out of the south-west were a fearsome storm, ready to sweep all before it onto the coast of Spain.'

'Storm?' she said, twisting in his arms to see his face.

Clay and the River of Silver

'What storm were this?'

'The papers don't speak of it,' he explained. 'They be too full of bombast an' ginger at the defeat of Boney an' the death of Lord Nelson. Day and night it blew, for the best part of a week. I tell 'ee, a sight more ships foundered an' souls drowned than ever perished in the battle.'

'But that's terrible,' she said, shuddering at the thought. 'How did you fare?'

'Our part were to take in tow one of the prizes, a big Frog ship named the *Redoubtable*, as had gone toe to toe with *Victory* an' had been beaten into a hulk in consequence. She were like a charnel house inside, with hundreds of wounded lying among the dead, and the water flooding in faster than the men at the pumps could clear it. She lasted the first night, but sank the following day.'

'Whatever became of the poor souls on board?'

'We took off a few, but most drowned. We could hear the piteous cries even above the fury of the storm, right up to the moment the water cut off their noise. I tell you, Ann, hell must be a lot like the inside of that there ship.'

*****

Heaven must be very like the interior of St James's Palace, Clay decided, as he passed through a set of double doors and into the throne room with Lydia beside him. Above them was a lofty ceiling, richly decorated with gold stucco. The walls stretching away on either side were lined with scarlet damask the same shade as the thick carpet that deadened their footfalls. On the walls huge portraits of previous monarchs in their coronation splendour peered down at the new arrivals. From above, the glow of innumerable candles glittered off the uniforms and jewellery worn by those stood around the empty throne at the far end.

'Captain and Mrs Alexander Clay,' roared the chamberlain by the door, at a volume Clay would have kept for hailing a masthead.

A few of the guests looked around, and one elderly figure with a shock of grey hair detached himself from the nearest group and came over, a naval lieutenant quietly behind him. 'There you are, Clay,' said the man in a Scottish accent. 'Alas, His Majesty is having one of his turns again, so it will be the Prince of Wales to whom you will be presented. But we're in luck. He's yet sober. Let us get this ceremony done before he finds the port.'

'My dear, may I present Lord Barham, First Lord of the Admiralty,' said Clay, drawing his wife forward. 'Your Lordship, my wife, Mrs Lydia Clay.'

'Not plain Mrs Clay for much longer, eh?' said Barham, bending over the hand Lydia held out. 'Your servant, ma'am. I fear I shall have to borrow you husband for a wee while. Becoming a knight involves a deal of tomfoolery, after which I shall have need of him at the Admiralty. Are you staying in town?'

'We are residing with my aunt, Lady Ashton, in Piccadilly,' said Lydia.

The admiral waved forward his flag lieutenant. 'Morris, kindly attend to Mrs Clay here, and see she gets home safely after the ceremony.'

'Yes, my lord. Good evening, Mrs Clay. Delighted to make your acquaintance.'

Clay exchanged a reassuring smile with his wife and then set off in Barham's wake, deep into the crowd close about the throne. All around him were uniforms, the scarlet of the

Clay and the River of Silver

army mixed with the more familiar dark blue and white of his own service. Dotted among them were bold women in satin dresses and long gloves, their dark eyes looking appraisingly at the tall naval captain. Eventually they arrived at the centre of the group, where a stout man with moist lips and sly blue eyes stood, the sash of the Order of the Garter stretched across his bulging waistcoat. Clay supressed a smile at how closely the Prince of Wales resembled his caricature in Gillray's cartoons.

'Good evening, Your Royal Highness,' said Barham, bowing low. 'May I present Captain Alexander Clay.'

'This is the officer you spoke of with such enthusiasm, Lord Barham?' lisped the Prince Regent.

'Aye, the very same, Your Highness. Few men in the service have burnt more powder to greater effect. He has served with distinction for many years. The late Lord Nelson was a particular admirer of his.'

'And I thought he saved all his admiration for himself, what?' commented the prince, to titters from some of the courtiers. 'Was you ever at court, Captain?'

'I had the honour of being presented to the king, Your Highness. That was in Weymouth, where he was taking the waters for his health. I brought him word of our victory at the Battle of the Nile and he was good enough to present me with a sword.'

'And have you slain our country's enemies with it?' asked the prince.

Clay coloured a little, conscious of all the eyes resting on him. 'On occasion, when it has been required of me, Your Highness.'

'Damn me, but I daresay you could tell a tale or two, eh? When we are done here, would you care to join me for a bite of supper and a game of whist?'

Philip K Allan

'Alas, I fear I must deprive you of the pleasure of Captain Clay's company, Your Highness,' said Barham. 'I have Mr Vansittart awaiting us at the Admiralty, on urgent business that cannot be delayed.'

'You sailors are always in such perishing haste,' complained the prince with a pout. 'Oh, very well, let us get the ceremony done. All this talk has given me a damnable thirst.'

Clay turned to see a procession of solemn figures approaching, dressed in scarlet robes. One carried a sword, another something glittering on a velvet cushion. A footman appeared and unrolled a square of carpet in front of him.

'Kneel, Captain,' whispered Barham beside him.

Clay sank down, hoping that he was doing so without trembling, despite the thumping of his heart. He bowed his head and felt the weight of the sword rest on each shoulder in turn.

'Arise, Sir Alexander, Knight Companion of the Most Honourable Order of the Bath,' ordered one of the robed men, and Clay got to his feet amid polite applause. He bent his head so that a ribbon could be dropped across his shoulder, and a glittering star was pinned to the front of his coat. Someone draped a scarlet cloak over his shoulders, and he was given a vow to repeat and a document to sign. And then the ceremony was complete. From now and for the rest of my life I will be Sir Alexander Clay, he reflected. He felt a twinge of sadness, wishing that his father had known of his success, but then he caught a glimpse of Lydia through the crowd, her beautiful face shining with pride.

*****

Clay was in something of a daze as he entered the main Admiralty building, the unfamiliar star thumping against his

Clay and the River of Silver

chest every other step as he followed Barham up the main staircase. A clerk jumped up from behind his desk as they arrived in an anteroom. 'Your visitor is awaiting your Lordship,' he said, ushering them towards an imposing door.

'Thank you, Fox,' said Barham. 'Pray serve a little port to celebrate the captain's spurs, if you please.'

'Yes, my lord.'

The room beyond was much as Clay remembered from his meetings with previous First Lords of the Admiralty, although this was his first visit after dark. The heavy curtains had been drawn, muffling the sound of passing carriages in the street outside, and several oil lamps had been lit. In their light he could see some familiar objects – the tell-tale wind gauge linked to the weathervane on the building's roof and the large canvas maps of the world's oceans that hung from the walls.

Vansittart rose from his seat by the fire and came over with a welcoming smile. 'Upon my word, but a star and ribbon does rather suit you, Alex, or should I say Sir Alexander,' he said, seizing Clay's hand. 'Well merited, and long overdue, if I am any judge. Well done, sir. Well done.'

'The honour almost came at a fearful price,' observed Barham. 'Prinny was in playful mood, and was all for inviting the captain to play a hand of whist. Fortunately, I was on hand to save him from a ruinous evening.'

'A deuced narrow escape, what?' chuckled Vansittart, turning to Clay with an explanation. 'The Prince of Wales holds his generous allowance from Parliament to be quite inadequate, and supplements it by cheating at cards. At a shilling a point, I might add.'

'I find it a little cool tonight,' said Barham. 'Shall we take our ease by the fire? Fox, pray bring over the port.'

When they were settled in comfortable chairs and the

drinks had been served, the clerk quietly left them. Once the door clicked shut Barham turned to Clay. 'What did you make of this evening?' he asked.

'In truth, it passed in a whirl, my lord,' said Clay. 'Although I did think His Royal Highness rather disrespectful of Lord Nelson's memory. His Lordship gave his life in the service of his father, after all.'

'That is Prinny all over, I'm afraid,' commented Vansittart. ''Tis pure jealousy. I daresay witnessing the multitudes that turned out for Nelson's funeral got him pondering on how few would mourn his own passing.'

'Alas, Nelson is no more,' said Barham. 'But the war continues, and it falls on us that remain to make the best of his great victory. What would you do, Captain, were you in my shoes?'

'Go on the offensive,' said Clay, without hesitation. 'After Trafalgar, the balance of naval power has shifted decisively in our favour. Now we are no longer obliged to keep so much of the fleet guarding the enemy's ports, we should take the war to them.'

'Do you have a particular object in mind?' asked the admiral.

'Southern Africa, my lord,' said Clay. 'We should take the Cape of Good Hope back from the Dutch, and retain it this time. I was most inconvenienced by not being able to touch there returning from Madras last year. In my view it was folly to have returned such a valuable place to the enemy. It is the best position between Europe and our possessions in India. Holding it would provide both supply and sanctuary to our ships, while also denying such comfort to our enemies.'

'Its return was a condition of the Peace of Amiens, of course,' said Barham.

Clay and the River of Silver

'Ah, yes,' said Vansittart, 'the peace which passeth all understanding.'

Barham sipped thoughtfully at his port for a moment as he gathered his thoughts. 'I am of your way of thinking regarding the Cape, Sir Alexander, and we do have a suitable force available to achieve that very object. When word reached us last summer that Villeneuve had broken out and was heading for the Caribbean – intelligence that you supplied, I believe – we took the precaution of gathering a wee force of troops in Ireland, under the command of General Sir David Baird. Our intention was that they would be despatched to recover any of our possessions in the West Indies seized by the French. As it turned out, Villeneuve's manoeuvre was in the way of a feint, and he returned to Europe to be defeated by Nelson. Which leaves the general and his men kicking their heels.'

'What force does he have, my lord?' asked Clay.

'Not above four thousand men,' said the admiral. 'Foot, for the most part, together with some artillery and a detachment of light dragoons. Too small a force to make much impact in Europe, but sufficient to conquer some out of the way spot like the Cape. And as luck would have it, further troops are due to be sent out to India shortly. They could help seize the Cape, before continuing on their way.'

'He would need naval support for protection and to help land such a force,' mused Clay. 'The enemy are certain to have some ships of force in the area.'

'I'm minded to send a squadron under Captain Popham,' said Barham. 'Two or three ships of the line, together with a few smaller vessels. He is regarded as something of an expert on the landing of troops, not least by himself. Are you acquainted with him, Sir Alexander?'

'Only by reputation, my lord. His signal book was of

Philip K Allan

considerable use at Trafalgar. Without it there would not have been the "England expects" message so beloved by the press.'

'Ah yes,' smiled Barham. 'A dramatic moment worthy of Mr Garrick in his pomp. And very Nelson.'

'Will Captain Popham be promoted to commodore for the expedition, my lord?'

'Oh, I think not. He has sufficient seniority on the list, and such a rank will only encourage him to exceed his instructions. Don't misunderstand me, Sir Alexander. He is a talented man. Capable, of course, but prone to be somewhat reckless. If I was to send him, I would want to pair him with a reliable deputy, who might counteract such tendencies. Which is why I thought of you.'

'I am flattered that you regard me in that way, my lord,' began Clay, but Barham waved his comment aside.

'Lord Nelson spoke very highly of you, and you are a senior captain yourself, now,' he said. 'With plenty of experience and a knighthood to boot. I have no doubt you are up to the task. How soon can the *Griffin* be ready?'

'Her hull is made good, and she is presently being re-rigged by the dockyard, my lord. I daresay she can depart by the month end. I am a little under compliment, but I have been promised twenty landsmen from the press. And I still need to replace Lieutenant Blake who fell at Trafalgar.'

'The artist cove?' queried Vansittart. 'That is a shame. He was excellent company and prodigiously talented. My commiserations to you, Alex.'

'Do you have a replacement in mind?' asked Barham.

'Mr William Russell, my senior midshipman, has been serving as acting lieutenant. He is due to take his lieutenant's exam presently, and is well acquainted with the ship.'

The First Sea Lord made a note of the name. 'I'll see

Clay and the River of Silver

that the senior examining captain is aware of your preference,' he said.

'I trust my presence on board the *Griffin* will not inconvenience you, Captain?' said Vansittart. 'I too am being sent. Not to wade ashore, musket in hand, I may add. I value my attire too highly for that. But there are sure to be political matters needing attention. Popham has offered me a berth in his ship, of course, but he will also have Baird and his staff to accommodate. Besides, I do find his society trying after a while. His discourse seems restricted to his achievements and the current state of his fortune.'

'I am sure that Mr Taylor will extend the hospitality of the wardroom to you once more,' said Clay.

'Good, that is settled,' said Barham, rising to his feet. 'We have taken quite enough of your time, Sir Alexander. Lady Clay will be wondering if you have been waylaid by footpads set on relieving you of that handsome-looking star upon your coat. I will have your orders sent across in the morning.'

'Thank you, my lord,' said Clay. 'Good evening to you, Mr Vansittart.'

'And to you, Captain.'

Once Clay had left, the old admiral and the young diplomat resumed their seats.

'You are still resolved to use this expedition to the Cape to explore possibilities in South America?' asked Barham.

'I believe it to be worth trying, my lord,' said Vansittart. 'For my part, the Cape is but a tavern on the passage to India. It is what may follow its capture that is of more interest. When we shall have a little army on hand with nothing to occupy them.'

'And you believe they can secure this river of silver you have spoken of?'

Philip K Allan

'Pizarro conquered Peru with three hundred men. What might a few thousand redcoats not achieve? Even just seizing a year's silver production from the treasure houses of Buenos Aires will provide a most welcome addition to the government's coffers.'

'Absolutely,' said Barham. 'But the cabinet have declined to issue any instructions to the expedition that go beyond the conquest of the Cape. You know politicians, sir. The whole South American adventure seems so uncertain that no one wishes to put their name to it. Although all will claim it as their own if it succeeds.'

'It was ever thus, my lord,' said Vansittart. 'In some ways, I prefer to operate in that way. Let Popham and I judge how matters lie when we are out there.'

'And you think him the best man to lead the expedition? He can be an awkward character, you know.'

'It was he who first introduced me to the opportunity, my lord. He would be certain to resent our giving such a plum to anyone else. Also, the fewer who know of our plans, the better.'

'Indeed, I note you didn't see fit to discuss your wider ideas with our friend,' observed the admiral. 'Why was that, pray?'

'Clay is a splendid commander, but is altogether too honest for the more, shall we say, political aspects of warfare. Our objectives and those of Mr Pueyrredon and his fellow patriots may well diverge at some point. If betrayal is required, it is best left to those familiar with life in the shadows, or those like Popham, who only have regard for themselves.'

Barham looked at the younger man with distaste, and then shook his head. 'Thank the lord I am too old to serve at sea. In my day it was enough to fight my country's enemies,

Clay and the River of Silver

without considering the more dubious parts of statecraft. Well Clay will do his duty and obey his orders, as every king's officer must, whether he likes them or no. But pray do not press his loyalty too far.'

Philip K Allan

Chapter 2
Preparations

With her towering masts and her long rows of big eighteen-pounder cannons, the thirty-eight-gun Griffin was one of the finest frigates in the Royal Navy. Freshly painted, newly rigged, she had been warped out of Plymouth dockyard, and rested at her mooring on the River Tamar. A broad strip of new copper gleamed along her waterline, indicating that she still had plenty of stores to load before she would be ready for her long voyage to the South Atlantic.

In the middle of her bustling deck stood George Taylor, her first lieutenant, running a hand through his iron-grey hair as he tried to organise the work of the day. A lighter had just arrived alongside, loaded with heavy casks of salt beef and sacks of ship's biscuit, replacing the one that had delivered the boatswain's stores that lay strewn across the deck. And just at this moment of maximum chaos, he had caught sight of the flapping red flag at the masthead of the powder-hoy as it left its berth on the far side of the river, coming to fill the frigate's magazine with gunpowder.

'Mr Hutchinson!' he roared towards the grizzled boatswain, the proud owner of the ship's longest pigtail. 'Kindly have your stores cleared from around the main hatch, if you please. They can be stowed properly later.'

'Aye aye, sir.'

'Mr Preston!' continued Taylor. 'Pray have the largest

Clay and the River of Silver

block and tackle rigged from the main yard and those hogsheads of beef lowered directly into the hold.'

Down on the main deck a good-looking officer with dark hair raised a hand in acknowledgement. The other sleeve of his lieutenant's coat was empty and pinned across his chest.

Taylor next turned to a young midshipman with a shock of blond curls crammed beneath his hat. 'Mr Todd, go and find Mr Faulkner. Give the purser my compliments, and tell him his provisions will be coming on board directly. Ask him to make his way to the hold to supervise their stowage.'

'Aye aye, sir.'

'That damned powder-hoy is definitely coming our way,' Taylor muttered to himself. 'We'll have to dump the galley fire over the side, just as cook will be starting to prepare the men's dinner …'

'Mr Taylor, sir?' said a nervous voice behind him.

'What the hell is it now!' exclaimed the first lieutenant, rounding on the unfortunate person who had broken into his thoughts.

Before him stood a young man with auburn hair neatly combed back from his pale face. His midshipman's uniform had recently been brushed, his shoes shone like mirrors, and his neckcloth was starched to the point where it offered the same comfort as a hangman's noose. 'S-sorry to disturb you, sir. But it is time for my lieutenant's exam.'

'Of course it is, Mr Russell,' said Taylor, clapping a hand to his forehead. 'What with all our provisions coming at once, I had clean forgot. Are you fully prepared?'

Russell indicated the bundle of documents he held under one arm. 'I believe so, sir. I have my journals, my certificates of sobriety and good conduct from the captain, and a copy of Norie's *Epitome of Navigation* in case I have a

Philip K Allan

moment of leisure to revise. How do I look, sir?'

'Like a most creditable candidate, William,' said Taylor, looking over the midshipman with a kindly smile. 'Although you might think to loosen that neckcloth a touch. Where is the examination to be held?'

'At the Commissioner's House over in the dockyard, sir. I had hoped to avail myself of the jollyboat to row across.'

'The jollyboat?' queried the first lieutenant. 'By no means. It is much too modest. We must see you delivered in the style expected of a future lieutenant of this ship. The longboat is available at present, and you can return with the extra hands we have been promised. There should be twenty pressed men awaiting transfer. Mr Preston! Belay that next cask of beef, and get the longboat in the water!'

'Eh, aye aye, sir,' said the lieutenant, the huge barrel in question hanging perilously in the air above the deck.

While the boat was lifted from its place on the skid beams and lowered over the side, most of the crew took the opportunity of the break in activity to gather and watch Russell depart.

'Just you blow them buggers out of the water, sir,' urged Jamali Jim, his voice now bearing little trace of his native Bengal after so many years in the navy.

Russell smiled weakly in response, and followed the boat crew down the frigate's side. As he made his way to join Sedgwick in the stern sheets, he heard Ezekiel Davis, the oldest member of the crew, talking to his neighbour a little louder than he intended. 'I remembers when Rusty first came aboard the old *Titan*. Naught but a nipper, he were, as couldn't tell a Turk's head from a turd. But look'ee now? Up to be a Grunter, if you'll credit it.'

'Where we be heading, sir?' asked Sedgwick once the

Clay and the River of Silver

midshipman had taken his place.

Russell pointed mutely towards the steps in front of Commissioner's House, not trusting himself to speak. The coxswain got the launch under way, rowing diagonally across the running tide. Soon they were out on the broad river and could see the long line of moored warships that curved away from them towards the sea. There were other frigates like the *Griffin*, with a single yellow gundeck, mixed in among bulky two- and three-decked ships of the line. Many of these bore the scars of Trafalgar, as they waited their turn to be seen by the dockyard.

As they approached, Russell could see it buzzing with activity. Every one of the drydocks that lined the bank was occupied by a warship, their high gilded sterns facing towards him and the sound of caulking hammers echoing over the water. Further along, a sheer hulk had been warped next to a battered seventy-four, its big crane slowly drawing the stump of a broken foremast from out of the hull like a dentist pulling out a rotten tooth. And then they were approaching the bottom of the flight of steps.

'Easy there, larboard side,' ordered Sedgwick. 'Row on starboards. Handsomely now.' He pushed over the tiller, and the launch turned up into the stream. 'Oars in! Clap on in the bow!'

The way came off, and the boat bumped gently to a halt. A bored-looking marine sentry looked down on them from above. Russell sat transfixed, clasping his bundle of journals to his chest.

'Commissioner's House be just up there, sir,' prompted Sedgwick, indicating the steps.

'Yes,' said the candidate, fingering his collar. 'What of these extra hands that need collecting?'

Philip K Allan

'Don't you go a fretting about them, sir. You just worry about that there promotion board. Me and the lads will fetch them back to the barky. I daresay that Lobster up there will show us where they be.'

Russell considered the marine sentry for a moment, and thought how much simpler the life of a soldier or a coxswain was. No examinations for them.

'Best not to keep them waiting, sir,' continued Sedgwick.

'N-no, that's right,' said the candidate, wishing that his legs would stop trembling.

'You'll do fine, if I can be so bold, sir,' said the coxswain. 'It be a test of seamanship, right? Well you've been through no end of storms and sea fights. More than the run-of-the-mill snotty they gets up afore them. An' true seamanship ain't learned from books, but out there, beyond the harbour wall.'

'You're right, Sedgwick,' said Russell, rising to his feet. 'I shall be back presently.'

'An' we'll be here a waiting. Good luck, sir.'

Sedgwick watched the young officer make his way up the steps with a shake of his head. 'Strange to see young Rusty afeared like that,' he commented to his friend Adam Trevan, who was sitting facing him, nursing the stroke oar on his lap. 'He's always been game enough in a fight, even when he barely reached above my belt.'

'Ain't the same though, is it?' said the Cornishman. 'Fears as we can see plain be a sight easier to master than them as we build up in our minds.'

Sedgwick looked at his friend in surprise. Trevan had the same startling blue eyes as always, but he noticed for the first time some threads of silver among the blond hair of his

Clay and the River of Silver

pigtail. 'Aye, that be the truth of it. Now, we best be seeing about these new hands. O'Malley and Evans with me, the rest of you stay here. Adam be in charge.'

The two sailors he had named clambered out of the boat and followed him up the steps. They made an odd pair. Sean O'Malley was a small wiry topman, with the curly hair and dark eyes of a gypsy. By contrast, his companion, Sam Evans, was comfortably the tallest man in the ship, with the build of the champion prize-fighter he had once been.

The marine sentry at the top of the stairs pointed Sedgwick in the direction of the Impressment Service's receiving ship, an old hulk from the time of Marlborough moored against a wooden jetty at the very edge of the dockyard. The vessel would have looked magnificent in its prime, to judge from the elaborate carved figures and interweaving foliage that still adorned its towering stern. But the bright colours and gilding were lost beneath layers of thick black paint, and nothing remained of her once towering masts. All her ports had lost their guns and lids, replaced by iron gratings through which the occasional pale face gazed out on the world. At the bottom of the gangway two armed sailors stood guard, together with a petty officer with heavily tattooed arms and a cutlass by his side.

'What are you lads looking for?' he asked.

'We be from the *Griffin*, over the water,' explained Sedgwick. 'Lieutenant Taylor sent us to collect our share of the press.' He pulled an indent from his pocket and passed it across.

The petty officer took the paper and glanced at both sides briefly, his face devoid of any comprehension.

'Twenty landsmen,' added Sedgwick, after a pause. 'That's what be set down.'

'So it is,' said the petty officer. 'Best you wait here

Philip K Allan

while I take this to Lieutenant Chisholm.'

It was some time before he returned, accompanied by a shambling line of men all dressed in a variety of ragged clothes, their hair long and unkept, their faces filthy.

'Bleeding hell,' muttered Evans. 'They looks like jailbait to me. An' I should know. I lived among enough of them, back in Seven Dials.'

'Just what the barky needs,' added O'Malley. 'Fecking cut-purses and murderers, is it? Trust the English to man their ships with such vermin.'

'Here we go,' announced the petty officer as the men shuffled to a halt on the jetty. 'A fresh batch just delivered from Nottingham Assizes, each one a volunteer for the king's navy.'

'These men volunteered?' queried Sedgwick, looking over the dejected recruits.

'Well, it were that or transportation. Between you and me, I'd have sooner chanced Botany Bay, but each to his own. I shall need them signed for. Your mark will do.'

Sedgwick took the proffered docket, read through it, and then signed his name at the bottom.

'Bleeding hell,' said the petty officer, taking it back. 'A blackamoor with his letters. Now I have seen it all. Any road, they're your responsibility now, so I'll thank you to get them off my jetty.'

'Come on you lot,' said Sedgwick, leading the way back towards the longboat. 'We've a Grunter to wait for before we return to the barky.'

'A Grunter? What's a Grunter?' queried one of the recruits.

'Or a barky, for that matter,' asked another.

'Grunter be what we call an officer, though not to his face, mind, and the barky is the ship,' explained the coxswain.

Clay and the River of Silver

'Once we be back there and you lot are read in, you can swab that filth away under the deck pump and get some clean slops to wear.'

'Are we free, then?' asked one, his face brightening.

Evans and O'Malley laughed uproariously at this. 'Free, is it?' said O'Malley. 'Well, what passes for freedom in King George's navy. Free to be beaten with a fecking rope's end when you slack and to be flogged for trifles.'

'Free of the skillet and into the bleeding fire, more like, shipmates,' agreed Evans, leering at the nearest man. 'Still, no more than you gaolbirds deserve. What you lot done? Thieving, was it? Or worse, maybe? Coz if you try any of that on the lower deck, you'll wish you had boarded that ship to Van Diemen's Land sharp enough.'

To his surprise, several of them rounded on the huge sailor, bristling with fury.

'It's us as has been robbed!' said one, jabbing Evans in the chest. 'Edward Pembleton's my name, an' I've had my trade taken by those damn mill owners. The only crime I've ever done was to stand up for the right to put bread on the family table.'

'So how comes you all wound up in fecking chokey, then?' demanded O'Malley.

'Coz every one of us is a proud follower of Ned Ludd,' said Pembleton.

'Ned who?' queried Evans.

'Ned Ludd,' repeated another. 'We're machine-breakers.'

'Fecking hell,' said O'Malley. 'We best be after keeping you lot away from the capstan, then.'

*****

Philip K Allan

The Commissioner's House was a long, three-storey building that faced on to the river. The imposing entrance was framed by a portico, above which rose a clocktower. Clerks in britches and stockings came and went as Russell made his way inside. The walls of the entrance hall were panelled with dark wood and hung with oil paintings of various ships the dockyard was associated with. Stood just inside the entrance was a marine with bristling sideburns. 'Excuse me, Sergeant,' Russell said. 'I am here for my lieutenant's exam.'

'You don't say, sir,' said the soldier, taking in the immaculate state of his uniform. 'Best join the other young gentlemen through that door over there.'

There were six midshipmen in the anteroom, all smartly dressed and each with a bundle of journals beside them. Most were a similar age to him, although two were considerably older.

'Seven of us,' exclaimed a candidate with thinning hair as Russell came through the door. 'And they never accept more than two. Pray God there are no more after you.'

'I ... I didn't see any others waiting,' said Russell.

'I doubt they will even pass a brace of us,' said another who was sitting near the window. 'Abandon Hope walked past earlier. He has already failed me twice.'

'What did he ask you about last time?' asked thinning hair.

'Some nonsense about calculating the phases of the moon,' said the unsuccessful candidate. 'Might as well have been Greek.'

Several of the midshipmen pulled out their copies of *Epitome of Navigation* and thumbed through to the relevant passage. Russell was tempted to do the same, but then his good

Clay and the River of Silver

sense returned to him. He had studied that passage only this morning, so instead he came across to join the midshipman by the window.

'Any other captains you recognise?' he asked. 'I've been away a few years. In the Indies.'

'That will be why you look brown as a Turk,' said the young officer with a friendly grin. 'Well, Captain Fanshawe from the dockyard usually presides over these panels. He's amiable enough, so what we truly need is that the third captain is not a tartar like Abandon Hope. I'm Richard Lamb, by the way, of the *Dragon*. That's her moored over there.'

'William Russell of the *Griffin*,' he replied, taking the proffered hand.

'The *Griffin*! You've served under Captain Clay?' exclaimed Lamb. 'Damn it all! What hope do we Channel Fleet johnnies have? I might as well leave now.'

Before Russell could answer, a door at the far end of the room opened and an elderly clerk came in. He peered across the top of his spectacles at them, and then down at a list he held in his hand. 'The panel will examine Mr Lamb first,' he announced.

'Here we go,' muttered his companion, picking up his journals and tweaking his neckcloth a little straighter. 'Midshipman Lamb to the slaughter.'

'Good luck,' whispered Russell.

Lamb seemed to have been away an age for those waiting dry-mouthed for their turn. Russell sat listening to the dry tick of the clock above the fireplace, and the murmur of voices from next door. When Lamb eventually returned, pale-faced from the ordeal, Russell was surprised to see he had barely been away for twenty minutes.

'Six months more sea time for me,' announced the

unsuccessful candidate. 'Abandon was on particularly savage form.'

'What did they ask you?' demanded one of the midshipmen, but before Lamb could answer, the clerk interrupted.

'No conferring, I pray, gentlemen,' he urged. 'It will avail you naught, for they never repeat the same question. Kindly return to your ship, Mr Lamb. The panel will see Mr Rotherham next.'

Rotherham, who was the officer with thinning hair, was away for half an hour, but returned with the beaming smile of success. He picked up his hat and cloak and fairly danced out of the anteroom, leaving a funereal atmosphere in his wake.

'If they only promote two, the odds are five to one against now,' muttered one midshipman gloomily.

Candidate followed candidate as the shadows lengthened outside, all returning with the same response – not ready for promotion, another six months of sea time required. Finally only Russell was left, his mind steadily emptying of all he had crammed it with over the last few days. He jumped up as the door opened, but it was only a young boy coming in to light the lamps. Then the penultimate candidate appeared. He was one of the older ones, his face flushed with anger. He snatched up his hat and left muttering to himself.

'Mr Russell, 'tis your turn,' said the clerk. 'Pray make haste. The panel wish to conclude their work for the day.'

The room he entered was dominated by a large table covered by a green cloth, behind which sat the three naval captains. In front of it was a chair, while off to one side was a small desk.

'This is the final young gentleman, sirs. Mr William Russell of the *Griffin*,' announced the clerk. He then took a

Clay and the River of Silver

circuitous route to his desk, passing behind the row of captains and pausing to whisper something in the ear of the officer sat in the middle.

'Ah, yes, of course,' muttered the captain, the oldest of the three, before turning to address the candidate. 'My name is Fanshawe, commissioner of this dockyard. The gentleman seated on my right is Captain Hope of the *Defence*.' Hope was a thin, red-faced man who stared intently at Russell. 'And this is Captain Williams of the *Ulysses*,' he continued, indicating a younger man on his left with an easy, lopsided smile. 'Pray be seated, so we can proceed.'

Russell dropped into the chair, aware only of the banging of his heart.

'Very well,' said Fanshawe. 'The panel is satisfied with the candidate's certificates and that his journals have been kept in a seamanlike manner. Are we agreed on that, gentlemen?'

'Quite satisfactory,' said Captain Williams, while Captain Hope restricted himself to a savage nod, his eyes never leaving Russell.

'Very well, let us proceed to the first question. Captain Hope, will you begin?'

'Can you tell the panel what is meant by a rhumb line?'

Russell opened his mouth to reply, but found that he had nothing to say. He knew he had heard the term before, but the context now escaped him. He closed his mouth once more and urged himself to think. Captain Hope's eyes seemed to grow even larger as they bored into him. From somewhere to his right the clerk's pen scratched to a halt, leaving a desert of silence in the room. He cleared his throat. 'A rum line, you say, sir,' he repeated. 'Eh … m-might that be the proper manner of organising the men so as to collect their spirit ration in an orderly fashion?'

Philip K Allan

'I beg your pardon?' queried Hope, his face growing even redder. 'What nonsense is …'

'Hear him!' chuckled Captain Fanshawe, his laugh edged with desperation. 'How amusing! Why I declare Mr Russell is making game of us. A rum line rather than a rhumb line, indeed! Very diverting.'

'That is all very well,' protested Hope, 'but I still wish for an answer. Without any further jesting, if you please, young man.'

'Of course, sir,' said Russell. Fanshawe looked significantly at him, and then down at where his hand rested on the table. His index figure was idly drawing an imaginary cross, and Russell's mind cleared a little. 'A rhumb line is one drawn upon the earth's surface which intersects all the meridians at the same angle.'

'Quite correct,' beamed Fanshawe. 'Captain Williams, do you have a question?'

'I wish to know what the candidate understands by plane sailing?'

As luck would have it, Russell had asked Jacob Armstrong, the *Griffin*'s American sailing master, to take him through that passage the night before. 'Plane sailing is the art of navigating a ship upon principles deduced from the supposition of the earth being an extended plane,' he began, offering up a word-perfect rendition of the original text.

'Hmm, I see Mr Russell can parrot his Norie well enough,' sniffed Hope. 'Which is not the same as comprehension …'

'But it is all that is required for this examination, Captain,' said Fanshawe. 'Why, if he has chosen to cast that passage to memory, surely that is to his credit? Kindly mark the question down as answered to the panel's satisfaction, if you

Clay and the River of Silver

please.'

'Noted, sir,' said the clerk.

'Good, then let us move on to practical seamanship,' said the commissioner.

'I have a question,' said Hope, smiling for the first time. 'Mr Russell, I want you to imagine that you have command of a frigate, close-hauled on the larboard tack with reefed topsails. You have another stricken ship under tow which carries no sail, nor can it steer itself. A gale is blowing from the nor'east, and Ushant lies two miles directly under your lee. Do you understand your situation?'

'Eh ... I believe so, sir,' said Russell.

'Good. The masthead reports dangerous reefs two miles directly ahead. Pray tell the panel what you would do, and the orders you would give.'

Russell closed his eyes for a moment, visualising the scene. The sea pounding against the ship's side, the howl of the wind through the rigging, the dead hand of the mast-less hulk astern. Sedgwick had been right, he decided. Seamanship wasn't something learned from books. The *Griffin* had been in just this situation the night after Trafalgar, when she had the doomed *Redoubtable* under tow. In his mind he was back on that wildly pitching deck, listening to the orders given by George Taylor and Jacob Armstrong as they had conned the ship.

'I would wear ship, sir,' he began. 'Any attempt at tacking with such a burden would see my command caught in irons.' Calmly he gave the flow of orders, explaining each in turn, until the last sail was sheeted home and the frigate was sailing away from danger. When he finished, the three captains were silent for a moment.

'Was the answer to your satisfaction?' asked Fanshawe.

Philip K Allan

'Very much so,' said Hope, his face betraying a hint of admiration.

'Do we have any further questions for Mr Russell? Captain Williams?'

'Not on my part, sir.'

'Then let us conclude matters, as it grows late,' said Fanshawe. 'I am of the opinion that Mr Russell has demonstrated he is worthy of promotion. Does anyone demur? Captain Hope? No? Excellent. Then let me be the first to congratulate you, Lieutenant Russell. Well done, sir. Your commission will be drawn up in due form and sent across to the *Griffin*.'

*****

It was fortunate that *Señor* Pueyrredon had arrived at Garraway's Coffee House early enough to secure one of the private booths that lined the wall. Soon after, it began to fill with London merchants and traders, all noisily discussing the business of the day. Harassed waiters passed among them, distributing fresh pots of coffee, clay pipes of tobacco or the latest editions of the papers. Among all the bright calico waistcoats and periwigs, the merchant captain he had come to meet was obvious as he came through the door dressed in a plain blue coat and britches. He studied him for a moment through the crowd, taking in his solid frame and weathered brown face before waving him over.

'Mister Pueyrredon?' said the man in a Boston accent. 'My name is Thomas Waine, master of the *Cape Allerton*.'

'I am pleased to meet you, Captain,' said the Spaniard, rising to take his hand. 'Please join me. Would you care for some of this coffee? It is quite good.'

Clay and the River of Silver

'A dish would be most welcome, sir,' said the American. 'The brew my steward serves is blacker than soot and about as palatable.'

Pueyrredon poured him a cup, to which he added several spoons of sugar. 'My, but that is good,' he concluded. 'So, I understand you have need of a ship.'

'Yes, of a neutral state, such as America. Would you perhaps start by telling me a little about your vessel, Captain?'

'The *Allerton*?' said Waine, his eyes lighting up. 'Why I'm happy to jaw about her all day, if it pleases you. She's a real beauty. Boston-built and only three years old. She's a shade over eight hundred tons, but brisk for her size. Handles easy as kiss my hand, too. If you care to look over her, she's just a step down the way. Moored in the Pool and waiting to unload.'

'And how do you find business at present?'

'Well, the war ain't helping any, but if you choose the right cargo, I find I can turn an honest dollar.'

'What cargo does she carry at present, Captain?' asked Pueyrredon.

'Grain this trip. Seems that what with all the soldiering going on in these parts, and so many menfolk not available to work the land, the price is pretty good. But I can carry just about anything.'

'Would you consider shipping a more valuable cargo?'

'More valuable, you say?' Waine regarded the Spaniard across the top of his coffee cup. 'What exactly did you have in mind, mister?'

'Me,' said Pueyrredon, meeting his gaze. 'And a consignment of weapons that I have recently purchased. Powder and shot. A thousand stands of muskets. Some pistols. All to be taken back to my home in the Rio de la Plata. Discreetly.'

Philip K Allan

'Oh, is that all?' said the American. 'What in God's name would you want with an arsenal like that? You figuring on starting a revolution, mister?'

'Let us call it an insurance policy,' said Pueyrredon, calmly refilling the cups. 'Are you interested? I will pay well.'

'How well?'

'Enough to cover the inconvenience to you, Captain.'

'The inconvenience!' exclaimed Waine. 'Is that all it is? There's a goddamn war going on in Europe, in case it had passed you by. The sea is crawling with Royal Navy cruisers, an' most don't care for us Yankees. I wouldn't get past the Downs without being stopped!'

'Place my purchases in the lower part of your hold, and keep a few layers of sacks from your current cargo to cover them well. Then, if we are stopped, all they will find is a ship out of Boston carrying grain, just as your documents state. I did ask my agent to recommend someone with a flexible attitude on such matters. He thought that you would be ideal, but if I am misinformed, I have several other masters I can talk to.' Pueyrredon started to rise from his seat, but Waine stopped him.

'I ain't said no yet, mister,' he said. 'If we get these guns out of Europe, what happens when we reach Buenos Aires? The Dons won't be too obliging when I try to unload all that weaponry of yours.'

'Oh, we shall not be landing them at Buenos Aires, Captain,' said Pueyrredon. 'We will dock fifty miles down the coast, at a little port called Ensenada.'

'And how exactly will that help us?'

'Because I own most of the land around there, and the head of customs is my nephew.'

Clay and the River of Silver

Chapter 3
Madeira

The wardroom of the *Griffin* occupied the stern end of the lower deck. Rows of doors ran along the sides, each one opening into an officer's cabin smaller than the meanest monk's cell. The narrow space between them was filled by a long table. It was gloomy now that the frigate was at sea, and the two ports at the rear of the space had to be bolted shut. The natural light and fresh air they supplied in harbour had been replaced by less welcome smells. The tang of bilge water and musty provisions wafting up from the hold beneath. The feral reek of poorly washed humanity from the packed lower deck just beyond the wardroom door, overlaid by a fishy note from the whale-oil lamps that hung from the beams.

    At one end of the table was Charles Faulkner, the frigate's purser. He was playing an intense game of piquet with Vansittart, each card wordlessly snapped down. Both men were well matched in appearance, for the purser still retained the aristocratic bearing that hinted at the family fortune he had squandered in his youth. Watching them was William Russell, sat a few places away in the lieutenant's coat he had bought in haste just before the ship left Plymouth. A carefully mended hole close to the heart and a stiffness in the lining hinted at its previous owner's fate. He jumped to his feet as Lieutenant Thomas Macpherson, commander of the *Griffin*'s contingent of marines came through the door.

Philip K Allan

'I see the cardsharps are hard at it,' said Macpherson, unbuttoning his tunic. 'I trust no money is at hazard, Charles? Remember your pledge?'

'Of course not,' replied the purser. 'I play purely for honour, my Caledonian friend, which I seem in want of. Vansittart here has the Devil's luck with cards.'

'Skill always trumps luck in the outcome of piquet, Charles,' corrected the diplomat, playing his last card with a flourish. 'My *partie*, I believe?'

'Again?' muttered Faulkner, gathering the cards together to shuffle them. 'Why are you on your feet, William? I didn't hear the watch change.'

'Sorry,' said Russell, retaking his place. 'My error.'

Macpherson took the chair next to his. 'Was it because I came in just now, laddie?' he asked, a kindly smile on his face.

'I suppose it was. The force of habit from all my years in the gunroom.'

'Well, you are among brother officers now, and need only stand for the captain. But I daresay it will take a wee time to adjust.'

'A while longer than that I fancy, Mr Macph— Tom, I mean,' said Russell. 'I may have his cabin, but how am I truly to take the place of Mr Blake among you all?'

'You passed your examination, did you not?' asked the Scotsman. 'You have the confidence of the captain, who favoured you above the other midshipmen? You understand your duties? And I have little difficulty sleeping in my cabin when you stand watch, in sole charge of the ship amid the peril of the sea.'

'To be sure, I can do all that well enough, but Mr Blake was so much more than a competent officer. He painted pictures. He had such an easy manner with the men. He was

Clay and the River of Silver

clever. I am just … well me.'

'Clever, you say?' said the marine. 'With an easy manner? An artist? That is a fair portrait of the friend we lost last year, but he was none of those things when I first made his acquaintance. It was back in ninety-seven, on board the *Titan*. You were a wee lad of thirteen, I recall, newly come to sea.'

'I remember you arriving, Tom,' smiled Russell. 'At the head of your men, and how much I admired your whiskers. I so wanted to grow some myself.'

Macpherson ran a hand over his still magnificent sideburns. 'You're no' the first man to covet these beauties, laddie. But to return to John Blake, he too had just been promoted. And in truth he was a sad fellow, quite in awe of that bully Morton. Why, he barely had an opinion in his head that wasn't put there by the second lieutenant.'

'Morton was a tartar to us midshipmen,' confirmed Russell. 'He would have us beaten for any trifling error. I'm ashamed to say it, but his passing was little mourned in the gunroom.'

'Aye, that is sad to hear. But my point was that Blake was no different to you. It was only once he was no longer in thrall to Morton that he grew into the splendid fellow whose society we all miss. Just be yourself, William, and all will turn out well.'

'Sound advice, Tom,' said Edward Preston, the *Griffin*'s second lieutenant, as he emerged from his cabin, dropping into the chair opposite the two officers.

'Was it not you that encouraged John to take up painting, Edward?' asked the marine.

'Yes, it had been his passion until Morton persuaded him that it was not a suitable accomplishment for a gentleman.'

'Perhaps I should take up something to fill my leisure

Philip K Allan

hours,' mused Russell. Preston and Macpherson exchanged a glance tinged with alarm.

'I would caution that the confines of a wardroom are ill suited for some activities,' said the marine. 'I once heard of an officer who decided to teach himself the German flute on a long commission. It didn't finish well.'

'And this from a man accustomed to the skirl of the pipes,' smiled Preston. 'How have the men reacted to your promotion, William?'

'They seem pleased for the most part, although many are still very familiar with me. But then they have known me since I was a boy. Some even feel able to discuss my instructions, or to call me Rusty to my face.'

'Then you must check them,' said Macpherson.

'Tom is right,' said Preston. 'For a time of crisis will come, in action or in heavy weather, when your orders must be acted on without hesitation. It is best to form that habit in the men now.'

'They call you Rusty, eh?' said Faulkner, running a hand through his own auburn locks. 'Heaven only knows what they must call me then, what?'

'Pinch-Farthing Faulkner, I believe,' said the marine.

'Pinch-Farthing!' exclaimed the purser. 'Me? Why, the ungrateful dogs! Do they think it easy to feed and clothe them on the pittance the Navy Board provides?'

'Oh, I dare say it is said with affection,' chuckled Vansittart.

'Can I say how welcome it is to have your company in our wardroom again, Nicholas,' said Preston.

'The pleasure is all mine, gentlemen,' said the diplomat, bowing in his place.

'Not least as it gives us a chance to find out more of our

Clay and the River of Silver

future,' continued Preston.

'Ah, and there was I thinking it was my wit you had missed,' said Vansittart. 'Don't look to me for intelligence, I pray. I am here in a very humble capacity – to provide advice, should it be required, that is all. But surely the captain has told you that we sail for Madeira to join with the rest of Popham's squadron, together with General Baird and his men?'

'Aye, but where are we bound after that?' asked Macpherson. 'Madeira can be a departure point for so many parts of the world. My shilling says we head for the Cape.'

'Now, Lieutenant,' said Vansittart. 'You may speculate, but I must not. Surprise is the greater part of victory, is it not? Then you must know that we shall squander such advantage if our object is openly spoken of. Have patience, gentlemen.'

'Will you give us no hint, sir?' asked Faulkner. 'Is Tom here right about the Cape?'

'All I can say is that the future will be full of interest for us all,' said Vansittart with a smile. 'Yes indeed. To the brim.'

*****

Clay was pacing the weatherside of the quarterdeck enjoying the early morning sun. It had only just cleared the horizon but it was already warm with the promise of a fine day ahead. The damp of a European winter seemed far behind, left in the *Griffin*'s wake as they sailed southwards. Each day he had watched the rolling Atlantic change in tiny increments from grey to green and finally to the deep blue of the approaching tropics.

'Land ahoy!' bellowed the lookout from the masthead. 'A point off the larboard bow!'

'What do you make of it, Dawson?' called Russell, who

Philip K Allan

was officer of the watch. Clay stepped across to hear the response.

'An island, sir. A mean little rock, in truth, just now raised, but I reckon there be a bigger 'un beyond it. I can see a deal of cloud sitting like a nest upon a chimney.'

'Porto Santo isle, with Madeira behind, I should say, sir,' suggested Russell. 'I was studying the chart earlier.'

'Well done, William,' said Clay. 'Then kindly alter course to pass Madeira to the east and bring us around to Funchal, if you please.'

'Aye aye, sir.'

Madeira, thought Clay to himself, as he resumed his walk, remembering his previous visit to the island. Then he had been a first lieutenant, sick with love for Lydia. She had been a passenger on an East Indiaman and Madeira was where they had parted. But it had also been the start of everything. He had been promoted later that year and Lydia had returned from India in time, having waited for him just as she had promised. Now she was the mother of his children, and he was Sir Alexander Clay, a senior post captain, with a wonderful ship to command and a fresh adventure just beginning. He returned to the present, and was surprised at how close the islands had grown. 'Pass the word for Mr Armstrong, if you please, Mr Russell,' he ordered. 'I shall presently require him to take us into port at Funchal.'

'Aye aye, sir,' said Russell, and then, 'I believe I could see us in, sir.'

Clay turned to him in surprise. 'I daresay you could, William. But it is the sailing master's duty to see us safely to our moorings. Besides, the rest of the squadron may well be there to observe our entrance. Let us save your first approach to a foreign harbour for a calmer occasion.'

'Aye aye, sir.'

Clay and the River of Silver

The quarterdeck began to fill with officers as Madeira grew closer. Even Napoleon, the ship's pet mongoose, awoke from his place on the sun-warmed capstan head to sniff appreciatively at the air. The northern coast consisted of cliffs rising directly from the sea, giving way to scrubby green slopes above, dotted with pine trees. Lines of sea birds came and went, calling raucously to each other as they passed overhead. Then the frigate turned about the eastern end of the island and the first signs of civilisation appeared. Red terracotta roofs among the trees, fishing villages in sheltered coves with lines of coloured boats drawn up along the shore. Terraced fields on the heights above, rising like steps built for a giant.

'Vineyards, I fancy,' commented Faulkner, who had arrived early to secure the ship's best telescope. 'A few pipes of Malmsey will be a most welcome addition to the wardroom pantry.'

'Indeed,' said Vansittart. 'Particularly if it means we are to be spared that very indifferent port wine Britton served last night.'

'Deck ho!' roared Dawson from the masthead. 'I can see that Funchee, beyond the next headland. There be a mighty lot of shipping in the harbour.'

'Aloft with you, Mr Sweeney,' ordered Clay. 'With the best glass, if the purser can be persuaded to surrender it.'

'Aye aye, sir,' said the midshipman.

'A lot of shipping,' commented Taylor to Armstrong. 'Let us hope they have left enough of a channel for us, Jacob. You know what these ship's masters can be like.'

'Deck there!'

'What can you see, Mr Sweeney?' replied Clay.

'Four two-deckers, and two smaller warships, sir. They are moored apart from the rest.'

Philip K Allan

'The rest, Mr Sweeney?' queried his captain.

'Merchant ships, sir. A great tangle of them. Why, there must be over a hundred!'

'It would seem Captain Popham and General Baird have arrived before us,' said Vansittart, coming over. 'That is well. We should not tarry too long here, where we are so easily observed.'

'Then Captain Popham should have chosen a more discreet rendezvous than Madeira,' said Clay. 'Half the neutral trade touches here. Do you note the American flag on that ship ahead. I daresay her master will make free to pass on what he observes to anyone he encounters. Mr Russell, I'll have the topgallants off her. We will heave to in the offing and await a pilot.'

'Aye aye, sir.'

When they finally rounded the headland, Clay had rarely seen a port so packed with shipping. The cobbled streets and stone buildings of Funchal were lost behind a forest of masts. Every buoy in the main harbour had at least four ships moored to it, with others warped against their sides. Most had soldiers lining the rails, red-coated infantrymen for the most part, watching their arrival with casual interest.

'Packed tighter than the Pool of London,' commented Old Amos to his fellow quartermaster at the wheel. 'I reckon you could cross from here to the shore, deck to deck like, and not wet a toe.'

'Over to that side of the channel, *senhor*,' said their Portuguese pilot to Armstrong, indicating the part of the port reserved for warships. There were six there already, all Royal Navy.

'What vessels are these?' asked Vansittart. 'Are they the ones we seek?'

Clay and the River of Silver

'They are indeed,' confirmed Clay, pointing them out. 'First we have three ships of the line, although one barely deserves the name. She is the little fifty-gunner over there. The frigate behind them is the *Narcissus*, thirty-two, followed by the sloop *Espoir*. Then to complete the squadron at the end of the line is the other sixty-four, the *Diadem*, which Captain Popham commands. Now that is odd.'

'What is?' asked Vansittart.

'She is flying a broad pennant. That can't be right. When we met with Lord Barham, I understood his Lordship to say that he was not going to make Popham a commodore,' said Clay. 'Indeed, my orders only refer to him as captain.'

'Perhaps he has been promoted in the meantime,' suggested Vansittart. 'In any event, he is the naval commander.'

'Shall I have his flag saluted, sir?' asked Taylor.

'Yes, I suppose we had better,' said Clay.

The *Griffin* sailed on until she was level with the end of the British line. 'You tie at the red buoy there,' said the pilot, pointing.

'I see it,' said Armstrong. 'Stand by in the bow to pick up our mooring, Mr Hutchinson! Take in sail, Mr Russell!'

'Aye aye, sir.'

'Bring her round, helmsman.'

'Round to larboard, aye,' said Amos.

The *Griffin*'s way came off quickly as the big square topsail was gathered in by a row of sailors stretched along the span of the yard. The last push of the Atlantic served to carry her forward to her place among the line of warships. Hutchinson, the boatswain, waved his leather hat from the forecastle as the buoy was picked up, and the frigate turned into the wind.

'You may begin the salute, Mr Taylor,' said Clay, and

Philip K Allan

the first gun banged out, each puff of smoke echoed by the reply from the two-decker.

'Kindly make our number to the *Diadem*, Mr Todd,' said Clay, when the sound of the last shot faded away.

'Aye aye, sir,' said the signal midshipman. In response, a line of flags soared up the sixty-four's mizzen.

'*Diadem* to *Griffin*. Welcome,' reported the youngster.

'Acknowledge, and send thank you, if you please.'

'Another signal, sir. Our number again. Come on board and report.'

'Barge away!' roared Taylor. 'Swiftly now.'

'Mr Vansittart, I do not doubt the invitation is also for you,' said Clay. 'Would you care to accompany me?'

'We are not to meet ashore?' protested the diplomat. 'I am wearing my best satin britches!'

'No time for you to change,' said Taylor, pushing him forward. 'I'll not have my ship spoken of as tardy.'

Once the barge was in the water, her crew hurried down the ship's side to their places at the oars, all dressed in matching white shirts and straw hats decorated with green ribbons the colour of the boat's hull and oar blades. Sedgwick growled an order, and they set off.

Vansittart watched the coxswain as he stared ahead, deftly steering in a long curve towards the *Diadem*'s side. He followed his gaze towards the bulky ship of the line, its twin yellow strakes reflected in the water, and noticed something dangling down from the main yard and brightened at the sight. 'That looks to be a more convenient way of getting on board,' he said, pointing. 'How does it function, pray?'

'The boatswain's chair?' said Clay. 'Why the men bring it close, you clamber on, and are hauled aboard much as a sack of provisions would be. But no sailor would risk being thought

Clay and the River of Silver

off as a lubber by using one in such calm conditions.'

'Easy there!' ordered the coxswain, as the ship loomed over them. 'Oars up! Clap on in the bow.'

The boat came to a halt beside the column of slats built into the ship's side that led up to the entrance port and Clay made his way through the boat towards it.

'Was you wanting to use the chair, Mr Vansittart, sir?' said a sailor in the bow, who had stretched out to grab it.

'Eh, I don't believe I shall,' he replied, eyeing the lowest step, green and slick with weed, with distaste. 'Another ship's side to clamber up,' he muttered. 'What joy.'

'Welcome on board, Sir Alexander,' enthused Popham, once the last trill of the boatswain's calls had faded away.

'Thank you, sir, and congratulations on your promotion.'

'Promotion?' queried Popham.

'To commodore,' said Clay, indicating the masthead.

'Ah … well, between us, actual confirmation of it hadn't reached me before I was obliged to sail,' said Popham. 'An oversight on their Lordships' part, no doubt. Or a clerical error. I am sure that was the Admiralty's intention.'

'But … but in all good faith, I ordered a salute fired!' protested Clay.

'And it is well that you did. The Portuguese authorities become much more accommodating if they believe they are dealing with one who is virtually an admiral.'

'Virtually an admiral! But you are no such …' began Clay, but Popham had turned back to the entry port. 'And Mr Vansittart too. But … God bless my soul! Is that blood upon your stocking, sir? Are you wounded?'

'Only my pride is truly hurt,' said the diplomat, with a grimace. 'I successfully negotiated your lowest two steps, only

Philip K Allan

to be undone by the third. But my shin will recover sooner than my stockings. Best China silk, at a guinea a pair.'

'Let us see if a little madeira will not restore you,' said their host. 'Pray follow me, gentlemen. I have the generals waiting for us in my quarters.'

The great cabin of the *Diadem* was a magnificent space, running across the full width of the ship. It was furnished with careful elegance in fashionable cherrywood furniture, upholstered in pale grey satin. Light flooded in through the run of six windows across the stern, and bolts of matching grey material were draped in folds to conceal the ship's stern-most pair of cannons. As they entered, two men in scarlet coats rose to greet them.

'We are gathered at last,' beamed Popham. 'Pray let me make the introductions. I know that all here know Mr Vansittart, but this is Captain Sir Alexander Clay. Captain, let me introduce you to Lieutenant-General Sir David Baird, who commands our troops, and will, it is to be hoped, presently be our governor at the Cape. And this is Brigadier-General William Beresford, his deputy.'

Baird proved to be an elegant Scot with silver hair who matched Clay in height. His handshake was firm, although Clay detected a haunted, anxious look in his pale eyes. Beresford in contrast was a short, jovial man with cheerful dark eyes and a bald pate.

'I have not had the pleasure, Sir Alexander, although I have heard of your exploits, of course,' said Baird in a soft Highland burr. 'You have served in India, I collect?'

'I was sent there as the peace was ending, sir,' said Clay. 'To the Malabar Coast, where Mr Vansittart and I worked with a man who claimed your acquaintance. Colonel Macaulay? The company resident in Travancore?'

Clay and the River of Silver

'Indeed,' said Baird. 'The colonel and I spent two years as prisoners of Tipu Sultan, chained beside each other in a Mysore dungeon. Under such circumstances one either becomes the most particular of friends or the bitterest of enemies. Fortunately, we became the former.'

'Splendid,' said Popham, clapping his hands together in fear that the general might be about to embark on a lengthy anecdote. 'Now we are all introduced, shall we proceed to more important matters? How we shall liberate the Cape from the enemy? Pray take a seat, gentlemen. O'Shaughnessy, some refreshment for my guests.'

'Aye aye, sir,' replied the steward, bringing over glasses.

'Now, Sir David,' continued Popham. 'You are acquainted with the area. Would you share your knowledge with us?'

'Several members of my staff have served there before. Control of the Cape rests on ownership of Cape Town and the adjacent naval base. Apart from a modest hinterland, occupied by Dutch farmers, there are no other settlements of note. Seize the town, and the rest will fall, gentlemen.'

'That sounds straightforward enough,' commented Vansittart. 'How do we take it?'

'Cape Town possesses formidable coastal defences,' said Popham. 'Beyond anything that my squadron could subdue, but is vulnerable from the landward side, where the only real threat comes from the natives. I propose that we land Sir David's men further up the coast. There are plenty of beaches to the north. There they can assemble and descend on Cape Town.'

'But the place must be chosen with care,' cautioned Baird. 'Too distant, and my men will arrive exhausted, yet two

Philip K Allan

close and we may find the enemy waiting to repel us as we step from our boats.'

'Has a suitable landing beach been chosen, sir?' asked Clay.

'It has not,' said Popham. 'That coast can be plagued by surf, depending on the season and the state of the weather.'

'What forces can we expect the enemy to have at his disposal?' asked Beresford.

'With regard to ships, the last we heard there were three significant ones,' said Popham. 'A Dutch ship of the line, the *Bato* of sixty-four guns, and two heavy French frigates, the *Volontaire* and the *Valeureuse*. They will doubtless have other smaller vessels, but nothing that this squadron can't handle.'

'And what of their forces on land,' asked Baird, turning to Vansittart. 'I was informed that you would provide the latest evaluation, sir.'

'As indeed I can, gentlemen,' said Vansittart, drawing a notebook from his pocket. 'But pray do not press me to know from whence these particulars come, if you take my meaning. Now let me see ... General Janssens, he being the governor, has at his disposal one regular Dutch regiment, the er ... 22nd Foot; another regiment of mercenaries, commanded by a Colonel Waldeck, and several units of militia. They also have some native units – light infantry drawn from the local Hottentot population, and some artillerymen recruited in the Dutch East Indies. All told they have similar numbers to ourselves.'

'Similar numbers? said Baird, shaking his head. 'I told London that we needed a greater force,'

'Do you think so, sir?' said Beresford. 'I didn't hear anything to occasion alarm. A mixture of mercenaries, blacks and farmers? Apart from this line regiment, I can't see the rest detaining our men for very long once we are ashore.'

Clay and the River of Silver

'And the squadron can supply another five hundred marines if required, as well as sailors and naval guns to provide a siege train,' added Popham.

'And what if Mr Vansittart's wee notebook is wrong?' asked Baird. 'What if their numbers are superior?'

'Wrong, Sir David? Wrong?' queried the diplomat, his eyes hardening. 'You may be well versed in soldiering, but when it comes to obtaining intelligence, I flatter to say I have few equals. My source is quite impeccable. You have my word upon it.'

'My apologies, sir,' said the general. 'I did not mean to impugn your abilities.'

'Of course you did not,' said Popham, filling the silence that followed. 'Sir Alexander, do you have any observations to make?'

'It strikes me that time is of the essence, sir. I know our destination is being kept secret until we have left Madeira, but even the duller among my people have guessed it, and this huge armada can hardly be long concealed. We must assume that if this General Janssens does not already know we are coming, he will do so soon, and will hasten his preparations to receive us. We should make for the Cape with all urgency.'

'Aye, you have the truth of it there,' said Baird. 'I fear we shall face a very well-prepared enemy.'

'Urgency you say?' said Popham. 'Have you ever had to herd a large convoy, Sir Alexander? Glaciers advance swifter than these merchant ships made passage here from Ireland. And upon my word, who can blame them? These contracted troop transports are paid a daily rate, so the slower the passage, the more they gain.'

'How long will it take us to reach the Cape?' asked Beresford.

Philip K Allan

'Two months to reach the island of St Helena,' said Popham. 'For we shall have to stop enroute to replenish our water, what with so many men on board, and as for the light dragoons, their damn nags are thirstier than camels. From there it is at least another three weeks to the Cape.'

'The best part of three months!' exclaimed Beresford. 'And we will still be unsure where we should land, or what the enemy has been up to.'

'Drilling their militia into guardsmen and turning Cape Town into a fortress, I make no doubt,' muttered Baird.

'Might I make a suggestion, sir?' said Clay. 'The *Griffin* could make the passage in half that time. I could search for possible landing sites and see how many enemy warships are in the area. I could meet you all at St Helena and report my findings.'

'A fine proposal,' enthused Beresford. 'I like your style, Sir Alexander.'

'It would certainly expedite matters,' conceded Baird.

'I had hoped for the *Griffin*'s assistance with these wilful transports,' sighed Popham. 'Another sheep dog to yap at their heels would have been most welcome; but I must concede your idea is not without merit. Very well, we shall next meet at St Helena. I will have your orders drawn up directly.'

'And when shall we depart?' asked Vansittart.

'As soon as the ships have taken on stores,' said Popham. 'Let us say the day after next. Agreed? Then kindly raise your glasses, gentlemen. To our conquest of the Cape, and to whatever may lie beyond.'

'Hear him!' said Beresford, thumping the table.

Clay drained his glass, a puzzled look on his face. 'Whatever may lie beyond, sir?' he repeated. 'What does lie beyond the Cape?'

Clay and the River of Silver

'Just an elegant figure of speech, I have no doubt,' said Vansittart. 'Honours for us and a secure passage for our shipping to India, I am certain is what the captain meant.'

But once Clay had returned to the *Griffin*, and was reflecting on the meeting, he felt sure he had seen a warning in the glance the diplomat had given Popham.

*****

The tavern was still there, occupying one corner of an intersection of narrow cobbled streets in the heart of Funchal's old town. It was a low, single-storey building with a pitched terracotta roof that was now green with lichen. Food scraps and rubbish were strewn like leaf litter across its packed earth floor, and its ceiling was black with grime.

'Can we really be meaning to drink here?' queried Sedgwick, wrinkling his nose at the smell of sour wine as the sailors peered in through the door.

'Stinks like the morning after the Goose Fair back home,' added Pembleton, the former machine breaker who had joined their mess.

'This is the fecking place, to be sure,' enthused O'Malley. 'The wine was a touch rough, but cheap at a penny a pitcher, and the serving wenches were comely enough.'

'Leastways they were ten year back, when we was last here,' said Trevan. 'Mind, there were a deal less folk about then.'

Every table in the place was occupied, almost all by red-coated soldiers, playing dice, drinking wine and carousing together. Just inside the door, a group of kilted Highlanders broke off their animated discussion in lilting Gaelic to look the newcomers up and down.

Philip K Allan

'There's the place for us,' announced Evans, pointing to a table against the far wall that was only half occupied by a group of sailors.

The others followed in the huge Londoner's wake as he picked his way through the crowd. They deftly stepped over the sprawling legs, and detoured around the rim of a fight that had broken out between two corporals from rival regiments, both too drunk to be of much danger to the other. Eventually they arrived at the table.

'Afternoon, shipmates,' said Evans, raising his voice to be heard over a burst of singing from a nearby table. 'All right if we join you?'

'Sure you can,' said the nearest sailor, in a Boston accent. 'Good to have some reinforcements. We ain't seen this many redcoats since Yorktown.'

'Aye, there are a few,' agreed Evans, as the Griffins gratefully occupied the rest of the benches. 'Not that I don't care for the company of Lobsters, but each to his bleeding own,' he added for the benefit of those soldiers within earshot.

'They make me nervous,' said Pembleton. 'Too like the militiamen the justices sent against us, back home, like.'

'These lads be all right,' said Trevan, filling his pipe. 'They be just pleased to be off them transports for a bit. Packed in tight as a slaver, I've heard.'

'Not quite that close,' said Sedgwick, quietly.

O'Malley summoned over one of the harassed serving girls with a two-fingered whistle that cut through the background roar with ease, and a jug of wine with five cups soon appeared in front of them.

'You never did say as what it was you did, afore you took to rioting, Ted?' asked Evans.

'I were a lacemaker,' said Pembleton. 'The whole

Clay and the River of Silver

family were, me, my parents, uncles and aunts, brothers and sisters. It were a good trade, an' all. Hard work, mind, and it plays Old Harry with your eyes, especially in the winter. But Nottingham lace was much sought after, so we had a decent enough living.'

'So why take to crime?' asked Sedgwick.

'It all started a few years back, when this new mill were built, out on the edge of town. A right big place it were, with a chimney tall as a spire, belching out smoke faster than Adam's pipe. Inside, it were full of big looms all churning out lace by the yard. We laughed at first, for the product couldn't touch the quality of what we made. But it seems most folk aren't concerned with that, if the price is low enough. Another mill opened, and then a third, and the price of lace became so cheap we couldn't even pay the rent, let alone feed ourselves. That's when me an' some of the others decided to take matters into our own hands. Breaking in at night with hammers an' that and smashing up the looms.'

'Could you not have worked for the mill owners, like?' asked Sedgwick.

'Oh aye?' said Pembleton. 'For half the wage, an' but one in ten offered work. I'd sooner fight the bastards.'

'I like your spirit, there, Ted,' said the Irishman, clashing his mug against the lacemaker's. 'Haven't we Irish been after fighting the fecking English forever.'

'I ain't so sure as you done right there, Ted,' said Trevan. 'Mills an' progress an' that be just how matters stand. That be a strong tide to pull ag'in.

'It's strange what a man will do when it's that or the workhouse, lads,' said Pembleton. 'And now I'm a sailor, me who'd never seen aught bigger than a river before.'

'A landsman,' corrected O'Malley. 'You've a way to

Philip K Allan

travel before you'll be rated as a seaman. And you certainly don't drink like a fecking sailor. Why you've hardly touched your grog! Down the hatch, there.' The Irishman provided a demonstration for the novice, before banging his empty cup down and wiping his sleeve across his mouth.

'Easy there, Sean,' cautioned Trevan as he refilled the cups. 'This knock-me-down be stronger than you think. We doesn't want you milling with half the tavern, like last time we was here.'

'What happened last time?' asked Sedgwick.

'We be sat over there, by that window, minding our own, like,' continued the Cornishman. 'Me, Sean and poor old Rossie, as fell at the Nile. Sean got fighting-drunk, an' took a dislike to these Yanks at the next table. There being six of them, all of a size, matters were going ill. And then Big Sam appears, fists up, chin down, for all the world like Tom Cribb in his pomp. He knocks down two of them, quick as quick, and the others turned shy.'

'Has your friend got something against Americans?' asked the sailor from Boston, indicating O'Malley. 'Because that don't sit so well with me.'

'Steady there, mate,' said Sedgwick. 'We ain't here to cause no trouble. We tars should stick together.'

'Even if some tars are blacker than most,' replied the American, looking the coxswain up and down.

'Is the look of my mucker a problem?' growled Evans.

'Now, Sam, it be no more than a jest,' said Trevan, pushing his friend back. 'So where you lads be from, then?'

'We sail with Captain Waine on the *Cape Allerton*, outward bound from London,' said the American.

'Right you are,' said Trevan. 'We followed you in this morning. You be reaching a long way south, if Boston be your

Clay and the River of Silver

mark?'

'Who sh ... says we're heading there?' said another sailor at the table, his words slurred with drink.

'Take no heed of him,' said the Bostonian. 'The captain has some wine to collect, that is all. For our owner, who is inordinately fond of the liquor they make hereabouts.'

'I'll wager he ain't after this gut rot,' said Sedgwick, holding up his mug.

'What you lads be shipping?' asked Trevan. 'Aside from fancy grog for the master.'

'Grain,' said two of the American sailors together.

Sedgwick looked puzzled. 'I thought you lads said you be from London, heading home? Don't grain go the other way?'

'Aye, but wash iss under the grain?' said the drunk, closing one eye and trying to touch the side of his nose.

'Hush yer bleeding noise, Caleb,' urged another sailor to the drunk, his accent strangely familiar.

'Bleeding hell!' exclaimed Evans. 'You ain't no Yank! You was born in London, or I'm a Chinaman. Where you from, brother?'

'Whitechapel, but I'm American now. Ever since I jumped ship for the *Allerton*.'

'How's that work?' asked Evans.

'It were easy enough,' continued the man. 'Captain Waine spoke for me in Boston. Then some bloke made me stick a paw on a Bible and repeat what he said. I think it were about my health, for he seemed mighty concerned about my constitution. And after that, I were a Yank.'

'You should consider it, lads,' said the Bostonian. 'We can always use good hands.'

'I don't reckon my Molly would fancy leaving Cornwall,' said Trevan. 'An' I'll not risk being flogged for desertion.'

'The *Griffin*'s a sweeter birth than most in the navy, so I'll be after staying put for now,' added O'Malley.

The conversation became livelier as the drink took hold, and soon the two groups of sailors were mingling together, an island amid a sea of scarlet. Later, Sedgwick was returning from the privy when he met Evans coming the other way.

'Sam,' he said, drawing his friend aside. 'Would you be doing something for me?'

'Aye, mate. What you after?'

'Have a jaw with that tar from London. Make out as you might be thinking of jumping ship yourself, maybe. I'll try my luck with the drunk one. I wants to find out what their barky be about. What they be carrying and why they be so far south. Something ain't right. I can feel it in my bones.'

Clay and the River of Silver

Chapter 4
The Skeleton Coast

A month later the *Griffin* was closing with the shores of Southern Africa. She was beating into an easterly wind that grew steadily warmer with each mile the frigate covered. The horizon was lost in a golden haze, and the air flowing over the ship had a musty smell. Fine dust particles pattered against the sails and slid down onto the deck in a gentle rain. Clay and his first lieutenant watched them drift across the planking.

'Mr Sweeney, kindly organise a party of men to swab away this filth, before the ship resembles a snuff box,' ordered Taylor.

'Aye aye, sir,' said the midshipman.

'I fear you may be engaged in a losing battle, George,' said Clay. 'This dirt will surely come thicker as we approach the land.'

'Can we not stay a little further out then, sir? Where the air is more wholesome?'

'We could, but that is where we may encounter shipping bound for the Cape,' replied his captain. 'I wish to arrive unobserved, and this shore has an ill reputation that makes most give it a wide birth.'

'Deck there!' yelled the lookout.

'What can you see, Saleem?' called Clay.

'I am not being certain, but perhaps land is in sight. Off the bow.'

Philip K Allan

Clay collected a telescope and focused ahead. He could make little out at first, but as the frigate steadily approached, something more solid began to appear amid the murk. It looked like a huge yellow wave stretching across the horizon, the wind tugging streamers from its crest. Then he realised that it must be a sand dune, but one of unprecedented size to be visible this far out.

'Goodness, it must be taller than Beachy Head,' muttered Taylor beside him.

'Much taller, I fancy,' agreed Clay, as the ship sailed on, the wall of sand growing all the time. 'I'll have the ship follow the coast southward, if you please.'

'Aye aye, sir.'

The boatswain's calls twittered through the ship, summoning all hands to trim sails, but once the *Griffin* had settled on to her new course, many chose to stay on deck, lining the rail and watching the strange landscape sliding past. The blue sea lightened to topaz as it approached a shore that was quite devoid of any hint of life. No scrap of green, no bird on the wing, nothing but sand towering up far above the frigate's main mast. The sailors might have been observing another world. After a while the vast dune gave way, tapering down to reveal a frozen sea of huge yellow waves behind it, stretching away as far as the eye could see.

'Deck there!' yelled the lookout. 'Ship in sight!'

'Where away, Saleem?' asked Clay.

'Two points off the bow! Beyond the next hill of sand! But very strange. She is far from the sea.'

'Far from the sea! What nonsense is this?' fumed Taylor, turning his telescope towards the sighting.

The ship proved to be a wreck, and was indeed a good quarter mile inland. She looked like a model that had been

Clay and the River of Silver

arranged as part of a tableau, with her bow thrust into a dune as if about to founder beneath a wave of sand. Her hull lay tilted to one side, the elaborately carved stern towards the approaching frigate. A few rags of canvas flapped mournfully from her remaining masts. On the stump of her mizzen jutted up a long, steeply pitched yard.

'She has a lateen mizzen, sir,' exclaimed Taylor. 'No European ship has carried such a rig for half a century or more. Can she be a Barbary cruiser?'

'I believe she is from another age,' said Clay. 'Look at that high stern, and all that carving. She might have sailed with Rooke or Shovell.'

'It must be dry as a tomb hereabouts for her timbers not to have perished, then, sir,' said Taylor. 'But how did she come to be so far from the water?'

'This is a strange coast, George,' said Clay. 'Jacob tells me it has an ill reputation. Too much shifting sand and strange fogs that spring up unannounced. He was quite alarmed when I told him I meant to come this way. For his piece of mind, we should stand further out to sea, before it grows dark.'

The wind shifted as evening approached until it was coming down from the north. Once it was no longer blowing off the land, it became clear of dust. The strange coast continued to pass by, cross-lit by the setting sun into a tiger's pelt of amber dunes, each paired with its shadow. As it grew dark, the wind dropped to a gentle air just sufficient to send the frigate whispering forward beneath a growing vault of stars, numberless beyond count, silent as a held breath.

Much later, Russell climbed up on to the quarterdeck to relieve Preston as officer of the watch. He was disappointed to find that the sky was now overcast, the air chill and moist. The light from the binnacle seemed furry and diffuse, those stood around it anonymous shapes in the gloom.

'Good morning, William,' said the voice of Preston as he approached. 'Although there is precious little good about it. The Southern Cross was visible earlier, and then this wretched fog rolled up.'

'But the air was so warm and dry earlier,' protested Russell.

'It is passing strange. Apparently, the sea hereabouts is perishing cold, and it cools any wind that doesn't come from off the land. I recommend you try to keep us from the shore. We don't want passing ships a hundred years from now pondering on the wreck of the *Griffin*, lost amid the desert sands.'

'No indeed,' said his fellow officer.

'Turn and strike,' announced the midshipman of the watch, flipping the hour glass over, and eight bell strokes rang out from the forecastle. The ship burst into life as the boatswain's mates roused the watch below.

'Right, I'm for a couple of hours' sleep before breakfast,' said Preston. 'The captain's sailing instructions are on the slate, but in essence they are to carry on as we are.'

'Keep a little salt pork for me and see that Macpherson doesn't have more than his share of the coffee, if you please, Edward,' said Russell.

The departing figure raised an arm in acknowledgement and Russell went to read Clay's instructions, tilting the slate towards the oil lamp burning in the binnacle. Around him there was swirling movement as the watch changed over, and then stillness as each person on deck was replaced. The pool of lit planking around the wheel was like an island adrift in the dark. It was only through sound that he could sense the existence of a world beyond. The hiss of the hull through the calm sea. The

Clay and the River of Silver

creak and rattle from the rigging as the ship swayed in the gentle swell. And the shifting and quiet talk of the men at their posts.

Once he was certain all was well, the new lieutenant began to pace the deck, his mind wondering as he walked. He reflected on his good fortune in being commanded by a man like Clay, ready to push forward his officers on ability, rather than favouring the well-connected, as too many captains did. On another ship he might have remained as a midshipman almost indefinitely. He had served with such officers before, bitter, grey-haired men forced to obey fresh-faced lieutenants half their age and with a fraction of their knowledge. As he walked, his determination grew to reward Clay's faith in him, and he began to imagine how it might happen. In his mind's eye he led borders onto an enemy deck, or battled against storms. But his conversation with Macpherson and Preston in the wardroom came to mind. Would the men really follow him through such perils as he imagined?

The sound of the bell brought him out of his reverie. Three bells? Surely he hadn't been walking for over an hour? He looked around and realised that the night was almost over. Grey light illuminated the air around him, and tendrils of mist twisted across the deck. He could see the main mast at the front of the quarterdeck, its column vanishing into the gloom above, but he could see little beyond it. Then he thought he heard a faint echo of the *Griffin*'s bell, muffled by the fog from somewhere off to starboard.

'Anyone hear that?' he asked.

'Heard what, sir?' queried the helmsman.

'A ship's bell, off to starboard. Mr Drake? Mr Todd?' The midshipmen of the watch shook their heads.

Russell stood for a moment, wondering what he had truly heard. Perhaps he had imagined it, or it really was an echo

Philip K Allan

of the *Griffin*'s bell, reflected back from some distant wall of sand. Nothing would surprise him on this strange coast. Then he recalled the sound had come from the seaward side. 'Mr Todd. Kindly give my compliments to the captain, and ask him to join me on deck. Tell him that I believe another ship may be close by.'

Todd exchanged glances with Drake and then stepped closer to Russell, lowering his voice. 'Are you sure about this, Rusty? Pipe won't care to be woken at this hour on a whim. None of the rest of us heard it.'

Russell looked at Todd, only a few years his junior, and his close friend when they had been midshipmen together, a few short months before. Then he hardened his heart.

'What insolence is this?' he demanded. 'How did you just address me?'

Todd stepped back and froze at attention. 'Eh ... R-Rusty?'

'Sir! You call me sir to my face, and Mr Russell to another. Is that clear?'

'Y-yes, sir.'

'And how dare you presume to question an order?' he continued. 'Are you too dull to follow a simple instruction?'

'No, sir. Of course not, sir.'

'Then how should you have responded, Mr Todd?'

'With aye aye, sir. Sorry, sir.'

'We make progress,' said Russell. 'Now go and find the captain. And make haste. It will go ill with you if that ship has escaped us thanks to your stupidity.'

'Aye aye, sir,' said Todd, retreating to the companionway.

Russell watched him go, and then unclenched his hands from behind his back, rubbing life back into the fingers. He

Clay and the River of Silver

walked across to the side rail, hating himself for how he had treated Todd. Preston and Macpherson's advice made sense, but all he could see was the look of hurt in his friend's eyes.

'More ginger in Rusty than I figured,' he heard one of the afterguard mutter to a companion. 'That there Goldilocks were close to tears.'

He drew out his telescope and began searching where he thought the sound had been. The light was growing all the time, but the fog was so thick that he could make little out. Please be there, he urged, realising how ridiculous he would seem if there really was no ship. 'Masthead! What do you see to starboard?'

'Can't see aught, sir,' came the reply. 'Thicker than mutton stew, although it be lifting a touch to larboard.'

'Good morning, Mr Russell,' said Clay, his bare feet showing beneath the dressing gown he had thrown over his nightshirt. 'What is all this about a ship?'

'Three bells had just rung when I heard her, sir,' said Russell. 'I marked the sound to be on the starboard bow, though how far away was hard to judge.'

'Did others hear it?'

'No, sir,' said the officer. 'I suppose I might have imagined it. Fog can play odd tricks on the mind.'

Clay took in the anxiety in his officer's eyes, and clapped him on the arm. 'I trust you, William. You have young ears and quick wits. Mind, we will need to get within a biscuit toss to find anyone today. Bring the ship around to close with your best estimate of where the sound came from and turn up the watch below. But quietly, mind. No boatswain's calls or clamour. And have the guns manned. I shall go shift into some clothes.'

When Clay returned it was light enough for him to see

Philip K Allan

that the ship had been transformed. Down on the main deck the gun crews stood beside their weapons, with Preston pacing slowly along the lines of cannon, checking all was as it should be. On the quarterdeck Macpherson had his marines formed up in a solid block of scarlet and white.

Armstrong came over to him, his face full of concern. 'This is an ill-favoured coast for sudden changes in direction in weather as thick as this, sir,' he protested. 'And the Dutch chart I am obliged to use is very indifferent.'

'I understand, Jacob, but we are barely making steerage way,' said Clay. 'We shall be able to kedge off easy enough if we strike a sandbar. And I fancy the sun will burn off this murk soon.'

'I would sooner have the comfort of a lead going in the bow, sir.'

Clay shook his head at this. 'The noise will travel, and I would sooner come upon this one unannounced. The enemy have several ships of force based at the Cape.'

'Aye aye, sir.'

Clay stepped across to join Taylor and Russell where they stood by the rail, straining to hear any sound. 'Anything?' he asked.

'Nothing yet, sir.'

The *Griffin* ghosted on in near silence towards the wall of retreating fog. Clay searched it with his telescope, until his mind began to fill with swirling grey, but could find no trace of anything solid. Then Russell held up a hand.

'Was that the flap of a sail, sir?' he asked.

Clay strained his ears and heard a muffled thump. He turned to the others for confirmation.

'A hatch cover or grating dropped back into place, sir,' confirmed his first lieutenant. 'A touch off the bow. Shall I have

Clay and the River of Silver

the guns run out?'

'Not yet, Mr Taylor,' said Clay. 'Let us continue in silence.'

Clay returned his telescope to his eye. The fog was thinning faster. Now it glowed silver as the sun penetrated it, and patches of open water appeared amid the coiling mist. Then he saw a dark shadow of something large and solid. In his mind he pictured the side of the Dutch sixty-four Popham had mentioned in Madeira, the *Bato*. Its twin gun decks turned towards him, the gunners training her twenty-four pounders around, her officers joking to each other at the ease with which they had lured him down on to their guns.

The mainmast backstay began to vibrate, droplets of water spraying from it. He glanced up to see Dawson, the lookout, sliding down from the masthead, the rope gripped between his calloused feet. He dropped onto the deck beside his captain and knuckled his forehead in salute.

'There be a brig showing Butter-box colours a cable off the bow, sir,' he announced. 'I thought best to come down an' report, so they don't hear no hail. They be carrying on without a care in the world, seemingly.'

'A Dutch brig, you say?' queried Clay, looking back towards the looming shadow in the mist. 'Not a man-o'-war?'

'I can only see her mastheads proud of this reek, but there are but two, and no commissioning pennant.'

Thank you, Dawson,' said Clay, dismissing the sailor. 'Mr Taylor, kindly run out the starboard guns, and have an armed boarding party told off and ready.'

'Aye aye, sir.'

The silhouette continued to shrink as the *Griffin* bore down on it. Then the silence was broken by the rumble of gun trucks as the frigate's main armament was run out, immediately

Philip K Allan

followed by a hail in guttural Dutch.

'Heave to there!' roared Clay. 'Or I open fire! Mr Preston, give him a gun, so he understands we are in earnest.'

'Aye aye, sir.'

The tongue of orange fire that shot out from the bow eighteen-pounder was met with cries of consternation from the shadow in the fog, and then Clay could see the ship at last, her dark hull battered and stained, rounding up into the gentle wind, her sails flapping mournfully. Her Dutch ensign had spent too long in the African sun, to judge from the blue and red bands now faded to turquoise and pink. As Clay watched, it made its jerky way down to the deck. 'What ship is that?' he asked.

A large bearded man in shirtsleeves made his way to the side, and cupped his hands into a speaking trumpet. 'Trading brig *Willemstad* of Cape Town, *meneer*,' he said, in good English. 'Please stop shooting. We only have a pair of six-pounders.'

'And who are you, sir?'

'Captain Hendrik de Bruyn, master of this ship.'

'What cargo do you have, Captain?'

'Grain in sacks, and some casks of salt beef.'

'A nice little prize,' commented Taylor. 'That'll get bought, cargo and ship, when we send it into St Helena.'

'Send a crew across to take possession of her,' said Clay, 'and send that fellow back with his papers, if you will.'

'Aye aye, sir.'

'Mr Todd, run and find my steward and tell him I will have an extra guest for breakfast. And pray ask Mr Vansittart to join us.'

'Aye aye, sir.'

*****

Clay and the River of Silver

The Dutch captain's eyes widened in surprise as he was shown into the cabin, to find the table laid and a delicious aroma of fresh coffee in the air. He was a big man, not as tall as Clay, but substantially broader. His thick beard covered much of his neckcloth, and he now wore a battered pea jacket pulled over his shirt.

'Captain De Bruyn,' said Clay, rising to greet him. 'I imagine you will not have had the opportunity to break your fast this morning, so would you care to eat with us? My name is Sir Alexander Clay, and this is the Honourable Nicholas Vansittart, a guest on my ship.'

'The pleasure is all mine, to be sure,' said the diplomat, opting to bob his head towards the Dutchman, rather than shaking the none-too-clean hand their visitor had begun to extend towards him.

'Vansittart? Surely that is a Dutch name?'

'Quite so, although my people left your splendid country rather a long time ago. We are all children of Britannia now.'

'Do be seated, I pray,' urged Clay. 'Would you care for coffee, or I can send for a small beer if you prefer?'

'Coffee please, Sir Alexander,' said De Bruyn, taking his place. 'I haven't tasted a drop since the war resumed and your naval blockade was reimposed.'

'An unfortunate necessity while your home country is occupied by the French and forced to oppose us,' said Vansittart. 'But there you have it. So long as the House of Orange is in exile and Bonaparte rules in their stead, there will be no coffee. Splendid brew this, by the way.'

'It is not just coffee that runs short,' said De Bruyn. 'The harvest has been poor at the Cape these last two years. We have to survive on what food we can smuggle in.'

'Ah,' said Clay. 'That will explain your cargo, but not your presence on this coast. My sailing master tells me it has an ill reputation.'

'He is right,' said De Bruyn. 'We name it the Skeleton Coast in these parts, with good reason, for it has claimed many a ship over the years. But those who perish when their ship founders are the lucky ones. The survivors find themselves in an endless desert with no water and sand driven by the wind that will devour their bodies until only their bones remain, hence the name. You were brave to bring such a large ship this close to the shore.'

'If it is such an ill-favoured place, what in all creation made you come this way?' asked Vansittart.

'I was trying to avoid you,' said the Dutchman.

'Watching yourselves, kind sirs,' announced Harte, Clay's steward, entering the cabin with a pair of covered dishes held with cloths. 'Both being hot as hot,' he continued, banging them down on the table. 'That one has salt bacon, tother has the eggs. Ship's biscuit in the barge with two types of jam, an' the last of the Madeira butter in the crock, what is only a touch on the rancid side.'

'Thank you, Harte,' said Clay. 'Pray serve my guests first, and I believe the captain here would appreciate a second pot of coffee.'

Once they all had food, Clay resumed the conversation. 'When you say avoid, do you mean that you were expecting us? Had you received word that we were coming?'

'This ship, or another Britisher. We have been expecting you to try something ever since the war started again,' said De Bruyn, through a mouthful of bacon. 'You came and took the Cape before, so why not again?'

Clay and the River of Silver

'So your forces are well prepared to receive us, I collect?' said Vansittart.

'Governor Janssens was drilling the militia when I left Cape Town.'

'Successfully ...?' prompted Clay.

'Might I have some more of that coffee, Sir Alexander,' said De Bruyn. 'And another egg would be welcome.'

Clay waved Harte forward to serve his guest, and the Dutchman resumed the conversation. 'Many have chosen not to answer the call, and farmers and shopkeepers are not soldiers,' he said.

'Even when defending their homes?' asked Clay.

'We know how to do that well enough,' said De Bruyn, a glint in his eye. 'We learn it young, living at the tip of a continent filled with naught but savages. But many say the Britishers didn't make war on people before and doubt they will do so again. Besides ...'

'Besides?' prompted Clay.

De Bruyn shrugged his shoulders. 'This damned blockade is killing us. Cape Towners live on trade, and that has all but dried up.'

'That is regrettable,' said Vansittart. 'Of course, under British rule trade would resume. Immediately. No more skulking along the Skeleton Coast, trying to avoid the captain here. Indeed, he would then be obliged to protect your vessel, rather than seize it.'

'That thought has occurred to some,' said De Bruyn. 'Others recall that when you were last here your garrison paid for all it needed, which is more than the French Navy do. And your Indiamen used to stop at Cape Town, full of passengers with gold in their purses.'

'Let us hope for a return to such profitable times,'

Philip K Allan

beamed the diplomat, before pausing, as if a thought had just occurred to him. 'But stay a moment. Perhaps we can do more than just hope, Captain.'

De Bruyn's eyes narrowed and he lay down his knife and fork. 'What are you suggesting, *meneer*?'

'As a man settled here in Africa, does it matter whether your governor is appointed by London or Amsterdam?' continued Vansittart. 'You said yourself how the colony benefitted under our rule. So why not aid the return of that happy situation?'

'Do you think you can buy me with a pot of coffee?' demanded the Dutchman.

'No, of course not. I was thinking more of your ship.'

'You mean his ship,' said De Bruyn, jabbing a thumb towards Clay. 'The *Willemstad* is his prize now.'

'Indeed, and will be condemned by a prize court in due course and sold off,' said Vansittart. 'At which point I could use my influence to see that it was offered back to its original owner ... at a favourable price. Of course, I would have to be able to vouch that person was a friend of my government, whose support should be valued.'

De Bruyn stroked his beard as he considered this, his eyes never leaving Vansittart. 'You truly have the power to do this?'

'Indisputably.'

'I will do nothing against the interests of my people.'

'I would never trust a man who would,' said the diplomat, holding his gaze.

'So what would you have me do, *meneer*?'

'Captain Clay here is anxious to find some suitable beaches near to Cape Town where troops could be landed,' said Vansittart. 'I understand the surf on the coast can be troubling.

Clay and the River of Silver

I thought that you might identify one for him?'

'Very well,' said De Bruyn. 'Losperd Bay is the best place. I can show it to you on the chart. Was that all?'

'Not quite,' continued Vansittart. 'I thought we might test the beach you recommend by landing you there. So you can return to Cape Town and discreetly prepare the ground for our arrival among your fellow citizens. I am sure you agree that an orderly transfer of power would be preferable to the damage and loss of life to be expected from a bloody siege.'

'General Janssens will never tamely surrender,' warned the Dutchman.

'No, he will need to be defeated in the field. You can leave that part to us. It is what will follow his defeat that concerns me. Will you help in that regard?'

De Bruyn hesitated for a moment more, before extending his hand across the table, and this time Vansittart accepted it.

*****

Dawn was just breaking as the *Griffin* stood out from Losperd Bay. Away to the south reared the solid mass of Table Mountain, its summit turning gold as the rising sun brushed it with light, the town at its feet lost in shadow. Behind Clay was the long stretch of empty beach, backed by low brown hills dotted with scrub, where they had left De Bruyn to make his way home. Even a few miles out he could still hear the thunder of the surf on the sand.

'Is this truly the best place for the army to effect a landing, sir?' asked Taylor. 'The launch returned shin deep with water, and Sedgwick says they nearly capsized bringing it off.'

'I daresay there may be somewhere better to the north,

Philip K Allan

but General Baird doesn't want to land his men more than a day's march from his objective,' said Clay. 'Let us hope the wind is kinder when that day arrives.'

Taylor looked up at the Dutch ensign streaming in the breeze in place of the frigate's usual colours. It had been made by her sailmaker in the hope that anyone spotting them from the shore would assume they were one of the warships based at the Cape. Then he looked out to sea and pointed ahead. 'Perhaps that island over there may afford a little shelter for the fleet,' he commented.

Clay turned his telescope towards it, a dome of grass and rock a scant two miles across. The rising sun began to light its western side as the ship approached.

'It is set down on our chart as Robben Island,' commented Armstrong, coming over to join them.

'I can't see much beyond a prodigious number of seals resting on the shore,' commented Clay. 'No, stay a moment. What is that catching the light near the summit?'

'A large tent, perhaps, sir?' offered Taylor.

'If it is, it will presently be blown away,' said the American. 'See how it flaps in the breeze.'

'What lubbers we are!' exclaimed Clay. 'It's a topsail, on the far side of the island! See, now it's being sheeted home.'

'Deck there!' yelled the lookout. 'Sail ho! Sail just beyond that there isle!'

'What do you make of her, Dawson?' demanded Clay.

'Ship from the look of her, three-masted and just getting underway, sir,' came the reply. 'She were only showing bare poles afore, which be why I missed her. Foretopsail sheeted home an' setting more to follow.'

'Do you think she has seen us, sir?' asked Taylor. 'Has that prompted her departure?'

Clay and the River of Silver

Clay looked around. To the east the sun had cleared the land, making him squint and throwing the long shadow of the *Griffin*'s towering masts towards the island. 'I think not, George. See how we lie in the eye of the sun. My guess is they anchored in a sheltered bay overnight to await daylight for their passage into Cape Town. Sail two points to larboard, so we come up with them as they clear the island.'

'Aye aye, sir.'

'Mr Sweeney, take a glass aloft and see what you can make of her.'

'Aye aye, sir.'

On her new course the frigate gathered speed, butting through the waves and sending clouds of spray pattering over her forecastle. The island was growing all the time, stretching across the water. Clay could see sheep grazing on the course grass now, and a little wooden jetty. Behind the island the other vessel was gathering pace. Clay watched as sails appeared on her other two masts. He stepped across to the binnacle and sighted over the compass at the other ship, calculating their relative speeds in his head.

'Mr Hutchinson!' he yelled towards the forecastle. 'Spill some wind from that topsail. I want the sun to hide us for a touch longer!'

'Aye aye, sir!'

'Deck there!' came a hail from the masthead. 'She's a warship! No colours yet, but she looks to be one of those French corvettes!'

'They carry twenty-two guns, as a rule,' commented Taylor. 'Eight-pounders, so no match for our long eighteens.'

'Beat to quarters if you please, Mr Taylor. Clear the ship for action.'

'Aye aye, sir. Shall I show our true colours?'

Philip K Allan

Clay glanced up at the Dutch flag above his head. 'Not yet, but have it bent and ready to raise. This one will flee the moment they realise who we are. The closer we can come, the better.'

From the deck beneath them came a long drum roll, and in response the *Griffin* began to transform herself. From under the quarterdeck came lines of sailors, carrying the contents of Clay's cabin towards the hold. As he watched, Sedgwick appeared to take charge of the gilt-framed portrait of Lydia, sliding it into its protective case before allowing it to go further. The glimpse of her face as it vanished from sight reminded him painfully of its creator. He looked towards the base of the main mast, which had been Blake's station. Preston stood in his place now, watching over the gun crews as they prepared their weapons for action.

'I have your sword, sir,' said a voice, and he turned to find Harte behind him, a glittering weapon in his arms. Once it was in place, he felt its familiar grip in his hand. He drew it out an inch to check it was free, and the bright steel glittered in the morning sun.

'Thank you, Harte,' he said, returning his attention to his surroundings.

'Ship cleared for action, sir,' reported Taylor, touching the brim of his hat.

Clay glanced across at Robben Island, so close now that some of the seals were raising their heads to inspect the new arrival. The other ship was only visible as upper masts, but would soon clear the end of the island. Through his telescope he found the tiny figure of her lookout, staring towards him with a hand shading his eyes against the low sun, and then gesturing towards the deck. A big ensign made its way aloft, the fly blood-red.

Clay and the River of Silver

'French colours!' yelled Todd from the masthead. 'And she's making more sail!'

'Set the topgallants, if you please, Mr Taylor,' ordered Clay, still watching the other ship.

'Aye aye, sir.'

Clay could see the flag, rippling in the wind. Then a row of three bundles were hauled aloft, breaking out from the mizzen topsail yardarm. 'She is signalling, gentlemen,' he announced. 'And only us in sight. A good sign, I believe – she has yet to smoke us.'

'Because she can only see our masts, sir,' commented Taylor. 'One glimpse of Tom's redcoats, and the scales will fall from their eyes.'

'I daresay that is true enough,' said his captain. 'Mr Todd, the flags have broken out! Note the signal down with care.'

'But ... but I can't read it, sir!' protested the midshipman. 'Two of the flags aren't ones we use.'

'Still record the order of the flags and their colour and form.'

'Aye aye, sir.'

Both ships reached the end of the island at the same moment, sliding clear from behind it. Clay's first glimpse of his opponent was of her round bow with an ornate figurehead of a man on a horse. Her black side was split by a long strake of white, broken at regular intervals by her open gunports. At each of them was a cannon, all run out and pointing towards the *Griffin*.

'Not totally foxed then,' commented Armstrong to Taylor.

'Mr Preston, run out the starboard guns,' ordered Clay. 'Quoins out and aim high. I want her disabled. Mr Taylor, our colours now, if you please.'

'Aye aye, sir!'

The moment the Dutch flag began its descent, the French ship vanished behind a boiling cloud of brown smoke. A ball whined over Clay's head and there was a loud crash from somewhere forward. Moments later the roar of the broadside reached him, and a cloud of seabirds rose into the air over the island.

'One hit below the mainchains,' observed Taylor, leaning over the side. 'Poor shooting, even for a Frenchman. The timbers should resist eight-pound balls at this range.'

'Edge her closer, helmsman,' ordered Clay. 'Mr Preston! Hold your first broadside until the range is more certain!'

'Aye aye, sir.'

Clay glanced ahead. Table Mountain was growing all the time, a dark slab against the glow of morning, like the silhouette of a monstrous giant's castle. The sun was higher now, picking out some of the roofs of the buildings in the town at its feet. Wisps of smoke rose in the air to show where embers in kitchen hearths were being brought to life. Closest to him was the low mass of a big fortress placed in the fork between the sea and a river estuary. He had visited Fort Good Hope in the past, when it had been in British hands, and remembered the big thirty-six pounder cannon mounted on its seaward walls. Then he looked across at the French ship beside him, bounding along on a parallel course. As he watched she fired again, just as a wave passed under her, throwing her broadside high. Some of the balls raised splashes from the sea between them but where the rest of the broadside went Clay could not tell.

'She's head reaching on us, I fancy,' said Taylor. 'Bolting straight for the safety of Cape Town.'

Clay and the River of Silver

'Quite right, Mr Taylor,' he said. 'Have that reef in the foretopsail shaken out and let her have her head. Helmsman, a point to starboard.'

'Aye aye, sir.'

With the *Griffin* on a converging course, and her extra sail thrusting her forward, the range came down steadily. The Frenchman was now hitting regularly, her shots punching holes in the sails, or thudding into the frigate's tough hull. Clay watched as a sailor was helped down the main ladderway beneath him by a comrade, blood dripping onto the deck from a splinter wound in his arm. He glanced again at the French ship, and then back towards Cape Town, coming ever closer. 'Now is the time, Mr Preston!' he yelled.

The lieutenant acknowledged the order with a wave. 'Make ready, starboards!' he ordered. A line of arms rose aloft from the gun captains and the crews crouched low. A moment of stillness as Preston waited for the deck to become level. 'Fire!'

In an instant the target disappeared behind a wall of flame and smoke as the broadside roared out. The *Griffin* heeled away from her opponent as the big cannon shot back inboard. Beneath Clay the deck erupted into a frenzy of activity. Guns were sponged out, ship's boys ran below for fresh charges, and cannonballs were rolled across the deck ready for the next broadside. Then the ship sailed free of the smoke and Clay looked across at his opponent. She had been hit hard by the well-aimed broadside. Shot holes pockmarked her hull and sails, and several severed shrouds trailed alongside her, but her speed was undiminished. 'Independent fire, Mr Preston!' he ordered. 'Fast and true, if you please.'

Each broadside was more ragged than the last as the faster crews outpaced the slower, until the *Griffin*'s fire became almost continuous as she pounded her opponent. By contrast, the French ship's discharges were beginning to fade under the remorseless barrage, but still she sped on.

'Surely she cannot long endure this, sir,' said Taylor. 'We must have four times her weight of broadside, not to count how briskly the men fire.'

'And yet nothing vital has carried away aloft,' said Clay, banging the rail in frustration.

'Sir!' called Russell from behind him. 'That fort has opened fire!'

Clay crossed to the other side of the ship to join him. Table Mountain filled the horizon, the bay at its feet opening before him. He could see other defences now, shore batteries placed along the coastline, and a second smaller fort on the far side of the town. But what disturbed him was how close Fort Cape Hope had grown. Through his telescope he could see a large Dutch flag floating above the ramparts and tiny figures running to their posts. A puff of smoke rose into the air and moments later a series of big splashes climbed from the surface of the water, well ahead of the bow. 'I need that Frenchman stopped, Mr Preston,' he roared towards the main deck. 'Now!'

But it was the enemy that struck the first telling blow. A loud crack sounded from above Clay's head, and he looked up to see half of the mizzen topsail tumbled down in ruin, the yard shattered by a lucky hit.

'Afterguard!' yelled Taylor. 'Aloft with you and secure that damage!'

'Aye aye, sir!'

Clay ignored the rush of men as they hurried past and concentrated on the battle. The enemy ship was steadily drawing ahead, now that the *Griffin* was robbed of a sail. More trial shots from the fort were raising tall columns of water, as

Clay and the River of Silver

the *Griffin* came ever closer. With time running out, he came to his decision. He turned to the midshipman standing by the wheel.

'Mr Drake!' he said. 'Make haste and find Mr Preston. Tell him to run out the larboard side guns, and send across his best gun-layers to serve them.'

'Aye aye, sir,' said the youngster in a piping falsetto.

'Mr Russell, I mean to cross the enemy's stern. You have at best two minutes to prepare.'

'Aye aye, sir.'

Clay watched the activity on the main deck beneath him. The flow of men crossing the deck to reinforce the guns on the disengaged side. Those still serving the starboard side guns levering their cannons further and further round as the French ship forged ahead.

'Up ports!' ordered Preston, once all the guns were fully manned. 'Run out, larboards!'

'You will have but a single broadside, Mr Preston,' he called. 'Pray make it count.'

'Aye aye, sir.'

Clay looked across at the enemy ship, judging the best moment to make the turn. 'When the stern passes that shroud … there,' he muttered to himself. More splashes from the fort, and then the moment arrived. 'Wheel hard over there! Now Mr Russell! Tacks and sheets!'

'Aye aye, sir!'

The *Griffin* swept around, turning across their opponent's stern with a volley of flapping canvas as the men hauled the yards around. The starboard side guns fell silent as their target vanished, while on the other side of the deck the crews readied to open fire. The stern of the French ship was painted royal blue with only minimal decoration around the run

Philip K Allan

of five window lights. Written in a curve of white letters across the counter was the ship's name, *Napoleon*.

'Let Boney have it, lads!' shouted Preston. 'Fire as you bear!'

The broadside was steady and purposeful, advancing down the side of the ship from bow to stern as each cannon bore in turn. The range was short enough for the carronades on the forecastle and quarterdeck to add their ponderous weight. Although the target was masked by smoke, Clay could hear each crash and the cries of the wounded as ball followed ball, smashing its way down the length of the enemy's hull.

'There she goes!' yelled Armstrong.

Through the smoke Clay saw the top of the main mast slowly lean to one side, like a man inclining his head, before gathering speed as it crashed down into the sea alongside. The mass of spars and canvas dragged the *Napoleon* to a halt.

'Back the foretopsail!' ordered Clay. 'Hold her thus!'

The smoke was rolling aside, revealing the shattered stern of the corvette. Only one window had survived, and the name of the ship was reduced to fragments of letters by the shot holes torn in the wood. A lone officer stood at the stern rail, waving his hat towards him, the motion becoming more frantic as the first of the reloaded eighteen-pounders was run up.

'Hold your fire, Mr Preston!' ordered Clay. 'I believe they mean to surrender.'

The shrill call of Preston's whistle coincided with fresh shots from the Dutch fortress, mercifully still falling short. On board the *Napoleon* her battered tricolour was lowered to the deck, amid cheers from the Griffins.

'Mr Russell, kindly take the longboat across with a prize crew and take possession of her, if you please,' ordered Clay. 'I will send the boatswain, carpenter and surgeon across

Clay and the River of Silver

presently to help restore her, but your first task will be to clear that wreckage and get her underway before we drift within range of the shore.'

'Aye aye, sir,' said the lieutenant. What course should I follow?'

'We shall make for St Helena and our rendezvous with the rest of the fleet, who will be arriving there presently. Good luck to you, William.'

'Thank you, sir.'

'No, stay a moment,' said Clay, looking around him. 'Mr Todd! What was that signal the Frenchman made?'

The midshipman consulted his slate. 'It was composed of three flags, sir. The first was blue over white, then came a plain one the same as our numeral eight, followed by a yellow flag with a black saltire.'

'Find them in the flag locker and send them back to me, if you please, Mr Russell,' said Clay. 'They may prove of use.'

'Aye aye, sir.'

Philip K Allan

Chapter 5
Invasion

If the expedition's ships had crowded the harbour at Madeira, they positively packed Jamestown Bay in St Helena. Clay could see their long ranks through the stern windows of the *Diadem* from where he sat. Beyond them was the island's main settlement, a ribbon of buildings lining the road that wound its way inland between headlands. He turned back to the map spread on the table in the great cabin of the sixty-four as Baird cleared his throat.

'And this beach will be suitable for my men to land, Sir Alexander?' asked the general, tapping a place with his finger.

'In truth, Losperd Bay is the best of a sorry lot, Sir David,' said Clay. 'When the wind blows strong, there is nowhere on this coast without a troubling surf, but there we found a channel through the waves that will serve. There is also an island close by that can provide shelter for the fleet if we are obliged to wait for the weather to ease.'

'Yes, I see it,' said the Scotsman, his finger moving on.

'The beach is but a day's march from Cape Town, as you requested,' continued Clay.

'Close, but perhaps too close,' muttered the general. 'Capturing those two ships was all very well, Sir Alexander, but have we tipped our hand to the Dutch?'

'You cannot censure a king's officer for taking a few prizes,' protested Popham, who had spent a pleasant morning

Clay and the River of Silver

calculating his share of their value. 'It is our duty to set upon the enemy when we find them.'

'And it is well that we did,' commented Vansittart, who sat a little apart from the others. 'Captain De Bruyn proved to be a most useful source of intelligence. It was he that showed us this beach, and as for alerting the Dutch, that goose was cooked some time ago. De Bruyn informed us that an attack has been expected ever since the peace ended.'

'And this Dutchman is to be trusted?' queried Baird.

'I trust no one until they have proved themselves, Sir David,' said Vansittart, eyeing the Scotsman. 'But the beach proved satisfactory. As for his efforts to turn popular opinion in our favour, that will only be shown if the enemy swiftly capitulate after we defeat them in battle. If they choose to withdraw into Cape Town and fight on, then I will have been deceived. But then you will be no worse off than if I had never met him.'

'A fair point,' said Popham. 'Perhaps we can finalise our plans, now that we have heard from Sir Alexander and Mr Vansittart? Sir David?'

'Very well,' said the general. 'We shall come ashore at this Losperd Bay and, once established, march on Cape Town from the north.'

'Good, we are agreed,' said Popham. 'I will naturally take charge of the landing itself.'

'Would it not be better for the *Griffin* to supervise that part?' said Beresford. 'Sir Alexander is the one most familiar with the area.'

'Aye, that would be preferable,' agreed Baird. 'He has scouted the landing site, while you have not been within a thousand miles of this beach.'

'Of course, there will be much to organise in the

Philip K Allan

squadron, sir, and I would be under your direction,' said Clay. 'But access to the shore is challenging.'

'You don't say,' muttered Popham, biting at his lip. 'Well, if Sir David insists …'

'That is settled then,' said Baird. 'Now, what if Mr Vansittart is wrong, and I am compelled to besiege Cape Town? I have nothing above a six-pounder in my artillery.'

'If your men can procure some draft animals to pull them, I daresay my *Griffin* can lend you some of her eighteen-pounders, together with the men to serve them,' said Clay. 'With your permission, sir?'

'Why not, Sir Alexander?' said Popham. 'You seem to have taken everything else upon yourself. Very well. General Baird and I will finalise detailed instructions on the voyage across, and I look forward to toasting our success in Fort Good Hope with the finest wine Governor Janssens's cellar can boast.'

'Hear him,' said Beresford.

'If that is all, I must be excused,' said Baird. 'General Beresford and myself are to dine with the governor shortly.'

'I trust you like made dishes,' said Vansittart. 'I dined with His Excellency last night and found he has a passion for mutton stew. But I confess it made a pleasant change from the salt pork, a half year in the barrel, that is being served in the wardroom of the *Griffin* at present.'

As the group began to disperse, Popham caught Clay's eye. 'Sir Alexander, might I have a word before you depart?'

'By all means, sir.'

'Mr Vansittart, would you care to take a turn on deck?' continued Popham. 'There is a service matter I need to discuss.'

When the two men were alone, Popham turned to his guest. 'I notice that you didn't feel obliged to salute my flag

Clay and the River of Silver

when the *Griffin* arrived yesterday.'

'That is so, sir. Given the confusion surrounding your status, I thought it for the best.'

'Confusion?' queried Popham, a frown forming. 'I'm not sure I have the pleasure of understanding you, Sir Alexander.'

'In Madeira you were unable to confirm your promotion, but if word has arrived from the Admiralty, I will of course be happy to honour your flag in the customary way, sir.'

The frown only deepened. 'Are you aware that every ship in the squadron will have noted your failure, and it will appear to them as a deliberate snub?'

'That was certainly not my intention, sir,' said Clay. 'If you have now been made commodore, I will have the appropriate salute fired.'

'I explained to you before that by some omission word of my promotion has been delayed.'

'Perhaps you might add an instruction to me in the orders you will be issuing to the *Griffin*, sir?'

'Why are you being so stubborn?' said Popham, his face flushing with anger. 'I am only asking you to fire some bloody guns.'

'Because a naval salute is not mere sport, sir,' protested Clay. 'It is either a well-merited honour, or it is naught but a waste of good powder. And you and I, as the senior naval officers here, should set an example in this regard.'

'Sir Alexander, I should warn you that I am not a man to vex.'

'That's as may be, but you are also a man seeking an honour for which you are not entitled. I know that there is no promotion. Lord Barham himself told me he did not intend to raise you to commodore. Mr Vansittart was present, if you care to summon him to corroborate what I say. But from your disinclination to give me a written order, I believe you know this already.'

Popham glared across the table at Clay, but found only calm defiance in the pale grey eyes opposite. In response his frown lifted. 'Oh ... very well. Salute me or not as you will.'

'I beg your pardon, sir?' said Clay.

'What do I care for such baubles?' continued Popham. 'Do as you see fit.'

'I see,' said Clay, after a pause. 'I'm obliged for your understanding of my position, sir. And as I say, the moment your promotion is confirmed ...'

'Yes, indeed,' said Popham, shuffling the papers on his desk. 'Good day to you.'

Clay was shaking his head when he joined Vansittart on the quarterdeck.

'Is all well?' asked the diplomat. 'You seem distracted.'

'I don't entirely know how I am,' said Clay. 'We argued over his absurd demand for a salute he has no right to, but when I stood my ground, he backed down in an instant. All very odd.'

'Did you mention our interview with Lord Barham, perchance?' said Vansittart.

'I believe I did, just before his volte-face.'

'Then there is your explanation. Nothing concerns Popham more than position and status, and the thought of you having direct access to the First Lord of the Admiralty has alarmed him. But have a care, my friend. Like many such men, he is not without a vicious streak.'

*****

It took three weeks for the fleet to sail across from St Helena to

Clay and the River of Silver

Losperd Bay, timing their arrival for just after nightfall. Clay emerged from his cabin in the dark before dawn and made his way up onto the quarterdeck. The jerky motion of the ship beneath his feet told him both that the *Griffin* was anchored at bow and stern, and that the wind had eased during the night. He glanced towards the east, searching for the first grey hint of dawn, before making his way across the deck.

A figure detached itself from the shadowy group standing around the binnacle. 'Good morning, sir,' said Taylor.

'Let us hope that it will be, George,' said Clay. 'Is the fleet in position?'

The first lieutenant indicated ahead of them, where a few faint lights showed in the night. 'The warships are moored in line with us, broadside on to the shore to cover the landing, and the transports are in the offing between us and that island, sir. And Mr Preston has just now returned.'

'How did you fair?' asked Clay as the officer came over.

'Well enough, sir,' said Preston. 'I was able to find the channel through the shallows that Captain De Bruyn indicated and mark it with the buoys.'

Clay couldn't see Preston's face, but he could guess at what a difficult task that must have been amid the surf on a dark night. 'Excellent work, Edward. See that you shift into some dry clothes before you take command of the guns that we are sending ashore.'

'Aye aye, sir.'

'Mr Sweeney, would you pass me the night glass.'

'Aye aye, sir,'

Clay searched towards the land with care. The eastern horizon was just starting to lighten, making the dunes above the beach appear as a dark, undulating line against the sky. The sea at his feet was black as pitch, restlessly moving towards the shore. Closer to the land he could see the white glimmer of breaking surf. He swept along the line of it, searching for the place where the waves were lower. 'I believe I have the channel now,' he said, his eye still to the telescope. 'A point off the beam.'

'That's where it lies, sir,' confirmed Preston. 'The first marker is a cable length away.'

Clay moved his attention to the shore beyond, searching for danger. The swinging lantern of a patrol making its way along the shore. The silhouette of a sentry gazing back towards him from the skyline, but the land seemed empty. Then he saw the light, a tiny point off to one side in the gap between two dunes. He was certain it had not been there earlier. He considered it for a moment and then remembered that when he had asked De Bruyn about securing draft animals, he had said there were several farms in the area. The grey light in the east was growing more pronounced and he imagined a sleepy maid lighting a lamp or blowing life into a kitchen fire before preparing breakfast. He closed the telescope and handed it back to the midshipman of the watch.

'My thanks, Mr Sweeney,' he said. 'Mr Taylor, are the ship's boats alongside?'

'They are, sir. The crews are armed and ready, and the signalling party have taken their places in the launch.'

'Excellent. Mr Macpherson, kindly have your marines man the boats. Mr Russell, you are with me. You have your speaking trumpet, I trust?'

'I do, sir.'

By the time Clay and Russell were settled in the stern sheets of the barge the eastern horizon was turning to pearl. It was just light enough for him to see the cross belts of the marines as they clumped down the ship's side to take their

Clay and the River of Silver

places in the boats. Once the last soldier took his place, Macpherson made his way along the boat and sat opposite him.

'All my men are present, sir,' he confirmed.

'Thank you, Tom,' said Clay. 'Give way, Sedgwick, if you please. You will find the first marker a cable off in that direction.'

'Aye aye, sir,' said Sedgwick. 'Push off in the bow there!'

The three boats formed into a line and headed for the shore, the sailors swinging backwards and forwards with the stroke in contrast with the static rows of marines between them. The light was growing all the time, revealing a sea of lumpy waves rolling towards the shore. From somewhere ahead came the distant rumble of surf breaking on the beach.

'I reckon that be the first of Mr Preston's markers ahoy, sir,' said Sedgwick, pointing forward.

Clay rose to a crouch and saw one of the whitewashed kegs that the *Griffin*'s cooper and boatswain had spent yesterday preparing to serve as buoys. 'Quite right. They mark the centre of the channel.'

As the boats pressed on, the light grew steadily stronger. Around them the waves were swelling in size as they neared the shore. Sedgwick pulled the tiller across to follow the strip of calmer water marked by the bobbing kegs. Clay looked behind him at the rest of the fleet. Close in were the warships in a widely spaced line, tugging at the anchor cables that held them parallel with the shore. He could see clusters of boats waiting in their lee. Further out, the bay was dotted with transport ships. Many more boats here, and a hint of scarlet on the decks of the nearest ones as soldiers formed up.

'Put your backs into it!' urged Sedgwick.

The roar of the surf was all around them now. The boat

rose as a wave passed under them, and Clay could see the beach just ahead, a broad belt of sand and shingle. Behind it was a fringe of dunes covered with thin grass and patches of scrubby bush.

'Brace yourself, marines,' ordered Macpherson as the boat ran down the wave and into the foam-flecked shallows. It ran on a little and then jerked to a halt.

'Oars in and over the side, lads,' ordered Sedgwick. 'Run us up as far as you can.'

Once the boat was stationary, and all the marines had disembarked, Clay stepped from his barge and was surprised by how cold the water was. The *Griffin*'s launch pulled up beside him, and more marines tumbled out, while behind him the larger longboat had grounded further out. He looked in both directions, but apart from the Griffins, the beach was empty.

'Corporal Edwards!' yelled Macpherson. 'I'll have a line of pickets thrown out to occupy the two sand hills ahead, and a reserve formed up in close order here.'

'Yes, sir!'

'Mr Russell, kindly signal to the fleet that the landing may proceed, and see that no one strays from the boat channel. I shall go and see the lie of the land,' said Clay. 'Sedgwick, come with me.'

'Aye aye, sir.'

The nearest sand dune was no more than thirty feet high, although the side facing the sea was steep. Clay scrambled his way up to the crest, pulling himself with the help of some of the vegetation. The wind flapped at the tails of his coat as he took out his spyglass and began to examine his surroundings. Away to the south was the familiar mass of Table Mountain, standing alone as if guarding the town at its feet. To the east of it was a low saddle connecting it to more mountains running away from

Clay and the River of Silver

him into the interior until they were lost in the light of the rising sun. The landward side of the dune was much gentler than the seaward face, and soon gave way to rolling pastureland, dotted with grazing animals and the occasional cluster of farm buildings. Halfway between where he stood and Cape Town, a winding river snaked its way inland. If it were not for the marine skirmishers hurrying to form a thin line below him, the scene would have been one of pastoral calm. Then his attention was caught by a flash of movement. He swung his telescope in that direction and saw horsemen.

There were about twenty of them, standing in a group a half mile away. They wore civilian clothes of homespun browns and greys that blended into the landscape, so that if it had not been for the toss of a horse's head, he might not have noticed them at all. With his telescope he could see they were mounted on shaggy-looking animals and armed with a collection of weapons. A few had proper cavalry carbines, the rest shotguns and fowling pieces. Only one, better mounted than the rest, had a sword. This last man also had a telescope, and as Clay examined him, he swung it towards him. For a moment the two men looked at each other, then the cavalryman gestured to his men, his mouth working soundlessly in Clay's eyepiece. Two of the enemy turned their mounts and rode off, one towards the interior, the other to the south. The others began slowly advancing towards him.

Clay looked out to sea, and was reassured by what he saw. The warships had their guns run out and manned, while from across the bay numerous boats were heading towards him, each with a block of scarlet-clad men. The nearest were those from the *Diadem*, carrying Baird and his staff, and were already close to the shore. The voice of Russell came back on the wind, bellowing through his speaking trumpet. 'Boat ahoy! Follow your orders! You pass the markers to starboard! Always to starboard! So that boats can both come and go up the channel!'

'Sedgwick, run down to the beach and tell Mr Macpherson that we have a party of irregular cavalry approaching,' Clay ordered. 'And bring the general and his staff up here once they land.'

'Aye aye, sir.'

The horsemen had spread out into a loose formation as they approached, while the two that had been sent off were visible only as puffs of dust galloping across the plain. From off to one side Macpherson appeared at the head of his reserve of men. He drew them up into a line on the slope just beneath where Clay stood. Then he raised a hand to shade his eyes from the rising sun and considered matters. 'Corporal, go around the skirmish line,' Clay heard the Scotsman order. 'Tell the men they are to hold off the enemy with musketry, but if pressed they are to fall back on me here.'

'Yes, sir!' said Edwards, saluting smartly and then hurrying away.

Macpherson took his place at one end of the line. 'Marines will fix bayonets,' he barked, before drawing out the claymore he favoured, the long blade glittering in the sunlight. From ahead came the first bang of a musket as one of the skirmishers tried his luck.

'What is all this about enemy cavalry, Sir Alexander,' demanded Baird as he appeared beside him, his face flushed to the colour of his tunic by his scramble up the dune. Behind him came Beresford together with a collection of officers who soon filled the top of the hill.

'I am not sure they can be dignified as cavalry, Sir David,' observed Clay, pointing towards the east and handing across his telescope. 'Farmhands and ploughboys might be

Clay and the River of Silver

nearer the mark.'

The sound of musketry intensified as the enemy approached. Then a horseman jerked to one side in his saddle, clutching at his shoulder, and the line came to a ragged halt. More shots rang out from the marines and the Dutch retreated back the way they had come.

'Your men seem to have the situation under control,' said Baird, returning the telescope. 'If a dozen such poor fellows is the best the enemy can boast, my men will soon be ashore.'

'I fear they will be reinforced, sir,' said Clay. 'Two of them have ridden off, one for the Cape, and another towards the interior. And if I am not mistaken, I can see something away in that direction.' He pointed inland where a long dust cloud had appeared further out in the plain.

Baird snatched back the telescope. 'A deal more of these horsemen riding in column,' he concluded. 'Perhaps two hundred strong.'

'Closer to a hundred, I should say, sir,' supplemented Beresford, who had his own telescope out. 'But there is also movement in the direction of Cape Town. I fancy the enemy is alert to us.'

'Who is first to be landed?' demanded Baird.

'The 71st Highlanders, then the 59th Foot, Sir David,' said one of his aides, referring to a notebook. 'The light companies to be landed in advance of the rest. I believe I see the first of them now.'

'Lieutenant Dalrymple,' said Baird to a subaltern. 'Kindly find Colonel Pack when he lands and tell him I want his Highlanders to relieve the marines. He is to advance to the edge of that field there. The 59th can form up to the right of them.'

Philip K Allan

'Yes, sir!'

'Sir Alexander, can I trouble you to return to the beach and expedite the landing?' said Baird. 'The sooner I have the men to defend a perimeter, the happier I shall be. Also, our chargers would not go amiss, so we can leave this wee hillock of yours.'

'Yes, sir.'

*****

'We are in position now, Mr Hutchinson,' called Preston from the stern sheets of the *Griffin*'s longboat.

'Aye aye, sir,' growled the boatswain from the rail above him. 'Lower away handsomely there!' he ordered to the straining men, and the barrel of the final eighteen-pounder started to descend the frigate's side. 'Ease off on that line a touch, Jack,' he added to Powell, his heavily scarred boatswain's mate, who had charge of a second rope that checked the cannon's stubborn tendency to twist in the air. Slowly, it made its ponderous way down the ship's side to settle on the cradle prepared for it, the longboat sinking deep into the water under its weight.

'Lash it tight there,' ordered Preston to the men in the boat. 'We don't want it coming loose and rolling us over on the way to the shore.' While the men secured it into place, he glanced down at the breech, where a name had been painted in flowing script by its crew. 'Brimstone Belcher,' he read. 'That will be gun number six, starboard side. Throws a trifle to the left.'

'All made fast, sir,' reported the petty officer in charge.

Preston experimentally pushed the end nearest him with his foot. 'Very good, Jamieson. Cast off the tackle and take your

Clay and the River of Silver

places, men, and let us get this one ashore. Mr Todd, you take the helm.'

'Aye aye, sir.'

The men had to strain to get the boat in motion, the oars foaming through the water as the longboat crept towards a beach that was now utterly transformed. Most of the soldiers had been landed earlier, but still there was an endless line of ships' boats coming and going. Just ahead of the *Griffin*'s longboat was a flat-bottomed lighter being towed towards the boat channel. On board where three miserable-looking horses, being comforted by riders in the blue tunics of the light cavalry. The boat immediately behind him was full of bundled tents.

On the shore ahead he could see mounds of equipment in crates and casks, and lines of picketed horses and solemn-looking oxen taken from the nearby farms. Between them, the beach was alive with activity. There were parties of red-coated soldiers hurrying up the dunes to rejoin their units. There were quartermasters and officers scurrying around, many clutching fluttering sheeves of paper, all bawling orders at their harassed men. And in the middle an exhausted-looking Russell, speaking trumpet drooping from his hand.

'Row steady there,' said Preston, as water slopped over the low freeboard of the boat. Fortunately, the wind had dropped considerably since the morning, or it would have been impossible to land any guns at all. The swaying lighter of horses was in the boat channel now, and Preston hastened to follow it. Both craft made it through the worst of the surf, the horses plunging for solid land the moment the lighter grounded in the shallows, despite the best efforts of their riders to control them. Preston turned to one side and steered parallel with the beach towards where the *Griffin*'s shore party had a substantial tripod of ship's timbers set up in the shallows. The first two eighteen-

Philip K Allan

pounders were already mounted on their land carriages, while an empty one awaited the arrival of the last gun.

Burdened as it was, the longboat grounded well short of the tripod, but once the crew had all scrambled out, they were able to haul it forward underneath the heavy block and tackle that hung from the apex. Rudgewick, the *Griffin*'s gunner, came forward to fuss over the Brimstone Belcher. Then, with the help of the combined effort of most of the shore party, the barrel creaked slowly up until the longboat could be hauled out from under it, and the last gun carriage rolled forward to take its place.

'Wheel that carriage a touch forward, lads,' said the crouching gunner, the tip of his tongue protruding from the corner of his mouth as an aid to concentration. 'Now lower her a bit. Avast! That carriage needs to come an inch my way. Lower again, handsomely!'

Just as the trunnions projecting from the barrel's sides were being eased into the recesses cut for them in the gun carriage, a fresh-faced young man in a smart uniform came galloping across the beach towards them, sand flying from his horse's hooves. 'Lieutenant Dalrymple,' he announced, as he pulled his mount to a halt. 'Are you in charge here, sir?'

'A moment if you please,' said Preston, watching the gun. 'Matters are at a delicate stage.'

The wheels of the carriage pressed deeper into the sand as the weight of the barrel transferred to them, and then the rope holding the Brimstone Belcher went slack as it dropped into place. Rudgewick and his mate clapped the heavy iron capsquares over the top of the trunnions to secure the barrel, and the final gun was complete.

Preston let out a sigh and turned to the figure looming above him. 'I am in command here. How can I help you?'

Clay and the River of Silver

'I bring word from General Baird, sir,' said the officer, bursting with importance. 'Are your guns ready for action?'

'They will be presently, but I understood we were to provide the army with a siege train,' said Preston. 'Surely we cannot have reached Cape Town already?'

'No, but the enemy are fast approaching over yonder, and none of our field guns have been unloaded yet. Sir David saw your pieces and wondered if they might be hurried forward instead.'

'Hurried forward?' queried Preston. 'My dear sir, these are naval eighteen-pounders! They weigh the best part of two tons each, not to mention the powder and shot they require. How do you propose we hurry them forward?'

'That young toff could always lend us his fecking nag,' muttered O'Malley to Evans.

The comment seemed to animate Dalrymple. 'Oxen, sir!' he said, indicating the line of beasts picketed further up the beach. 'Those were captured this morning. There are your beasts of burden.'

Preston eyed the animals uncertainly. Many had flopped down on the sand, the rest were shifting restlessly, their tongues lolling. 'Did you also seize any harnesses?'

'I don't believe so, sir. Is that important?'

Preston contemplated the officer but saw only innocent vacancy in the face above him. 'I take it you have ridden in a carriage before?'

'Oh, many a time, sir. Father has quite the collection.'

'And did you ever notice how the horses were connected to the vehicle?'

'Lord, no!' laughed Dalrymple. 'I leave all that to the dashed coachman, what?'

'I see. Well kindly give my compliments to Sir David,

and tell him that if the oxen can be made available to me, and Lieutenant Macpherson and the *Griffin*'s marines can offer me their protection, then I shall do my best to join him with my guns.'

'Thank you, sir,' said the subaltern, saluting with a flourish. 'Much obliged, I'm sure.'

'Blooming army!' exclaimed the gunner, as they watched the youngster gallop away. 'Not a clue, as usual, sir. No harnesses, and them bullocks tethered all morning in the sun without so much as a drop of water. I doubt they could pull the skin off a bowl of gruel. How are we meant to move these here guns with them?'

'Fortunately, Mr Rudgewick, we are the blooming navy,' said Preston. 'And are used to shifting for ourselves. Do you have all you need to serve the guns in action?'

'Aye, pretty well, sir, although a dozen rounds of canister would be a comfort, in case the enemy should press us close.'

'Very well. Kindly return to the ship in the longboat to collect them, and give Mr Hutchinson my compliments. Tell him to give you as many leather buckets and as much manila line as he has.'

'Buckets and line? Aye aye, sir. I'll bring you back all I can.'

'Mr Todd, kindly organise some parties of men to search for fresh water. The local farms must have wells, or you may find a spring. The rest of you get those beasts moved over into the shade of that dune. Swiftly now.'

*****

It was while they were searching for water among the low,

Clay and the River of Silver

undulating scrub that the sailors found the nest. O'Malley saw it first, as he came over a rise in the ground and stopped in amazement. Just below him was a broad circular scrape in the ground, where powerful claws had torn the yellow grass aside to create a dish-shaped depression ten feet across in the sandy soil. In the centre of the nest was a clutch of eggs twenty strong, each the size of the hefty eighteen-pounder cannonballs that the Irishman had spent much of the morning unloading on the beach. He glanced around, fearful that some monstrous bird might be standing over him, but finding none he dashed forward, placed an egg under each arm, and went off to join the others. 'Will you look at these beauties?' he exclaimed. 'How big must the fecking hens be hereabouts?'

'I never saw the like,' marvelled Trevan, taking one of them and hefting it in his hand. 'Three pounds if it be an ounce.'

'Well, I'm after eating one of these, if I can get into the fecker,' said O'Malley. 'I've not had a thing since an hour before dawn. There's plenty for yous all, lying on the ground for the taking, just over there.'

'I've not tasted egg since before I left Polwith,' said Trevan, as the men gathered around the rim of the enormous nest.

'What becomes of the eggs them hens lay in the coops by the wheel?' asked Pembleton.

'Pipe and the Grunters scoff the bleeding lot, mate,' said Evans. 'None of them ever get forward of the wardroom.'

'I don't suppose we could cook them,' asked Trevan. 'Raw be fine, mind, but coddled be better.'

'Nah,' said O'Malley, already sawing away at the top of his egg with his knife. 'Light a fire here, and half them fecking Lobsters will be down on us in a blink. Besides, what we going to cook it in? Our hands? Just tuck, afore anyone notices we're missing.'

The sailors ate quickly, spooning the rich yolk into their mouths with their hands and letting much of the white dribble into the dirt. They were well into their second egg each, when Trevan, who had taken his to a position from where he could keep watch, came scrambling back down to join them.

'Avast there, shipmates,' he hissed. 'Goldilocks be coming this way!'

The sailors plunged their hands into the dust, rubbing furiously to clean off the clinging egg, before appearing on the skyline and hurrying towards the officer. Midshipman Todd eyed them suspiciously as they trotted down the slope.

'There be no sign of a spring over there, sir,' reported Trevan, touching his hat to the officer.

'No indeed,' said Todd. 'Nor would I expect to find one at the top of a hill. What have you men been about? Why, you are all filthy!'

The sailors wiped their hands guiltily on their shirts, but the mixture of dirt and raw egg was thick as glue, and drying fast in the warm air. The midshipman's eyes narrowed with suspicion as he regarded their efforts to get clean.

'It were my fault, sir,' said Pembleton, stepping forward. 'Back home in Nottingham, my father were known as a diviner. Folks used him to find the best place to dig a well, or to help search for missing jewellery. I had the strangest feeling that there were some water up there, and had the lads dig for it with their hands, but it were no use. It don't seems as the gift has passed to me.'

'Hmmm,' said Todd. 'This all seems very strange. You would have done much better to have gone directly to that farm down there, as I did. There you would have found a perfectly serviceable well.' He pointed down the slope to where a ring of

Clay and the River of Silver

thatched buildings was grouped around a square of beaten earth, not two hundred yards away.

'To be sure, the farm might have been better, sir,' conceded O'Malley. 'But what's going on out on the plain?'

A track led away from the farm towards the south. After a few miles it crossed a line of low hills, their crests occupied by red-coated soldiers, with more marching to join them. Beyond the line of hills was another long column raising clouds of dust into the air, and coming from the direction of Cape Town.

'Bleeding hell,' said Evans. 'That must be the Butterboxes! Is there to be a battle, sir?'

'There will be soon, and we must be part of it,' said Todd. 'Trevan, run back to the beach and find Mr Preston. Tell him that we have found both water for the oxen, and a track to follow for the guns. We shall come behind. Make haste, now!'

'Aye aye, sir.'

Philip K Allan

Chapter 6
The Battle of Blaauwberg

'I say,' enthused Dalrymple. 'You nautical chaps certainly know your stuff, sir.'

'In my experience, there are few tasks sailors cannot turn their hands to,' agreed Preston.

The aide had dismounted from his horse, the better to appreciate the work the men were engaged in. A relay of buckets of water from the farm on the far side of the dunes had revived the oxen sufficiently for them to be arranged in double-lines in front of each gun. The animals seemed to respond well to the unfamiliar shouts of the Griffins. 'Two points to starboard, there, Nelson,' urged one sailor, gripping the horn of an ox like a tiller to steer him into place. 'Now, easy there! Hold fast on Bill Pitts beam.'

Other sailors sat in groups on the sand, busy knotting and splicing the coils of rope that Rudgewick had brought back from the frigate, turning them into head collars and traces for the animals.

'Will all this suffice to get your guns to the army, sir?' queried Dalrymple. 'The enemy have brought up some field pieces, and Sir David is anxious that we should be able to match them in kind.'

'In truth, I am uncertain,' confessed Preston. 'I know exactly how many hands are needed to haul the *Griffin*'s main yard aloft, but how many oxen are required to pull an eighteen-

Clay and the River of Silver

pounder was never part of my training. Let us hope that a team of eight prove sufficient for each, once we have them on the track Mr Todd has found.'

Dalrymple looked at the long slope leading up from the beach to the gap between two dunes, a puzzled look on his face. 'But how will you get them from here to your track, sir?'

'Ox herding may be a novelty to my men, lieutenant, but when it comes to hauling on ropes, they are masters,' smiled Preston. 'Watch and learn!'

Once a team of oxen were harnessed to the first gun, Preston began organising the rest of his men. 'Mr Rudgewick, kindly follow close behind with a party equipped with bolsters of wood. If we should falter, you are to place them behind the wheels so the gun cannot roll back. Is that clear?'

'Aye aye, sir.'

'Mr Todd, I'll have a drag rope tied on either side of the gun carriage, and the men divided between them.'

'Aye aye, sir.'

'Mr Macpherson, can you have your men ready to help, should they be required? They can clap on to the sides of the carriage.'

'Corporal Edwards! Have the men leave their muskets and equipment, and stand ready to assist!'

'Yes, sir!'

When everyone was in position, Preston took his place a little way ahead, where he could see all the parts of the operation. 'Very well. Drivers, get your beasts in motion!'

With cries and slaps, the oxen lurched forward, pulling the wheels of the gun free from the clinging shallows, and across the beach towards the bottom of the slope.

'Keep it rolling!' urged Preston. 'Take up the slack on the drag ropes, there!' The gun began to slow as the slope increased, the wheels churning deep into the sand. 'Now pull you men! Pull! Marines! Now is your moment!'

The gun ground its way up the slope, and then came to a stop on the last, steepest part, the men straining and cursing, leaning forward like participants in a tug of war.

'Hold her there, Mr Rudgewick!' ordered Preston.

The gunner and his party hastened forward to stop the gun running backwards. 'Gun's holding, sir!'

'Stand easy all!' said Preston. 'Catch your breath, lads.'

'That's a dashed pity,' commented Dalrymple. 'Shall I go and tell Sir David that the guns can't be moved?'

'Certainly not,' said Preston. 'We have but a short way to go before the slope eases and the grass commences. It's this damned sand that is the problem. See how the wheels have sunk in? But a dozen good heaves will answer.' He turned to the sweating sailors. 'Almost there, lads. We only need get it in motion and then run away with her. Heave and stamp will answer, just like back on the old *Griffin*. But we must pull as one. Take your timing from me.'

'Aye aye, sir.'

Preston waited for the men to line up on the drag ropes, spitting on their hands and digging their feet in for grip. 'Marines, take your places! Drivers ready? Drag ropes ready? On three! One, two and three! Heave!'

The gun lurched forward a half turn of the wheel before halting once more. 'And again! Heave!' Another half turn. 'Heave!' Again and again the men threw their weight on the rope, bodily heaving the stubborn mass up the slope.

'Once more and we are there, lads!' urged Preston, just as the men were flagging. 'Heave as one! Now!' The gun jerked forward, and this time rolled on. With a grunt the sailors ran it up to the top of the slope before collapsing to the ground.

Clay and the River of Silver

'Easy all!' said Preston. 'Well done, men! Mr Todd, I'll have those drag ropes untied, and let us collect the second gun.'

'May I speak, sir,' gasped Trevan, raising a weary hand.

'Yes, what is it?'

'I'm thinking it'll be tougher pulling up the next one, now this here slope be all churned up and us proper winded, sir, begging your pardon.'

'What of it, Trevan?' said Preston. 'There's a battle about to start, and these guns are required for it.'

'I ain't shirking, sir,' said the Cornishman. 'But hauling these here guns would be a sight easier if the wheels ran true.'

'I dare say it would. And if oxen could sprout wings, that might serve us too.'

'What if we be stretching a bit of canvas over the steepest part, sir. Stop the wheels sinking in by spreading the load, like. An old jib should answer. Maybe the longboat's sail, at a pinch.'

Preston stared at Trevan for a moment, and then back at the heavily rutted slope. 'That may well answer,' he conceded. 'In fact, it is a very good suggestion indeed. Thank you for making it. Mr Todd, let us get the longboat mainsail up here and put it to the test.'

'Aye aye, sir.'

'Lieutenant Dalrymple, I believe you can inform General Baird that the *Griffin*'s guns will presently be on their way to him.'

'I will do so with pleasure, sir.'

*****

When both armies had manoeuvred into place, calm descended over the battlefield. The British had the higher ground. Their

Philip K Allan

six battalions occupied the crest of a chain of hills that ran from the last spur of Blaauwberg mountain towards the sea. A small squadron of the 20th Light Dragoons, all those whose mounts had been unloaded in time, covered the seaward flank. In the centre of the British line, where the dirt road to Cape Town crossed the hills on its way south, stood Preston with the three eighteen-pounders from the *Griffin*, loaded and ready.

In front of him, drawn up on the flat veldt between the British and Cape Town, were the Dutch, also with a battery of guns deployed straddling the road. The armies were matched in overall numbers, but little else. Where the British formation had a look of well-drilled uniformity, the enemy's was much more varied. Only two units were dressed in uniform coats and cross belts, one of European soldiers in trousers, the other of black soldiers with bare legs. Among the rest only a handful had military tunics, the remainder boasting a variety of civilian clothes. From their loose formation, Preston guessed they must be the militia. Finally, at the ends of the Dutch line were swarms of the irregular horsemen who Clay had seen earlier.

A cool wind blew in from the open ocean, hissing through the brown grass and raising little dust devils in the space between the two armies. All that could be heard was the jangle of harnesses as horses shook their heads to clear the flies clustering around their eyes, and the thump of hooves as messengers rode to and fro behind the lines with last-minute instructions for the various units. One such messenger was Lieutenant Dalrymple, who came rushing along the ridge towards the *Griffin*'s guns.

'Does that laddie ever ride his horse at a regular pace?' asked Macpherson, whose marines were drawn up on the slope behind the guns.

'I very much doubt it, Tom,' said Preston. 'What can I

Clay and the River of Silver

do for you, Lieutenant?' he added, as the young officer pulled his mount to a halt.

'Sir David orders you to commence your bombardment, and requests you concentrate on the enemy's artillery.'

Preston took out his telescope and examined the gun line below him, each one surrounded by its crew. 'Ten small pieces, six-pounders at best,' he commented. 'It will be long range for them, firing uphill back at us. The gunners don't look very Dutch. Why, most are wearing turbans.'

'They are Malay, I believe, sir,' said Dalrymple. 'From the Dutch East Indies.'

'All those masses of soldiers would make for a better target, but I'm sure the general knows best. In any event, it will be good to get started, having dragged our cannon all this way. Mr Todd! Have the men man their pieces. Our mark is the enemy guns.'

'Aye aye, sir.'

Most of the crews had been dozing in the sun, but they jumped up smartly and hurried to take their places around the guns. As each cannon was manned the captain raised his fist aloft.

'Gun one! Fire!' ordered Preston, standing downwind of the battery.

Gun one roared out, raising a puff of dust well to the left of the target. The ball bounded on, and there was a sudden flutter in the ranks of one of the militia regiments. A gap appeared and two figures lay prone on the ground.

'A hit of sorts, but you'll need to aim better than that, Abbott,' said Preston, as the crew raced to reload. 'A battery is a thin target when compared with hitting a ship. Mr Rudgewick, can you oversee the laying of gun one, if you please.'

'Aye aye, sir.'

Philip K Allan

'Gun two, see what you can do.'

Another tongue of flame, and this time the puff of dust came midway between two of the guns, harming neither. 'Better,' declared Preston. 'Your range is good. See you run the gun back to the same place for your next shot.'

'Aye aye, sir.'

'Gun three now ... Gun three? O'Malley, where are half your crew?'

'Evans and Pembleton had an urgency, you might say, sir. For the heads,' said the Irishman, indicating where the big Londoner and the ex-lacemaker could be seen squatting behind a bush among the oxen.

'What about Trevan? Where has he gone?'

'Over there spewing faster than the village pump, sir,' reported O'Malley. 'But he'll be right soon enough. I felt a deal better after I had meself a puke.'

'What the hell have you lot been eat—' But the rest of Preston's question was lost in a roar as the Dutch battery opened fire. Dust flew up from the slope in front of them, and a few shots whined past overhead. 'Oh ... never mind, O'Malley, just fire as swiftly as you are able. Mr Todd! Go and tell Evans and Pembleton to return to their posts at the double, and then find Trevan.'

'Aye aye, sir.'

'The rest of you fire as swiftly as you can. Let us show them how briskly a navy crew can handle a gun.'

The battery at the bottom of the hill were firing slowly but steadily. He watched a European officer moving from one gun to the next, checking the aim, before giving the order to fire from the end of the row. Then the whole battery vanished behind a curtain of smoke, the sound only reaching him on the heels of the barrage of cannonballs as they thudded into the

Clay and the River of Silver

slope beneath him. The target slowly emerged again as the breeze sent the smoke rolling away.

By contrast his cannons were firing more quickly, even gun three, now that its crew was back to full strength. He was pleased to see that the captains were pausing before firing, checking their aim was true, and that the guns had been run back up to the same place each time. There were gunners lying on the grass at the bottom of the hill, while he had lost no one yet. He heard O'Malley shout a warning to his crew to stand clear, and moments later the eighteen-pounder roared out. One of the enemy's guns vanished under a cloud of dust, and when it cleared it was heeled over with one wheel reduced to a tangled mess.

'Good shooting, gun three!' said Preston. 'We're getting on top of them, lads.' He turned to congratulate the crew. Evans was busy sponging out, his suntanned face strangely pale, while Trevan stood beside him with the next charge sweating profusely. He wondered again what had made them so ill. Clay had given strict instructions against looting, although Preston knew that many of the crew would ignore that if alcohol was involved. Had they stolen drink from a farm? But Trevan was one of the steadier men, and they were not behaving as if they were drunk.

'Sir,' said Todd beside him. 'Something is going on down there.'

Preston returned his attention to the battle. More gunners were down, and the rate of fire from the Malay battery was slowing. A group of horsemen in more elaborate uniforms grouped around a man with a red, white and blue sash around his waist. Preston decided he must be General Janssens, the enemy commander. Just at that moment gun two boomed out, the shot ploughing through the crew of one of the enemy six-

Philip K Allan

pounders as they were gathered to wheel it back into position. The gun was unharmed, but more gunners now lay on the veldt. Janssens looked at the carnage, and then turned to address someone. A horseman broke away and galloped along behind the Dutch lines. Preston followed him closely until he arrived among the cavalry drawn up on the flank. He closed his telescope and returned it to his pocket. 'Mr Rudgewick!'

'Sir?'

'Would you issue those rounds of canister to the guns please. I believe we will have need of them presently.'

'Aye aye, sir.'

'Tom, a word of advice if you please.'

The marine came over to join him, and Preston pointed out the situation. 'We have been making good progress towards silencing the enemy's guns, which has prompted their general to send an order to those horsemen over there. I presume he wants them to stop us.'

'Aye, I dare say that's the case,' said Macpherson calmly. 'Cavalry is the natural enemy of artillery. They come on so fast that they are upon a battery before it can fire more than a few shots, and a rammer is poor defence against a well-honed sabre.'

'That doesn't sound very reassuring,' said Preston. 'Look, I'm just a naval officer, you're the soldier. What do you suggest I do?'

'Make sure the shots you have count,' said the marine. 'Especially the last one. Hold your nerve for as long as you can.'

'Right,' said Preston. 'Oh, my! They are starting to move this way!'

'So they are,' said Macpherson. 'I shouldn't be too alarmed. If these are the same horsemen my skirmishers saw

Clay and the River of Silver

off this morning, the sight of your great guns primed and ready may well prove enough. But in case I'm wrong, and they have found the pluck to charge home, I'll have my lads drawn up in close order just here. Your men can take refuge behind us if pressed.'

'Right,' said Preston, swallowing hard. 'Thank you, Tom. New target! Those horsemen approaching over there. Fire ball for now, but be ready to load with canister when I give the word.'

'Aye aye, sir.'

'Marines will form a two-deep line on me!' ordered Macpherson.

Preston had assumed the cavalry would simply charge directly towards them, down the corridor between the two armies, but then he realised that this would have exposed them to musket fire from the British infantry lining the crest to his right. Instead, they were moving along behind the Dutch line in a mass, perhaps two hundred strong, trailing clouds of dust as they came. 'They mean to come straight up the slope towards us, lads,' he warned.

'Aye aye, sir,' grunted the gun captains, helping heave the heavy cannon around until they pointed towards the new target.

The guns fired one after the other, their crews leaping forward to reload without pausing to see where the shots had fallen. The target was a much better one than the widely spaced guns, despite the longer range. Preston watched a horse suddenly crumple and fall, the rider tumbling over its neck. Then another rider vanished from his saddle as if plucked off by an invisible hand. 'Good shooting lads!' he urged. 'Give them another!'

Now the horsemen were coming closer, trotting jerkily,

Philip K Allan

the individual riders rising and falling in the saddle. Beside him, the loading of the guns was almost complete. A sailor on the nearest one was driving a fresh ball down the barrel. An instant later he was gone, dashed away by a shot from the Dutch battery, leaving his rammer still protruding from the muzzle. 'You, Anderson! Take his place,' he ordered. 'Get that gun loaded and run up!'

The sailor stepped over the broken body and seized the wooden shaft. 'That's home!' he reported, pulling the rammer clear.

The guns banged out again, the heavy balls bounding through the mass of horsemen, knocking more animals and riders down like toys as the cavalry arrived behind the Dutch battery and wheeled round to face him. Preston could see Janssens, sword in hand, flourishing it in the air, and pointing his way, and he felt his throat go dry. 'Canister now!' he ordered. 'Run the guns forward 'til they point down the slope. Quoins fully in. And hold your fire 'til I give the word.'

'Aye aye, sir.'

The enemy battery fell silent as the crews ran clear of the approaching cavalry. The horsemen flowed around the guns like water through rocks and collected again at the bottom of the hill. They were a motley lot on a variety of different-sized horses, many of them sporting beards. Among the broadbrim hats that predominated, Preston could make out the odd top hat and even a tricorn. Those who had swords drew them and the horsemen broke into a trot.

'Marines will fix bayonets!' ordered Macpherson's voice from somewhere behind him.

Preston heard orders being barked from the battalions on either side, but ignored them as he concentrated on the approaching enemy, trying to decide the best moment to open

Clay and the River of Silver

fire. A canister round was a thin copper cylinder packed with hundreds of musket balls that would spread out like a cone when they left the muzzle. But timing was all important, he reminded himself. Fire too soon, and the cloud of balls would be wide and thin. Fire too late and it would only hit the few directly in its path. He could hear the drum of the horses' hooves as the cavalry gathered pace, growing all the time as they came up the slope. He glanced to either side, but the red-coated infantry had folded themselves into hollow squares bristling with bayonets, leaving a wide gap with only his guns and Macpherson's little party of marines to stop the wall of horsemen. He forced himself to be calm, and chose a point in front of him when he would order the guns to fire.

'Steady lads!' he urged, more for his own benefit. 'Gun captains ready!'

The enemy were coming on like a wave towards a beach. The thunder of their hooves was filling the air, making the ground tremble beneath his feet. He looked at the officer leading them on, his curved sabre held above his head, his face distorted as he yelled to his men. Preston felt an overwhelming urge to turn and flee. His hand was shaking like a leaf as he tried to draw his sword. Then the officer reached the rock that Preston had chosen as his mark. 'Fire!' he yelled.

Three lanyards were jerked back as one. Three flints snapped forward, and three guns roared out in a single deluge of smoke and fire. He stared into the fog of brown, expecting the tide of cavalry to appear at any moment, sweeping towards him. Nothing. Then the smoke cleared a little and he saw a solitary horse standing riderless below him. The wind blew the rest away to reveal a tangled mass of men and fallen horses dotting the slope, and the rest fleeing back the way they had come.

Philip K Allan

'I said they would give you no bother, laddie,' said Macpherson, appearing beside him. 'But that was very well done.'

'If you say so, Tom,' said Preston, still mesmerised by the carnage beneath him. After the initial shock, the first of the wounded were starting to moan and cry out for help. He looked around as Dalrymple came galloping up.

'By Jove, bravo, sir,' enthused the subaltern. 'Sir David was most impressed and asked to know your name, which I was pleased to give him. He orders you to cease firing, as the army are going to advance.'

Preston had been so focused on the attack that he had not noticed what was going on elsewhere. As he looked around him, he saw that the battalions on either side had come out of their squares and were busy being dressed back into formation by bawling sergeants. From further off came the sound of bagpipes, and he saw a solid line of red marching down the slope at a steady pace. Then the next battalion began to advance, followed by the one beside him. Soon the air was filled with the beat of drums and the squeal of fifes. 'What are we to do, then?' he asked.

'Oh, the navy has done quite enough, sir,' said Dalrymple. 'Your captain ferried us ashore in good order and your guns have played their part. Now it is our turn. Observe the battle from up here, if you will. I must return to the general.' And with that, he was away again.

'Not a bad spot to watch from,' said Macpherson. 'Look how boldly the Highlanders come on.'

But his companion was distracted by the remnants of the cavalry charge just below them. 'Mr Todd, once you have secured the guns, the crews can attend to those poor souls down there. And have a message sent back to the captain on the beach.

Clay and the River of Silver

Give him my compliments, and let him know we will be bringing wounded back for the surgeons to attend to.'

'Aye aye, sir.'

'My men can assist,' said Macpherson, waving them forward. 'They shan't be needed in battle, from the look of things.'

The long scarlet lines had reached the Dutch positions now. Where they were opposed by militia, the enemy units dissolved away before their remorseless approach. Preston could see swarms of tiny figures running across the veldt, casting aside their weapons and equipment as they fled. Only a few units were still in good order, trading crashing volleys of musketry, but they were heavily outnumbered. The Malay gunners were fighting hard with whatever equipment came to hand. Then the tide of red flowed over them, leaving the ground littered with their bodies. And almost as soon as it had started, the battle was over.

*****

The little thatched cottage was much too small to accommodate everyone, so a table and chairs had been set up outside on the beaten earth of the courtyard. It was positioned in the pool of shade cast by a spreading milkwood tree. Sitting along one side of the table were General Baird and Captain Popham, both resplendent in full dress uniform, together with Nicholas Vansittart in much lighter attire. Behind them stood various officers, including Clay. Facing them across the table was a row of empty chairs.

'Are the Dutch ever going to appear?' asked Baird, fanning himself with his hat. 'Damned close today, I find,'

'That is because you military coves will swathe

yourselves in broadcloth, whatever the conditions, Sir David,' said Vansittart. 'I find it rather agreeable.'

'But what can they be discussing?' said the Scotsman. 'Our terms were set down clear enough. They surrender the colony intact and we ship their garrison home. We are hardly barbarians at the gate.'

'I daresay it is mostly for effect,' said Popham. 'The blushing bride's show of reluctance before hopping into the nuptial bed, what?'

'Guard! Attention!' bellowed a corporal. In response, the sentries on either side of the cottage door slapped their muskets up in front of them, as a grey-haired man in a blue uniform emerged from the building accompanied by several civilians. One of those following was Captain De Bruyn, dressed more smartly than when he had breakfasted with Clay and Vansittart.

'Have you concluded your deliberations, Colonel von Prophalow?' asked Baird, indicating the chair opposite his. 'Can we get the agreement signed?'

'Almost, Sir David,' said the Dutchman. 'Just a few points to clear up.'

'Go on,' said the general, crossing his arms.

'The agreement says all Dutch and French soldiers and sailors will be sent home, while civilians have the option to stay and become Britisher, yes? But what of those in the garrison who have wives in the colony? There are many who have married local girls, even some of my officers.'

'Ah ... well now ...' said Baird, looking pleadingly towards Vansittart.

'If they are Dutch they can stay, provided they too swear allegiance to the Crown,' said the diplomat. 'But all French citizens and their dependents must return to Europe, without

Clay and the River of Silver

exception.'

'Yes, that sounds reasonable,' said Baird. 'Just what I was going to suggest. Pray amend the treaty, Cooper.'

'Yes, sir,' said the general's clerk, scratching furiously.

'Do we have an agreement then?' asked Baird.

'Not quite, Sir David,' said Von Prophalow. 'De Bruyn here speaks for his fellow sea captains. They are worried that when Cape Town becomes British, their sailors will be pressed into your navy.'

'Naturally,' said Popham. 'Being a citizen comes with obligations as well as rights.'

'But perhaps in this case we might make a concession,' said Vansittart. 'What if we were to make Cape Town sailors exempt from impressment for a period of, say ten years? The war might well be over by then? Would that answer Captain … was it Brown?'

'Captain De Bruyn, and that would be satisfactory.'

'Draft another clause, if you please, Cooper,' said Baird.

'Yes, sir,' sighed the clerk.

'Surely that must be all, Colonel?' said Baird.

'One more point, please. Here it says all public property to be handed over. Does this include warships?'

'Absolutely,' said Popham.

'Because the *Bato* was sunk to avoid capture.'

'The Dutch sixty-four?' spluttered Popham. 'But that was my prize! Our prize, I mean. Who was responsible for this outrage?'

'French sailors at Simon's Town.'

'We must find the culprits, Sir David,' urged Popham. 'The *Bato* should be raised at their expense, the rogues!'

'That is as may be, but it is hardly a matter for a treaty,' said the Scotsman. 'Were there any other substantive issues, Colonel?'

Von Prophalow looked to his companions and then returned to the document. 'No, Sir David. We are ready now.'

'At last,' said Baird, pulling an inkstand towards him. 'Treaty please, Cooper. Let us get this wee paper signed ...'

'I have a question,' said Vansittart.

'Of course, you do,' sighed Baird, returning the pen to its place. 'How foolish of me to think otherwise.'

'In what capacity will you be signing, Colonel?' asked Vansittart.

'I am commander of the garrison,' said Von Prophalow.

'But not governor of the colony,' said Vansittart. 'It may seem a formality, but such treaties should be ratified by the official representatives of our two governments. That is Sir David here as our governor-designate. Where is General Janssens for the Dutch?'

'After the battle, he fled into the mountains with some followers,' said the colonel, pointing airily towards the east. 'He wishes to fight on, I think, but he has few men. Just this morning deserters were arriving in town.'

'I have sent Beresford to bring him in,' said Baird. 'Once he sees the game is up, he will surrender soon enough.'

'Very well,' said Vansittart. 'Clerk, kindly note that the colonel is signing as acting governor in the absence of General Janssens, who has abandoned his post.'

Baird signed the much-amended treaty with a flourish, and pushed the document across the table. The Dutchman spent a little longer checking the various changes, and then signed too.

'Excellent, sir,' said the general, holding out his hand. 'My men will take possession of the various fortifications

Clay and the River of Silver

around Cape Town immediately, Colonel. It will be good to have the Union flag flying over Fort Good Hope once more.'

'Might I suggest that the fortifications continue to fly the Dutch flag for now, Sir David,' said Clay. 'It will be some time before word of our victory reaches the enemy, and there are still two French warships unaccounted for.'

'A trap, eh?' enthused Beresford. 'Let them sail in under our guns, thinking nothing is amiss?'

'Actually, I was going to make that very suggestion, General,' said Popham, turning to glare at Clay.

'Then we shall make it so,' said Baird.

*****

The *Cape Allerton* had made a good passage from Madeira. She had spent no more than a few days becalmed in the doldrums at the equator, waiting for the first breath of the south-east trade winds. Then she had stopped briefly at Recife in Brazil to replenish her fresh water and had headed south, following the coast. The sea had been tropical blue for most of the voyage, but had turned to green as the wide mouth of the Rio de la Plata opened up to the west of her.

Captain Waine slipped an extra disc of smoked glass into his sextant, and brought the sun carefully down to the horizon, rocking easily on his feet against the swell of the sea. When he was satisfied, he clamped the instrument and consulted the curved gauge. 'This is your River Plate, right enough, but I'm going to need a pilot from here on in. My chart shows her to be mostly shallow as a pan, and I ain't planning on leaving the *Allerton* stuck on no mudbank.'

'Of course, *señor*,' said Pueyrredon. 'The best pilots are to be found on the northern shore. You can pick one up off

Philip K Allan

Punta del Este. Just over there.'

The pilot who came aboard later was dressed in a shabby coat and britches, with lank dark hair showing from beneath his battered hat. He bowed low when he saw Waine's passenger. 'Don Pueyrredon, a thousand welcomes! I had not expected to find you on board a Yankee ship, *señor*. Are you returning to Buenos Aires?'

'Not immediately. I will first visit my estate near Ensenada. I have some cargo to unload there.'

'Forgive me for mentioning it, *señor*,' said the pilot, with a troubled look on his face. 'But this fine vessel will never pass through the entrance to the port at Ensenada without touching bottom.'

'No, which is why I would like you to take us to my private jetty, just east of the port,' explained Pueyrredon. 'Arriving at night, if you please. It would be best to avoid meeting the *Guardacosta*.'

'I know the place exactly, *señor*. Captain, could you put your ship before the wind, and steer west by south.'

'Not until I know what's going on here. Back in London you said this was all going to be easy. Now there's talk of ports too tight for the *Allerton*, and unloading by night to avoid the coast guard. I thought you said you owned this place?'

'I do,' said Pueyrredon, patting the American on the arm. 'Relax, Captain. All will be well. I only wish to avoid unnecessary questions.'

'And I don't intend to see my ship wrecked in the dark if this feller here don't know his business,' said Waine, indicating the pilot.

'We are early enough to arrive at dusk, *señor*, if that would make the captain feel easier,' suggested the pilot. 'The *Guardacosta* will have returned to port by then.'

Clay and the River of Silver

'That might answer for the navigation, but this is sounding a deal more troublesome than you spoke of,' said Waine, folding his arms.

'Which is why I am paying you so handsomely, my friend,' said Pueyrredon. 'Don't play the innocent. You knew exactly what you were getting into. Besides, I have a little gift for you, once my cargo is unloaded.'

'A gift? What sort of gift?'

'You will see, Captain. West by south, I believe the course was.'

Despite his shabby appearance, the pilot knew the area well, and laid out a course across the estuary using a combination of dead reckoning and the few landmarks visible from the ship. The colour of the water darkened towards chocolate brown, and marker buoys began to appear as they sailed deeper in, showing the presence of the more dangerous shoals. It was only as the sun was beginning to set, and the American ship was nearing the southern shore, that he asked Waine to reduce sail and station a reliable man with a lead in the forechains.

'By the mark, fifteen!' called the sailor as the ship passed over the lead. He hauled it back up and inspected the base. 'Mud bottom!'

'No need for your man to report on that, Captain,' observed the pilot. 'He will find nothing else around here. Come a point to starboard, please, helmsman.'

The *Cape Allerton* sailed on, following a shoreline of slick mud, rising to a flat land dotted with trees. Only a church tower surrounded by a small settlement broke the monotony. Faintly on the wind came the tolling of a bell.

'That is Ensenada, Captain,' explained the pilot. 'Behind that mudbank lies the river that leads there. Our way lies a little further along the coast. A point to leeward now.'

'By the deep, thirteen!' called the man in the bow.

Now a small shabby boat sailed by, trailing a net. Two men in ponchos watched them idly, before returning to their fishing.

'And the mark, twelve!'

'Our destination lies just ahead, Captain,' said the pilot. 'Beyond those trees.'

'All hands! All hands to reduce sail!'

The American ship was every bit as handy as her captain had claimed back in London, and rounded into the sheltered bay with ease. Jutting out towards them was a short stone quay, with a building at the landward end. A dirt track led inland towards a low hill in the near distance. On its summit was a large walled complex of buildings. A few lights were shining out from the windows.

'Home at last,' breathed Pueyrredon.

'And the mark, eight!' added the man in the bow.

'There should be just enough depth for you to moor against this side of the jetty, Captain,' said the pilot. 'Or you could anchor here and unload by boat.'

Waine thought for a moment, gauging the wind and the state of the tide. 'I'll come alongside,' he decided. 'The sooner I can unload and be away from this damned coast, the happier I shall be.'

As the *Cape Allerton* pressed on, several men emerged from the building at the jetty's end and hailed the ship across the water. Pueyrredon's reply in Spanish was met with waves of greeting, and one man ran behind the building, emerging on a horse. He rode away quickly in the direction of the complex on the hill.

'All is well, Captain,' explained Pueyrredon. 'My men

Clay and the River of Silver

will help you moor, and I have sent someone to fetch carts and horses. And there are no coast guard patrols in the area.'

'Very well. First mate! Get the foretopsail off her! And have warps and springs prepared!'

'Aye aye, sir!'

It was dusk by the time the *Cape Allerton* was secured alongside. Waine had lanterns hung in the rigging and the hatch covers removed. By the time the first boxes of muskets were being swung up from the hold, a line of horse-drawn carts had appeared on the wharf. The American had expected them to be empty, but to his surprise they were full of sacks. He looked enquiringly at Pueyrredon.

'I said I had a gift for you, *señor*,' he explained. 'It is grain, from my farms, to add to what you already have. It is what you usually carry, is it not? And will serve to explain your presence here if you are stopped when you leave.'

'And where am I to sell all this grain?' asked the American.

'I should take it to Cape Town, before you return to Boston,' said Pueyrredon. 'You will find a good market for it there. Unless I am very much mistaken, the Royal Navy blockade will be lifted by now, and there will be many more mouths to feed. And in return, you can deliver a message from me to the British naval commander at the Cape. His name is Popham. Tell him that I have returned and that soon the Rio de la Plata will be ready to rise.'

Philip K Allan

Chapter 7
The *Volontaire*

The *Griffin* was at sea once more, much to the delight of her captain. Clay had left Baird, Vansittart and Popham behind in Cape Town, battling with all the minor details that accompanied the transfer of power. His ship was fully provisioned and the eighteen-pounders sent ashore were back in their usual places on her main deck. He had dined well, and was now walking on his quarterdeck enjoying a cigar. The sun was in the sky, the sea was blue, and his ship was running free, hunting for the two French frigates that had been operating out of Cape Town before the invasion.

Their captain's good spirits were shared by his men. It was a Sunday afternoon, traditionally a time of leisure for the crew. Many of them had taken the opportunity of fine weather to wash their clothes, and the standing rigging of the foremast was alive with a flapping bunting of garments. The forecastle was dotted with men, most engaged in activities familiar to Clay. There were the men sitting quietly working at a piece of scrimshaw, or repairing their clothes. There were those in pairs who had washed their hair, one waiting patiently while the other gathered their billowing mane back into a neat pigtail. There were groups of sailors fishing from the catheads or gathered around a literate shipmate to have a letter home composed for them. But for one group he couldn't place their activity. At its heart he recognised some of the former convicts that had come

Clay and the River of Silver

on board in Plymouth. 'Mr Taylor,' he called. 'A moment of your time, if you please.'

'Yes, sir?'

'Pembleton and his associates have drawn quite the crowd,' said Clay, nodding towards the forecastle. 'What do you suppose they are up to? I'll have no seditious talk on my ship.'

'I believe they are teaching their shipmates how to make lace, sir,' said the first lieutenant.

'Lacemaking? Really?'

'Yes, sir. You know how the men like to adorn their shore-going clothes. Ribbons in their shirt seams and the like. Now it seems their fancy has run to lace.'

'But they will look like so many fops.'

'They will, sir. Although it would be a brave man to say as much to Evans or Powell.'

'True,' said Clay, smiling at the thought. 'I believe I may have done the new hands a disservice. And Pembleton at least may have the makings of a sailor.'

'If the war lasts that long, sir,' said Taylor.

'Sail ho!' came a cry from the masthead. 'Two points off the bow!'

'What do you make of her, Dawson?' yelled Clay.

'A fair-sized ship, I reckon, sir.'

'Up you go, Mr Sweeney,' said Taylor. 'Mr Russell, have the men take their clothes down from the rigging and strike their possessions below.'

'Aye aye, sir.'

'A point closer to the wind, helmsman,' ordered Clay.

'Point to the wind, aye, sir.'

Clay walked forward along the starboard gangway and searched the horizon for the distant ship. He swept the line

Philip K Allan

where the deep blue of the sea touched the pearl of the sky, paused, and tracked back again. As the *Griffin* rose to a wave, a tiny square of white appeared, and then vanished. It was the briefest of glimpses, yet Clay knew he had seen the bulging fore topgallant sail of a ship much the size as his own. 'Mr Sweeney!' he called aloft. 'Is she alone, or does she sail in company?'

A pause while the midshipman searched the rim of the world visible to him from the top of the main mast. 'No other sail in sight, sir.'

Clay returned his telescope to his eye. The sail was above the horizon all the time now, tribute to how swiftly the ships were converging. He glanced forward. The foremast had been stripped clear of washing and the last of the men were disappearing below. He returned to the quarterdeck.

'One of the French frigates, sir?' asked Taylor.

'Seven chances in ten that she is, George,' said Clay.

He resumed his walk, but this time he was pacing with purpose. He pitched his cigar over the rail and clasped his hands behind his back. The sighting could be anything, of course. A stray merchantman, for example, or a large whaler. But such a ship would be wary of the *Griffin*, yet this one was coming boldly towards him, which made it certain she was another hunter like him. There was a remote chance she might be the *Narcissus*, the squadron's other frigate who was also searching for the French, but her patrol area was further to the east.

Clay swung around just before he reached the foremost of the quarterdeck carronades, and paced back along the deck. Of course, the other captain would probably be reasoning just like him. Even now he might be pacing too, pondering why the *Griffin* had not altered course. If she was indeed one of the French ships, far from land and sailing alone, her captain might

Clay and the River of Silver

decide to flee. Clay needed to delay that moment for as long as possible, until it was too late for her to escape.

'Deck there!' yelled Sweeney from the masthead. 'She's a man-o'-war for certain. I can see her topsails.'

'Still alone, Mr Sweeney?' asked Clay.

'Yes, sir.'

'Mr Taylor, kindly clear the ship for action, if you please. But no marines in the tops yet, and keep the guns run in.'

'Aye aye, sir.'

As the drum roared out from the deck below, Clay found his walk interrupted by the crews of the carronades rushing to get their weapons ready. He stopped level with the frigate's flag locker, where Todd stood with his signal rating, slate ready. The blond midshipman would have little to do if Clay was right and this was an enemy ship. And then he realised how he might lure the enemy closer.

'Deck there!' called Sweeney. 'She's a frigate, sir! Much the size of us.'

'The odds shorten, George,' said Clay. 'Nine chances in ten, I believe.'

'Yes, sir. She might be the *Valeureuse* or the *Volontaire*. Both are forty-gun heavy frigates. And the ship is ready for battle.'

'French colours!' yelled Sweeney. 'Just breaking out now!'

Clay stepped across to the rail. The enemy was well over the horizon, showing her bow and her long starboard side, black with a strake of deep scarlet running along her gundeck. Her big topsails were braced around on their long yards, her masts towering high.

'Shall I have our ensign hauled aloft, sir?' asked Taylor.

Philip K Allan

'I think not. Dutch colours, if you please.'

'Aye aye, sir.'

'Mr Todd!'

'Yes, sir,' said the signal midshipman, coming across.

'Do you recall the signal that corvette made off Robben Island?' asked Clay. 'Mr Russell brought the flags back once she was captured.'

'I do sir,' said Todd. 'And I kept the flags as you ordered. There are three. The first was blue over white, then ...'

'I see you have it committed to memory,' interrupted Clay. 'Kindly make the signal now.'

'Aye aye, sir.'

There was a buzz of conversation across the quarterdeck as the unfamiliar flags rose to the mizzen yardarm, and those around him guessed what their captain was doing.

'Will it answer, I wonder,' said Armstrong, pointing his telescope towards the other ship. 'It may not be the enemy's recognition signal at all.'

'It need only confuse him, Jacob,' said Taylor. 'Another ten minutes on this course and she will be under our guns. See, she responds. A good sign, I think.'

'Enemy signalling, sir,' reported the signal midshipman. 'I can't read it, begging your pardon. It's made up of two flags, neither of which we use.'

'No matter, Mr Todd,' said Clay. 'The correct response, I don't doubt. Note it down for me.'

'Aye aye, sir.'

The French ship was growing all the time as she came on, so that Clay no longer needed his telescope. She sat heavy in the water, and was being handled well, he decided. A picked crew and many months at sea would have ensured that.

'Surely she must smoke us soon,' said Taylor. 'Our

Clay and the River of Silver

open bow is as English as beef and ale, not to mention our navy rig. Ah! There we go!'

The Frenchman had abruptly changed course, heading closer to the wind to gain the weather gauge, and a fresh signal broke out from her rigging.

'The enemy is signalling again, sir,' reported Todd, 'but I have no notion …'

'Thank you, Mr Todd,' said Clay. 'The game is up. I'll have our own ensign, Mr Taylor. Run out the guns and the sharpshooters may deploy.'

'Aye aye, sir.'

Clay ignored the marines as they made their ponderous way aloft, dragging extra pouches of ammunition with them, and returned his attention to the enemy. She was broadside on to him, her hull stretching long and low across the sea as she beat up into the wind. Among her mass of sails were two huge ensigns, their colours bright against her sails. Then she dropped off, declining battle and turning away.

'Follow her, Mr Taylor. As close-hauled as she will lie.'

'Aye aye, sir.'

As the *Griffin* settled on to the same course as her enemy, Clay found himself looking at her broad stern, no more than a mile and a half ahead. He could see the sweep of her windows amid the gilded carving that surrounded them, and her name, *Volontaire*, in white letters, just beneath them.

'She seems reluctant to make our acquaintance, sir,' said Taylor. 'Do you suppose we shall catch her?'

'French ships are generally swift, but she looks heavily laden to my eye,' said Clay. 'And we have Mr Hutchinson on our side.' He pointed forward, to where the boatswain was fussing over the headsails, minutely adjusting them to maximise their draw.

Philip K Allan

'A stern chase is a long chase, they say,' said Taylor, before turning to the men at the wheel. 'You can come closer to the wind than that! Don't you like the feel of prize money?'

'Aye aye, sir.'

The frigates rushed onward, under every sail they could carry, two things of beauty as they scored the deep blue of the ocean with long comet tails of white. Yard by yard, at a pace that was barely perceptible, the *Griffin* overhauled her opponent. After an hour of hard battling, a sailor ran along the gangway from the bow and came to a halt, knuckling his forehead to his captain.

'What is it, Hobbs?'

'Mr Hutchinson's compliments, like, an' he reckons that there Frenchie could be in range of the long nines, sir.'

Clay looked at the stern of the *Volontaire*, and noticed it had grown broader. He could see several officers looking back at him. Above their head, in the mizzen top, sat several soldiers, nursing their muskets.

'I believe the boatswain may be right,' he said. 'My thanks to you, Hobbs. Mr Taylor, let us try our luck with the bow chasers.'

'Aye aye, sir.'

The *Griffin* was equipped with two nine-pounder guns, mounted each side of her bowsprit and pointing directly forward. They were the nearest thing to precision weapons the age had to offer, their long barrels carefully milled in smooth brass. But conditions were far from ideal, with the frigate heeled over and her bow crashing through each successive wave. The first two shots banged out almost together, but when the smoke cleared their splashes were far apart. One was in line, but well short, the other wildly off to one side. 'Mr Russell, kindly go and take command of the forecastle,' ordered Clay.

Clay and the River of Silver

'See if you can improve their practice.'

'Aye aye, sir.'

Whether it was the presence of the young officer, or the gun crews were becoming accustomed to the lively motion, the next few salvos were better aimed.

'A splash, hard alongside, sir,' announced Taylor. 'That is better. I think that was the larboard gun.'

'We must slow them a little,' said Clay. 'Or it will be dark when we come to fight them in earnest.'

'Indeed, sir,' said Taylor, as the next salvo was fired. 'Only one splash, so the other ball must have struck home. I wonder where?'

'Mizzen topsail,' said Armstrong. 'See, a hole punched clear through, close to the leech.'

Clay looked at the tear, and noticed the canvas around it had a blush of amber. The officers lining the stern rail were sheltering their eyes beneath levelled hands. He looked behind him and saw the sun was dropping towards the horizon. The nine-pounders banged out again, and a fresh hole appeared in the mizzen topsail.

'Why do they not try and reply?' asked Macpherson. 'They have stern ports in their wardroom, just as we do?'

'They lie too tight to the water to be used close-hauled like this, Tom,' said Taylor. 'She would ship water faster than if we had holed her below the waterline. See, the lee port is almost under. Besides, she would need to move a pair of guns from her main battery, and she will be needing all of those presently.'

'Darn good shooting, there!' exclaimed Armstrong. 'Both balls, clean through her stern!'

The run of glass windows were glowing in the low sun, making the shattered frame left by the nine-pounder ball

Philip K Allan

obvious. The other shot had struck lower, leaving a gash of white close to the rudder.

'I wonder what she is carrying?' mused Clay. The other officers looked at him quizzically.

'Sir?' queried Taylor.

'Well-handled French frigates like this one are generally swifter than ours, yet we have been overhauling her steadily,' he explained. 'And those stern ports seem too low for me. It is true they can only be used on an even keel, but I doubt if the *Griffin*'s ones are awash like that. Yet we are fully provisioned.'

'Treasure?' offered Taylor. 'From New Spain? That would be grand.'

'Heavy guns, for their garrisons in the Indian Ocean, knowing our luck,' added Macpherson.

'I prefer George's treasure,' smiled Clay. 'But no matter, we will know presently.'

As the range closed, the nine-pounders were hitting her stern again and again, sending broken gilding and splinters of wood flying. One shot struck the mizzen mast a glancing blow, leaving a scar like a bite from an apple.

'I suppose those wee cannon will knock any ship to pieces given enough time,' said Macpherson.

'If the enemy will let us,' said Clay. 'She must surely turn and fight soon?'

But the enemy seemed content to run on, towards the approaching night. When the two chase guns fired again, Clay noticed how bright their muzzle flashes had grown. Behind him the molten sun was close to the horizon. He looked at the brightly lit stern of the *Volontaire*, just ahead of him now, and saw that the officers who had been watching him had vanished. In the mizzen top the marines were firing down towards the

Clay and the River of Silver

deck, the bang of their muskets drifting over the water.

'What in all creation …' began Armstrong.

'Mr Sweeney!' roared Clay. 'What is happening on board the enemy?'

'Fighting, sir!' called the midshipman. 'I can see the flash of pistols and, I'm not certain, but I think I can see redcoats!'

'Redcoats!' exclaimed Macpherson. 'What nonsense is this?'

The long bowsprit of the *Griffin* seemed to be almost touching the stern of the French ship. In the growing dusk the flash of small arms was bright on the enemy's deck, and Clay began to hear the clash of weapons and the sound of shouting. 'Helmsman! A point off the wind! Bring the enemy alongside to larboard.'

'Alongside to larboard, aye, sir.'

'Mr Taylor! Secure the guns …'

'Secure the guns, sir!' exclaimed the first lieutenant. 'But they will be able to fire into us unopposed!'

'Secure the main deck guns, and have the crews armed for boarding,' ordered Clay. 'I'll not fire into a ship full of friends. Do it now.'

'Aye aye, sir.'

Port lids were banging shut beneath him as the eighteen-pounders were run back in. Then the first of the gun crews came up from below, stuffing pistols into their waistbands and slinging cutlass belts over one shoulder. Preston was urging another group to take boarding pikes from the racks around the base of the main mast. Further forward Russell and Hutchinson were organising the men on the forecastle. Clay pulled out his own sword, glittering like fire in the last of the sun, and went to join the men gathering along the rail.

Philip K Allan

They were overlapping the battered stern of the *Volontaire*. An officer on her quarterdeck turned as the loom of the *Griffin*'s towering foremast appeared beside him, and he yelled a stream of orders. Some soldiers in blue tunics ran to the quarterdeck rail, levelling their muskets towards the new threat, but they were quickly despatched by the marines posted in the *Griffin*'s foremast and the frigate swept on.

Now the French ship began to respond to the frigate appearing beside it. The soldiers in her mizzen tops began firing down on the British sailors massed along the gangway, and several were hit. Clay watched as one fell backwards with a cry down onto the main deck. The stern-most guns on the *Volontaire* roared out, sending their heavy balls crashing across the *Griffin*'s abandoned gundeck, filling the space between the ships with brilliant flame. Clay strained to see what was happening on board the enemy. There seemed to be a melee down on the main deck, with more fighting up on the forecastle. Pistols banged and flashed in the gloom, and edged weapons screeched against each other.

The ships were no more than forty yards apart. Macpherson's marines were firing steadily across the gap at any target that appeared. A few of the enemy's guns fired again, and more balls crashing into the *Griffin*'s hull. Then the gap was twenty yards. Some of Clay's top men were climbing up the shrouds with grappling hooks swinging from their fists.

'Ready, Griffins?' yelled Clay, receiving an animal growl in reply.

Fifteen yards, then ten. More of his men were falling as French sailors rushed to line the side. A big man with thick stubble aimed his pistol directly at Clay, and for a moment he wondered if this was when his life would end. He instinctively raised an arm to ward off the shot, and felt a hot rasp across the

Clay and the River of Silver

back of his hand, like the lick of a cat. He looked in disbelief at where the bullet had grazed him, leaving a brown line across his unbroken skin. Not today, it seemed. Not today.

To his left Macpherson's marines were fixing gleaming bayonets to their muskets. To his right the gun crews jostled for position, led by the huge Evans who had jumped up into the main chains, a drawn cutlass in his fist. In the bow Russell was at the head of another party that included Hutchinson, his leather hat pushed back, making trial sweeps through the air with an axe. Above his head topmen had gathered at the ends of the yardarms, ready to leap across into the enemy's rigging. And behind him stood the solid figure of Sedgwick, at the head of his barge crew, ready to follow him across.

'Let fly, lads!' Clay bellowed. 'Make us fast!' Grappling lines flew through the air, and the hulls ground together. 'Up and at them!'

With a collective roar the crew of the *Griffin* swept across the narrow gap left by the ships' tumblehome and down onto the enemy's deck. Immediately in front of Clay was the man who had tried to shoot him, a drawn cutlass in his hand. Clay leapt up on to the rail and across the gap before the sailor could cut at him, holding his long sword out in front with a stiff arm. He dropped down on his opponent, his momentum giving the blow a deadly weight. The point struck the sailor in the shoulder, sinking in deep, and with a cry he fell back. From the corner of his eye he saw the tip of a boarding pike thrust towards him, and he tried to twist from its path. Then a cutlass blade crashed down from behind his shoulder, knocking the shaft aside. 'My thanks, Sedgwick,' he gasped.

Clay steadied himself and looked across the broad quarterdeck of the *Volontaire*. The initial fury of his men's attack had driven the French back, but now they were rallying

Philip K Allan

around the wheel, urged on by their officers. Down on the main deck a separate fight was going on, between more French sailors and red-coated opponents, many of who seemed to be poorly armed. He could see one thrusting with a flexible rammer, another armed with a crowbar. Up on the forecastle the fight was over, and Russell was leading his men down onto the main deck to help their unknown allies.

'Come on, lads!' Clay urged to those around him. 'Take the wheel and she is ours. Follow me!'

The members of his barge crew formed a solid phalanx around their captain, and as they drove forward, more and more Griffins joined them until their advance became as irresistible as the tide across a beach. Preston appeared off to one side, at the head of his gun crews, his one-armed fighting style jerky and strange. Then Macpherson appeared on his other side, his marines back in close order, thrusting and jabbing with their bayonets and driving the enemy back. A French sailor ahead of Clay dropped his cutlass to the deck and backed away, holding his empty hands towards his attackers. Then another did the same, until all across the deck French sailors were laying down their weapons and retreating. By the time Clay had reached the wheel the fight was over.

'I am Capitaine Jacques Bretel,' said a neatly dressed officer of about Clay's age. He bowed stiffly and held out his sword. 'My ship is yours.'

Clay took the weapon and passed it to Sedgwick, who thrust it under his arm. 'My condolences, Monsieur. I am Sir Alexander Clay, of His Majesty's Ship *Griffin*, although I wonder if you should be surrendering to me. Had fighting not broken out before we came alongside?'

'You mean the prisoners,' exclaimed the Frenchman. '*Quelle bande de salauds!* I should have left them to drown!

Clay and the River of Silver

When all my men were preparing to fight you, they revolted behind our backs. Of course, we could have defeated them, or defeated you, but not both together! Here comes their leader now.'

Clay turned to see Preston approaching with a ginger-haired officer dressed in a filthy scarlet tunic with green facings. His face was pale and gaunt beneath its covering of stubble, but there was no mistaking his grin of triumph. 'Well met, sir,' he enthused, grabbing Clay's hand. 'Captain Augustus Duckworth of the 54th West Norfolk regiment. By Jove, but that was a close-run thing! For a while there I thought we had caught a tiger by the tail, but your chaps arrived just as things were turning sour.'

'And what is a captain of the West Norfolks doing off the Cape?'

'Off the Cape you say, sir?' exclaimed Duckworth. 'As in Southern Africa? I'm dashed if I know. By rights we should have been in Gibraltar these last three months. We were part of a convoy that got scattered by a nasty storm a week out from home. Next morning there were just our two transports with not a sign of the rest. Then we spotted a sail and our fool of a captain made towards it. It turned out to be the *Volontaire*, who snapped us up. Since when we've been treated quite abysmally. Cooped up in the hold with barely enough to eat for month after month. When we heard gunfire and the odd shot striking home, we guessed it must be the navy and decided to lend a hand, what?'

'How many are you, Captain?'

'At the start of the fight I commanded two hundred and seventeen, sir. Rather less now, of course.'

'So many?' exclaimed Clay. 'In fairness to Captain Bretel it would be a terrible burden to accommodate such

Philip K Allan

numbers, even on board a ship of this size. But your men are free, and we should have you back on dry land within the week. Now, if you will excuse me, I must attend to securing our prize.'

*****

Popham had left his cabin on the *Diadem* and was now working in an office provided for him in the newly designated Government House in Cape Town. He was working with his clerk on a mountain of supply indents for the squadron, when there was a knock at the door. 'Come in!' he ordered.

An army corporal marched in, stamped to a halt and saluted smartly. 'Lieutenant Thomas's compliments, sir, and we've got this 'ere American gentleman at the gate what's asking for you.'

'Asking for me, you say?' queried Popham. 'Did he give a name?'

'A Captain Waine, master of some ship called the *Allerton*, sir.'

'That will be the *Cape Allerton* of Boston, sir,' added his clerk, consulting some notes. 'It arrived this morning with a cargo of smuggled grain. General Baird is due to decide on whether to permit it to discharge its cargo. Given the state of supplies hereabouts, I imagine he will give his permission without much need to enquire further.'

'This is a bit rum,' said Popham. 'Why would a grain smuggler want to meet with me? Where was this cargo from, Dobson?'

'I believe from the Viceroyalty of the Rio de la Plata, sir,' said the clerk.

'Was it, by Jove! That changes matters. Kindly let him through, Corporal.'

Clay and the River of Silver

'Yes, sir!'

'Dobson, give my compliments to Mr Vansittart and ask him to join me,' continued Popham. 'Then show this American fellow in, if you please.'

'Yes, sir,' said the clerk, gathering up his papers and making for the door.

'You must be Captain Waine, I presume?' said Popham a little later when his visitor was shown in. 'I am Commodore Popham, and this gentleman is the Honourable Nicholas Vansittart. Pray be seated. Might I offer you some refreshment?'

'Mighty kind, sir,' said the American.

'Dobson, kindly serve some of the Constantia,' said Popham. 'It's a very passable local wine, Captain, not dissimilar to madeira.'

'That sounds most acceptable,' said Waine, taking a glass from the proffered tray. 'Good health to you.'

'And you,' said Popham, raising his glass. 'I understand you wished to see me?'

Waine turned to Vansittart. 'I did, but no offence to you, Mister Vansittart, but I was asked to bring word to the commodore here. No one mentioned you.'

'Good,' said Vansittart. 'I much prefer my name not to be bandied around.'

'It is quite all right, Captain,' said Popham. 'You can speak freely in front of my friend here.'

'Well, I was recently employed by a Spanish gentleman by the name of Pueyrredon.'

'Pueyrredon!' exclaimed Popham. 'That is very interesting.'

'Pray continue, Captain,' said Vansittart.

'He asked me to tell you that he has returned to the Rio

Philip K Allan

de la Plata, and that it is ready to rebel. I hope that means something to you folks.'

'Those are most welcome tidings, Captain Waine,' enthused Popham. 'Thank you for bringing them to us.'

'Was that the entire message?' queried Vansittart.

'Pretty well.'

'And what evidence did you personally see of rebellion when you were there?' continued the diplomat.

'In truth I didn't see any, but then I hardly left my ship.'

'I see,' said Vansittart. 'One more question, if you please. What exactly was the nature of your employment by Mr Pueyrredon?'

'I don't believe I am at liberty to say, sir. It being a private arrangement, and the gentlemen concerned not being present to give his consent.'

'I think we understand, Captain,' said Popham. 'Thank you for delivering your message, and I will be sure to speak with the governor about the cargo you wish to land.'

'Much obliged, gentlemen,' said Waine, rising to his feet and heading for the door. 'Good day to you.'

'That is splendid tidings, is it not?' said Popham when they were alone.

'It is encouraging, but then we already knew that Pueyrredon wanted us to come,' said the diplomat. 'Captain Waine's message hardly added to that.'

'Is that a lawyer's caution I detect, sir,' said Popham. 'Come now. The board is set, and the game is afoot. A river of silver is waiting for us, just as we planned for in London.'

'Yes, I suppose so,' agreed Vansittart. 'But I would like to know what Pueyrredon and this American fellow were up to. Surely if it was just shipping grain, Waine would have told us, would he not?'

Clay and the River of Silver

'It matters little,' said Popham. 'Come, let us go and see General Baird.'

Philip K Allan

Chapter 8
The Spark

With the onset of evening, the sea breeze blowing across Table Bay was replaced by a warmer flow from the land. It gently swung the ships at anchor around their mooring cables. Clay sensed the movement from his chair in the great cabin of the *Diadem*. He looked up and saw the view through the stern windows change from the brooding bulk of Table Mountain to the open ocean, pale as topaz in the evening light. But the beauty of the scene was lost on his host, whose mind was on more pecuniary matters.

'Ah, prizes,' sighed Captain Popham, beaming at those gathered around his dinner table. 'Two handsome ones in as many weeks, if you will credit it! While Sir Alexander was helping the West Norfolks capture the *Volontaire* ...'

'Helping the Norfolks?' protested Clay. 'What has Duckworth been saying?'

'Nothing, Captain,' said Popham. 'I am merely summarising from your report. As I was saying, while the *Volontaire* was being captured, her sister ship the *Valeureuse* fell into my lap in a most agreeable fashion. It was Tuesday last, when two ships were reported approaching the bay under full sail. I confess I thought it might be an enemy squadron come to interrupt our fine work, for the lead ship was a big frigate showing French colours, with a second frigate hard astern. But

Clay and the River of Silver

as they drew near, we saw it was our *Narcissus* hotly pursuing an enemy who was fleeing for the safety of Cape Town. You will recall I had arranged for all the fortifications to fly Dutch colours, and in consequence, the *Valeureuse* sailed right in. Why, she was so thoroughly deceived that she even hailed this ship as she passed! Once there was no prospect of escape, we replaced the Dutch ensigns with our own, and with so many guns trained upon her, she was compelled to surrender without a shot fired. What do you make of that?'

Beresford and Vansittart exchanged an awkward glance, while Clay resumed his staring out of the window.

Eventually Vansittart filled the silence. 'Let us raise a glass to the prizes, however they were obtained,' he said. 'I know how beloved they are among sailors.'

After the toast had been drunk, polite conversation resumed around the dinner table. Clay turned to Beresford, who was beside him. 'Tell me, sir, how do matters progress here at the Cape?'

'Tolerably well, in truth. Janssens surrendered to us a few days after you sailed, and he and the former garrison are all now on their way back to Europe in some of the transports that brought us out. As for the citizenry, they seem perfectly content with the change in regime. It helps that General Baird has seen fit to leave most of the local officials in post, and has opened the port to trade. In fact, the first neutral ship arrived the morning before your return. An American vessel carrying grain, I believe. You can see her in the harbour.'

'Indeed, all is going splendidly,' beamed Popham. 'With both of the more troublesome French ships in the area *hors de combat*, and the Dutch and French prisoners sent packing, we are free to consider what more we might achieve, gentlemen.'

Philip K Allan

'More?' queried Beresford. 'Is the conquest of the Cape not sufficient?'

'Oh, 'tis but a flesh wound for Boney,' said Popham, waving his wine glass airily. 'A change in the flag over a governor's residence ain't going to bring him down. We need to strike an altogether lustier blow.'

'Do the French have anything vital left in this region, sir?' asked Clay.

'No, but their principal ally does,' said Popham, pointing towards the setting sun. 'Spain has a whole empire in South America. Do you know that due west of where we sit lies the River of Silver – the Rio de la Plata, as the Dons would have it. And it is well named, for bullion flows down that river from their mines in the Andes to the port of Buenos Aires. Consider what a blow it would be for the enemy if that treasure went into the vaults of the Bank of England instead of the war chest of the Corsican tyrant.'

'But can such a thing be done with the resources we have?' asked Beresford. 'Two of our foot battalions were only loaned to us for the duration of the campaign at the Cape, and must now be released to continue to India. And a decent garrison is required to be left here to prevent the enemy recapturing Cape Town with the same ease that we did.'

'I discussed the matter yesterday with General Baird,' said Popham. 'He has agreed to provide the 71st Highlanders and a half-dozen pieces of Royal Artillery ordinance.'

'One battalion and six guns!' exclaimed Beresford. 'To invade South America!'

'Not quite. You forget the resources of my squadron. Our warships can put over three hundred Royal Marines into the field between them, as well as armed parties of sailors and additional guns and crews as required. And what I propose is

Clay and the River of Silver

more in the way of a raid than a formal invasion.'

'And who is to lead this rash expedition?'

'You are, General.'

'Me!' choked Beresford, wine spilling freely onto the cloth. 'You jest, sir?'

'By no means,' said Popham. 'The operation will need a general to command it, and Sir David cannot leave Cape Town. Do you know of any other generals within a thousand miles of here?'

'I am not here to interfere in military matters,' said Vansittart. 'But I can say that taking Buenos Aires from the Spanish and capturing the bullion believed to be there is an objective supported at the highest levels of the government.'

'And when considering the merits of the expedition, we should also reflect on the opposition we will encounter,' continued Popham. 'What military resources the Spanish have are widely scattered, and one of our battalions is surely worth any two of theirs. Look how well things went here.'

'Actually, the Dutch infantry fought very courageously,' said Beresford. 'It was the locally raised troops that let them down. But how prepared are we for such an attack? Do we even have maps of the area?'

'I can do better than that,' said Popham. 'As luck would have it, the *Diadem*'s carpenter spent several years living in Buenos Aires.'

Beresford looked around for support and latched on to Clay. 'Sir Alexander, what do you think of all this?'

'It certainly sounds bold, even foolhardy,' said Clay. 'Unless we can be assured of the likely attitude of the local population. When Mr Vansittart and I met with Captain De Bruyn, it was clear that the people of Cape Town were unlikely to resist a change of regime. That explains the militia's

Philip K Allan

unwillingness to fight, and the town's rapid surrender. Only a fool risks his skin for a cause he doesn't believe in.'

'Absolutely,' agreed Beresford.

'So perhaps the key here is whether a column of redcoats arriving at the gates of Buenos Aires will be welcomed as liberators, or resisted as invaders,' concluded Clay.

'Well said, sir,' enthused Popham. 'You have put your finger upon it! That American ship you spoke of earlier did not just deliver grain. Her captain also brought me a message from a local landowner that Mr Vansittart and I met with in London, informing me that the Rio de la Plata is ready to throw off the chains of Spanish rule. No one expects us to liberate a whole continent, Beresford. But we may very well provide the spark for the fire that will do that. Why, I daresay they will be putting up statues to you in Buenos Aires in years to come. Think of that, man!'

*****

The dining hall of the hacienda was a cavernous space. The floor was of glazed terracotta tiles set in a pleasing geometric pattern and the ceiling was held up by beams of mountain cedar. One wall was lined with a mixture of heavy chests and solid furniture, the other contained a huge fireplace. The long table that ran the length of the room could have comfortably accommodated many more than the four men who sat clustered around one end, taking their ease with the contented air of those who have dined well.

'More wine, my friends?' asked Pueyrredon, summoning forward a servant.

'My thanks,' said Cornelio de Saavedra, the oldest of the four, his thinning brown hair starting to grey across his

Clay and the River of Silver

temples. 'I try to avoid Portuguese wine, but I confess this madeira is excellent. How did you come by it?'

'The ship that brought me back from Europe stopped at Funchal, so I purchased a few cases. It was there that I saw the fleet of the *Inglés*, on its way to the Cape.'

'And you are certain they will come here next?' asked Manuel Belgrano, a tall darkly handsome man.

'Oh, yes,' said their host. 'When I met with *Señor* Vansittart and Captain Popham in London, I gave them the most compelling of arguments. The *Inglés* may have obtained a veneer of civilisation now, but they are all still pirates at heart. I had only to mention the treasure to win them over.'

'Do we have a formal agreement in place with them?' asked Juan Castelli, leaning forward, an anxious look on his face.

'Only a civil servant could ask such a question,' said Saavedra, rolling his eyes to the others.

'Such matters are never committed to paper, Juan,' explained Pueyrredon. 'Remember that we dabble in treason. A document like that would be our death warrant in the wrong hands. Especially for you, working for the viceroy.' The others nodded at this, their faces grim.

'When can we expect them to arrive?' asked Belgrano.

'Any day now,' said Pueyrredon. 'The armada I saw in Madeira will have quickly swept the Hollanders into the sea.'

'I must tell you that the viceroy knows there is an *Inglés* army in these waters,' cautioned Castelli. 'I was with Don Sobremonte when word arrived that their fleet had been seen. He has given orders for the navigation buoys that mark the way into Buenos Aires to be removed, and is recalling troops from the interior.'

'As captain of the urban militia, I can try and make sure

that they fight poorly,' said Belgrano. 'But I have no authority over the army.'

'I brought guns back from Europe with me, and I have started training my supporters,' said Pueyrredon. 'But they will not be ready to fight for some time, and besides, I don't think that it would be wise for any of us to fight beside the *Inglés*.'

'Why not?' queried Saavedra. 'I thought they were to be our allies, like the French were to General Washington?'

'The French agreed to support the Americans for as long as it took,' explained Pueyrredon. 'I have no such agreement from *Señor* Vansittart. They come for the treasure, my friends, not for us. Let them defeat the viceroy and his Spanish troops, and keep our own forces ready to seize power when they go.'

'He is right,' said Castelli. 'If we openly support them, and the *Inglés* should fail, we will soon find ourselves in front of a firing squad, and the rebellion will perish with us.'

'Very well,' said Belgrano. 'I have waited this long, I can be patient. But we must do our best to make sure the *Inglés* do not fail, comrades.'

'What if we could persuade the viceroy to send his troops to defend Montevideo instead?' suggested Saavedra. 'Then they would be away on the north bank of the Rio de la Plata. With *Inglés* warships in the area, they would not be able to cross back to Buenos Aires, and would need to march far into the interior, which would take many weeks.'

'Why would Don Sobremonte agree to do that?' protested Castelli.

'You are his principal advisor,' growled Belgrano. 'Advise him to do it!'

'It is not as easy as that.'

'Say it is because the waters near Buenos Aires are too shallow for their biggest ships, which is true,' suggested

Clay and the River of Silver

Saavedra. 'And that is why they will attack Montevideo first.'

'Tell him that the merchant community have picked up rumours about the enemy attack,' urged Pueyrredon. '*Inglés* agents asking for information about Montevideo. The approaches to the city, the size of the garrison. That sort of thing.'

'Perfect,' said Belgrano, indicating Pueyrredon and Saavedra. 'And there are your sources! We have the heads of two of the biggest merchant houses in the city sitting at this table, ready to swear to the viceroy's face about the truth of what you say.'

'Yes, that might work,' mused Castelli. 'In fact, I am sure that it will. He is worried about his position in Madrid. If I hold out the prospect of him outwitting the *Inglés* and winning a great victory, he is sure to follow my advice.'

'Do you remember when we first formed our secret society, all those years ago?' asked Pueyrredon. 'Belgrano and Castelli were fresh-faced law students; I had just taken over running the family business after my father died. Now look at us. So close to achieving our dreams.'

'If the *Inglés* come,' said Castelli.

'They will come,' continued their host. 'And when they do, they will sweep Spanish rule aside, take their treasure and go. But they will also be the spark that will set this land ablaze! And from the ashes of that fire will be forged a new country, ready to take its place among the family of nations. Let us drink to the future, my brothers. Let us drink to the United Provinces of the Rio de la Plata!'

*****

Two months later, the British fleet was approaching the coast of South America. It was a grey morning, the sun veiled by cloud, and the water over the side was dotted with patches of rotting vegetation. As they crept onwards, a strange sound grew from somewhere lost in the mist to the north.

'What on earth is that clammer?' asked Clay. 'It sounds like Smithfield's the week before Yuletide.'

'That will be the island of Lobos, sir,' said Jacob Armstrong. 'The sailing directions speak of it being thick with seals, some the size of oxen. A good spot if we stand in need of fresh meat, and a useful mark in close weather. It means that we are entering the River Plate, right enough. And there are few more godawful stretches of water in creation.'

'Why so, Jacob?' asked Vansittart. 'It seems fairly benign to me.'

'Because the Plate is uncommon shallow for such a huge expanse, sir,' said the American. 'Stiff with hidden mudbanks, strange tides, and blessed with the most indifferent of winds.' He indicated the big sixty-four following astern, an elephantine shape in the mist. 'Our ships of the line will struggle to get up to Buenos Aires, especially as we can hardly ask the Spanish to lend us a pilot.'

'We discussed the matter last night on board the *Diadem*,' said Clay. 'Captain Popham has decided that the sixty-fours will remain in deeper water blockading the estuary and preventing any shipping from Montevideo interfering with our landing. It will just be the troopships, with ourselves, the *Narcissus* and the *Encounter* that will continue to the objective.'

'Two frigates and a brig, sir,' said Taylor. 'That seems a little thin as an escort for an attack on a city of over forty thousand souls.'

'I'm inclined to agree,' said his captain. 'But I have

Clay and the River of Silver

some more welcome tidings for you, Jacob. We do have a river pilot.'

'Really, sir?' queried Armstrong. 'Some Spanish turncoat?'

'A Scottish turncoat, actually,' said Clay. 'The *Encounter* stopped a Portuguese trading brig bound for Rio de Janeiro and found him on board. He has been working these waters for twenty years or more. We will have need of him, for he said the Dons have removed most of the navigation markers. He also reported that Buenos Aires is both poorly defended and full of treasure.'

'You hear that, Bartholomew White,' whispered Old Amos at the wheel to his fellow helmsman. 'Pipe says that there Boney Hairys be stuffed tight with chink.'

'Aye, that'll be proper grand,' smiled his companion, his attention wavering as he contemplated the prospect.

'Steer small, there!' roared Taylor, as the frigate fell off the wind.

'Beg pardon, sir,' said White, returning to his duty.

Once the frigate was safely back on course, the first lieutenant resumed his conversation with the other officers. 'But surely Captain Popham and General Beresford are on the *Diadem*, sir,' he said. 'Are they not to accompany us?'

'As soon as we are off Montevideo, they will transfer across,' said Clay. 'The pilot to lead us in the *Encounter*, while Captain Popham, the general and his staff will be on the *Narcissus*.'

'We have escaped lightly,' said Taylor, brightening. 'I was wondering how the wardroom could accommodate any more persons.'

'Not exactly. There is also the small matter of our share of the squadron's marines, which we will be obliged to take on board. All those from the *Diadem*'s marines and half of those from the *Raisonable*.'

'But ... but that must be over a hundred men, sir!' protested Taylor.

'Closer to a hundred and twenty,' said Clay. 'It will only be for a few days. There is also Captain Gillespie, their commander and his two lieutenants, so the wardroom has not escaped entirely.'

'But where ...'

'Deck ho!' called the lookout. 'There be a proper town just a looming up through the murk. A point off the bow. Several ships in harbour, an' all.'

'Ah, that will be Montevideo,' said Clay. 'And this mist seems to be lifting.'

'*Diadem* signalling, sir!' reported Todd. 'Fleet to heave to and await transfers as agreed.'

'Are we ready to receive those marines, George?' asked Clay.

'Yes, sir. It will be beyond tight, but I daresay we shall manage.'

'Kindly acknowledge, Mr Todd,' ordered Clay. 'Bring the ship up into the wind, if you please, Mr Taylor.'

'Aye aye, sir.'

It took over an hour before the final boatload of marines had clambered up the side, and the *Griffin* sat appreciably deeper in the water. Clay gazed across his ship, and saw scarlet-coated figures wherever he looked. They sat in lines along the hatch combings, in groups on the deck, or stood taking their ease against the side. Every one came festooned with equipment that comfortably doubled the space he occupied. By the main mast were all their hammocks, each one neatly bundled up, but collectively making an appreciable mound.

Clay and the River of Silver

'This will never do,' protested Clay. 'Captain Gillespie, a word, if you please.'

'Yes, sir,' said Gillespie, a handsome marine officer with auburn hair. He came across the deck and saluted smartly.

'We cannot possibly work the ship with so much clutter on deck,' explained Clay. 'Mr Taylor, pray join us. Let us see about creating some order.'

'It'll not be easy, sir,' warned the first lieutenant.

'And yet it must be done. Captain, your men can be without their equipment for a few days?'

'They can, so long as they can be reunited with it before we land, sir.'

'Very well, kindly give the order for them to surrender it all. The armourer will need to find space for the weaponry, the boatswain for all these extra hammocks, and the packs can go in the hold.'

'And the men, sir?' queried Taylor.

'Must go to the lower deck. They can sleep beneath the crew's hammocks.'

'My officers and I have managed to reduce our baggage to a single sea chest each, sir,' said Gillespie. 'Where are we to be accommodated?'

Clay was about to say the wardroom, when he caught the look of despair in his first lieutenant's eye. 'Mr Taylor. Kindly make free to use my great cabin to accommodate these gentlemen. I will be quite content with the coach.'

'Aye aye, sir.'

*****

Don Rafael de Sobremonte, viceroy of the Rio de la Plata, scratched irritably at his periwig, and wondered when the

Philip K Allan

performance would end. *The Mayor of Zalamea* was his least favourite Calderon play, and the actors were making heavy work of it. The atmosphere in the theatre was close and stuffy, thanks to the multitude of lamps illuminating the stage. Around him sat seven of his twelve children, fidgeting and bored. He considered slipping away, but the viceregal box was placed centrally to command the best view of the stage and was visible to most of the audience. He had just stiffened his resolve to remain to the end when the door at the back of the box opened.

A shard of light fell across the youngest Sobremonte daughter as one of his aides slipped in. 'My apologies for disturbing Your Excellency's enjoyment of the performance,' he whispered.

'Please don't mention it, Carlos,' replied the viceroy. 'An urgent matter requiring my immediate attention has arisen, I don't doubt.' Without pausing for a reply, he turned to his wife. 'My apologies to you, my dear, but I must be excused. Alas, work before pleasure, but do not let my absence disturb your enjoyment.'

For a man of sixty he showed surprising agility as he jumped up from his seat and out of the box. The aide closed the door behind him, cutting off both the drone of the actors and Doña Sobremonte's protests. In the corridor were several of his officials headed by his chief advisor with an open letter in his hand.

'*Señor* Castelli,' he said. 'What is the matter?'

'A dispatch has arrived, Your Excellency, from the governor of Montevideo. The *Inglés* fleet has been sighted.' He handed it across and the viceroy scanned the contents.

'No word of any landings yet,' mused Sobremonte. 'Perhaps they plan to come here to Buenos Aires after all?'

'I think not, Excellency,' said Castelli. 'Remember that

Clay and the River of Silver

both *Señor* Pueyrredon and *Señor* Saavedra reported their objective was Montevideo. Besides, the governor also mentions the fleet having three ships of the line. Such vessels are much too large to reach up here, even if the enemy had pilots.'

'True,' said the viceroy, returning to the dispatch. 'Three of the line, two frigates and diverse smaller ships. What do you advise I should do then?'

'I believe this is wonderful news, Excellency,' enthused Castelli. 'The enemy is falling into the trap you have so cleverly laid for him. Montevideo is well defended with our best troops. A bloody repulse of the enemy there will fully restore the king's faith in you after that unfortunate native uprising. I would urge you to press home your advantage and make your triumph certain. There is still the flotilla of gunboats we keep here to protect the approaches to the city. Send them downriver to help the governor, for they could make all the difference.'

'But that would leave Buenos Aires almost defenceless!' protested Sobremonte.

'Victory favours the bold, Excellency. And we can always mobilise the city militia. Shall I send word for Captain Belgrano?'

'No, I will only call on him as a last resort. Arming the Creoles is dangerous. Too many of them are influenced by these revolutionary ideas from France and America. Few have the interests of the Crown at heart like you, my friend.' Sobremonte patted his adviser affectionately on the arm. 'Very well, have the gunboats crewed and sent downriver.'

'It will be done, Excellency,' said Castelli, bringing his heels together and bowing his head.

'But we should also think about moving the treasure,' added the viceroy. 'Just in case we are wrong about the *Inglés*.'

Philip K Allan

*****

The British squadron formed a long line astern as they sailed deeper into the huge estuary. The armed brig *Encounter*, with her shallow draught and Scottish pilot on board, was at the head. Next came the troopships, with the *Narcissus* in their midst, and finally the *Griffin*, with the deepest draught and the most resources should any of the ships need help.

Clay had never sailed across such strange waters. The mist had cleared away to reveal an endless expanse of brown. Only from the masthead could the southern bank be seen, a thin line on the far horizon, while to the north the Rio de la Plata might stretch on forever. At first, they sailed confidently westwards for several days, dropping anchor at night, or if the wind wouldn't serve. But then they came to the upper reaches of the estuary and entered more difficult waters. Long banks of brown mud appeared around them proud of the oily surface. Now they were following a coiling path, full of twists and turns, with each change signalled by the *Encounter*. Clay looked at a pair of bull sea lions sunning themselves on a passing mudbank as they briefly raised their heads to watch the procession of ships. 'Mr Preston, kindly get a lead going in the bow.'

'Aye aye, sir.'

'By the deep eight!' called the sailor after the first cast of the lead. He carefully examined the weight before starting to whirl it in the air again. 'Mud with shell, and the water be sweet!'

'Fresh water,' marvelled Preston. 'And yet we are so far from land.'

'Only two fathoms under our keel is a worry,' said Taylor. 'She's drawing more with all these marines on board, and fresh water will only make her sit deeper.'

Clay and the River of Silver

'Fortunately, Mr Faulkner tells me they are eating their way through our stores at a prodigious rate, which may lighten us by an inch or two,' said Clay. 'Mr Todd, the *Encounter* has a fresh signal for us, I believe.'

'Aye aye, sir.'

'And the deep nine!' called the leadsman.

'That is better,' said Taylor.

'General signal, sir,' reported the midshipman. 'Turn to larboard in succession.'

'Acknowledge, if you please, Mr Todd,' said Clay. 'Mr Preston, mark where the *Encounter* turns and have the men ready.'

'Aye aye, sir.'

'And the deep nine!' repeated the leadsman.

'How does this pilot know where the channel turns, sir,' marvelled Taylor. 'I haven't seen any buoys for a while.'

'We are indeed most fortunate to have found him,' said his captain. 'Now, what is the *Willington* about?'

The transport ship immediately ahead of the *Griffin* had drifted off course, so that Clay could see the stern of the ship in front of her in the line.

'Shall I signal to her, sir,' suggested Todd.

'Too slow,' said Clay. 'Mr Drake, take this speaking trumpet and go to the bow. Hail the *Willington* and tell her to keep better station. Run now!'

The midshipman dashed off down the gangway, threading his way through the groups of marines whose turn it was to exercise on deck. But he had only just reached the forecastle when the troopship shuddered to a halt, her stern slewing around to block the channel. Plumes of darker water blossomed around her.

'Back the foretopsail!' roared Clay. 'Make haste, Mr

Hutchinson, before we run aboard her.'

'Aye aye, sir!'

'Thank the lord it is slack water,' said Armstrong. 'Else we would be joining her in the shallows.'

'*Narcissus* signalling, sir,' reported Todd. 'Commodore to *Griffin*. Why are you not following instructions previously issued?'

'God damn and blast that man's eyes!' thundered Taylor. 'Can't he see what is amiss?'

'Reply "*Willington* aground", if you please, Mr Todd,' said Clay. 'Then "am about to give assistance".'

'Aye aye, sir.'

'Sorry, sir,' reported a crestfallen Drake, the unused speaking trumpet dangling from his hand. 'She was hard aground before I could fill my lungs.'

'No matter,' said Clay to the returning midshipman. 'I'll take that.' He relieved him of the speaking trumpet, and pointed it towards the stricken ship, now just ahead of them. '*Willington* ahoy! Are you able to refloat without assistance?'

The master of the troopship came to the rail to reply. 'I've tried backing the sails, but she is too hard aground for that to answer in these indifferent airs, sir. It might help if we lightened her. I have two hundred Highlanders on board that you could take off?'

Out of the corner of his eye, Clay saw Taylor cross his arms at this. 'Let us see if we can haul you off before we try that, Captain,' he said. 'I'll send across a cable.'

'Thank you, sir.'

'Pass the word for Mr Hutchinson, if you please,' ordered Clay.

'*Narcissus* signalling again, sir,' reported Todd. 'When will you be able to proceed?'

Clay and the River of Silver

'What is the matter with that man, sir,' said Taylor. 'I'm starting to regret he ever invented his damn signalling system!'

'Reply "answer not known", Mr Todd,' ordered Clay. 'Ah, there you are, Mr Hutchinson. We need to haul the *Willington* off with the capstan, but first the *Griffin* must provide a secure purchase. Might we anchor her by the stern? Take the best bower out in the longboat and drop it a distance astern? This mud should provide good holding ground.'

The boatswain rubbed at his chin as he regarded the troopship. 'That bower might not be enough, sir,' he said. 'For a heavily laden barky like yon *Willington*. I'd sooner have two anchors, one on each quarter. Bower and kedge should answer.'

'Make it so,' said Clay. 'Mr Taylor, could you have the longboat launched and the anchors readied.'

'Aye aye, sir.'

'Mr Hutchinson, kindly have a suitable cable roused out and passed across to the *Willington*.'

'Aye aye, sir.'

It took the best part of an hour and four further hectoring messages from the *Narcissus* before the huge anchors had been dropped astern of the *Griffin*. At the same time one end of her biggest cable was taken across and made fast on board the troopship and the other end was brought aft through the frigate to her capstan. This consisted of two drums, one on the quarterdeck and a second mounted on the main deck directly below. They were connected by a thick oak shaft that pierced the deck between them. Around each capstan head were square recesses into which long bars had been fitted like the spokes of a wheel. Clay took his place on the starboard gangway, from where he could see all parts of the operation. 'Mr Taylor, is all ready?'

'Yes, sir.'

Philip K Allan

'Very well. Mr Hutchinson! Man the capstan.'

'Aye aye, sir.'

The squeal of the boatswain's calls sounded through the ship, summoning all hands. They arrived from various directions, lining up along the bars. Clay watched as the crew took their places, lithe topmen standing beside portly cooks, booted marines mixed with cooper's mates. In front of him a deeply tanned seaman contrasted with his neighbour, a pale-faced carpenter's mate who spent much of his life below decks. Napoleon the mongoose even appeared, attracted by the fuss. He scampered along a bar and jumped up on top of the upper capstan head to better observe proceedings.

When everyone was in place, the boatswain turned towards him. 'Capstan manned, sir,' he reported, touching the brim of his leather hat.

'Carry on, Mr Hutchinson.'

'Take up the slack there! Handsomely!'

The capstan began to turn, with a steady clack, clack from the iron pawls at its base. Clay looked ahead, watching the heavy rope that led to a stern port on the *Willington* as it was drawn in, rising dripping from the water. As it straightened, the *Griffin* was slowly pulled forward. Then the anchor cables astern grew tight, with a creaking groan from the bits.

'Here it comes, lads!' cautioned Hutchinson. 'Heave, now!'

The angle of the men at the bars changed as the strain came on. The capstan gave one more, reluctant clack. Clay looked at the cable, now straight as a rod, water spouting from it as it was squeezed from between the fibres.

'Heave, you bastards!' roared the boatswain, bringing his cane down on the back of a sailor he thought was slacking. Men were crying out with the effort. Another clack, and then

Clay and the River of Silver

nothing. The bar nearest to Clay was bending like a bow under the pressure being exerted on it by Evans and the big marine private in shirtsleeves beside him. Clay looked at the marine for a moment, and then an idea came to him.

'That will do,' he ordered. 'Stand easy and recover your wind, men. Mr Hutchinson, Mr Taylor, a moment please.'

'We ain't going to shift that there *Willington* like this, sir,' reported the boatswain, removing his hat and wiping his brow with the back of his arm as if he had been manning the capstan himself. 'There be a sight too many blooming Lobsters on board her.'

'On the *Griffin* too,' said Clay. 'Which made me think that we should be using them. We have over a hundred marines sitting idle on the lower deck. Can we not have them to help?'

'Maybe not a hundred, but if the men squeeze up I daresay I could find place for the sixty with the broadest backs, sir,' said Hutchinson.

'Excellent,' said Clay. 'Pass the word for Captain Gillespie, there!'

'Aye aye, sir!'

'Then I thought we could do the same at the *Willington* end. They have two hundred strapping Highlanders on board.'

'I doubt there is enough cable to lead back to their capstan, sir,' said Taylor. 'And it will only be modest in size.'

'But what if all two hundred were to run from one side to the other? The transfer of their weight might loosen the grip of the mud.'

'Well worth a try, sir,' said Taylor. 'Shall I send Mr Russell across to organise it?'

'If you please, Mr Taylor. Ah, Captain Gillespie. I have need of sixty of your sturdiest men, if I may.'

With the new recruits taking their places, the capstan

bars were uncomfortably crowded. Clay could sense a grim determination among his men to see the task through as they slapped backs and bumped fists, before lowering themselves into position to apply the maximum force. There was no slack to take up this time. The cable was heaved so tight from their last effort that it felt as if cast from bronze to Clay's touch. He looked across to where Russell stood on the stern of the troopship beside her master, speaking trumpet in hand, looking his way. All along her rail was a thick line of scarlet figures, making her masts dip noticeably to that side. 'Ready, Mr Russell?' he called.

'Ready, sir,' came the reply.

'Pray continue, Mr Hutchinson.'

'Aye aye, sir,' said the boatswain, flexing his cane. 'Take your places, and this time put your backs into it, or I'll want to know the reason why. One, two and three! Heeeeave!'

The men threw themselves at the bars but might as well have been pushing against the side of a church.

'Heave!' roared Hutchinson. 'Like those whores did when they brought you bastards into the world! Heave!'

When the groans from the men at the capstan reached a crescendo, Clay hailed the *Willington*. 'Now, Mr Russell!'

In a wave from stern to bow the Highlanders vanished from the rail and the ship rocked a little. Clay watched as the pawl on the capstan slowly lifted, hesitated a moment, and then dropped with an audible clack. Someone on the capstan cheered.

'If you've wind for hollering, you ain't doing yer part!' yelled the boatswain, extracting a yelp from the guilty party with a well-placed stroke of his cane. 'Now heave!'

Clay watched the Highlanders reappear in a mass, and the capstan clacked again. Then the soldiers were off once

Clay and the River of Silver

more. Another clack. Pause and then a second. And a third as the capstan began to inch around. 'That's it!' he cried. 'You're shifting her, men.'

The speed of the capstan slowly increased as the *Willington* slid free of the mud, until she was rocking gently on the water once more.

'Mr Taylor, I'll have that cable secured. Mr Todd, kindly signal the *Narcissus*. *Willington* afloat.'

The men at the capstan all cheered at this, and began to disperse, until they were halted by an angry blast on Hutchinson's boatswain's call. 'Where are you lot going?' he demanded. 'Back to your places! There still be two anchors astern to raise. Lord only knows how set they'll be with all that heaving.'

Philip K Allan

Chapter 9
Buenos Aires

It rained for most of the night as the squadron waited for dawn. They had reached far up the Rio de la Plata, although the river was still endlessly wide, and had moored as close to the shore as their pilot dared take the *Griffin* and the *Narcissus*. In the gloom of his cabin, Clay stood in his oilskins, draining the last of his coffee prior to going outside. He returned the cup to Harte with a grunt of thanks and headed for the door. Up on deck the first grey light of dawn was washing across the sky. The rain continued to fall, drumming on the planking and forming silver threads of water that flowed down the standing rigging.

'Good morning, sir,' said Taylor, touching the brim of his hat. 'It's actually easing a little, if you will credit it. I have the ship's boats in the water, and Mr Preston is busy trying to reconcile Captain Gillespie's men with their equipment. He pointed towards the main deck, where the lieutenant was presiding over a scene reminiscent of an eastern bazaar, as red-coated figures scavenged through various piles of equipment, looking for their own.

'And what of our contribution to the landing party?'

'Ready, sir,' said Taylor, indicating where Macpherson stood at the head of the frigate's marines. Drawn up next to them was a party of thirty sailors, all armed with muskets. Russell was slowly making his way down the lines, checking each man's equipment.

Clay and the River of Silver

'Excellent. That seems to be in hand. Any word from the *Narcissus*?'

'No signals yet, sir.'

'That is not like Captain Popham,' smiled Clay. 'Perhaps he is still abed.'

The two officers stared out over the rail. The frigates were moored in deeper water, with the troopships and brig closer in, perhaps a mile from the shore. Beyond them stretched a wide, flat land with only the occasional stand of trees or little settlement to relieve the monotony.

'Hard to credit that a city of forty thousand souls lies a dozen miles from here, sir,' said Taylor. 'Somewhere beyond those low hills to the west. Perhaps Saleem can make something out. He has keen eyes.'

Clay tilted his head back. 'Masthead there! What do you make to the westward?'

There was a pause while the Indian sailor considered this. 'Very difficult, sir, with all this rain. But perhaps I am seeing little smoke and some towers?'

'And maybe the glint of som'it more fecking precious,' whispered O'Malley to Evans as they stood among the shore party on the main deck.

'Message from the *Narcissus*, sir,' announced the signal midshipman. 'Proceed with landing as previously agreed.'

'Acknowledge please, Mr Todd,' ordered Clay. At that moment a brief scuffle broke out between two marines each with a strap on the same pack. It was quickly resolved by an outraged sergeant bawling at them from close range.

'Captain Gillespie's men seem ill-prepared to depart at present, sir,' observed Taylor. 'Shall we send our shore party across first?'

'Good idea, George,' said Clay. 'Mr Russell! Mr

Philip K Allan

Macpherson! Kindly man the boats!'

'Aye aye, sir.'

The *Griffin*'s boats set off on the long pull for the shore, each one packed with armed sailors and marines. They were soon followed by those of the *Narcissus,* bringing more. As they approached the cluster of transport ships, they could see Highlanders making their uncertain way down into other boats drawn up alongside. They passed them, the steady rock and pull of the men at the oars sending them hissing across the flat water. The rain had eased to a fine drizzle, but the low pewter sky was heavy with the threat of more. The longboat was in the lead. She was the largest of the squadron's boats, and in consequence had the deepest draught.

'Easy there, lads,' ordered Sedgwick, as the tiller juddered in his hand. The crew stopped pulling, their oars held in a fan above the water as the boat glided on.

'Is there a problem?' asked Russell, who was sitting beside him in the stern sheets.

'I reckon the keel touched bottom, sir,' reported the coxswain. 'Only brushed it, mind, but we don't want to run aground rowing hard. This may be as far as the longboat can go, burdened as she be.'

'Are you sure?' queried Macpherson, from his other side. 'But we must still be a good four hundred yards out.'

In answer the boat ground to a halt, the bow noticeably higher than the rest. The frigate's launches glided past on either side for another twenty or so yards before they too came to a halt. 'That be as far as we can go, sir,' reported Sedgwick.

'The chart did show this bay was shallow,' commented Russell. 'Very well, it shall have to be shank's pony from here. Shore party! Over the side!'

The marine seated in the bow stared gloomily at the

Clay and the River of Silver

water, swishing the fingers of one hand through it, as if gauging the temperature of a bath.

'What are you fecking waiting for?' hissed O'Malley. 'Get your arse over the side! While you're sat there, the Dons are sure to be stashing all their chink!'

'What if there's creatures in there?' asked the marine. 'Sanchez in the afterguard spoke of giant water serpents hereabouts, as can swallow a man whole.'

'Fecking Lobsters, afeared by a puddle of water,' muttered the Irishman, handing his musket to Trevan before pushing past the soldier and hopping over the side. At the same time Macpherson swung himself out of the stern sheets.

'A wee bit viscous underfoot, but smooth enough to walk upon,' reported the officer, as he stood knee-deep beside the boat. 'Marines will disembark! Corporal Edwards, see that the men hold their pieces high.'

'Yes, sir!'

With little befalling the men in the water, other than thoroughly soaked trousers, the rest of the party left the boat, the sailors laughing and joking at the strange sensation of standing in the sea so far from the shore. Free of their weight, the lightened boat drifted free.

'Quiet there!' ordered Russell. 'Sedgwick, kindly return to the boat to collect Mr Todd and the rest of the shore party.'

'Aye aye, sir.'

Russell and Macpherson waded off, leading their men towards the shore, a thin line marking where water gave way to sky. The other groups from the launches fell in behind them, along with those from the *Narcissus*. As they advanced, Russell wrinkled his nose. 'This water smells abominably,' he said. 'And we still have a good cable's length to go.'

'The filth of Buenos Aires has to go somewhere,'

Philip K Allan

commented Macpherson. 'But you can take comfort in the thought that others are less fortunate than yourself, William. Pity the poor Highlander, who must follow you dressed in a kilt.'

'I hadn't thought of that,' grinned Russell.

They waded on for another hundred yards or so before Macpherson brought them to a halt with a raised hand. The Scotsman pulled a small telescope from his pocket and examined the coast ahead. 'We are fortunate not to be opposed,' he commented. 'This mud makes for slow progress. A few dozen sharpshooters on the beach to greet us would have made matters interesting. But there is not a soul. No, beg pardon, there is a pair of men on horses.' He passed the glass across to his companion. 'Just by that wee hut, there.'

'They look to be civilians,' said Russell. 'And in no hurry to depart.'

'I daresay they are amazed to find so many grown men choosing to wade through this filth,' said Macpherson, reclaiming his telescope and waving the party forward. The water level steadily dropped as they advanced until they stumbled ashore. Russell contemplated his ruined white britches, while Macpherson organised the men. 'Corporal Edwards, form a line of pickets a hundred yards in from the shore. I suggest you keep your sailors together here for now, William, until we are reinforced.'

'Good idea,' said Russell. 'And here comes one of your horsemen.'

Macpherson looked around to see a rider trotting towards him. He was a tall man with a gaunt face framed by sideburns. His horse was a magnificent animal, sleek and well groomed. He pulled up near them and politely touched the brim of his hat with a gloved hand. 'Good morning, *señores*,' he said.

Clay and the River of Silver

'You have chosen a very strange place to come ashore.' He indicated the bay behind them, now full of wading soldiers. 'The Rio de la Plata has many shoals, but few as shallow as this one. I take it you are the *Inglés* soldiers come to attack Buenos Aires?'

Russell and Macpherson exchanged startled glances. 'I'm not sure who you are, sir,' said Macpherson. 'But I am not at liberty to discuss our presence with you.'

'My apologies,' said the man. 'In my excitement at your arrival, I quite forgot my manners. My name is *Señor* Pueyrredon. And I quite understand your need for discretion. Very wise, my friends. But if you have guns or horses in your ships to bring ashore, there is a jetty close to here that you will find much more convenient. My man can show you. Unless you prefer walking through mud?'

'And why would we trust you, Mr Pueyrredon?' asked Macpherson.

'Because I am an acquaintance of your Captain Popham. Is he with the armada?'

'How the devil …' began Russell.

'If you care to wait here, sir, General Beresford, who is in command of our forces, will presently be coming ashore,' said Macpherson.

'Of course,' said Pueyrredon. 'May I at least know your names?'

'This is Lieutenant William Russell of the Royal Navy, and my name is Thomas Macpherson of the marines.'

Pueyrredon stooped low in the saddle to shake each by the hand, before looking with contentment at the growing numbers of invaders forming up around them. 'Will all your men be landed before nightfall?' he asked. 'It would be best to advance quickly. Your presence will have been reported to the

Philip K Allan

authorities, and while Buenos Aires is poorly defended now, that can change.'

'We will be ashore long before then,' said Russell. 'Why, a good quarter are here already.'

'A quarter?' exclaimed Pueyrredon. 'But ... there cannot be more than a few hundred here? *Santa Madre*! Please tell me you have come with more troops than this?'

*****

'The *Inglés* are landing at Quismes?' exclaimed Sobremonte. 'Impossible! Why, that is less than a day's march from here!'

'There is no mistake, Excellency,' said Castelli. 'They began coming ashore at dawn. Of course, it may just be a feint, and the main attack will still be against Montevideo. Their squadron is contemptibly small, and can only contain a trifling number of troops.'

'But ... but a small number may well be enough!' exclaimed the viceroy, jumping up from behind his desk. 'The city is virtually undefended. Why, even the gunboats have been sent to protect Montevideo.'

'We have the militia, and the garrison of the fort. And mounted volunteers are coming in from the countryside as word of the invasion spreads.'

'Creole peasants and shopkeepers,' snorted Sobremonte. 'Why did I send so many troops away? Why did I listen to you, Juan? You are a lawyer, for goodness' sake, not a general!'

'I apologise if I have failed you, Excellency,' said Castelli, bowing his head. 'If you would like me to step down, I will do so.'

'I want you to do your job, my friend. I agree that your

Clay and the River of Silver

counsel has been poor. So, give me some good advice. It is what I pay you for, after all. What should I do now?'

'Excellency, if the city should fall, it would be a calamity if you were to be captured,' said Castelli. 'You are the viceroy. The king's representative here. May I suggest we temporarily move the seat of government to somewhere safer. Cordoba, for example.'

'Leave Buenos Aires to the *Inglés*?' exclaimed Sobremonte. 'Run away? This is what you want me to do?'

'Buenos Aires is only one city of many, Excellency. If you are captured, who will rule the Rio de la Plata?'

The viceroy walked to the window as he considered this. His palace looked out on to the wide stone-flagged Plaza Mayor in the heart of the city. Beneath him, citizens were hurrying across the square, or gathering in concerned groups. Opposite was the main cathedral, its bells clanging in alarm, while off to one side he could see some of the militia being drilled. He took in their ragged lines and the uncertain way they held their muskets, and wondered how long they would resist a serious attack by professional troops. It seemed impossible to think that the redcoats might soon be here, taking control of one of Spain's richest cities. He drew himself up a little straighter and turned from the window.

'It may be only one city among many, but it is my capital, and I will not abandon it without a fight. You can go and make the necessary preparations to move the government, but first fetch the military commander and let us see what sort of an army we can put into the field.'

'It will be done, Excellency,' said Castelli, hurrying from the room. Outside in the corridor bewigged footmen were taking down paintings and beginning to roll up the carpet under the supervision of a butler in an elaborate coat. 'Put it all back,'

Philip K Allan

he ordered. 'The viceroy is staying.'

'Really?' queried one of the servants. 'I mean, yes, *señor*.'

The advisor strode on until he reached the anteroom to his office. His clerk looked up enquiringly from his desk as he approached. 'We carry on for now, Pablo,' said Castelli. 'Send word for Colonel de Acre to come and report immediately, but continue with the preparations for moving the administration to Cordoba.'

'It will be done, *señor*,' replied the clerk. 'And you have visitors. *Señor* Saavedra and Captain Belgrano are waiting for you.'

Castelli went through into his office and closed the door carefully behind him. The two men jumped to their feet as he came in.

'Well?' queried Saavedra. 'What on earth is happening? The city is full of rumours.'

Castelli waved them back to their seats and headed to a decanter that stood on a table beneath a large framed print of King Charles IV, his pudgy hand resting nonchalantly on a globe. 'A drop of amontillado, gentlemen? The Holy Mother knows, I need one.' He sloshed generous measures into three glasses and passed them across. '*Salud!*'

'But are the *Inglés* coming?' persisted Belgrano.

'Yes, but in such trivial numbers I am at a loss to know what to do,' said Castelli. 'If we rise up and join them, and the *Inglés* are defeated, we shall all be executed, and that will be the end of our cause. But then if we do nothing, will we not hasten the very defeat we fear?'

'What is Pueyrredon doing?' asked Belgrano. 'He has all those weapons he smuggled in, and has been training his men in secret.'

Clay and the River of Silver

'He helped the *Inglés* to land, but says he will not lift a finger beyond that until it is clear that they will win.'

'Sound advice,' said Saavedra, 'and what of the viceroy? What will he do?'

'That old fool is all for staying and fighting,' said Castelli. 'God knows, but I tried my best to persuade him to go.'

'Then we carry on as we have been, gentlemen,' urged Saavedra. 'Keep our powder dry. Appear to support the viceroy loyally, but be ready to act.'

'I can ensure the city militia are poorly prepared for action,' said Belgrano. 'And who knows? Perhaps the *Inglés* will be victorious.'

*****

Once the field guns had been unloaded, and the officers had been reunited with their chargers, Beresford's little army set off towards Buenos Aires. The 71st Highlanders led the way, almost a thousand strong in their swishing kilts and feather bonnets, lustily singing along with the popular airs played by their pipers. Rumbling behind them was a battery of six field guns that seemed like toys when compared with the huge naval guns used at the Battle of Blaauwberg. Then came General Beresford and his staff, well mounted, their harnesses jingling. Bringing up the rear was the Royal Navy's contingent. There were three hundred marines, striding out in perfect step, eyes to the front and a hundred sailors strolling along behind them, taking in their surroundings with a keen and noisy interest. And that was the extent of the column. Barely more than one and a half thousand strong, with the muddy bay they had landed behind them and the vastness of South America ahead.

'So how much chink do you reckon we'll find in this

Philip K Allan

here Boney Hairys?' asked Evans, returning to the sailors' favourite subject.

'The Grunters say it's lying there in fecking piles,' enthused O'Malley. 'Mounds of treasure heaped like slag about a furnace, so it is. Leastways according to what Old Amos was telling Harte.'

'Them two old gossips?' queried Evans. 'I might have bleeding known.'

'But will we be getting a share?' queried Pembleton. 'Like from them prizes we took?'

'Not a chance,' said Trevan. 'Bullion be droits of the Crown, just like when that frigate squadron took the Dons treasure fleet back in the year four. Those lads didn't get so much as a farthing of all the chink on board.'

'Hark the sea lawyer,' scoffed the Irishman. 'Spouting his dog-Latin like a fecking priest at mass. Droits is it? All I'm after saying is that if there's piles of chink, and no watch set, it would be awful strange if a few coins didn't go astray.'

The others considered this pleasant thought as they marched on across a land as flat as the ocean in every direction save ahead, where a low ridge lay across their path. After a while Trevan stepped out of the column for an uninterrupted view forward, shading his eyes. Then he ran to retake his place. 'Never mind stealing chink, lads. I reckon we've some fighting to do first. There be Don soldiers on that ridge ahead.'

As the little army approached, fresh details became apparent. It was little more than a gentle rise, only made prominent in contrast to the surrounding land. At the end that overlooked the Rio de la Plata stood a hamlet of whitewashed buildings with thatched roofs, while at the landward end the ridge dropped lower until it vanished altogether. A small inlet fed a marshy area at its foot. Drawn up along the skyline were

Clay and the River of Silver

about two thousand defenders, with a battery of field guns in the middle. The column came to a halt, while Beresford and his staff cantered ahead to examine the position.

'We should just up and at 'em,' suggested Evans. 'Look at that rabble. Even I can see they ain't proper soldiers. I reckon they'll bolt like them Butter-boxes did, soon as we press close.'

'You has the truth of it there, Big Sam,' confirmed Trevan, who had the best eyesight. 'Apart from them gunners in the centre, the rest are all dressed anyhow. Lots of horsemen, mind. But they didn't give us much bother at the Cape.'

'We did have eighteen-pounders then, Adam,' observed Pembleton.

'I see Lacy Ted's a fecking expert,' commented O'Malley, indicating Pembleton with a jerk of his thumb. 'A sailor after ten days at sea and now one battle makes him a general.'

'Listen up, lads,' said Evans. 'Here comes that toff from the Cape come to see Rusty.'

Lieutenant Dalrymple's uniform was not quite as immaculate as before, but he was still comfortably better turned out than the mud-splattered sailors. He galloped down the column and jangled to a halt in front of Lieutenant Russell. The Griffins shamelessly worked their way forward to better learn their fate.

'The army is to deploy and attack immediately, sir,' announced the aide. 'We only appear to have local militia opposing us. A guinea against a farthing they forget to aim low when firing downhill and their volleys pass over us.'

'That sounds promising,' said Russell. 'Where do you want us?'

'Plumb centre, with the 71st on your right and the marines on your left. That way your flanks will be protected from the enemy's horse, of which he is well supplied.'

Russell assessed the situation. 'So, we are to advance directly at their battery, then? Will we be helped at all by our artillery?'

'Regrettably the ground is too swampy for moving guns.'

'But fine for moving fecking sailors, is it?' muttered O'Malley.

Russell ignored the Irishman. 'Very well, lieutenant,' he replied, trying to adopt the nonchalant calm he had seen Clay and the *Griffin*'s other officers show on the eve of action. 'Thank you. That seems very clear. Follow me, men!'

They resumed their advance, passing the redundant guns, pulled off the road to let them through.

'Don't fancy soiling your fecking boots, lads?' asked O'Malley. 'Or was it your trousers?'

'Silence, men!' ordered Russell as laughter burst out. Beresford and his staff were gathered ahead by the roadside, and the marines were saluting smartly as they passed. Russell touched a hand to his hat and received a kindly smile from the general. Ahead of them the Highlanders were peeling off to the right and the marines to the left. Suddenly there was nothing between him and the enemy.

The Spanish battery vanished behind clouds of smoke, and clods of dark earth flew up just ahead of the sailors. A moment later the sound of the barrage reached him, the bark of the guns high-pitched to men used to the deeper roar of naval ordinance.

'Form up here!' ordered Russell, indicating the gap left between the end of the Highlanders and the marines to his left. 'Two ranks, and check your priming! Mr Todd, take your men away to the right.'

Clay and the River of Silver

'Aye aye, sir!'

The sailors took their places with none of the precision of the redcoats around them. When they were in position, Russell placed himself in the middle of the front row.

'Marines! Fix bayonets!' called the voice of Captain Gillespie.

'Sailors, fix bayonets!' ordered Russell, glad of the reminder. He drew his sword, noticing the dullness of the edge, and wished he had been able to afford something better when he was promoted. The battery ahead fired again, and for a moment he glimpsed a dark smudge rocketing towards him. Then he was blinded as mud erupted just in front of where he stood, cascading down over his head. He looked around in disbelief, astonished that he was still alive.

'You be all right, sir?' said a concerned Trevan to his right, taking his arm. 'That were mighty close, but I reckon this marsh be a blessing.' He indicated the black scar just in front, arrowing straight towards the officer. 'That ball vanished into the mud quicker than a penny into a miser's purse.'

'I'm fine, thank you,' said Russell, knocking dirt from his hat, while his heartrate slowed a little. Off to his right the pipes of the Highlanders squealed into life, accompanied by the steady beat of drums and the shout of orders. 'Sailors, advance!' he yelled. 'Nice and steady!'

It soon transpired that "nice and steady" was the fastest that troops could advance across the marsh. The men's feet vanished from sight with each step, and had to be wrenched free before another stride could be taken. The guns continued their bombardment, sending clouds of smoke rolling down towards them, and showering the advancing sailors with soil. Most of their projectiles were swallowed by the mud, but every so often a ball found its mark, and the ground behind the advancing

Philip K Allan

British was soon dotted with the fallen. Then the sailors reached firmer ground and their pace quickened.

The guns fired again, shots ripping past Russell, and out of the corner of his eye he glimpsed a file of Highlanders collapse backwards. Volleys of musketry crashed out from above, and more red-coated figures fell to the left and right of him. Through the billowing smoke he could see the gunners frantically reloading their cannon, and he recognised the copper cylinders being passed forward.

'Come on, lads!' he yelled. 'Follow me!'

The men surged up the slope behind him, but after a few paces he realised that the Spanish field guns were being loaded much faster than the huge eighteen-pounders he was used to. He felt cold dread as he saw that they would never reach them before they fired. Preston's account of the Battle of Blaauwberg told around the wardroom table came back to him, with its description of the devastation three well-aimed rounds of canister had caused. The line of guns ahead was being wheeled back into place, each muzzle a dark "O" as it was trained towards him.

'Halt!' he roared, spreading his arms wide. The ragged line of sailors stopped in confusion, looking around at each other. To either side, the Highlanders and marines were continuing to press forward. 'Everyone lie down!' he said, putting as much authority into the command as he could. 'Do it now!' Uncertainly at first, the sailors began to drop. 'Quickly!' urged Russell, as the last gun was wheeled into place. He heard a shouted order from the battery and threw himself on the ground.

The roar of the guns was deafening, and the air filled with a howling blizzard of musket balls that seemed to skim just over his head. A choking pall of smoke rolled down over them,

Clay and the River of Silver

and the swarm of canister was gone. 'On your feet!' he roared, leaping up himself. A few sailors were left writhing on the ground, but most of them picked themselves up, a little dazed, and looked to him, many with a respect that had been absent before. 'Don't let the bastards get off another of those, lads!' he yelled. 'Charge!'

He turned and ran up the slope, his sword raised high, and with a cheer the sailors followed. To either side of him the Highlanders and marines had paused fifty yards short of the Spanish line, raising their muskets to their shoulders in a single rippling motion, but he carried on. Then the British volleys crashed out, blanketing the hill with smoke once again.

Through the fog a gunner in a dark blue coat appeared, his rammer thrust down the muzzle of a six-pounder. He desperately tried to wrench it free but Russell was on him too fast, thrusting at the Spaniard with the point of his sword. There was a cry of pain and the man staggered backwards, clutching at his thigh. Then a wave of sailors flooded past him. Evans was in the lead, his musket like a toy in his hands, slashing with the bayonet to right and left. Pembleton was just behind him, using the butt of his like a club. Trevan arrived beside him, and promptly dropped down on one knee to fire at an advancing sergeant with a thick moustache. For a moment Russell was surrounded with swirling fights, but nothing could withstand the fury of the Griffins. Within a few minutes, the sailors found themselves alone among the abandoned guns.

The smoke began to clear a little to reveal two solid walls of red coming on at the double to the left and right of them. A few ragged shots banged out from the lines of Spanish militia, but most of them turned and fled. Russell continued up to the top of the crest, with the sailors of the *Griffin* crowding around him. The reverse slope was covered in fleeing figures and abandoned equipment. He paused there, sword in hand and looked out. To his right was the Rio de la Plata, with the three warships and the transporters out on the water. And ahead lay the city of Buenos Aires, now defenceless before him.

*****

The viceroy was trying his best to complete a normal lunch with his wife and children, but it was difficult to maintain any sense of normality in the strained atmosphere within the palace. The sound of gunfire from somewhere to the east had been hard to ignore, but then it had petered out, leaving an ominous silence in its place. Now the whole city around them seemed to be holding its breath, waiting. He took another morsel of food from his plate, although his appetite had long gone, and smiled encouragingly at the rows of dark eyes looking back at him from both sides of the table. 'Eat up, my children,' he urged. 'This fish is really very good.'

'Are the *Inglés* coming to murder us, Papa?' asked Maria, the oldest of his daughters.

Before he could answer, the sound of rapid steps came from the corridor outside, and the dark eyes transferred their attention to the dining room door. The knock that followed was urgent and firm. 'Let them in,' ordered Sobremonte to a footman.

'Your pardon for the interruption, Doña Sobremonte, but I must speak with the viceroy on a matter that cannot wait,' said Castelli, bowing low.

'Please excuse me, my dear,' said her husband, rising from his place and dropping his napkin on the table. 'Let us go next door, *señor*,' he said, leading the way. As soon as they were alone, he looked enquiringly at his adviser. 'The battle?'

Clay and the River of Silver

'Lost, Excellency,' said Castelli. 'The militia broke and ran at the first volley. The enemy captured all our guns and are now marching for the city. I expect them to arrive in a matter of hours. I have taken the liberty of ordering carriages for you and your family.'

'Yes, I must go,' agreed Sobremonte. 'But you must stay, my friend.'

'Excellency?'

'I need someone here I can trust,' said the viceroy. 'Listen carefully, for we haven't much time. Gather all the officials in the city, military, civic and religious. You are to surrender to the *Inglés*, without a fight. Accept their demands, provided that the enemy agree that the people and the buildings are to remain unharmed.'

'But Excellency …'

'I need Buenos Aires intact, Juan,' said Sobremonte. 'I have been reflecting on your words to me. When you said that this city was just one of many. You were right. The *Inglés* may take it, but will they be able to keep it? I think not, for I still rule the Rio de la Plata. I have troops at Montevideo, and the gunboats we sent there, but most of all I have the people. I will call on them to rise up against the invader and drive him back into the sea from whence he came. We may have lost a battle, my friend, but we have not yet lost the war. Keep our city safe for the day when I will return.'

Philip K Allan

Chapter 10
The River of Silver

The little fort and mission church built an age ago had long since been absorbed within the growing city. A combination of wealth flowing from the interior and settlers flooding in from Europe had fuelled that expansion until Buenos Aires sprawled along the southern bank of the Rio de la Plata. But today the population was tense and fearful, wondering what the future would bring. They had watched their viceroy and his family drive away, his splendid coach leading a column of heavily laden wagons. They had heard the tales of defeat spread by fugitives from the battle. Those who lived on the eastern side of the city could even see the approach of Beresford's little army.

The citizens reacted to all this in different ways. Those wealthy enough to have haciendas in the countryside followed their viceroy's example and fled. The pious crowded into the churches, to light candles at the feet of their favourite saints and beg for their protection. The rest retreated behind shuttered windows and locked doors, abandoning the streets to stray dogs and redcoats alike. But this was not an option for the civic leaders. They had been ordered to congregate on the outskirts and await the arrival of the invaders.

It was mid-afternoon when Beresford's men reached them. First came a thin cloud of skirmishers detached to scout ahead of the column. They reacted with blank astonishment as

Clay and the River of Silver

they took in the group of Spanish dignitaries dressed in their finest clothes, with the ribbons of various orders draped across them and glittering chains of office around their necks. In the midst of them was the archbishop, robed and mitred in cloth of gold. They quickly recovered and surrounded the dignitaries, muskets at the ready, fearing a trap of some kind. Others watched the nearest buildings, or took up position among the kitchen gardens that lined the road. Then a young officer approached the group. 'Does anyone speak English?' he asked.

'I do, *Señor*,' said one, stepping forward. 'My name is Castelli, and I serve the Viceroyalty of the Rio de la Plata. These other men represent the city. I must speak with your general, before there is any more unfortunate bloodshed.'

The officer looked Castelli over while he considered what to do. Then he recalled that, as a lowly subaltern, he could exercise the timeless privilege of junior rank. When in doubt, pass the problem on. 'Corporal Fraser!' he barked. 'Go find the captain, and tell him there is a delegation here asking for the general.'

'Yes sir!'

Captain sent word to major; major sent word to colonel; and colonel sent word to general, until Beresford himself came riding up with his staff, by which time most of his army was drawn up around the officials.

'I'm General Beresford,' he announced. 'Who wishes to speak with me?'

'I do,' said Castelli. 'I represent Don Rafael de Sobremonte, viceroy of the Rio de la Plata. I wish to offer you congratulations on your victory, and to discuss an end to hostilities.'

'And why is the viceroy not here to speak for himself, sir?'

Philip K Allan

'He left the city this morning, but instructed me to negotiate on his behalf. I am authorised to offer you the surrender of Buenos Aires in return for certain conditions.'

'Conditions, eh?' said Beresford. 'I fancy, after this morning, I could simply march in and seize your city, and the devil take your conditions.'

'Perhaps you can, General,' said Castelli. 'But I can offer you the active cooperation of the city authorities. And my terms are not unreasonable.'

'Indeed? And what are they, pray?'

'If you agree to respect all private property and citizen's rights, I am authorised to offer the surrender of all state and military facilities within the city. Naturally, the exact terms will need to be drawn up, which may take a little time.'

'Fine, but while that is happening, as a gesture of goodwill, my men will occupy all the key points within the city,' said Beresford.

Castelli bowed at this. 'That would be reasonable, in light of the completeness of your recent victory.'

'There are also some urgent matters we require your assistance with. I want pilots to guide our ships into the harbour, and I want immediate access to the state treasury.'

'The city has no harbour in the formal sense, General. The silt of the river prohibits it, you understand. We have mooring buoys for large ships out in deeper water, and a port area with jetties for boats to transfer people and goods between them and the shore.' Castelli indicated one of the officials behind him. 'If your men will permit the harbour master to pass, he can arrange to guide your squadron to the buoys. As for the state treasury, that gentleman there is the royal treasurer. He is at your disposal.'

Beresford called forward one of his aides. 'Dalrymple,

Clay and the River of Silver

was it those plucky sailors from the *Griffin* that reached the enemy position first this morning?' he asked.

'It was indeed, sir.'

'Then they should have the honour of this. Pray go and get them.'

'Right away, sir.'

From behind the immaculately dressed ranks of the Highlanders the sailors appeared, doing their best to look soldierly as they marched over to stand in front of the general.

'Ah, Lieutenant Russell,' said Beresford, reaching down to shake his hand. 'I was most impressed with your chaps' assault on that enemy battery earlier. Capital show, by Jove.'

'Thank you, sir,' said Russell, colouring with pride.

'I will naturally call Captain Clay's attention to your performance, but I also have another service that I need you to perform. Do you see that portly chap in a red weskit? I wish you to go with him and take possession of the royal treasury. You should find it contains a substantial fortune. Keep it safe.'

The general's request provoked contrasting reactions among his audience. The sailors listening on grinned broadly at the news, while Russell's face showed only alarm. He stepped closer and dropped his voice. 'Do you think that is entirely wise, sir?' he asked. 'Might a party of marines be a better choice?'

'Don't you trust your men, Lieutenant?'

'I do, sir. But I would caution against exposing them to excessive temptation. Three were in prison awaiting transportation to Botany Bay not six months ago.'

Beresford chuckled at this, and indicated the redcoats behind him. 'I daresay many of my soldiers have pasts that don't bear scrutiny. There are few honest men prepared to be shot at for a shilling a day. Just keep a watchful eye on them,

Philip K Allan

and all will be well. But pray go now. I need that place secured.'

'Aye aye, sir.'

So it was that the shore party of the *Griffin* were the first to enter Buenos Aires. The treasurer led the way, followed by a solemn-faced Russell and his high-spirited men. Behind them came detachments of Highlanders, heading off to occupy various points within the city. The outskirts were semi-rural, with modest little houses surrounded by kitchen gardens. Then, by degrees, the buildings became closer packed, and the streets laid out in a more formal pattern. But of the population, there was little sign.

Soon, even the boisterous sailors fell silent in the oppressive atmosphere, hushed by how loud their voices sounded in the empty streets. Yet they all sensed that they were being watched. Shuttered windows held ajar, swiftly closing as they approached. A face peering around a door frame, vanishing the moment they were looked at. The sound of running feet from a side alley and the glimpse of a retreating back. Some of the sailors unslung their muskets and held them ready across their chests.

'Cheery fecking place,' commented O'Malley. 'Is the plague in town, or do you lads reckon we're not welcome?'

''Tis only to be expected,' said Trevan. 'I daresay folk back in Polwith wouldn't take kindly if the Dons came marching up Church Lane.'

Their guide turned to the right at the next intersection on to a well-paved street that led down towards the water. Ahead the sailors could see the port area, with piled goods awaiting shipment and a stone jetty with a few moored boats and lighters alongside it. At this more familiar site they hastened forward, happy to leave the gloomy city behind. The brown water was not the clean sea they were used to, but as they

Clay and the River of Silver

emerged on to the quayside, they could see the familiar sight of the *Griffin* in the distance, working her way towards them, with the rest of the little squadron around her.

'The treasury is this way,' said their guide, pointing to a solid-looking stone building set back from the water. It was surrounded by a low stone wall, topped with iron railings. Only the first floor of the building had any windows, all of which were barred. The walls of the ground floor were blank and smooth, with a single entrance. Guarding the perimeter were a number of armed sentries.

'Thank you, sir,' said Russell. 'I take it the treasure is normally stored in the basement?'

'Indeed, *señor*. The quantities are so large, and very heavy. It arrives on river boats from the interior, and is stored here for shipment back to Spain. Please to follow me.'

'Looks much like a prison,' commented Pembleton as they approached the entrance.

'Never mind the look of the fecking place,' hissed O'Malley. 'Hark to what old fatty had to say! So much chink they can barely shift it!'

'I heard,' said Evans, with a gleam in his eye not unlike that of polished silver.

As they reached the iron gates to the compound a burly sergeant stepped forward to block their path. The treasurer spoke to him in rapid Spanish, after which he saluted smartly and wheeled away, bawling orders to his men. The treasurer turned to Russell. 'I have explained to him that you are now responsible for guarding the building, and he and his men are to return to barracks. What further do you require of me?'

'I would very much like to see inside the basement, sir,' replied Russell, ignoring the low growl of assent from the Griffins at his back. 'Mr Todd, kindly take twelve men and post them around the perimeter. No one is to enter without my leave.'

'Aye aye, sir,' said the midshipman.

'The rest of you, follow me.'

'Just try and fecking stop us, Rusty,' whispered O'Malley.

Set in the centre of the wall was a pair of solid oak doors, thick with iron studs. The treasurer fished a ring of large keys from his coat pocket, unlocked the door, and handed them to Russell. 'The doors are very heavy, *señor*,' he explained. 'You will need some of your men to push them op—' Before he could complete his sentence, a rush of willing sailors crowded past him and the doors were swung wide.

'Stand back there!' yelled Russell. 'O'Malley! Evans! Back to your places!'

When calm was restored, the officer entered the vault with the treasurer beside him. A floor of heavy stone flags stretched away from them, lit by burning oil lamps hung on some of the pillars. As Russell advanced, the sound of his footfalls echoed in a curious, empty fashion. He stared into the gloom around him with increasing alarm. 'I don't understand, sir,' he queried. 'Where is the treasure?'

'The bullion, *señor*?' asked the official.

'Yes, of course. You spoke of it earlier. Is it not kept here?'

'It was, *señor*. A little over four million in silver dollars and bagged gold dust. His Excellency ordered it removed from the city some days ago. His men came and loaded it onto wagons. As you see, they left not one *centavo*.'

*****

Clay and the River of Silver

It had taken little time to transform the viceregal palace in Buenos Aires into the headquarters of General Beresford's administration. Most of the city's officials had been re-employed after swearing an oath of allegiance to George III that few understood. The only visible signs of change were the Union flag that had taken the place of that of Spain on the roof and the Highlanders now on duty outside. The former viceroy's large office still had its fine view over the Plaza Mayor. It was here that Beresford was in earnest conversation with Popham and Vansittart when there was a knock at the door.

'Come in,' said Beresford.

Castelli entered. 'Thank you for summoning me, General,' he said, bowing stiffly. 'I have several important citizens waiting who are anxious to discuss the future with you. One is *Señor* Pueyrredon, who had the pleasure of making the acquaintance of Captain Popham and *Señor* Vansittart in London.'

'Never mind that, sir,' snapped Popham, rising from his chair. 'Where the bloody hell is the river of silver I was promised?'

'The Rio lies just over there, *señor*,' said Castelli, pointing. 'I believe you can see it from that window.'

'I don't mean that damned muddy ditch,' exclaimed Popham. 'I mean the bullion. The silver and gold that Pueyrredon said we would find here. Where is it?'

'Its removal was ordered by Don Sobremonte in great secrecy as soon as your fleet was sighted, Captain. But where it was taken, even I do not know.'

'Did it go by land or sea?' asked Vansittart.

'Lieutenant Russell said the treasurer spoke of wagons,' said Beresford.

'In which case it cannot have gone very far,' said the

Philip K Allan

diplomat.

'So where the bloody hell is it?' thundered Popham.

'Pray resume your place, sir,' urged Vansittart. 'Before you make yourself quite ill.'

Once the naval commander had sat down, his face still flushed, the diplomat turned to their visitor. 'Mr Castelli, although the general represents Great Britain, I advise the government,' he explained. 'I was present when Mr Pueyrredon first asked for our intervention here. I took that request to the highest level on his behalf, on the basis that our coming to Buenos Aires would provide a much-needed supply of bullion to assist in our war with Napoleon. I do not take kindly to those who fail to meet their obligations.'

'I am sure *Señor* Pueyrredon was quite truthful when he spoke of the treasure,' said Castelli.

'I daresay he was, yet here we are,' said Vansittart, his face devoid of its customary good humour. 'So let me be very clear. Captain Popham's ships will be returning home with the promised sum, which can come in one of two ways. The easiest is for you and your friends to locate someone in the city who knows where the treasure has gone. I am sure a shrewd cove like yourself will know who to approach, and how to unlock their tongue. You return and tell us, the money is recovered, and cordial relations are restored, after which I see no objection to discussing the future with you and your associates.'

'And the second course you spoke of, *señor*?'

'Oh, I am quite sure you don't want to go down that path. We might start by seizing the contents of the merchant's warehousing down on the waterfront. That might fetch a portion of the required sum. The rest would have to come from a punitive levy on the wealthy, along with sundry other acts of unpleasantness.' Vansittart indicated the window. 'I daresay

Clay and the River of Silver

that cathedral across the square must have a fair collection of altar plate, for example.'

'You wouldn't dare!' exclaimed the Spaniard, crossing himself.

'You think not? Well, let us hope you can locate the treasure, and so won't have to find out what we are capable of. But be swift. I am not known for my patience.' Quiet followed Castelli's rapid departure.

'You are not really expecting my men to steal from a church?' queried Beresford.

'I doubt it will come to that,' explained Vansittart. 'We have our redcoats, and they do not. Mr Castelli is a bright fellow. He understands that, and I expect he also knows where the treasure has been taken.'

'Really?' queried Popham. 'Why do you say that?'

'The viceroy will hardly have soiled his hands shifting the loot himself, which means he would have got a close confidant to do it for him.'

'Then why the devil did Castelli not say?' asked Beresford.

'I remember his name from the letters pledging support for independence that Mr Pueyrredon brought with him to London,' explained Vansittart. 'He is one of the republicans, so I suspect he doesn't wish to declare his hand and fall out irrevocably with Spain until the right moment. Openly helping us find the treasure might place him in a difficult position. That is why I had to apply some pressure.'

As the others were absorbing this there was another knock at the door.

'There you are, gentlemen,' said Vansittart, bowing in his place to them. 'The power of diplomacy.'

'Come in!' said Beresford. 'Ah, Mr Castelli. That was

quick work.'

'Yes, General. It turns out that an acquaintance of mine, *Señor* Belgrano, who commanded the city militia, was responsible for moving the treasure. It is in Luján. The monks of the Monastery of San Benito have it in their keeping.'

'Luján,' repeated Popham. 'Is that far from here?'

'Perhaps two days by wagon? I can supply a guide to show you the way.'

'If you please,' said Beresford. 'Along with transport to bring the bullion back again.'

'Yes, General. I will go and make the arrangements now.'

'Who will collect it?' asked Vansittart, once they were alone. 'I would not trust Mr Castelli's loyalty just yet.'

'My men are fully engaged in holding down the city,' said Beresford.

'Then I suppose it will need to fall on the navy,' said Popham. 'But who shall we send?'

'Lieutenant Russell of the *Griffin* is a steady man,' said Beresford. 'But it could be a very hazardous expedition. We barely control Buenos Aires. What is happening in the surrounding area is a mystery, let alone in a town two days march away.'

'Hazardous, you say?' said Popham. 'Then we should send the *Griffin*'s marines too. And a competent man to lead them all. I will order Captain Clay to take command.'

'Sir Alexander?' queried Beresford. 'Surely it is too dangerous to risk such a valuable man?'

'I trust this has nothing to do with not firing damned salutes?' added Vansittart.

'Of course not,' said Popham. 'I am merely thinking of the treasure. And pray do not interfere in how I manage my own

Clay and the River of Silver

people, gentlemen. My mind is made up, Clay will be in command. In fact, I believe I will go and tell him myself. Good day to you both.'

'Please wish him luck on my part,' said Beresford.

*****

Although it was not far to Luján, it proved a depressing journey for the little column of Griffins as they followed their captain along the dirt road that ran towards the west. The market gardens and fields that surrounded Buenos Aires soon gave way to flat, scrubby grassland dotted with the occasional tree beneath a wide sky of grey clouds. Late on the first day the rain returned, dripping from the sailors' hats, darkening the coats of the marines, and turning the road beneath the wheels of the wagons to mud. As they passed through the occasional little settlement, their welcome was as chill as the weather. Men in ponchos paused from their work in the fields to glare at them, while women shooed their bare-footed children inside, slamming doors behind them.

On the second day the rain eased and a line of hills appeared on the horizon, growing steadily as they approached. At midday Clay called a halt, and while the men ate their rations, he climbed up on one of the wagons to study the way ahead.

'Luján is close, *senor*,' explained their guide, who had clambered up beside him. 'Between here and the hills.'

'I can see a deal of trees ahead,' said Clay, his telescope to his eye.

'Trees, yes,' agreed the Spaniard. 'There is nice river, and always trees grown close to water here. The town is on the near bank.'

Philip K Allan

'And the monastery? Where does that lie, pray?'

'Outside the town. The monks, they make good wine.'

'I daresay they do,' smiled Clay. 'All that chanting must give them a thirst.'

'Fecking grog as well as chink,' commented O'Malley returning to his companions from loitering within earshot of his captain. 'I'm starting to like this little jaunt.'

'How big is this bleeding town?' asked Evans through a mouthful of ship's biscuit. 'I'm as game as the next man, but there ain't many of us if it comes to a mill.'

'Aye, an' the locals aren't exactly welcoming,' added Sedgwick.

'No need to be after fretting, lads,' said the Irishman. 'We'll be giving the town a wide berth. 'Tis a monastery we're heading for. How much fight can fecking monks put up?'

A few hours later the column arrived outside the Monastery of San Benito. It stood on a low rise in a loop of the river, a cluster of buildings beside a solid-looking church, all surrounded by a high stone wall.

'Mr Macpherson,' said Clay. 'Kindly post your marines around the outer wall. No one is to leave.'

'Aye aye, sir.'

'Mr Russell, keep your men together while I speak with the abbot.'

'Aye aye, sir.'

The main entrance was easy to find, a large wooden door set in the wall. Above it in a niche was a painted statue of a monk, a hand raised to bless Clay as he approached. Finding no obvious way in, he was about to hammer on the door when his guide cleared his throat and looked significantly towards a length of rope dangling by the frame. Clay pulled on it and a bell clanged somewhere inside. After an age, a small square of

Clay and the River of Silver

wood opened in the door and a face with tonsured hair appeared.

'*Si?*' said the monk.

'My name is Captain Sir Alexander Clay of his Britannic Majesty's frigate *Griffin*, here on behalf of General Beresford, governor of Buenos Aires. I wish to speak with the abbot.'

'*Qué?*' said the monk.

'You there. Pedro,' said Clay, waving forward his guide. 'Kindly translate for me.'

Clay stood back from the grille while the Spaniard respectfully removed his hat and spoke to the monk. When he had finished, the opening banged shut, and Clay found himself standing in front of a blank door once more. 'Well?' he asked.

'He has gone to find the abbot, *señor*,' explained Pedro. 'He is probably at his prayers.'

'Having siesta, more like,' snorted Clay. 'Will he be long?'

The guide shrugged his shoulders and Clay began examining the lock to see how easily it could be forced. But before long the door swung open. A monk in a habit so dark it was almost black beckoned him to follow.

'Mr Russell, secure this gate, if you please,' he ordered. 'Mr Todd, come with me.'

'Aye aye, sir.'

The monk led them into a calm oasis. Ahead Clay could see a square cloister with beds of herbs growing in its open centre, and more black-clad monks walking around its perimeter, or sitting in silence. Off to one side other monks were working in a vegetable garden, watering plants or hoeing the few weeds that grew between them. The monk led the officers along one side of the cloister to where an elderly man in much better-quality robes stood waiting for them. 'I am Reverend Father Francisco,' he said in reasonable English. 'You are welcome here, *señores*.'

'You have a lovely monastery, sir,' said Clay. 'How long has it been here?'

'We were founded over a hundred years ago by a mission from the motherland. I am the twelfth abbot. But how may I help you?'

'I am here to recover a large quantity of bullion brought recently from Buenos Aires,' said Clay. 'It is state funds that must be returned by order of the new governor.'

'Who is the *Inglés* soldier I have heard of, no? Brayasford?'

'General William Beresford. That is correct.'

Father Francisco looked concerned. 'I am sorry, but your men have had a wasted journey, *señor*. There is no money here.'

'Yet the information I have is quite definite,' said Clay. 'I trust you have no objection if my men make a thorough search?'

'*Señor*, this is a sacred place! A house of peace and prayer!'

'My men will be as brief as possible. It would be best if you were to cooperate. Opening locked doors and so forth. To avoid excessive damage to your property.'

'This is outrageous!' spluttered the abbot.

'Consider your outrage noted,' said Clay. 'Now, kindly provide me with any keys we may require, and call your monks together. It might be best if they were to wait in the church until we have finished.'

Father Francisco considered Clay for a moment, his face flushed with anger, but he found his gaze held by cold grey eyes

Clay and the River of Silver

the pale shade of a wolf's. With a shudder he turned away to call over a monk, and spoke rapidly to him in Spanish. Then he turned back to the Englishman. 'Very well, *señor*, for the sake of my monastery it will be as you ask. And I hope God will forgive you for bringing men of violence into this place.'

'Thank you, sir,' said Clay. 'Mr Todd, my compliments to Lieutenant Russell, and please ask him to bring his men here.'

The monastery was not large, and with parties of sailors despatched under a petty officer to each building, the results of the search soon came back.

'Naught but beds and chests of togs on the lower deck, sir,' reported John Powell, the scar-faced boatswain's mate.

'That will be the monks' dormitory, sir,' translated Russell for his captain.

'Galley be clean, sir,' said Josh Black, the captain of the foretop, returning from the kitchen and refectory.

'As is the great cabin,' added the last petty officer to return, who had been sent to search the abbot's house.

'Are you satisfied now?' asked Father Francisco, a serene smile playing across his lips.

'You make wine here, do you not, sir?' asked Clay.

'Yes, a little. The money it brings in helps our work with the poor.'

'So you must have a wine cellar?'

'Of course. It lies under the storerooms over there, *señor*.'

'Begging your pardon, sir, but I found the ladderway down into that hold,' said Powell. 'Plenty of barrels, but not so much as a farthing in chink.'

'Did you check inside them?' asked Clay.

'Yes, sir. O'Malley and Evans did, quite thoroughly.

Philip K Allan

Nothing but wine.'

'I bet they did,' muttered Russell, darting a glance at the pair of seamen, who were both grinning broadly.

'In which case there is only one more place to search,' said Clay. 'We must proceed to the church.

'Have a care for your mortal soul, *señor*,' warned Father Francisco, 'before you violate the house of God!'

'Thank you for your concern, but I have no unease in that regard. Follow me with a party of your men, if you please, Mr Russell.'

'Aye aye, sir.'

The interior of the building was cool and gloomy. Light filtered down from a few narrow windows set high in the walls. The stone floor was strewn with rushes, and the only furniture comprised rows of simple wooden choir stalls where the monks had gathered, some with heads bowed in prayer, others watching the entrance of the sailors with unease. At the eastern end of the church was an altar below a painted panel showing an elderly monk being beckoned upwards by the Virgin Mary. He was probably Saint Benito, Clay decided, given the halo that encircled his bald pate. But the only glint of treasure came from where the picture's gold leaf sparkled in the light of the candles on the altar. There was nowhere in the bare interior to conceal wagon loads of anything.

'Are you satisfied at last?' asked the abbot. 'I think it might be best if you left, before the locals hear of what has happened here. They are very protective of our monastery.'

Clay nodded at this, defeated at last, and started to turn away. Then he stopped as a thought came to him. 'Did you say that you were the twelfth abbot of this place?'

'Yes, I have that honour,' said the cleric.

'So where are the tombs of the other eleven?'

Clay and the River of Silver

'Tombs, *señor*? Oh, we are a simple order. We have no need for such worldly things. They are buried in the monks' cemetery down by the river.'

The explanation came out pat enough, but Clay had seen Father Francisco's eyes flicker down for the briefest of moments, before he regained his composure. 'Mr Russell. Kindly have your men search this place for a crypt.'

'A crypt? Aye aye, sir.'

'There be some manner of iron grating in the floor over here, sir,' reported Trevan. 'Smells proper musty.'

'Pull aside these rushes, men,' urged Clay. 'Mr Todd, go and find me a lantern.'

Soon the interior of the church began to resemble a threshing floor as the sailors set to with a will. 'Iron ring over 'ere, sir,' reported Black, from close to the altar. 'Set in a wooden 'atch.'

'Open it please,' ordered Clay.

The petty officer swung back the heavy trap door, to reveal stone steps leading down into the dark. A dank, musty smell wafted up from below.

'Lamp please, Mr Todd.'

'Here you are, sir,' said the midshipman, handing it to his captain.

'Thank you,' said Clay making his way down into the dark. The crypt had a dirt floor beneath a low roof of stone vaulting. It covered a similar footprint to the church above, and had a line of simple stone tombs running part way along one wall. Stacked all around them were line after line of bulging canvas sacks. Clay gave the nearest one an experimental push with his foot, and the heavy bag fell over, the length of cord securing its mouth giving way as the contents surged against it. A rush of coins spread across the floor, glittering like the scales of a fish.

    'A river of silver indeed,' marvelled Clay. 'Ahoy, Mr Russell! Have the wagons brought through into the courtyard if you please. We have found what we came for.'

Clay and the River of Silver

Chapter 11
New Arcadia

The former viceroy's dining room was pleasantly situated, with a row of tall windows along one side looking out on to the gardens. Some of the more valuable pictures were missing from the walls, bundled into one of the carts when Don Sobremonte made his rapid departure, but enough remained to give the room a homely air. Replacing the viceroy's numerous children at the table were only two diners.

'I could become accustomed to this lifestyle,' sighed Beresford. 'Beef steak for luncheon, cooked to perfection, and enjoyed in this rather agreeable setting.'

'The fruits of victory, my dear chap,' said Popham. 'The promised treasure has been returned to us, and Spain's principal city in the Americas captured, all with relative ease.'

'Relative ease!' spluttered the general. 'Says the man who was safe on his ship while my lads were in the heat of battle and Clay was recovering the loot. Not to mention absenting yourself from the tortuous negotiations over these damned terms of surrender!'

'Have they been concluded yet, William?'

'They were signed this morning, thank the lord,' confirmed Beresford. 'But it has been a trial, with every Jack-in-the-pulpit here holding an opinion at variance to the others. Dealing with the Butter-boxes was easy as kiss my hand by comparison. Do you know what the final objection was? The archbishop had a problem with our offer to respect freedom of religion!'

'Why, for all love?' asked Popham.

'Because a papist don't hold with it. You either follow their church, or you may as well be a Mohammedan! Anyway, it is done now.'

Popham regarded his companion as he sipped his wine. 'What do you suppose they will make of all this in London?' he asked.

Beresford put down his knife and fork to consider this. 'They will certainly be pleased when they learn of the treasure, and of course the capture of the Cape, which was the prime objective.'

'Ah yes. The Cape. I daresay you and I shall get a little reflected glory from that, but if I know General Baird, he will have composed his account of the action so that most of the credit will go to him.'

'As is only fair,' said Beresford. 'For he would also have been the one censured if the invasion had failed.'

'Of course,' agreed Popham. 'But the capture of Buenos Aires, my friend. That is all down to us. You and me. Indisputably it was my idea, and the military execution was your achievement. If we play our cards soundly, it could be the making of us.'

'Do you think so?' asked Beresford. 'But we will be away from here soon, will we not? A raid, you named it back in Cape Town. While General Baird's will be a permanent occupation.'

'William, you need to think bigger. For centuries our merchants and manufacturers have wanted to trade with the Spanish Empire, and been blocked at every turn by the Dons. But now we hold this city, the perfect entry point for trade with

Clay and the River of Silver

a whole continent. Are we truly going to give it up and walk away? Surely it will be us that will be censured. For throwing away the greatest opportunity to come our nation's way since the first East India Company merchant set foot in Bombay.'

'What are you about, Popham?' asked Beresford. 'Is this why you didn't want Clay or Vansittart present?'

'I find in a discourse with many, all becomes a ceaseless debate. Like your discussions over the surrender treaty. Clay is my junior, so will do as he is told. And the last thing we need is Vansittart, with his lawyer's caution. Let us, the military commanders on land and sea, decide what is for the best, and then inform the others.'

'Very well,' said the general. 'What do you propose?'

'I confess that it was the treasure that first attracted me to the River Plate. But I believe we might achieve so much more.'

'Such as?'

'The city has been legally surrendered to us. Why should we not stay? Why not declare Buenos Aires to be the newest of His Majesty's colonies?'

'But … but I can barely hold the city as it is with the resources I have,' protested Beresford. 'God only knows what is happening in the countryside around us.'

'Very little, to judge from the want of opposition that Clay encountered in his jaunt to Luján.'

'But that is surely because we have caught our opponent off balance. Their viceroy is still at large, and we have yet to encounter any regular Spanish troops. Castelli tells me they were gathered around Montevideo, but by now some at least are sure to be on their way here.'

'We have defeated the Dons once, I daresay we can do so again,' urged Popham. 'Particularly if we can gain the

Philip K Allan

support of the people. Declare Buenos Aires a free port and offer the populous sound government. Once this place is the most prosperous city in America, you will be able to recruit no end of locals for its defence.'

'And until then? I doubt if Viceroy Sobremonte will grant us the time for all that to answer.'

'Then let us ask for reinforcements,' said Popham. 'From General Baird in the first instance and then from London. I can send the *Encounter* with our dispatches.'

'But the risk if this should go wrong,' said Beresford shaking his head.

'It is bold, I grant you,' said his companion. 'But think of the rewards that will accrue to the men who opened up a whole continent to British trade? The thanks of Parliament? The freedom of the City of London? Knighthoods from the king? Or in all probability something better. Lord Beresford of Buenos Aires? Or what about Viscount Popham of the Plate, eh?'

'Lord Beresford, you say?' mused the general. 'It does have a certain ring to it.'

*****

The following morning, in one of the city's grander town houses, the birth of a nation was under discussion. The house stood close to the cathedral, set back from the road, with a sweeping half-moon of cobbled drive that led to an imposing door, designed so that coaches could deliver and collect their passengers with the minimum of inconvenience. In the large drawing room three men had gathered.

'I have had some thoughts about our flag,' said Saavedra, whose home this was. 'It came to me yesterday, and my daughters were kind enough to stitch an example for us to

Clay and the River of Silver

consider.' He held out a piece of fabric composed of broad sky-blue-and-white stripes. 'The blue is for our beloved river, and the white represents silver, symbolising our new country's wealth. Rio and Plata, you see?'

'But the river is always brown,' observed Belgrano.

'We can't have a brown flag!' protested Pueyrredon. 'It will just look dirty.'

'The colours aren't meant to be taken literally, but more symbolic,' said Saavedra. 'They could represent other things. Truth and purity, for example?' He held the flag out at arm's length for a moment, his head on one side. 'Does anyone else think it needs something in the middle. A lion perhaps, or a sun?'

'Don't we really need to decide on a constitution before we choose a flag?' said Pueyrredon.

'Flags are much more important for rallying the masses to our cause, my friend,' warned Saavedra. 'No freedom fighter ever went into battle behind a sheaf of papers.'

'That is true, but we should wait for Castelli before deciding such things,' said Belgrano. 'What can be keeping him?'

'He was meeting with the *Inglés* this morning to discuss when they plan to leave, but I would have expected him to be here by now,' said Saavedra, glancing towards the clock that stood on the mantlepiece. 'The viceroy's palace is very close.'

'When the *Inglés* leave, we will need more than a flag,' said Belgrano. 'We must be ready to raise an army to defend our new country from Spain the moment we declare independence.'

'The training of the men on my estates is proceeding well,' offered Pueyrredon.

'And I ensured that most of my militiamen kept their

Philip K Allan

weapons hidden in their homes in the city, rather than returning them to the armoury in the fort,' said Belgrano. 'But we will need more than this. Artillery, for example. Reserves of ammunition. Uniforms. All that is in the safekeeping of the *Inglés*.'

At that moment a wigged butler opened the door and Castelli marched in, his face red with anger.

'New Arcadia!' he roared. 'We have been betrayed, my friends! Betrayed!'

'New Arcadia?' queried Pueyrredon. 'Where the devil is that?'

'Here, that is where!'

'You're not making any sense,' said Saavedra. 'Come, sit down and compose yourself, and tell us what has happened. José! Bring a glass of wine for my guest.'

'Yes, *señor*,' said the butler, hurrying across with a drink on a tray.

'New Arcadia is the name the *Inglés* plan to call our beloved country, comrades,' explained Castelli. 'Popham seemed very pleased with it. Said that it had a classic ring.'

'But what need have we for a new name?' asked Belgrano. 'And why do the *Inglés* think they have any right to choose it for us? It isn't even Spanish!'

'Because they have no intention of leaving,' said Castelli. 'They are drawing up the proclamation as we sit here. They will claim the city for their king, and declare it a free port.'

'There must be some mistake,' said Pueyrredon. 'They never mentioned this when I met with them in London. Indeed, *Señor* Vansittart was most reluctant for them to come at all. No, the whole thing is absurd.'

'Is it?' said Saavedra. 'What fools we have been! Inviting the *Inglés* here and smoothing their path to victory.

Clay and the River of Silver

Now they have grown drunk on it, and fancy our city will make a fine addition to their empire. Compensation in the south of America for what they have lost in the north.'

'There can be no mistake,' said Castelli. 'I had it from General Beresford and Captain Popham. Just now.'

'The traitorous dogs!' exclaimed Pueyrredon. 'I told them of our dreams of independence, and not once did they hint at this. They lied to my face! Even that snake Vansittart, who supposedly speaks for their government.'

'In fairness he was not there,' said Castelli. 'It was only Popham and Beresford.'

'What did you say when they told you?' asked Saavedra.

'Naturally I protested in the strongest terms, but they would have none of it. They reminded me that I, along with every other official in the city, had sworn allegiance to their king. It was a condition of the peaceful transfer of power.'

'And did you take such an oath?' asked Belgrano.

'I did. Just as I once swore allegiance to Charles IV of Spain. And I would swear loyalty to the emperor of China, if it brought the United Provinces of the Rio de la Plata a day closer. But when we have our own country, I will only swear one more oath, which I will keep for the rest of my days.'

'Oh, what a fool I have been!' said Pueyrredon, plunging his head into his hands. 'I thought that after they took the treasure they would only be interested in trading with us.'

'With the *Inglés*, it always starts with trade,' continued Saavedra. 'A few baubles for the natives. Silver for spices. Then a little enclave that brings in wealth to benefit the locals, and buys their support. Next come the troops, to protect the traders. The acquisition of land so that their settlement can grow. And gradually their tentacles extend out, until a whole continent is under their sway, and they have become too powerful to resist. Is this not how the *Inglés* conquered India, comrades?'

'But this isn't India, and Buenos Aires isn't Bombay!' protested Belgrano. 'They lack the military force for such a bold project. Their redcoats fight well, but they are too few for this.'

'They are too few at present,' corrected Saavedra. 'But what reinforcements might be coming? Perhaps sailing up the Rio de la Plata even now?'

There was quiet for a moment, as the four would-be revolutionaries absorbed what had happened. Castelli was the first to break the silence.

'We must act, my friends,' he urged. 'We should never have trusted the *Inglés*, but now they are here we must drive them out quickly. I never doubted that we could gain our freedom from Spain. Half the soldiers in the Spanish regiments here are sympathetic to our cause. But these redcoats are much tougher. Once there are more of them, I doubt we will ever be free.'

'For my part, if it is a choice between Spanish chains or ones forged in England, then I would sooner have Sobremonte back than have the *Inglés* in power,' growled Belgrano. 'I say we fight them!'

'You are right, my friend,' said Pueyrredon. 'No one is more disappointed than me at this turn of events. But our dispute with Spain is like a disagreement within a family. Now our very way of life is threatened by outsiders. What will the *Inglés* change next? Our language? Our religion? Our culture? We must come together to protect ourselves. I will return to my estates and raise the countryside against the invader.'

'I will do the same in the city,' said Belgrano. 'Start the

Clay and the River of Silver

resistance here in Buenos Aires.'

'Agreed,' said Castelli. 'I will share the situation with the viceroy, and beg him to send us aid. And I will pay a visit to the archbishop on my way home. He was angered by the text of the original surrender agreement, and by the raid on the monastery at Luján. It could be very useful if the priests were to condemn this "New Arcadia" to the faithful at mass on Sunday.'

'Excellent plans, gentlemen,' said Saavedra. 'For good or ill, we have invited a wolf cub into our home. We must kill it before it grows too powerful to resist.'

*****

Private Conway, a marine serving on the *Griffin*, was not the cleverest of men. He was the bane of Corporal Edwards's life. If there was a soldier on parade with smeared pipeclay, or a single unpolished button, it was sure to be him. On the odd occasion when Conway was not at fault, then it was certain to be his close friend Private Roberts, the second-dimmest marine on the *Griffin*. The years went by, but no matter how loudly Edwards bawled at the pair, or how frequently he stopped their grog, the pair showed no sign of improvement. Which was why, a week after the foundation of New Arcadia, they were selected to patrol the area of warehousing and slum dwellings closest to the river.

'Not the river bank again, Corporal,' protested Roberts.

'Be nice to see another part of town, for a change, like,' supplemented Conway.

'And have to call out the guard again, because you two have taken a wrong bleeding turn?' said Edwards. 'Lieutenant Macpherson would have me guts for fiddle strings. No, it's the

Philip K Allan

docks for you beauties. Not even fools like you can get lost with a bleeding river this big to lead you home.'

'What about the beat up by the market?' asked Conway. 'Just this once, like. We'd find the way back easy enough.'

'I doubt if you could find a tit in a bawdy house, Conway,' observed their corporal. 'Now quit your whining and get a move on.'

The two marines shouldered their muskets and set off on patrol. At first they followed the riverbank, where a few old men were fishing with rods down at the water's edge. Roberts raised his hand to wave at them, but was met by solidly turned backs. A little further on they passed a cart piled high with root vegetables being pulled by a pair of mules. The driver turned away as they greeted him, and whipped his animals into a trot.

'You reckon we should have stopped him and searched the cart, mate?' asked Roberts.

'Why would we be after doing that?' queried Conway. 'It was plain to see what your man was taking to market.'

'Aye, but he could have had a stand of muskets concealed under that lot,' said his friend.

'And why would he be doing that?' queried Conway. 'He'd hardly be selling firelocks alongside his spuds, would he?'

Roberts considered this, but the wheels of his mind turned at a modest pace. By the time he had identified the flaw in his friend's argument, the cart was long gone, and the two marines had turned away from the river. The dirt road they followed was scarred with the ruts of cart wheels. At first it ran between a warehouse and a rickety boatshed, before narrowing as it climbed away from the water. Alleyways ran off the road on either side, where stray dogs lay panting in the shade and barefoot children stared at them with wide, dark eyes. Men in

Clay and the River of Silver

tattered britches and open shirts paused their conversations to watch them pass. The warm air was filled with a hum of indistinct sound, as if the marines occupied a circle of quiet within a busy hive.

They had just paused at an intersection when Roberts caught sight of a flash of movement out of the corner of his eye. He turned to peer down a passageway where a young woman beckoned to him from the far end. 'Aye aye,' he said to his companion. 'What you reckon that wench is about?'

Conway considered matters for a moment, and the urgency of the waving increased. 'I'm after thinking that colleen needs our help, what with her flapping like a bird.'

They plunged down the alleyway in single file towards the girl, past openings on either side. The smell of cooking came from one, an old lady sat at the entrance to another, her head thrown back, apparently asleep, to judge from her gaping, toothless mouth.

'Fast!' urged the girl when they reached her. 'My *madre*! She fall down!' She plucked at Conway's sleeve and set off at a run, turning this way and that. The passageway twisted and divided like the root of a plant, until the marines were hopelessly lost in the heart of the labyrinth. At last, they arrived panting in front of a battered wooden door in a wall. Their guide plunged through it and the marines followed close behind.

On the far side was a large, dimly lit room, bare of any furniture. It might have been a kitchen once, to judge from the dilapidated range set in a brick fireplace. Now dirt and rubbish lay piled against the walls and what light there was came in narrow shafts through the crude boards nailed across the broken windows. It fell on the raised weapons of the group of men that stood facing the door. The girl went and stood beside one of them, a burly man with a thin moustache. He pointed the bell-shaped muzzle of a large blunderbuss towards the new arrivals.

'Where ... where's your fecking mother?' asked Conway, trying to catch his breath.

The marginally brighter Roberts went to pull his musket from his shoulder, but froze as he felt a pistol jab against his back. He turned to see two more men, standing either side of the entrance. The other one closed and bolted the door.

'You give gun, powder, knife, everything to the men,' ordered the man with the blunderbuss. 'Or boom, understand?' He raised his weapon a little to show where his finger rested on the trigger.

'I got yous,' said Conway, passing across first his musket, and then the rest of his equipment. 'Although I'll be in for a flogging for losing it.'

Roberts followed suit, passing his weaponry to the man with the pistol, who examined the musket with obvious enthusiasm. 'Can we be going now?' he asked.

'Going?' said the man with the blunderbuss. 'Where you want go, *Inglés*? You come steal my land. Now you pay price.' He nodded to the others, who closed in on the pair of marines.

*****

It was a tense group who met a few nights later in Beresford's headquarters. The viceregal palace was a darker place than it had been in the days of Don Sobremonte. The blaze of candlelight that used to shine out on to the square was concealed behind drawn curtains, as a precaution against sharpshooters willing to try their luck. Outside, the few Highlanders on sentry duty had been reinforced in numbers, and a regular flow of mounted messengers arrived and departed

Clay and the River of Silver

with word of the goings on in the restless city that lay all around.

'New Arcadia?' queried Vansittart. 'What on earth were you thinking of, General?'

'In truth, it was Popham who first made the suggestion,' observed Beresford.

'Because I thought it had considerable merit,' said the naval commander. 'An argument which, as I recall, you found persuasive when the possible advantages to you personally were enumerated.'

'What are you suggesting, sir?' demanded Beresford, his face colouring.

'Gentlemen, please,' said Vansittart. 'Little will be achieved by our falling out. But my question remains unanswered. What were the pair of you thinking of?'

'For my part, I assumed the population would welcome the change,' said Popham. 'Much as the Dutch did in the Cape. Mr Pueyrredon seemed deuced keen on our coming when we met with him in London.'

'Met him in London?' said Beresford and Clay together. 'When were you going to tell me this?' continued the general.

'Oh, the meeting was of little consequence,' said Popham. 'He told us of the treasure, and wanted some help against the Spanish.'

'How selective your memory is!' exclaimed Vansittart. 'As I recall, he spoke with considerable passion of wanting help to gain independence from Spain. And he certainly never spoke of a desire to trade one imperial master for another. Detail is everything in the diplomatic world.'

'So what would a diplomat have done, when Buenos Aires dropped into his lap with so little fuss?' asked Popham.

'Had you chosen to share your project with me in

advance, I would have advised prudence,' said Vansittart.

'Prudence ...' repeated the naval commander, rolling his eyes.

'Even if I thought that annexing the city was a good idea,' continued the diplomat. 'Which I don't, to be clear; I would have still counselled a more ambiguous position. Keep those in favour of independence hopeful of achieving their goal, so as to buy time to gain the government's approval, or permit any reinforcements to arrive.'

'Dissembling, in other words,' scoffed Popham. 'As oppose to the straight talking I favour.'

'If by a little dissembling I can achieve an objective without it costing the butcher's bill you men of blood charge, then my conscience is clear,' said Vansittart. 'And to be clear, I never fail to keep my word, by making sure to never giving it in the first place.'

'But to return to your meetings with these revolutionaries, am I to understand that commitments were made that have now been betrayed?' asked Clay. 'If so, I start to understand their fury.'

'I am of your way of thinking, Sir Alexander,' said Beresford. 'No one saw fit to tell me of these secret meetings in London. Why did you not mention it before you let me declare New Arcadia, Popham?'

'Because you would never have had the courage to do it if I had, General.'

'I beg your pardon?' said Beresford, rising to his feet. 'I lacked courage? Pray withdraw that comment, or shall I require satisfaction.'

'Enough!' said Vansittart, banging the desk. 'We will not turn on each other! Only our enemies here, of which we seem to have many, will rejoice. Popham, you meant no

Clay and the River of Silver

disrespect, did you?'

'Of course not, and if I have offended you, sir, I apologise.'

'Handsomely said,' added Clay. Beresford slowly sat down again, still eyeing the naval commander.

'For good or ill,' resumed Vansittart, 'we have publicly declared the existence of New Arcadia, with all the authority of General Beresford's position as the government's official representative here. My immediate concern is what we do next?'

'Do you have the resources to hold the city, sir?' asked Clay.

'I do, for now, but only just,' said Beresford. 'But I shall need to be reinforced soon. There are rumours of men being raised in the countryside around us, and the citizenry grow bolder by the day.'

'Two of my marines were relieved of their weaponry recently, and were found severely beaten,' said Clay.

'They were lucky to have survived, Sir Alexander,' said the general. 'One of my Highlanders was killed and three were wounded in an exchange of fire early this morning. And those rogues without firelocks are content to use any weapon that comes to hand. Knives, pikes... why another patrol was pelted by stones thrown by children, if you will credit it.'

'Reinforcing our position seems to be key, sir,' said Clay. 'But where is such aid to come from?'

'I have sent the *Encounter* away with urgent dispatches for Sir David at the Cape, requesting aid,' said Popham. 'They also carry letters to the Admiralty in London appraising them of our urgent need.'

'I doubt that General Baird will agree to weaken his command further,' said Beresford. 'In the 71st he has already given us his strongest unit. While there is any prospect of a Dutch rising or a French intervention, he will want to keep the rest of his forces to hand.'

'And help from home will take many months to arrive, gentlemen,' said Vansittart. 'On top of the distances involved, we must also consider the leisurely speed with which the wheels of government turn. I fear we shall have to shift for ourselves.'

'What about more help from the squadron?' asked Beresford. 'Can you do more, Sir Alexander?'

'You already have all the *Griffin*'s marines and a third of her sailors,' said Clay. 'Which leaves me with just sufficient men to work my ship. And the same proportion of the *Narcissus*'s people too.'

'And what of the other ships?' asked the general. 'Those two-deckers we left behind?'

'You have their marines,' said Popham. 'And it is their presence in the Rio de la Plata that prevents the Spanish regular units at Montevideo crossing to attack us here. I fear we would rue the decision to weaken their crews further, if the result was several thousand soldiers marching on Buenos Aires.'

'So, you offer me nothing?' said Beresford. 'Yet more forces I must have. How shall we square this circle?'

'Could we not raise some troops locally?' suggested Vansittart. 'As John Company do in India? Or the Butter-boxes did with their Malay gunners and Hottentots?'

'We do have plenty of muskets in the city armoury,' said Beresford. 'But training troops takes time.'

'There is also the question of how reliable they would be,' said Clay. 'Might we not be simply arming and training our opponents?'

'Shall we seek the opinion of Mr Castelli?' said Vansittart.

Clay and the River of Silver

'That gentlemen is long gone,' said Beresford. 'He stormed off in a rage when Popham and I informed him about New Arcadia. I understand he has quit the city for his family estate, as have many of the better sort. Including this Pueyrredon chap you spoke of.'

'All of them raising the country against us,' said Popham. 'And pray, where do they find the weaponry to arm their supporters? Surely it cannot all come from waylaying marines?'

'They have been smuggling in arms, sir,' said Clay. 'From home, if you will credit it.'

'How the deuce do you know that?' asked Beresford.

'From my coxswain, Sedgwick, who is an uncommonly clever fellow.'

'The Negro?' queried Popham. 'Really?'

'There was an American ship named the *Cape Allerton* in Madeira when I joined the squadron, sir,' explained Clay. 'Some of my people on a run ashore became friendly with her crew, and found that she was carrying a cargo of arms bought in London. When pressed, they claimed they were for the American government, but Sedgwick thought it odd they had sailed so far south if that was their true destination. Later, the same ship appeared in Cape Town, now with a hold full of grain from the River Plate. It doesn't require much imagination to deduce what cargo they unloaded here.'

'Do we know the nature of these weapons, Sir Alexander?' asked Beresford, but it was Vansittart who replied.

'A thousand stands of muskets, a deal of powder and shot and numerous cases of pistols, if I recall correctly,' said Vansittart.

'By Jove, you know about this?' spluttered the general.

'I had Pueyrredon watched while he was in England,

and learned of his purchase,' said the diplomat. 'Since I thought they were to be used against the Spanish, and that he was an ally, I took no further action. In truth I had forgotten all about them until Sir Alexander mentioned this damned Yankee ship.'

'You criticise my actions, and yet you have armed our enemy!' exclaimed Popham.

'May I remind you that they only became enemies thanks to this New Arcadia folly of yours,' said the diplomat.

Popham began to say something else when Clay held up a hand. 'Do you hear that?'

The others paused to listen. From somewhere in the distance came a series of faint bangs. Clay went to the window, pulled back the curtain and opened it, the sound immediately growing louder.

'Musket fire, or I have never heard it,' said Beresford, coming to join him. 'Some way off, mind you.'

From beneath them came the sound of horse's hooves clattering across the square, and a shouted challenge from one of the sentries. A little while later, booted feet approached the door and there was a thunderous knocking. 'Come in!' ordered Beresford.

Lieutenant Dalrymple entered, his spurs clattering in his haste. 'Trouble I'm afraid, sir. One of our patrols came under fire, so Captain Arbuthnot took a company to investigate. He reports a large force of men gathering outside the city towards Perdiel. Several hundred to judge from their campfires. It is their skirmishers exchanging fire with ours that you can hear.'

'Thank you, Lieutenant,' said Beresford. 'Kindly ask Colonel Pack and Captain Gillespie of the marines to join me.'

'Yes, sir,' said Dalrymple, saluting again before hurrying from the room.

'I trust this matter will not prove overly troublesome,

Clay and the River of Silver

gentlemen,' said the general, rising to his feet. 'But it may be best if you return to your ships until the city is quiet once more.'

Philip K Allan

Chapter 12
Perdiel

The marines seemed clothed in black in the moonlight, their uniforms only turning to scarlet when the light from the lantern Corporal Edwards carried fell on each man in turn as he accompanied Macpherson along the line.

'Only thirty-five other ranks on parade,' mused the Scotsman, once the inspection was over. 'Sykes and Reynolds fell in battle the day after we landed, of course, and O'Sullivan was wounded when his patrol was ambushed yesterday.'

'An' Conway and Roberts are still in the care of the surgeon, sir,' added Edwards. 'Lord preserve us, but I never thought I'd be missing them two wiseacres.'

'Any port in a tempest, Corporal,' smiled Macpherson. 'Very well. Have the men form a column of march and let us get underway.'

'Yes, sir.'

The marines followed their officer out into the deserted street. It was past midnight, and the sound of musket fire from the edge of the city had petered out, leaving an ominous silence in its place. The footfalls of his men and the clink of their equipment sounded unusually loud to Macpherson as he led them, alert for any danger. Would the barrel of a musket slide out from behind that partially open shutter? Or did that passageway's well of darkness conceal a gang of rebels fingering their weapons? His hand felt for the reassurance of his

Clay and the River of Silver

sword hilt. But the city remained quiet, save for the sound of marching boots as the various contingents of troops headed towards the western edge.

'Lieutenant Macpherson?' asked a well-mounted officer, walking his horse forward from the shadow beside a church. 'My name is Dalrymple. Your men are to join Captain Gillespie and the rest of the marines in that large barn over there.'

The Scotsman looked in the direction the officer had indicated. 'I see it. What force do we have gathered?'

'Besides the squadron's marines, a half battalion of the 71st. It is all the general can spare and still retain some grip on the city. Colonel Pack is in command.'

'A bare seven hundred then,' concluded Macpherson. 'And what of the enemy?'

'Hard to say. Greater numbers, for sure, with plenty of horsemen. After a brisk exchange with some of our Highlanders, they have withdrawn towards the west. It will be dawn soon, and we march in pursuit of them at first light.'

'Thank you, Mr Dalrymple. My men will be ready.'

The barn was packed with sleeping marines, so Macpherson led his men to a nearby walled orchard where they could get some rest. Some fell asleep quickly, rolled up in their greatcoats in the pools of shade beneath the fruit trees while others sat around in small groups in the moonlight talking quietly, or checking over their equipment. Once he was sure all was as it should be, Macpherson left them and walked into the fields to the west. A line of pickets was posted out here, while further on he could see campfires in the distance, like rows of glowing eyes in the darkness. 'I wonder,' he said to himself, addressing the distant fires. 'Were you truly driven off, or do you wish to draw us out to fight on ground of your choosing?'

Philip K Allan

A cold wind blew in from the open water of the Rio de la Plata to his right, flapping at his coat as he turned to rejoin his men. On the way back, he was attracted by a glow of firelight from in front of the barn. A few marines had got a brazier lit and were warming their hands on it. Several of his fellow officers were standing nearby talking quietly, including Captain Gillespie of the *Diadem*, the senior marine. 'Ah, Macpherson, there you are. Are your men up for a little Don hunting?'

'They are certainly ready for regular soldiering, after all this wretched patrolling of the city streets, sir.'

'Hear him!' agreed Gillespie. 'My lads have had their fill of playing at Bow Street Runners too. Let us hope the enemy has the courage to stand his ground and fight this time, so we can resolve matters once and for all.'

'What happened earlier, sir?' asked Macpherson. 'I heard a deal of firing, and then the order came for us to come and join you.'

'Stuff of nothing, really,' said Gillespie. 'Some of their mounted irregulars – gauchos, the Dons call them – jumped a patrol of the 71st. After a bit of a fusillade, the guard was called out, and the enemy cut and run back to their camp away over yonder. They ain't blessed with much pluck, these horsemen.'

'Dawn soon, sir,' said another marine lieutenant, rubbing his hands at the prospect. 'It will be good to get stuck in to them.' There was a general rumble of approval at this, but Macpherson held his peace.

'You seem thoughtful, Lieutenant,' observed Gillespie.

'I am as impatient for battle as any of these gentlemen, sir,' said Macpherson. 'I only hope the enemy will oblige us with the stand-up fight we desire.'

'You think they may not?'

Clay and the River of Silver

'I wouldn't in their position, sir.'

'Why the devil not?' asked one of the other officers.

'Because it plays directly to our strength,' explained Macpherson. 'They are wearing us down effectively enough without any need to hazard battle.'

'Well, for good or ill, we must march out to meet them,' said Gillespie. 'Let us hope Mr Macpherson is out in his reckoning, and our time is not wasted.' He pulled out his pocket watch and angled it towards the flames. 'Half an hour before Colonel Pack wishes us to begin our advance. Kindly rejoin your men, gentlemen, and have them assembled in good time.'

*****

Pueyrredon pulled his cloak around him against the wind from the river as it came hissing through the grass, sending a flurry of sparks slanting upwards from the campfire. On the far side of the little blaze Castelli gave the embers a rake with a stick, and looked around for more fuel.

'Let it die, Juan,' said Pueyrredon. 'It will be dawn soon.' He pointed to the east, where the moored British ships near Buenos Aires sat on calm water the colour of polished steel. Their masts and heavier spars were just starting to show, black against the pale eastern sky. His companion turned to watch. By tiny increments, the ships' standing rigging appeared, as if being sketched in by an invisible hand.

'I wonder what battle is truly like,' mused Castelli. 'We have talked of fighting so much over the years, and yet I have never actually experienced it.'

'Dreadful and very confusing, from what I have heard,' said his companion. 'But remember, our war will be one of many fights and petty triumphs. We win today if we draw the enemy out from the city so that Belgrano's men have the freedom to create fresh mischief behind them. If we can slay a few dozen *Inglés* before we slip away, so much the better.'

'It is hardly very glorious,' muttered Castelli. 'We seem to be fighting like footpads.'

'Patience, my friend,' urged his companion, getting to his feet. 'Most of my men, and all of yours, have never heard a musket fired in anger. We know they are not ready to beat the redcoats. Whatever happens today will be a valuable lesson for them, and for us too. But before battle, breakfast! I told my servant to have it ready the moment the sun was up.' He bellowed over his shoulder towards a man in an embroidered waistcoat, who was busy at a nearby fire. '*Hola!* Salazar! Where is our food and coffee?'

'Just coming, *señores*,' said the man, loading up two plates. 'Have a care. The cornbread is very hot.'

The two men began eating, while the light grew behind the distant city. Pueyrredon ate with obvious pleasure, but his companion only toyed with his. Instead, he watched the camp as it came to life around them. At the picket lines of horses, men in broad-brimmed hats were saddling their animals, or leading them towards a nearby stream to drink. Elsewhere, militiamen were rolling up their bedding, before tying the ends together and looping it across their chests. They wore all manner of clothes and hats, the only hint they were a single army coming from their muskets resting together in tripods of three, all identical and new.

The two freedom fighters surrendered their plates to Salazar as officers began to appear, seeking orders. They were only distinguishable from their men by the better cut of their clothes and a white sash tied around their waists.

'Ah, Ramirez. Your men are to line the crest, between

Clay and the River of Silver

the buildings there, and the six-pounder cannons over there,' ordered Pueyrredon. 'Major Castelli here will be in command of your position.'

'The crest,' repeated the officer, rasping a hand through the plentiful stubble on his chin while he considered Castelli. '*Si señor*. I will deploy my men now.'

'What about my gauchos, *señor*?' asked another officer, in scuffed boots and spurs.

'You will be with me, Garcia,' explained Pueyrredon. 'We will ride out to meet the *Inglés*, and then do what your lads do best. Skirmish and harry, and see if we can make their march here as uncomfortable as possible. When they arrive, we form up behind the hill. Ready to cover Major Castelli's men when they are forced to retreat.'

'A good plan,' said Garcia. 'I will gather my men on the road and wait for you, no?'

'I'll just finish my discussions with the major here, and come and join you,' said Pueyrredon.

'I'm … I'm not sure if I will be able …' began Castelli when they were alone.

'Of course you will,' said his friend, placing an arm around his shoulders.

'I feel like a child whose play-acting at being a soldier has suddenly become real. I'm only a civil servant. Calling me "major" doesn't make me one!'

'And I'm really a merchant, Garcia is really one of my ranchers and Ramirez was once a sergeant in the army, who has only ever fought Indians,' explained Pueyrredon. 'We are all play-acting, my friend, because there is no one else to take our places today. All you need do is stay calm, show no fear in front of the men, and get them to hold their fire until the *Inglés* reach the ditch at the bottom of the slope. Then they can retreat. You

Philip K Allan

can do that? For your country?'

Castelli was quiet for a moment, and then nodded. 'For my country,' he repeated. 'Thank you, brother. I'll will act my part.'

'Good! Salazar, fetch the horses!'

'*Si señor!* Right away.'

As they waited, Pueyrredon drained the last of his coffee, while Castelli retied his sash. 'Bourbon white,' he commented. 'I would sooner fight in the sky-blue and silver of the Rio de la Plata than this Spanish rag.'

'All in good time, my friend,' said Pueyrredon. 'First we must chase the *Inglés* out.'

The wind had backed towards the east with the arrival of day. As the two friends mounted their horses, it brought the smell of the city to them, together with the faint sound of bagpipes.

*****

The gauchos were a thin cloud of movement around the advancing British column. Macpherson watched one of them come trotting towards him. The man brought his horse to a halt a few hundred yards away and raised a carbine to his shoulder, aiming directly at him. Macpherson forced himself to march onwards as if nothing was happening. The man vanished behind a gush of flame and powder smoke, the crack of the shot arriving a moment later. Macpherson let his breath out and looked around to see where the ball had gone. Meanwhile, the gaucho calmly turned his horse away and retreated, feeling in his saddlebag for another cartridge.

'They couldn't hit a barn with a shovel, I reckon, sir,' commented Corporal Edwards beside him. 'Mind, two hundred

Clay and the River of Silver

paces is a touch long for a carbine, especially when yer bobbing around on a nag, but I daresay they don't fancy coming no closer 'case we gives them a volley.'

'Yet their efforts are not entirely without reward, corporal,' said the Scotsman, indicating a kilted body lying face down beside the road.

'Aye, that do seem the way of it, sir. The Dons whittling us down, one man at a time.'

More shots banged out, this time from the other side of the column, and Macpherson heard a cry of pain from somewhere ahead. A little while later he drew level with a marine seated on his pack. A comrade was tying a bloody rag into place on his arm, while a sergeant stood over the pair.

'There you go, Charlie,' said the second marine, drawing the knot tight. 'Only a scratch. With luck the sawbones will let you keep the arm. Have a draught of water, mate.' He unscrewed the cap on a canteen and passed it across. It shook as Charlie took a pull, water cascading down his chin.

'All right lads,' said the sergeant, reaching down to help the wounded man to his feet. 'Best fall back in. You doesn't want to be left behind with these mounted buggers waiting to pounce.'

At that moment the column came to a halt, and the little group took the opportunity to make their way forward, the sergeant carrying the wounded man's musket. Macpherson stepped to one side to see what was happening. A mile ahead was a gentle rise in the ground. On the crest he could see a line of men stretched between a cluster of whitewashed buildings and three small field guns. He made a rough estimate of numbers and concluded that the enemy had several hundred more men.

Riding down the side of the column from its head was a

young officer. Lieutenant Dalrymple, he decided, taking in the rider's reckless speed. The aide pulled up where Captain Gillespie stood at the head of the squadron's marines, and then came thundering back towards the *Griffin*'s contingent, his horse sending clods of earth flying from the soft turf of the verge. 'Good day to you, sir,' he said, pulling on his horse's reins with one gloved hand and saluting with the other.

'And to you, Lieutenant. What orders do you have?'

'Colonel Pack is troubled by all these damned horsemen potting at the column for sport,' said the officer. 'He wants skirmishers sent out to push them back. The light company of the 71st will deploy ahead, and he wishes the marines to do the same on the flanks. Captain Gillespie ordered the men from the *Narcissus* to deploy on this side of the column and your men to protect the other.'

'Aye, that makes a deal of sense,' agreed the Scotsman. 'My compliments to the colonel, and I will position my men directly.'

With a half wave, half salute, Dalrymple was off again and Macpherson began issuing orders. 'Corporal Edwards, I'll have the men drawn up in skirmish order along this flank of the column.'

'Yes, sir!'

Macpherson advanced towards the enemy horsemen, examining the ground for cover, but what he found was disappointingly flat and featureless. Several shots came his way as he approached and a puff of soil spat up from the ground beside him. He glanced backwards to see the thin line of his marines advancing behind him, muskets held across their chests. As he watched, one was shot full in the face, falling backwards without a murmur to lie crumpled on the grass. Macpherson forced himself to look at the mess that was left of

Clay and the River of Silver

the man's face, struggling to recognise which of his soldiers it was. 'Jones,' he concluded. 'Poor laddie. Only thirty-four of us now.'

While the main column resumed its progress, Macpherson deployed his men in a line fifty yards out. They kept pace with the column with little rushes of movement between shots and bouts of reloading.

'Take your time, there!' ordered Edwards, as one marine dropped his ramrod in his haste.

'Good shot!' enthused Macpherson, as a gaucho slumped over his horse's neck and then tumbled to the ground. Another horseman sheared away, his mount limping badly. One rider, bolder than the rest, spurred towards them, but the moment he pulled up to take aim, three shots rang out together, and he fell to the ground. His horse sniffed at his body, and then turned to trot away, whinnying with fear.

The gauchos were still mainly firing at the marching column, a much better target than the widely spaced marines, but with considerably less enthusiasm now they were under fire themselves. Macpherson could sense the change. The rate at which the enemy was shooting was steadily dropping. He watched one man take aim from impossibly long range before retreating to reload. 'Marines will advance twenty paces towards the enemy!' he ordered.

'That's it, Lieutenant,' said a voice behind him. 'Drive them back! You seem to be gaining the upper hand.'

Macpherson turned to see Captain Gillespie approaching. 'Aye, I believe we have the better of them, sir,' he said. 'Of course, a man on a horse will always present a superior target than a lone skirmisher, but my lads have performed well. Now, who is this chap coming up?'

A tall, better-mounted rider was galloping along behind

the gauchos, dressed in a long coat with a white sash tied around it, apparently giving orders to judge from the way he was waving his sword.

'Well, that's a bit rum,' said Gillespie, examining the new arrival through his pocket telescope. 'I may be mistaken, but I declare that is the chap who helped us land when we first came to this wretched place. The arrogant fellow who told us about his jetty.'

'Mister Pueyrredon, sir,' said Macpherson, dredging the name from his memory. 'I thought him an ally. Why the deuce is he fighting us? Ah, but now he is ordering his men to retreat.'

'Only because we have reached the battlefield,' said Gillespie. He pointed to the low ridge, now just ahead. At that moment a cloud of smoke erupted from one of the guns at the end of the line and earth was thrown up close to the head of the column. 'Recall your men, and have them fall in behind mine. Things are about to get interesting.'

*****

Castelli urged his horse forward along the summit of the low ridge to inspect the position his men were occupying, with Ramirez walking along beside him. He started with the hamlet of Perdiel, no more than a cluster of low buildings that protected the militia's left flank. All around the perimeter men were cutting loopholes in the plaster walls with bayonets under the supervision of their officer. Bright Sheffield steel flashed in the early morning sun as their new weapons cut through the wattle and daub with ease.

'Who is that officer, Ramirez?' Castelli asked.

'Tocalli, *señor*,' said the former sergeant. 'He served two years as a French marine, until he ran when his warship

Clay and the River of Silver

touched Montevideo.'

'Well, he may be a deserter, but he seems to know his craft,' commented Castelli.

Ramirez looked up at his commander and shrugged. 'Buildings can help make the men brave. Until they realise that a mud wall you can cut with a knife will never stop a musket ball.'

Castelli gave a few words of encouragement to the defenders, and turned his horse away to ride behind the soldiers strung out along the crest. They looked more like a queue of farm labourers waiting for casual work than a military formation. Many were lying on the grass, hats pulled over their faces in the hope of more sleep, while others sat around in groups talking. One close at hand was puffing on the stump of a thin cigar.

'Idiot!' hissed Ramirez, hauling the man to his feet by his collar, and brandishing the cartridge case that hung from his cross belt under his nose. 'You have thirty rounds of powder about your neck, and you're smoking?'

The man dropped the butt into the grass and hastily stubbed it out with the heel of his shoe. 'Sorry, Captain.'

'Are they ready for battle?' queried Castelli as the two men moved on. 'Shouldn't they be standing up at least?'

'The *Inglés* are still far away, *señor*,' said Ramirez, pointing vaguely towards the east. 'I would let them rest while they can. When the artillery start to fire will be the time for them to stand to arms.'

'Ah yes, the guns,' said Castelli, spurring his horse forward. 'Now that is more like it.'

There were three cannon, small field guns drawn up in a row on the right flank of the militia. On the reverse side of the slope was a collection of mules, some hitched up to the gun

Philip K Allan

carriages, others with wicker baskets hanging from their sides loaded with charges and cannonballs. The battery looked much more martial than the militia from a distance, with its gun crews standing ready and their officer watching the enemy's approach through a large telescope balanced on the shoulder of one of his men. But as Castelli approached, he realised it was as rag-tag as the rest of the little army. The three guns were all different designs and only a few of the men had any sort of uniform. He vaguely recognised the officer as a friend of Belgrano's. 'When do you believe you will be able to open fire?' he asked.

The man looked up from his telescope. 'Not until the *Inglés* come a lot closer, *señor*,' he reported. 'Perhaps when they reach that tree down there?'

Castelli got down from his horse, throwing the reigns to Ramirez, and went to join the man. He followed his arm and saw the lone tree beside the road. In the distance beyond it he could see something moving out on the plain, trailing dust in its wake. Faintly on the wind he heard the bagpipes again, this time accompanied by the crackle of small arms fire. 'May I?' he said, indicating the telescope.

'Of course,' said the artilleryman, stepping to one side.

First Castelli saw only swirling movement. Horsemen flitting across his vision in the grey morning light. Then he saw something more purposeful, coming towards him like a vast millipede, its numberless legs moving in a regular, flowing rhythm. As the light grew, and the enemy column became clearer, he could see the swish of hundreds of kilts and the swinging of many arms. Fear gripped him as he watched the remorseless advance, and he paused for a moment, his head still bowed to the telescope while he let the banging of his heart subside. Then he turned to the others.

'They come on with no guns or cavalry that I can see,'

Clay and the River of Silver

he said brightly. 'And they don't have our numbers. General Pueyrredon's gauchos have already shot several of them.'

Ramirez scratched at his stubble. 'That may be true, *señor*, but …'

'Come with me, Ramirez, and let me give you your orders,' said Castelli, glancing towards the nearest gunners. He took the reins of his horse and walked out of earshot. 'I know what you were going to say,' he whispered. 'Of course the *Inglés* will win the battle, whatever the odds. But our job is to win the war. Time is on our side, my friend. All we need do this day is kill as many as we can, and escape to fight again. General Pueyrredon will soon pull his horsemen back behind the ridge to cover our retreat. Remember, the enemy have no cavalry to chase down our men when they run.'

Ramirez nodded at this. 'Very well. What must we do, *señor*?'

'The men are to hold their fire until the enemy reach the ditch at the foot of the ridge. We shall give them a volley, and in the confusion we fall back.'

'I am not sure the men have the *cojones* to wait so long, *señor*. They fear the enemy greatly, especially the Scottish barbarians.'

'Then we must help give them courage.'

Just then one of the field guns roared out, filling the air with the reek of sulphur, and Castelli almost lost his mount as it shied away from the noise, circling around him at the limit of its reins. 'Hold him steady for me,' he ordered, patting the horse's neck.

Once he had remounted, he trotted forward to rejoin the ragged formation of militiamen. They were all on their feet now, pointing nervously towards the long snake of scarlet as it came ever closer. Pueyrredon's gauchos were flooding back

Philip K Allan

towards him, dividing into two streams to flow around the ends of the ridge, like the tide around an abandoned sandcastle.

'Close formation there!' ordered Ramirez as he walked behind the militia. 'Sergeants, do your bloody job! This line should be straighter than this! Three ranks with one man every pace!'

While the soldiers were pushed and shoved into something resembling a military formation, Castelli sat on his horse watching. Below him, the drone of the pipes was joined by beating drums as the column broke into two distinct formations each side of a group of mounted officers, Highlanders on one side and soldiers in trousers on the other. He had to admire the effortless way the men ran to their places, forming two straight lines. Even a well-placed cannonball from the battery caused only momentary confusion as it ploughed through the Highlanders. The fallen were dragged aside and the survivors shuffled inward until the gap had vanished, leaving Castelli wondering if he had witnessed any casualties at all. The militiamen were silent, transfixed by the redcoats beneath them. Part of the line began to shuffle backwards, until halted by an outraged Ramirez. Others fingered their weapons nervously, or looked backwards over their shoulders. Castelli touched his spurs to his horse's flanks and rode along just behind them.

'Lovely, isn't it?' he called loudly. 'These *Inglés* invaders with their pretty red coats and their dreadful music.' A few men chuckled at this, and Castelli rode on. 'Look at them? Dressed in skirts, like our women.' A few more laughs at this. 'You know what they fight for?' continued Castelli, turning his horse around at the end of the line to retrace his path. 'For money, like common whores. They are no more than filthy mercenaries, come here to steal from us. To take the food from our plates, the wealth from our mines, the soil from beneath our

Clay and the River of Silver

feet. Are we going to let them?'

The growl in answer was weaker than Castelli had hoped for, but it was something to build on. 'My brothers, we can be stronger than them,' he urged. 'Do you know why? Because we fight for something more precious! Our homes! Our people! Our country! *Viva la Rio de la Plata!*'

Some cries of *viva* broke out, and men brandished their muskets on high. Several of the more enthusiastic fired into the air.

'Stop that!' ordered Ramirez. 'Keep your bullets for the enemy! Sergeants, see those men reload their pieces!'

But it was too late for that. The tone of the drums became more urgent, the bagpipes began a fresh tune, and the wave of scarlet swept towards them.

'Steady, my brothers,' urged Castelli. 'No one is to fire until I say so!'

The gun battery roared out and smoke drifted across their front, masking the enemy, leaving only the unearthly sound of the pipes and the steady thump of the drums, coming ever closer. Then the fog cleared a little, revealing a glimpse of scarlet amid the grey, and a dozen muskets went off together.

'Stop that!' yelled Castelli, riding behind the men. 'Hold your fire, I say! We wait until they reach the ditch at the foot of the slope.'

The last of the smoke cleared, revealing the twin lines of soldiers, still out on the flat but now close enough so the collective tramp of their boots on the ground sounded clearly. The sunlight glittered on their bayonets. The wind ruffled the feathered bonnets of the Highlanders that made them seem so much taller than the marines beside them. Castelli pulled his horse to a halt, transfixed by the sight. Every fibre of his being wanted to do something to halt the remorseless advance, but in

Philip K Allan

his heart he knew nothing could stop them. More militiamen began firing, even though the enemy line was well short of the ditch.

'Don't fire!' pleaded Castelli. 'Wait! Wait!'

But it was no use. His voice was lost beneath the growing ripple of musket fire. A few of the enemy fell, but their ranks always closed to fill the gaps and their pace never wavered. When they reached the ditch, almost every one of Castelli's men were frantically trying to reload their discharged weapons. At a barked command, the line of red halted and then raised their muskets in a single wave of movement. A pause to settle their aim, and then the volley crashed out. All around Castelli, men were tumbling to the ground, some crying in pain, others inert. Ramirez was one of these, his lifeless eyes staring upwards, a dark stain spreading across his tunic. Those who had survived the blast of musketry turned and fled, leaving the young freedom fighter alone, struggling to control his horse. Then through the grey haze of smoke left by the volley came a charging line of Highlanders, and he turned his horse about to join the rout.

The plain behind the ridge was a mass of fleeing men as Castelli spurred his horse through them. The militia were mixed with gunners from the battery, some riding mules they had cut free from their traces. Ahead of them was a skirmish line of gauchos, with Pueyrredon in their midst. As the fleeing men flowed between the horsemen they slowed their pace, and a few of the braver ones began to form up again behind the riders. Castelli glanced over his shoulder and saw that the ridge was packed with British soldiers, some securing the three captured guns, others herding prisoners from out of the buildings, or helping the wounded, but none seemed to be advancing any nearer. He pulled his horse up to walking pace and rode over to

Clay and the River of Silver

join his friend.

'I am sorry, Juan,' he said, drawing up beside Pueyrredon. 'I have failed you. I tried to make them wait for the *Inglés* to reach the ditch, but the enemy's advance was too much for them.'

'No need for an apology, brother,' said Pueyrredon. He waved his riding crop towards the soldiers dotted all over the plain behind him. 'Most of them survived to fight again, which is more than can be said for the fifty or so *Inglés* we left on the battlefield, perhaps more. And now our men have been blooded. They know what a battle is truly like, as do we. Next time they will do better.'

Philip K Allan

Chapter 13
Death by a Thousand Cuts

The sailors from the *Griffin* had been ashore for over a month now, and the novelty of the experience had long since worn off. At first, they had been able to spend their leisure time enjoying the grog shops and brothels to be found close to the banks of the Rio de la Plata. But the increasing hostility of the population and growing number of attacks had put these delights off limits. Now when they were not guarding the city treasury, they hastened back to their barracks, always travelling together, with their weapons to hand.

It was a week after the battle, and the men had just been relieved. Trevan was leading the way down the middle of the street, peering into each alley they passed. 'I hate this place,' he muttered. 'We ain't wanted here. Why, barely a watch passes without another taken, or found with his throat cut. The day we be safe back on the old *Griffin* can't come swift enough, I tell 'ee.'

O'Malley, by contrast, was striding along with his musket casually slung over one shoulder. 'Of course, I have little to fear from the locals,' he bragged. 'Being a fellow catholic, like.' To demonstrate the point, he raised his hat politely to an old lady in black who emerged from a side street with a large basket. 'A thousand blessings on you, mother,' he said. 'That's an awful heavy-looking burden. Can I be carrying it for you, at all?' To aid understanding he held out his hand,

Clay and the River of Silver

accompanying the gesture with his most winning smile.

The lady snatched the basket close, her jaw working for a moment as she summoned enough saliva to spit at the Irishman's feet. Then she hissed a stream of Spanish before making off, still muttering.

'Ain't "*diablo*" som'it to do with the devil?' queried Evans, picking one word from the flow of invective.

'Aye, that be so, Big Sam,' confirmed Trevan. 'Still, not as unkind as being told you been whelped from a bitch. I thought *hijo de puta* were a greeting, afore Lopez in the starboard watch put me right.'

'Perhaps she's not a papist after all,' suggested Pembleton, with a wink to the others.

'Aye, that'll be it,' agreed O'Malley, brightening at the notion. 'And here we are. Home sweet fecking home.'

The barracks was a modest affair, set back from the street. It consisted of single-storey buildings grouped around a small dusty parade ground and was surrounded by a high wall. The sailors marched past the marine sentries on the gate and hastened towards the hut allocated to them. It was well situated, close to the perimeter, in the shade of a large tree that grew just beyond the wall in the grounds of an adjacent convent of friars.

When they had moved in it had been recently abandoned by its former residents, a Spanish artillery company disbanded when the British took over the city. The departing gunners had left the barrack room in a filthy state, but with the industriousness of sailors the Griffins had transformed it. The narrow wooden beds with their lice-ridden mattresses had been removed and replaced with hammocks strung between the beams. The mouldering paint on the walls had been renewed with whitewash taken from a nearby storeroom. Best of all, a daily regime of copious water and scrubbing had revealed honest wooden planking beneath the dirt floor they had inherited.

'Not quite the fecking barky, lads, but a sight better than how we found it,' pronounced O'Malley, abandoning his musket and cross belts, and climbing into his hammock with a sigh of contentment.

'Aye, that be so,' agreed Trevan. 'But we still need to find where them rats is coming from.'

'Fecking rats again!' exclaimed the Irishman. 'Haven't we searched all about for them buggers? And we've not found so much as a rat turd.'

'They be here, right enough,' protested his friend. 'You ain't got ears as sharp as mine. I can hear them at night. Scratching away, like.'

'I've heard them too, Sean,' added Pembleton.

'Maybe we should fetch Napoleon,' suggested Evans. 'Ain't no ratter to match that bleeder. Cats ain't in it!'

'An' risk the ill luck as will follow taking him out of the fecking barky?' protested O'Malley. 'Are yous after brewing up a tempest the moment we set sail? And me having lost me feather an' all.'

A silence descended as the sailors considered this. The only sound in the room came from Pembleton, who was cleaning his musket, a puzzled look on his face. 'Sean,' he said eventually, 'what's all this about a lost feather?'

'My wren feather. It was stowed nice and tight in the band of me hat, an' now the feckers gone. I tried to replace it, but it seems they don't have wrens hereabout. Some bugger in the market offered me one from a cock's tail. A chicken feather! I ask you?'

Pembleton carried on with his cleaning, his puzzled frown even deeper than before. 'I don't follow, mate,' he said

Clay and the River of Silver

eventually. 'What need would you have for a wren feather?'

'Will you hear the lubber?' exclaimed the Irishman. 'You've a lot to learn, Lacy Boy. Every jack should carry one of them feckers.'

'But why?'

'Because your wren's feather be a certain way to preventing drowning.' explained Trevan. 'I always carry one.'

'Really? And does it answer?'

'Aren't Adam an' I the living proof?' exclaimed O'Malley. 'Two jacks as have sailed every fecking sea in creation, an' yet here we are.'

'It took me a while to get used to their nautical horseshit, Ted,' commented Evans. 'Feathers to hold back drowning ain't the least of it. You'll hear more sense in Bedlam, mate.' He reached over to give Pembleton a sympathetic pat on the shoulder, but his hand landed a little harder than he intended, jerking the ramrod from between his fingers. It dropped to the floor like an arrow, passing between two planks with barely a clatter and vanished from sight.

'Bloody hell!' exclaimed the Londoner. 'Where's that gone, then?'

Pembleton dropped to his knees and peered between the planks. 'I can't see it at all.'

'I said as we had vermin,' observed Trevan.

'But his bleeding ramrod's vanished!' protested Evans. 'It's the length of a musket barrel! How big do you reckon rats are in these parts?'

'We should go tell Rusty,' said Pembleton, shaking his head. 'Something about this ain't natural.'

Russell and Macpherson had only recently returned from a long row out to the *Griffin* and back to report to Clay. They were sitting in their waistcoats, neckcloths freshly

Philip K Allan

loosened, when the sailors were shown in. A newly poured draught of watered wine had just been set in front of them, still cool from the cellar to judge from the beads of condensation forming on the glass.

'What do you mean, it vanished?' asked Russell, his eyes resting on the drink.

'One moment it were heading for the floor, the next it had gone, sir,' explained Evans. 'A conjurer at Barnet Fair couldn't have done it better.'

'Surely it has simply passed between the boards,' observed Macpherson, sipping from his own glass. 'The armoury here is well stocked. I daresay an appropriate replacement can be issued, provided it is looked after properly in future.'

'No, sir,' supplemented Pembleton. 'It weren't any lack of care on my part. It fell straight as a die, plumb through the floor. An' when I put my eye to the crack, I felt air moving down there.'

The two officers exchanged glances, and then both rose to their feet.

'I'll call out the guard,' said Macpherson. 'You had best procure a brace of crowbars, William.'

'Right,' said Russell. 'You men, come with me.'

A few minutes later a crowd had gathered outside the sailors' hut. Macpherson was there, with a dozen marines at his back, while Russell had been joined by the third lieutenant from the *Narcissus*, whose shore party shared the barracks. Their curiosity piqued, many of the sailors and marines off duty had also wandered over to see what was afoot.

'We are going to look like damned fools if all we discover is a ramrod lying in the dirt,' whispered Macpherson to his fellow officer. 'Pembleton, is he not one of the felons who

Clay and the River of Silver

came aboard in Plymouth?'

'He is,' confirmed Russell, leading the way into the barrack room. 'Now then, where did this miraculous event occur?'

'I was stood here, sir,' said Pembleton, taking up a position on the floor. 'Big Sam hit me shoulder a bit brisk like, and the ramrod dropped just about … there.' He indicated a place with the point of his shoe.

'Evans, O'Malley,' ordered Macpherson. 'Crowbars, here. Let us have these boards up.'

''Tis an awful shame, sir,' said the Irishman with a shake of his head. 'That wood's come up lovely, what with all the holystoning we've been doing.'

'Carry on, I say!'

The two sailors drove the teeth of their crowbars into the gap, and with a splintering crash the floorboard lifted. O'Malley shifted his point of purchase, while Evans grabbed the loose end and heaved upwards. The plank came free, leaving a long slot in the floor. The smell of damp earth flowed up from below.

'That be odd,' commented Trevan.

Russell leant forward and peered downwards, expecting to see flat dirt just beneath the planking. Instead, he found himself staring into a dark void. 'Pembleton, go and find a lantern and some rope,' he ordered. 'Mr Macpherson, have your men stand to. Evans and O'Malley, carry on. Let's have the next plank up.'

By the time that Pembleton returned, a large square opening had been made in the floor, revealing a round chamber, five foot deep, beneath the barrack room. Russell lowered the lantern into the space and more details emerged. A criss-cross of planks shoring up the walls from collapse. A discarded spade

Philip K Allan

left on the ground beside a leather bucket. Pembleton's ramrod, stuck like an arrow at a shallow angle in the ground. The dark mouth of a tunnel, leading towards the perimeter wall and the convent beyond. And stacked against one wall, a number of small kegs.

'That's never fecking gunpowder?' asked O'Malley.

*****

The senior leaders of New Arcadia were gathered once more in Beresford's headquarters, in the heart of an uneasy city, while a furious Clay strode up and down in front of the windows. 'Barrels of gunpowder, if you will credit it, placed right beneath where my sailors were lodged,' he fumed. 'It was a plot worthy of Guy Fawkes himself, and was close to reaching fruition. Only a flame set to the trail was wanting to blow them all to kingdom come.'

'Most distressing, to be sure, Sir Alexander,' said Beresford. 'But pray step away from the windows and retake your seat. Only yesterday one of the sentries was killed by a sharpshooter on the roof opposite. I would not want you to fall in such a fashion.

'And this excavation originated from the convent next door, you say?' asked Popham, once Clay was back in his chair.

'From a gardeners' lean-to within the grounds that rested against the wall, sir,' he confirmed. 'Captain Gillespie found it when he raided the place. Those responsible had fled, of course, and the prior claimed to have not known a thing about it.'

'A likely tale,' scoffed Beresford. 'I know for a fact that his friars are busy urging the populous to oppose us. I will speak with the archbishop again, but I do not hold out much hope. He

Clay and the River of Silver

is always most agreeable to my face, while he continues to undermine me the moment I leave.'

'Then we should round up these damned clerics,' said Popham. 'Throw them into jail, the rogues.'

'That would be most unwise,' said Vansittart. 'I cannot conceive of an action better calculated to inflame the passions of a catholic population. They may not be casting rose petals at our feet, but let us not provoke them into throwing rocks.'

'We are long past that stage, gentlemen,' said Beresford. 'Bullets took the place of stones some weeks back. Truly I am at my wits end. I do my best to offer this wretched city superior governance over what has gone before, but these damned Spaniards will not have it. I recently ordered a reduction to the ludicrously high customs tariffs set by the viceroy, and damned me if a delegation of revenue officials didn't come to protest at the want of dues to collect! If you offered me the governorship of Sodom and Gomorrah rather than this place, I'd agree to the appointment in an instant.'

'Change is always troublesome,' commented Popham. 'But are things not starting to move in our favour, General? Did we not defeat the rebels a few days back? At this Perdiel place?'

'We did, at the cost of thirty dead, and a further fifty wounded. Those lightly hurt will return in time, but my force is still reduced by at least fifty.'

'Surely the enemy lost many more?' said Popham.

'Yes, but each victory leaves me weaker than before, no matter how trifling the loss,' explained Beresford. 'Every soldier of the enemy's we kill is made good as more join the resistance, while I cannot replace my losses. Each day one or two more fall to ambush or assassination here in Buenos Aires. In so wide a city it is impossible to check all the workings of the people. I know that they meet nightly to train in secret, and every day they grow bolder. I tell you, my command is suffering death by a thousand cuts.'

'Is it truly so bad?' said Popham.

'There are times when I wish I had never listened to your bloody notion of New Arcadia,' said Beresford. 'And that we had just taken the treasure and left.'

Vansittart smiled grimly at this. 'Do I detect remorse, that fatal egg by ambition laid?'

'And what, pray is that supposed to mean, sir?' demanded Popham.

'Oh, just a piece of bastardised verse. William Cowper in origin, I believe. But it seemed apposite to the occasion. Although you make a good point regarding the treasure. Perhaps it would be prudent to have it removed from the city treasury to the warships out in the river. The *Griffin* and the other one.'

'The *Narcissus*,' said Clay. 'I can organise that, although I will need a little time for the carpenters to build suitable strongrooms.'

'Good,' said Popham. 'Will two days suffice for the arrangements?'

Beresford looked from one to another of them. 'You gentlemen seem intent on abandoning me,' he said. 'Cutting and running with the loot, and the devil take my men.'

'By no means,' said Popham. 'It is merely a sensible precaution. But once the treasure is on board, perhaps we should just withdraw?'

'Just withdraw?' queried Vansittart. 'I think the time has come for us to be completely candid. Had you two seen fit to consult with me before formally declaring the existence of New Arcadia …'

'We know! You would have cautioned against it. This

Clay and the River of Silver

is old ground—' protested Popham, but Vansittart cut across him.

'Pray attend to what I have to say. General Beresford represents the Crown here. When he makes a formal pronouncement, he does so with the full weight and authority of the government. For good or ill, he has declared New Arcadia exists. That statement cannot be simply withdrawn on a whim the moment a few sentries are killed. Our whole empire rests on the concept of our prestige. When our governors and viceroys speak, they must be believed, else we shall have rebellions to deal with from Quebec to Calcutta, and not just here.'

'Then we must fight on?' queried Beresford. 'Whatever the cost?'

'Precisely so, General,' said the diplomat. 'It takes six months to recruit and train a regiment; it takes six centuries to build a nation's reputation.'

*****

There was a calm dignity about Captain Santiago de Liniers. He was a well-built man with a full head of silver hair that contrasted pleasingly with a face tanned from his years at sea. With his dark eyes and strong aquiline nose, he looked every inch the Spanish grandee, although he had begun life as Jacques de Liniers, the youngest son of a minor French noblemen from Niort. But that was an age ago, and for many years now he had been a trusted officer of the Spanish Crown. He stood looking out of the hacienda window as a fresh batch of recruits were put through their paces in the courtyard below, but turned as the estate's owner came into the room, accompanied by a friend. '*Señor* Pueyrredon, what a pleasure to see you again,' he said.

Philip K Allan

'I trust my arrival here unannounced has not inconvenienced you?'

'Not at all,' said his host. 'The men who accompanied you are being offered some refreshment in my kitchen. I believe you know *Señor* Castelli?'

'Of course. Don Sobremonte speaks very highly of your loyalty to Spain.'

Castelli smiled in response, but wondered if there had been a slight emphasis on the word "loyalty". Perhaps not, he decided, remembering that Spanish was not Liniers first language.

'Would you care for a glass of wine?' continued Pueyrredon. 'A bite to eat?'

'Not for me, thank you,' said their guest.

'Then please take a seat, Captain Liniers, and tell us what brings you so far from the sea?'

'General Liniers,' corrected the new arrival. 'The viceroy has seen fit to elevate me to that rank, and to place me in command of all Spanish forces in the province of Buenos Aires for the duration of this crisis.'

'General, you say?' queried Castelli. 'But surely you are a naval officer, *señor*?'

'I am, but I also have much experience at fighting on land. Against the Barbary pirates in Morocco, and the Portuguese in Brazil. As a young officer I was one of those sent to help the Americans in their struggle for independence. You will find that I fight the enemies of my king, wherever they are to be found.'

'Of course, General,' said Castelli. 'You will find no such enemies here. *Señor* Pueyrredon and I, together with our associates in the city, have been organising the resistance to the *Inglés*.'

Clay and the River of Silver

'So I have heard. Could you tell me what forces you command?'

'Sufficient to confine the enemy to Buenos Aires, General,' said Pueyrredon. 'Between us we have raised almost two thousand militia here in the countryside, along with several hundred gauchos. We also had a small number of guns, but they were captured when we fought last week.'

'You have done well, gentlemen. And what about in the city?'

'Our compatriots *Señor* de Saavedra and Captain Belgrano are organising resistance there. They have large numbers under arms, and take a steady toll on the enemy. Belgrano made sure many of the city militia hid their weapons when the *Inglés* arrived.'

'That is interesting,' mused Liniers, his dark eyes holding those of the others for a moment. 'I wonder why he did not use those arms to prevent the *Inglés* taking over in the first place? And I couldn't help but notice that the militiamen being drilled in the courtyard seem to have muskets of a British pattern. Brown Bess, if I am not mistaken? Newly made, which I found strange. I trust I can count on your complete loyalty to Spain, gentlemen?'

'How can you say such a thing?' demanded Pueyrredon. 'Haven't both of us risked our lives in battle? As for these Brown whatevers, I purchased them from an American gunrunner, at my own expense I might add, to arm troops to fight against the *Inglés*. Until you mentioned it, I had no idea as to their origins.'

'As for the militia, with no regular forces on this side of the river, the *Inglés* attack was so rapid they had little time to gather,' said Castelli. 'When the viceroy left, he asked me to organise resistance in the city, and I thought it prudent for

Philip K Allan

Captain Belgrano to get his men to hide their arms so they wouldn't fall into enemy hands. An action that is now reaping dividends, I might add.'

'I understand, gentlemen,' said Liniers, holding up his hands. 'There has been so much talk of revolution and breaking with the mother country in the last few years, that one can become over-suspicious. I still think the *Inglés* invasion with so few troops to be very odd, but there will be time after we have driven them away for such matters to be investigated. The main thing I wanted to discover was that I could rely on you.'

'Well, now that is established, can I ask what assistance you bring to our cause, General, besides yourself?' asked Pueyrredon. 'We have had no practical support at all until your arrival today.'

'That is because the *Inglés* ships control the Rio de la Plata, which has obliged my men to march the long way around from Montevideo. But they will be here soon. I left the column to ride ahead two days back. I have brought El Fijo's Regiment of Foot, two companies from the Blandengues Regiment of light infantry and three companies of dragoons, together with plenty of artillery. Almost two thousand men, all told.'

'Regular troops!' exclaimed Pueyrredon. 'That is most welcome. Our militia do what they can, but cannot long resist the *Inglés* redcoats, as we found to our cost at Perdiel.'

'You were most unwise to fight them in the open, my friends. I fought the *Inglés* during my time in America. A line of redcoats drawn up on good ground cannot be easily beaten.'

'Then how are we to defeat them?' asked Castelli.

'We must do as General Washington did,' urged Liniers. 'Wear them down, as you have been doing, and then fight them where they no longer have the advantage. On broken ground, in forests or in mountains. Ambush them in narrow

Clay and the River of Silver

places, where they cannot deploy properly.'

'But this is the Rio de la Plata,' protested Pueyrredon. 'There are no forests or mountains, just miles of grass.'

'That is why we will fight them in the city,' said Liniers. 'Let the buildings be our forests and the churches our mountains. A narrow street can be a very good place for an ambush, no?'

'I can see that Don Sobremonte chose wisely when he appointed you, General,' said Castelli. 'Where do we start?'

'First, I wish to inspect your men, gentlemen,' said Liniers, rising to his feet. 'Look them in the eye, and see if they are truly up to the task. Then, when my men arrive, we shall march on the city.'

'And drive the *Inglés* out!' exclaimed Pueyrredon.

'No, it is not enough to drive the enemy back to their ships,' said Liniers. 'The dignity of our king requires that they be crushed in so complete a fashion, they will never dare to return.'

Philip K Allan

Chapter 14
Barricades

Thunder clouds, heavy with rain, had been rolling in from the Atlantic for much of the day. But as evening approached, the sun cut through them, sending long beams across the water to shine on the *Griffin*'s longboat as it made another run out from the shore towards the anchored frigate. The light transformed the water dripping from the oar blades into droplets of falling gold. Russell and Todd sat relaxing in the stern sheets, enjoying the calm of the evening as each pull took them further from the oppressive feel and constant danger of Buenos Aires. The boat sat deep, thanks to the consignment of bullion that lay in rows of canvas sacks along the centreline, each one carefully weighed, secured with strong cord and heavily sealed.

'Longboat ahoy!' called the master's mate in charge of the anchor watch. 'Come along starboard side.'

'Starboard, aye,' bellowed Sedgwick in reply, tugging the tiller across to send the boat towards the whip that hung down from the main yard. 'Easy there!'

The men rested on their oars, and the way came off the boat as she bumped to a halt against the frigate's side. Trevan grabbed the end of the rope and made it fast to the first bag. 'Haul away, there!' he called, and the sack rose, turning slowly as it did so, until it was pulled over the side by those waiting on deck.

'Mr Russell, sir!' called a voice from the quarterdeck.

Clay and the River of Silver

'What is it, Mr Sweeney?'

'The captain sends his compliments, and asks if you would join him in his quarters, sir.'

'Carry on here, Mr Todd, and keep an eye on the men,' ordered the lieutenant. 'If so much as a farthing goes missing, there'll be the devil to pay.'

'Aye aye, sir.'

When Russell entered the great cabin he found Clay sitting at his desk lost in thought, while Taylor stared gloomily out of the stern windows at the ornate bow of the *Narcissus*. 'You sent for me, sir?' he asked, coming to attention in front of his captain.

'I did indeed, William. Thank you for coming so promptly. Pray take a seat. Can I offer you refreshment?'

'Thank you, sir. That would be most agreeable.'

'Harte!' called Clay towards his day cabin. 'A glass of wine for the lieutenant, if you please.'

'Aye aye, sir.'

'How does the transfer of the bullion proceed?' asked Clay, once his guest had his drink.

'The last bags of silver are being brought on board just now, sir. The *Narcissus* received her allocation earlier.'

'That is good to hear. And pray tell me how you find the situation ashore?'

'May I speak frankly, sir?'

'In all things, I hope.'

'Troubling, sir. Our presence has always been resented, but now we are encountering much more open hostility. The attempt to murder my men while they slept was bad enough, but today I doubt the enemy would bother to conceal what their intentions were so thoroughly.'

'I met with Tom Macpherson earlier, who said much the

same,' said Clay. 'His men come under daily attack, and he says the city has the same feeling that proceeds a coming storm.'

'He puts it much better than I have,' said Russell with a smile. 'But then Tom keeps the soul of a poet hid beneath that scarlet tunic of his.'

'Yes, I believe he does,' agreed Clay.

'May I ask a question, sir?'

'By all means.'

'I have always understood there is no dishonour in withdrawing in the face of a superior foe, sir. A frigate will do it, for example, if faced by a ship of the line. So now that we have the Don's treasure safely on board, why are we obliged to stay?'

Clay exchanged glances with Taylor, before replying. 'What you say is only partially correct. To take your example, there are occasions when this frigate has been compelled to engage a ship of the line, if an objective of sufficient import requires it. You have seen me forced into such an action more than once over the years.'

'And is this such an occasion, sir?'

'Why yes. Taking Spain's largest city in the New World is a lusty blow against our enemies. And there is reason to believe we may yet prevail in this fight. The 71st are an excellent body of men, and General Beresford is a determined leader.'

'Very well, sir,' said Russell. 'You can count on me to do my duty.'

'Thank you,' said Clay. 'There was something else I wish to discuss with you. Mr Taylor and I were speaking of it just now. While I have every confidence in our position, it is still possible that the Dons may get the upper hand. It is not a prospect I think likely, nor one I have discussed with Captain

Clay and the River of Silver

Popham or General Beresford, but I wish us to consider it now. What would you do under such circumstances?'

Russell considered matters for a moment. 'Most of the Highlanders are accommodated in the city fort or around the viceroy's palace, so I suppose we would fall back on them, sir. But I would hope for some direction from my superiors. Captain Gillespie commanding the squadron's shore party in the first instance and of course General Beresford.'

Clay considered the officer, before continuing. 'I cannot predict what may happen. All may go well, or turn to chaos. You may receive the clear orders you speak of, or become isolated and have to shift for yourself. But I want you to remember this. You will always have the safeguard of this ship. If all else fails, make for the port, where I can take you and any others in need off.'

'Thank you, sir. That is a comfort.'

'Good. But keep that to yourself. The only other persons I have spoken to about this are Tom and Mr Taylor here. Do I make myself clear?'

'I believe I understand, sir.'

'Then I have detained you long enough,' said Clay, rising from behind his desk and holding out his hand. 'You had best get back before this weather breaks. Good luck, William.'

'Thank you, sir. Goodbye.'

Once Russell had gone, Clay turned to his first lieutenant. 'How did you think that went, George?'

'I believe he understood the dangerous path you are treading, sir. William is a clever boy.'

'Yes, and growing into a valuable officer before our eyes. I am pleased we got him promoted.'

'You are quite certain there is no prospect of us prevailing here, sir?'

Philip K Allan

'None whatsoever, George,' sighed his captain. 'I wish I could say otherwise, but this intelligence of fresh forces approaching from the west will prove to be the final straw.'

'And what of our commander, sir? Captain Popham?'

'That pompous fool only has consideration for himself,' said Clay. 'This ridiculous New Arcadia was his idea, but you can be sure that he will contrive to be well clear when all comes crashing down. No, it is Beresford I feel sorry for.'

A patter sounded on the deckhead above them, and both men looked out of the stern windows as the long-promised rain began to fall.

'Well, it cannot be helped, George,' sighed Clay. 'They all outrank me, and will not countenance the only sensible course to follow.'

'Which is, sir?'

'To find some accommodation with the Spanish that allows us to withdraw with some shred of dignity,' said his captain. 'Which is why we must be ready to save our people at the very least. Have the armourer fit boat carronades in the longboat and launches, and keep them on the water, armed and ready. I'll be damned before I see my people left to die.'

*****

Russell had considerable difficulty sleeping that night. First there was the rain, falling with hissing fury on the city, cascading from the roofs of the buildings and turning all the many unpaved streets into muddy quagmires. When it eased, around midnight, it was replaced with other, more disturbing sounds. The persistent barking of dogs from the western suburbs. The sound of distant shouting and the occasional crackle of gunfire. It was not until just before dawn that he had

Clay and the River of Silver

drifted into sleep, only to be shaken awake moments later by his servant.

'Sorry to disturb you, sir,' said the youngster. 'Only we've all been ordered to stand to arms, urgent like. Mr Todd is assembling the men now.'

'Wh-what time is it?' croaked Russell, sitting up in bed and rubbing at his chin.

'Six bells, sir. I've only cold water for you to wash with, I'm afraid. All this rain's been an' done for the kitchen fire.'

'Don't worry, Godwin. Just bring me my clothes and something to eat.'

'Right you are, sir. It'll have to be bread and cheese an' a drop of wine, I'm afraid.'

Russell pulled on his uniform in the grey light filtering through the window, his coat and boots damp and clammy from yesterday's rain. As he ate his cold breakfast, he watched Macpherson stride past and then pause to eye the sky with obvious distaste. 'Corporal Edwards!' the Scotsman called across the parade ground. 'See the men protect their locks with oilskin covers.'

'Here you are, sir,' said Godwin, bringing in the lieutenant's weapons. 'I've renewed the priming, although that may not answer if this rain sets in again,' he explained as he passed a pistol across, before dropping to one knee to buckle the sword into place. Russell placed the pistol deep in his coat pocket and pulled on his hat.

'Good luck, sir. Give them bleeding Dons what for.'

'Thank you,' said Russell, making his way outside. The *Griffin*'s remaining marines were formed up in a double line, while his sailors were in a more nebulous group beside them, with Midshipman Todd at their head. He walked across to join Macpherson. 'What's happening, Tom?' he asked quietly.

Philip K Allan

'More trouble from the locals, laddie,' said the Scotsman. 'Apparently, they've been busy erecting barricades during the night. The shore party from the *Narcissus* have already gone to deal with one. We are to disperse the rogues manning another in Three Kings Avenue.'

Russell considered this for a moment. 'That sounds promising, if the Dons want a proper fight,' he commented. 'I'd sooner have that than all these attacks from the shadows.'

'Aye, but why are they acting so bold? That's what concerns me. I suggest you let my lads go first 'til we know what we are up against.'

'Be my guest,' smiled Russell, stepping back and holding out an arm to usher his friend towards the gate.

'Marines will form a column of march!' ordered Macpherson, and the Griffins set out.

Almost immediately they left the protection of the barracks, the two officers noticed a change in atmosphere. The street was strangely empty, and a pregnant silence hung in the air, as if the surrounding city held its collective breath.

'Where are the carts and drays bringing produce in from the countryside?' asked Macpherson. 'They are normally rattling along this street from well before dawn.'

'Perhaps the rain has delayed them,' suggested Russell.

'Maybe, but there are no locals out either. Does that not strike you as odd?'

The little column marched on, until they came to an intersection. "*Avenida Tres Reyes*" was painted on the wall of a house that stood at the corner. Macpherson ordered the column to halt while the officers looked down the street.

It was a narrow affair, a canyon between tall buildings with closely shuttered windows. Along one side was a colonnaded walkway lined with shops, all closed with their

Clay and the River of Silver

windows and doors barred. The road itself was of dirt, churned to rutted mud by the rain. At the far end, where the next intersection lay, it was blocked by a rough barricade of crossed beams and looted furniture with an upturned cart at its heart. Someone had tried to improvise a flag from a bed sheet which hung down sodden and limp over the front of the barrier. Behind it could be seen the heads and brandished weapons of those defending it. The sight of Macpherson's scarlet tunic brought forth a growl of defiance.

'Rather excited civilians,' commented the marine, as he focused his pocket telescope on the enemy. 'Some muskets, mixed with fowling pieces, but the majority have improvised pikes. Knives lashed to broom handles, that sort of thing. Nothing that should long detain us. I suggest my lads advance on them in close order, give them a volley, and then go in with the bayonet.'

'Very well. And what would you have my men do, Tom?' asked Russell.

'Have a care for our backs.' Macpherson eyed the buildings on either side. 'I don't like the feel of this place. Too tight and cramped. And what do you suppose lies behind all these shutters?'

'We could search each house as we advanced?' suggested his friend.

'No, that would take too long,' said Macpherson with a shake of his head. 'And these folk dislike us enough, without adding breaking and entering to their list of grievances. Come, William. Let us get it done. Corporal Edwards! I'll have the men drawn up in close order across the street here.'

'Yes, sir!'

Meanwhile, Russell divided his men into two groups. 'Half with me, the rest with Mr Todd. Each will take a side of the lane, watching the windows opposite. Is that clear?'

'Aye aye, sir!'

'Eh, what we looking for, exactly?' queried Evans in a whisper as they moved into position.

'Marines will fix bayonets!' ordered Macpherson.

'For the fecking enemy, of course. Taking potshots at the Lobsters once they have passed,' explained O'Malley.

'Marines will advance!'

At first the appearance of the soldiers at the end of the street had been met with a fresh storm of jeers from the barricade, and a few shots rang out as the more excitable of their opponents let fly. But this soon faded into a tense silence as the solid block of men came on, squelching their way through the mud. From nearby came the echo of small arms fire.

Russell paused to listen, and became aware that there was more distant firing to be heard across the city. He glanced at Macpherson, but he was focused on the battle in this street as he calmly marched towards the barricade, his gleaming claymore in his hand.

The tension was almost unbearable. The only sounds seem to come from the British. The suck and slosh from the marines' boots as they marched in step. The clink and rattle from the sailors' equipment, following in their wake. When the marines reached the midpoint of their advance, a few harsh braying notes rang out from a poorly played bugle behind the barricade, and everything changed.

From above Russell's head came the sound of shutters banging open. On the buildings opposite, figures appeared in the windows, taking aim at the backs of the soldiers. He glanced upwards and saw a man leaning out of the first-floor window immediately above him, musket in hand, looking for a target. 'Griffins! To arms!' he yelled, pulling out his pistol. 'Shoot

Clay and the River of Silver

these men!'

At the sound of his voice the man looked directly down at him. Russell had an image of a swarthy face, eyes wide with surprise. Then the soldier tried to turn his cumbersome weapon around, but the window was narrow and he was impeded by one of the shutters that had swung back from the wall. With a strange sense of calm, Russell raised his pistol until he held it directly upwards in both hands, like a priest holding a chalice aloft, and pulled the trigger. The pistol crashed out and he watched the man lean slowly forward, as if falling asleep. Then he gathered speed in a rush of whirling limbs and flapping equipment to smash down into the mud of the road. He was a tall, lean man, dressed in a blue military coat over a bright red waistcoat and leggings.

Russell wrenched his gaze from his dead opponent to see what was going on around him. At his cry of warning, the sailors had begun firing at those appearing above them. Across the road another soldier lay slumped over the frame of a window, his arms hanging down, pointing towards where his musket and hat lay beneath him. But more figures were appearing in other windows, some firing at the sailors, others leaning out to shoot at the marines. All Russell's men had fired off their muskets, and stood around frantically reloading while shots splattered into the ground around them, sending up little geysers of mud. Next to him, Pembleton was frantically working the ramrod that had fallen through the barrack room floor. Then he spun away from his weapon with a cry of pain as a musket ball slammed into his arm. Further down the street O'Brien from the afterguard lay face down and motionless, the dark stain on his back sending red threads into the mud around him as it started to rain again.

'We're being shot like fish in a bloody kettle here,'

Philip K Allan

Russell muttered, looking around for some cover. Then he saw the colonnaded walkway on the far side of the street. 'Over there!' he yelled. 'Take cover behind those pillars!'

The sailors scrambled across the road and into shelter as more shots rang out. The last to arrive were Evans and Trevan, dragging a moaning Pembleton along between them. More musket balls thudded into the dirt behind them as they staggered into cover.

They were in a sort of tunnel running along one side of the street, built to provide shelter for pedestrians On its inner side were the row of heavily boarded shops, many with owners' names painted above their doors. Above them the first floors of the buildings jutted out, supported by thick beams that rested on the stone columns lining the street.

'Trevan, get a neckcloth around Pembleton's arm between the wound and his heart, before he bleeds to death,' ordered Russell. 'Evans, see if you can break into this shop. There may be a way to the floors above that will let us come at these marksmen from behind. The rest of you, one column each, place it at your back and reload your pieces.'

'Aye aye, sir.'

While the men were busy, Russell looked back out into the road. There were two more sailors lying out in the rain, in addition to O'Brien. Further down the street at least four of the marines were down, but the rest were pressing on towards the barricade. He ducked back as a musket ball hit the stone pillar he was sheltering behind, sending a shower of dust and stone splinters into his face. 'Come along with that reloading!' he urged. 'I need those men in the windows brought under fire!'

O'Malley transferred the ball in his mouth into the barrel of his musket before replying. 'Nearly ready, sir,' he said, folding the cartridge into a wad and ramming it home. 'And I

Clay and the River of Silver

knows just the fecker I'm after getting. The one as shot our Ted Pembleton.'

'Fire when you are able, men, and make every shot count,' said Russell, before joining Evans. He had just hammered open the nearest shop door with the butt of his musket and thrust his head in.

'Fiddle maker, sir,' he reported, emerging again.

'Mr Todd, take three men and see if you can find a stair. One had best be Evans here, in case it comes to fighting at close quarters.'

'Aye aye, sir.'

'Go softly, mind,' added Russell. 'So as not to alert them you are coming.'

'Gentle it is, sir,' confirmed Todd.

'Might be a touch late for stealth, sir,' commented Evans, shouldering his musket and drawing out his bayonet. 'Me having bust down the door an' all. But if I give them a little poke with this, I daresay it'll answer.'

The sailors were firing steadily, peering around each column to loose off a shot, before ducking back into cover to reload. Each puff of gunsmoke drew a fresh fusillade from the street opposite, but at least these shots were no longer directed at Macpherson's men. Russell had just completed reloading his pistol when a cry of pain came from somewhere above, and another opponent fell crashing down to lie inert in the middle of the road, close to O'Brien.

'Looks like Big Sam found that stair, sir,' commented Trevan, who had left Pembleton to join the firing line.

But Russell was looking at the body of the new arrival. He wore a blue coat of the same cut as the man he had shot earlier with his pistol. From beneath the garments extended the corpse's legs, one twisted uselessly aside, clad in the same bright red leggings. 'Damnation,' he muttered to himself. 'Uniforms! These men aren't militia. They're regular soldiers.'

He glanced up the street and saw that the marines were no more than a hundred yards from the barricade. The limp white flag still hung down across the front, masking part of it, but as he watched it was pulled aside, to reveal the muzzle of a field gun. For a heartbeat nothing happened. Then the gun roared out, filling the narrow street with fire and smoke that rolled in a cloud towards him. A storm of grape swept out of the fog, sending splinters of stone flying from the faces of the buildings and scoring furrows in the mud. 'Tom!' yelled Russell, stepping into the street, blind to the musket shots splashing around him.

At first all he could see was acrid smoke drifting towards him. Then the rain began to thin it a little, and the first few marines appeared, shadows in the mist, growing as they ran back down the street. He advanced towards them, searching for his friend. First came the able-bodied, flowing past him. 'Get into cover!' ordered Russell, indicating the colonnade. Then slower figures appeared. A dazed private who had lost his hat. Another clutching an arm across his chest. Two more, carrying a wounded comrade between them. 'Have you seen Lieutenant Macpherson?' he demanded.

'I … I ain't sure, sir,' said one of the survivors. 'It's bleeding carnage back there.'

Russell hurried into the thinning smoke, searching. From ahead he could hear the cries of the wounded, and what might be pleading. He ducked at a sound like ripping cloth in the air, and a bullet fired from above splashed into the road beside him. And then he saw a familiar, upright figure limping towards him, using the long sword in his hand like a walking stick. 'Tom!' Are you hurt? Come, lean on me.'

Clay and the River of Silver

''Tis only a scratch, laddie,' said the officer, gratefully flinging an arm around Russell's neck.

'Come, step out and let's make haste to get into cover. It's not far, and you can tell me what happened as we go,' urged Russell, making for the colonnade as swiftly as they could.

'They've done for my poor boys,' gasped the Scotsman, as bullets continued to hit the mud around them. 'That canister blast must have felled ten of them. Then they came on like fiends, and it was too much for the rest.'

'Nearly there,' said his friend. 'Trevan! O'Malley! Come help.'

'Edwards fought like a tiger, 'til he was cut down from behind, and I accounted for a few with my sword. Can you hear the bastards now? Butchering the wounded!'

With the help of the two sailors, Russell got Macpherson into cover. 'Sit with your back to one of these pillars,' he suggested.

'No, laddie, not 'til I've checked on my men. Where are they?'

'In that shop Big Sam bust the door of, sir,' reported Trevan. 'There be a back door an' all, leading to an alley as looks a deal safer than this street. Should we need to scarper, like.'

Russell looked enquiringly at his friend. 'Shall we get clear of this hellhole, Tom?'

'Aye,' agreed the marine. 'The enemy have us in a false position. We can do no more here.'

*****

General Beresford had left the viceregal palace and set up his command post in the wide Plaza Mayor outside, where his men could deploy properly. Each of the streets leading into the square was held by a company of Highlanders drawn up in close order, supported by at least one field gun. Their scarlet tunics were hidden beneath the long grey coats they wore against the rain. The general sat on his horse with Colonel Pack beside him. Rain fell all around them, leaving broad puddles and gurgling in the drains. Behind him was the regiment's colour party, their precious flags left in their leather cases to protect them from the elements.

With his staff around him, and the square well-fortified, Beresford should have felt confident, but he was increasingly aware that his part of the city was the calm eye at the centre of a swirling hurricane. From all around came the crackle of distant small arms fire, punctuated with the occasional boom of a cannon. Then, down one of the streets came the sound of marching feet, and the defenders guarding that entrance parted to allow a group of two dozen dishevelled soldiers through, with a young Highland officer at their head.

'Is that not Captain Arbuthnot, Colonel?' asked Beresford, leaning towards Pack.

'It is, sir. I directed him to investigate those reports of crowds gathering close to the artillery park. But where the devil is the rest of his command?'

While his men went to get a drink from the fountain by the cathedral, Arbuthnot limped across to stand in front of them and raised a weary hand to his hat. His face was streaked with dirt, his coat stained with powder smoke.

'What has befallen you, man?' demanded Pack. 'I sent you out with half a company!'

Beresford raised a hand to restrain the colonel, and turned to his aide. 'Lieutenant Dalrymple, kindly bring some refreshment for the captain while he makes his report. And see

Clay and the River of Silver

his men get something hot to eat.'

'Yes, sir.'

'Now, kindly tell us what has befallen you?'

'We left at dawn, sir, as ordered,' began Arbuthnot. 'At first it seemed calm, perhaps excessively so, for the streets were strangely deserted. Then we encountered small bands of armed men roaming the city. They fell back before us, and as my instructions were to head directly to the artillery park, I left them be and pressed on. When I got there, I found it in the hands of their militia, so I was obliged to storm the place, driving the enemy off with minimal losses.'

'And what of Sergeant MacGregor, and the men left guarding the place?' asked Pack.

'All dead, I'm afraid, sir,' said the officer, his face a mask. 'Though butchered might be closer to the mark, for none were spared. The enemy stripped them of their muskets and equipment before leaving. But I can report MacGregor and his men put up noble resistance, to judge from the Don bodies strewn about the place.'

Beresford and Pack were silent for a moment, envisaging the scene. An orderly appeared at Arbuthnot's elbow with a tankard on a tray, and the officer drank from it thirstily.

'What of the guns they were protecting?' resumed Pack.

Arbuthnot wiped his mouth dry on his sleeve, and returned the tankard to the tray before replying. 'Taken, along with much powder and shot. The magazine had been broken into and the store house plundered.'

'Well, it cannot be helped now,' said Beresford, stirring in his saddle. 'The enemy have a dozen more six-pounders to vex us with, and our numbers decline further. What happened next, Captain?'

Philip K Allan

'With no guns to protect and no garrison to bring in, we set off to return, sir. Which was when our troubles truly began. Barricades pulled across our path. Sharpshooters picking us off from above. Volleys of musketry fired from side streets as we passed. Artillery too. It was truly hellish. We took steady losses for every yard of progress, until we were so reduced we were obliged to leave the worst of our wounded behind to have any prospect of the able-bodied returning here at all.'

'These militiamen grow damned bold!' exclaimed Beresford.

'They do, sir,' agreed Arbuthnot. 'But it was not their irregulars that did most of the damage. We were engaged by Spanish line infantry.'

'Really?' queried Pack. 'Are you sure, man?'

'Yes sir. They were well drilled and drawn up in formation, all in uniform.'

'Thank you, Captain,' said Beresford. 'I am sure you did your duty creditably under difficult circumstances.'

Arbuthnot saluted once more and turned away, to be replaced by Dalrymple. 'Apologies for bringing yet more ill tidings to you, sir,' said the aide. 'The messengers you sent to Captain Gillespie have returned. They were unable to get through to the marine's barracks, on account of large bodies of irregulars between us and them.'

'Then we have no way of knowing if they have succeeded in dispersing those various barricades in the port area?'

'I'm afraid not, sir.'

'The port area?' queried Pack. 'Is it cut off from us? I had hoped we might evacuate some of our wounded to the ships, sir. And perhaps some of the regiment's camp followers. Men's wives and the like.'

Clay and the River of Silver

'That may have to wait until the situation is resolved here, Colonel,' said Beresford.

But the Highlanders' commander was no longer listening. Instead, he was looking at something over the general's head. 'Where the devil have they come from?' he asked.

Beresford turned his horse around to face the cathedral. The soaring frontage was topped by a stone parapet. Behind it had appeared the heads and shoulders of a row of figures, each one holding a musket. It was an excellent position, with a commanding view out over the square, while they were partly protected. As he watched, a series of shots rang out, engulfing the firing line in smoke. A Highlander in the front rank of the nearest formation reeled away as he was hit. Next to Beresford a staff officer's horse crashed to the ground, its rider howling in pain with his leg trapped beneath the animal.

'Skirmishers!' bellowed Pack, spurring his animal forward. 'Skirmishers here! Bring these men under fire!'

'You should pull back, sir,' urged Dalrymple, appearing beside the general. 'They are sure to target you.'

'Not now, Lieutenant,' said Beresford, waving him away. 'Kindly attend to poor Major Jones and see he is pulled out from beneath his charger.'

'Yes, sir.'

Highlanders were running across the square to form a firing line facing the men on the cathedral roof, but Beresford found his attention drawn to other rooftops, where more figures were appearing. Then an officer came running over from the troops posted guarding the western entrance to the square. 'A large crowd is approaching our position, sir. Do we have permission to open fire?'

'Are they armed, Captain?'

'Very much so, sir.'

'Then pray do so,' said Beresford, his face grim. 'Let us pay them back in their own coin.'

Clay and the River of Silver

Chapter 15
Assault

The Griffins who had survived the attack on the barricade had paused in a small city square. While the wounded were attended to under the portico of a little church, their officers considered what to do next. The sound of firing was almost constant, mainly from afar, but occasionally much nearer, and gunsmoke drifted through the streets like dawn mist on the surface of a river. Russell did his best to ignore the sulphurous reek as he concentrated on the firing. 'It comes mainly from the heart of the city,' he concluded. 'The area around the cathedral, I would judge.'

'Aye, like enough,' said Macpherson. 'The Dons know this place better than us, and where the seat of power truly lies. Mind, the 71st will take some beating. Steady lads, those Highlanders.' He paused as a low rumble of sound echoed through the square. 'Artillery too,' he concluded. 'A battle proper, it would seem. That will explain why the enemy hasn't pursued us. Let us take our opportunity to get back to our barracks.'

'Should we not try and join the battle?' asked Russell.

'Our duty is to get these wounded to a surgeon, before they expire, and we need to report back to Captain Gillespie,' said the marine. 'Besides, I'm not sure how much fight my lads have left at present.'

'Very well. Mr Todd! Get the men on their feet.'

Philip K Allan

'Aye aye, sir.'

Macpherson limped to where the square opened on to the main street and peered around the corner. Then he waved the weary column forward. Most of the able-bodied were helping the wounded, leaving only a half-dozen marines with Macpherson to lead the way, and Russell with eight sailors to bring up the rear. At first the streets were largely deserted, with only the occasional roving band armed with knives and staves crossing their route. One group, bolder than the rest, tried to block their path, until the marines levelled their muskets at them and they shrank away down a side street. But as they approached the barracks, Russell turned to see a growing mob following behind. Beyond them was the city centre, lost under a cloud of gunsmoke, the crackle of distant firing now accompanied by the crash of volleys.

'Turnabout, rearguard,' he ordered.

He drew his sword and pulled his pistol from his pocket, while his men formed up behind him, muskets held across their chests. At this the mob halted. Most seemed content to shout abuse and shake their improvised weapons, but a few bolder individuals ran from the safety of the crowd to hurl stones towards them, before swiftly retreating. Russell glanced over his shoulder and saw the column was some way ahead. 'Start walking backwards,' he ordered. 'Slowly! Show them no fear.'

As soon as they began to retreat, the mob came after them, their pace gradually increasing. Russell ducked his head to avoid a rock. 'Steady lads,' he urged. 'Keep the pace steady.'

'Can't we give the bleeders a volley, sir?' asked Evans, itching for a fight.

'No one is to fire until I tell them,' ordered Russell. 'Nothing will bring them on faster than the knowledge that our pieces are empty.' He glanced over his shoulder again, and saw

Clay and the River of Silver

the wall surrounding the barrack compound at last. 'Not long now, lads.'

Another crowd came boiling out of an alleyway to join their compatriots, and the pace of the mob's advance quickened. Stones were raining down among the sailors, and O'Malley let out a stream of curses as one struck his arm. Russell watched a balding man in a dark green coat stop and level his pistol at them. His hand vanished in a ball of smoke, the shot raising a spurt of mud from the road surface at Russell's feet. 'Keep it steady, lads,' he urged.

The mob grew dangerously close, emboldened by the sailors' withdrawal. Russell desperately wanted to check on his progress, but like a matador facing an enraged bull, he felt if he let his focus waver for a moment, they would charge. 'Halt!' he ordered. 'Evans, tell me where the column is?'

'Eh, they've just reached the barrack gate, sir.'

'Prepare to fire!' he said, cocking his pistol. Eight more clicks sounded around him. But although he saw some hesitation on the faces opposite, the rest came on, driven forward by those pressing from behind. The pistol in his hand began to tremble as he sensed the bull was about to charge. 'Level your weapons,' he said, extending his arm and willing his hand to be steady. Eight muskets were brought up onto eight shoulders. A pathetic display of firepower against the hundreds now crowding the street.

But the mob came to a halt, as if some invisible force was holding it back. Russell felt his pistol grow steady in his hand. He pointed it at individuals before him, and saw them shrink back into the safety of the crowd. Then he heard movement behind him, but he still couldn't risk a look.

'Well done, laddie,' said Macpherson, limping to his side. 'Reinforce the line, marines!'

Philip K Allan

It was only the six men that had led the column, but their presence seemed to disconcert those in front of them further. He could see individuals breaking away from the rear of the mass, while others were pointing at something beyond Russell, and at last he risked a glance over his shoulder. Like ants from a nest, a steam of marines and sailors was emerging from the barrack room gate and hurrying down to join them.

'I took the liberty of calling out the guard before I came myself, William,' explained Macpherson. 'They are much reduced in numbers after this morning, as we are, but they should be enough to disperse this rabble.' He gestured towards their opponents, who were obviously of the same opinion. Like a cloud before a keen wind, the crowd was rapidly thinning.

*****

In the Plaza Mayor, Beresford and Pack had abandoned their horses. As the fight for the city centre had intensified, the animals made them too obvious a target for the enemy occupying the rooftops of the buildings around the square. Instead, they were making a tour of the various positions on foot, with their staff officers trailing behind them.

'We have driven them off the roof of the cathedral, sir,' explained Pack, indicating the baroque frontage towering above them. 'I was obliged to storm the place, much to the annoyance of the priests within, who did their best to thwart us. I have now posted men to stop the building being reoccupied.'

'Good,' said Beresford. 'And how do you propose to remove the damned sharpshooters from all the other buildings? They pick us off for pleasure.'

As if to make his point for him, a shot ricocheted off the ground between the men. It had stopped raining, and the ball

Clay and the River of Silver

left a powdery mark on the flagstones. Both men considered it for a moment. 'We had best keep moving,' said Beresford, 'if only to throw off their aim.'

'I have a half company storming each building in turn, but it is slow progress, sir. The enemy is stubborn, and are generally well barricaded in.'

'Can you not draw off more men to deal with them?' asked the general.

'From where, sir? We are assaulted down every street. I dare not thin the ranks of the defenders excessively, for fear that the enemy may break through.'

The men walked on and passed two Highlanders carrying the body of an artilleryman between them. 'Another gunner,' mused Beresford, turning to watch them adding him to the growing line of corpses in the middle of the square. 'We seem to be losing them at a disproportionate rate.'

'I've noticed that too, sir,' said Pack, flinching as another shot from above passed close to his head. 'These marksmen are targeting our gunners and officers. It is a shrewd play, for it is our artillery that is defeating their assaults. It speaks to me of a controlling mind behind these attacks.'

'I daresay that is right,' said Beresford. 'The enemy seem much better organised than before. They must have found a leader to follow with some understanding of warfare.'

'Stand to arms!' yelled the officer in charge of the next intersection as they approached. The call was taken up by his sergeants as they hurried the men back into a dense, two-deep line blocking the entrance to the square. In the centre of the infantry formation was a single six-pounder cannon. The few remaining gunners were supplemented by a pair of Highlanders on each wheel to help run it up. Beresford and Pack hurried forward to join the officer.

Philip K Allan

'What are you facing, Captain Mackay?' asked Pack.

'A fresh assault, sir,' said the officer, gesturing down the street.

It was one of the wider boulevards that headed downhill towards the port area, running straight for several hundred yards before it bent to the left. Appearing from around this corner was a solid mass of blue-coated soldiers, advancing to the steady beat of a drum. In front of them was a pair of field guns being wheeled forward by a large mass of civilians.

'Doubtless stolen from our artillery park,' commented Beresford.

'Come left a little,' ordered the gunner in charge of the British six-pounder. 'Down elevation a touch. Now stand clear! That means step back,' he supplemented to the soldiers by the wheels, who hastily moved away. 'Fire!'

The smouldering linstock came down and the field gun roared out, filling the street with smoke. The carriage rolled back a few feet, and the crew rushed to reload it while the Highlanders returned, ready to wheel it back into place. The three remaining gunners manning the cannon were painfully slow. One had gone to fetch a charge, another a fresh cannonball, leaving the third alone with the rammer swabbing the barrel out. Beresford turned away in frustration. 'Lieutenant Dalrymple!'

'Sir?'

'Run to the next entrance to the square, and if they are not engaged, bring back more gunners.'

'Right away, sir.'

Beresford returned his attention to the street in front of him. The smoke was only thinning gradually, sheltered from the breeze by the tall buildings. He had just registered that the attacker's drum had stopped, when twin flashes of orange

Clay and the River of Silver

appeared in the grey fog. A moment later masonry showered down from a nearby building, while the second ball bounded through the dense mass of Highlanders and away into the square. One man was killed outright, his body broken and bloody. Another was whimpering, his eyes wide with fear as he looked at where his foot had once been.

'Pull those men from there, and take Cowie to the surgeon,' ordered Mackay. 'Close ranks!'

It seemed an age before the British gun was reloaded, by which time the Spanish guns had fired again, causing fresh carnage among the defenders. 'Where are those extra gunners?' demanded Beresford, as his aide came running over.

'I'm sorry, sir, but the next entrance is also under assault, as is the one beyond that,' explained Dalrymple. 'As those guns only have four remaining crew each, I thought best to leave them in place. I trust I did right?'

Before answering, Beresford was forced to duck down, arms held up to protect his head as another shower of masonry cascaded down from the damaged building. Then he paused to listen and realised that the sound of artillery fire was becoming more general around the square.

'Sailors!' he exclaimed. 'If only we had a party of sailors. They all know how to serve guns. Why, our little six-pounders are like toys when compared to what they are used to.'

'A party of sailors would indeed be useful,' said Pack, stepping back to allow another wounded Highlander to be helped towards the rear. 'Regrettably, the Dons are between us and the port, and in some numbers.'

The remorseless barrage carried on, sending ball after ball up the street. After half an hour rubble was strewn across the road. Then a lucky shot destroyed one wheel of the six-

Philip K Allan

pounder, leaving the gun lying drunkenly on its side. The surviving crew looked around for orders.

'You men, go with Lieutenant Dalrymple,' ordered Beresford. 'He will reassign you to other guns that have need of crews.'

'Highlanders, close ranks where the gun was,' ordered Mackay.

Pack turned towards the centre of the square, where the regimental colour party stood. 'Pipe Major!' he roared. 'Let's have something to cheer the men. Play a reel or jig or the like.'

The sound of the pipes seemed to blend with that of the artillery and the crack of small arms fire, as if it was the surreal composition of a madman. Then the artillery fire from below stopped, to be replaced by the drum once more, its beat urgent, growing steadily louder as it approached up the street.

'Ready lads,' said Mackay, drawing his sword and peering into the dense clouds of smoke that filled the street.

Beresford looked at the infantry line. It was thinner now, thanks to the bombardment it had endured, but seemed steady enough. The drum beat grew louder, the sound multiplying as it echoed back from the walls of the buildings.

'Fix bayonets!' ordered Mackay, and in a fluid movement each man drew out his long blade and slotted it into place.

Still nothing but smoke, but now the beat of the drum was accompanied by the tramp of boots. Then there was something darker amid the grey, coming closer.

'Present!' bellowed Mackay. Each musket was brought up to a shoulder, those in the second rank fitting between the ones in front, so that every weapon could bear.

'Aim a wee bit lower, lads,' growled the sergeant in front of Beresford. 'The enemy is downhill, remember.'

Clay and the River of Silver

Now he could see the Spanish line, their white cross belts showing stark against their dark coats. The drummer boy was in the front rank, beside an officer with a drawn sword, a diminutive figure, his tunic thick with coloured braid. At the sight of the Highlanders standing so calmly to receive them, the enemy advance faltered.

'Fire!' yelled Mackay.

The volley crashed out, filling the air with smoke once more.

'Now charge!'

Immediately the Highlanders were bounding down the street to get at their opponents, who turned and fled, leaving the ground strewn with bodies.

'Halt there! Halt I say!' ordered Mackay, before the charge ran out of control. 'Back to your positions!'

Beresford watched as the Highlanders reappeared out of the smoke, and turned to Pack. 'That was handsomely done. You have a fine body of men, Colonel.'

'Thank you, sir. And now, if you will excuse me, I shall see how matters go on the east side. I believe an assault is imminent there too.'

'Please carry on,' said the general, returning to his position in the heart of the square. Beside him walked Dalrymple, now bareheaded. He looked at him for an explanation.

'It was shot through during the assault, sir,' he explained. 'A spent ball, I fancy, for it made a shocking big hole. Quite ruined it, in fact.'

'Well, let us rejoice it is just your hat and not your head that is quite ruined, what?'

'Yes, sir,' agreed the aide, but his smile was quickly replaced by a more worried expression. 'May I ask a question,

Philip K Allan

sir?'

'Please do.'

'I heard Colonel Pack say that the enemy were between us and the port. If that is so, how shall we get out of here, should circumstances require it?'

'That I don't know, Lieutenant. Which is why we must persevere.'

*****

It was evening now, but if anything the fighting in the city had grown more intense with the fading of the light. Clay looked across the water towards the shore from the entry port of the *Griffin* as he waited for Vansittart to make his careful way down the side. The port area seemed quiet, but the centre of the city smouldered like a volcano. Clouds of gunsmoke coiled upwards, lit from within by the flash of artillery and the prickle of musket fire, the noise an almost constant rumble. 'Poor bastards,' he muttered to himself.

Beneath him Vansittart was tottering along the middle of the barge, making free use of the oarsmen's shoulders for balance, until he collapsed gratefully into his place in the stern sheets. Clay waited a moment for the boat to stop rocking, and then clambered down to join him.

'Shove off in the bow,' ordered Sedgwick, as his captain took his place. 'Take a stroke, larboards. Now all together.' The barge gathered way across the darkening water and headed for the *Narcissus*. The frigate had become a thing of beauty, with orange lamplight spilling from her open gun ports and through the windows at her stern, to be mirrored in the calm water around her.

'Boat ahoy!' came a hail from her quarterdeck.

Clay and the River of Silver

'*Griffin!*' replied Sedgwick, followed by 'Larboard side!' to tell the officer of the watch that Clay wanted no ceremonial when he came on board.

'Good to see you, Sir Alexander,' said Captain Donnelly, her commander, shaking Clay's hand as he stepped down onto the companionway, 'and you too, Mr Vansittart. Pray follow me, and I shall take you to see the commodore. I should warn you, he is in low spirits tonight.'

Popham was slumped in his chair when his guests were shown in, his neckcloth loose and a half-full glass by his side. He was staring out of the stern windows towards the shore, and didn't seem to have heard their entry.

'Good evening, sir,' prompted Clay.

'And what pray do you find good in it, Sir Alexander?' queried Popham, turning to face his guests. 'That the city is thick with rebels, or that all communication has been severed with General Beresford?'

'It was but a civility, sir,' said Clay, his face colouring. 'A courtesy, if you will. Like offering those you have invited to your quarters a seat, or some refreshment.'

'Well, that is mended sooner than the debacle on shore,' said Popham waving them towards the chairs in front of his desk. 'O'Shaughnessy, pray bring my guests a glass of wine, if there is any left in the bottle.'

'Aye aye, sir.'

'Do you see no prospect of our prevailing, sir?' asked Donnelly.

'None at all,' said Popham. 'The forces that oppose us are too great, and resent us too much. Beresford has made a sad hash of things. I did my duty in helping him found New Arcadia, yet after barely a month it is all about to fall. And who, pray, will take the blame, eh? I fear this sorry tale will go very ill for me in London. Very ill indeed.' His eyes flickered across to Vansittart for a moment, looking for reassurance, but the diplomat's face was motionless.

'If I may speak frankly, sir,' said Clay. 'I agree with you that New Arcadia is doomed, although you treat the general harshly. But portioning blame is for tomorrow. More urgent is for us to attend to how we can bring some aid to those poor soldiers in the city.'

'Bring them aid?' scoffed Popham. 'My dear sir, the situation is quite futile. Captain Gillespie reports that there are thousands of enemies between him and Beresford. Simply thousands.'

'Then if it is as hopeless as you suggest, why can we not come to terms with them, while we have something to bargain with, sir?' suggested Clay. 'A free passage out for our people, in return for our immediate departure, for example.'

'An ignoble surrender! Is that your suggestion?' queried Popham, waving his steward over to fill his glass. 'Wonderful! There goes my bloody peerage.'

'What has that to do with anything?' demanded Clay.

'Hah! Says the man with a knighthood.'

'Awarded for attending to my duty, rather than the state of my prospects. To which end, may we return to the situation here. Surely, as a fellow naval captain—'

'Commodore,' corrected Popham.

'As a fellow naval officer, you will be aware that there is no disgrace in striking your colours to save lives in the face of overwhelming opposition, sir. What is the difference in this case?'

'I agree, sir,' said Donnelly. 'Captain Clay speaks a deal of sense.'

'He won't let me,' said Popham, pointing his glass

Clay and the River of Silver

towards Vansittart. 'You heard him as well as I did. When he spouted all that rot about the country's honour.'

'Pray do not seek to shift the blame, Popham,' said the diplomat, pulling angrily at the lapels of his coat. 'You chose to embark on this Arcadia nonsense without discussing it with me. All I did was explain the diplomatic consequences of your action. But even as we face defeat, there is a more pressing reason why we cannot seek terms with the Dons.'

'Which is …?' prompted Clay.

'Which is that any negotiation will certainly require the return of the treasure, and as that is now the sole benefit we have obtained from our being here, I cannot permit it.'

'A very good point,' said Popham.

'But we can't just abandon Beresford!' protested Clay.

'Then what do you suggest we do?' asked Popham.

'We have most of the crews of the *Griffin* and the *Narcissus*, sir. Together with what forces remain to Captain Gillespie in the port area, surely something might be attempted? We need only open up a single street for the survivors to retreat down.'

'Flinging good money after bad?' exclaimed Popham. 'Is that your suggestion? And if the ships' crews are captured too, what then? How will we make good our escape? All we would succeed in doing is adding the capture of two of the king's ships to the loss of a regiment. And in likelihood the transports as well. Then my career will truly be over.'

'Let me attempt something with my people,' urged Clay.

'My answer is still no. Vansittart is correct. The only good to come from this sorry affair is the treasure stored in the holds of the frigates. It cannot be put at risk.'

'Then are we to do nothing?' exclaimed Clay. 'We sit

safe out here on the water, while our comrades fight on? At the very least we should try and get our shipmates to safety.'

'I agree with Sir Alexander,' said Donnelly. 'I have thirty prime hands as well as my marines on shore, and they are not so far from the port. Surely something can be attempted?'

'It will also influence how events are seen in London, sir,' added Clay. 'Would it not be useful to report a limited success at the end of our time here. The Admiralty might view it more favourably than that no attempt was made at all?'

'Hmm, you make an interesting point,' mused Popham. 'Oh, very well. But you are not to go further inland than the port area, and are only to hazard a few boat crews. This squadron must be left with sufficient men to handle the ships should you fail. You had best lead it, Sir Alexander, to see that my orders are followed. Is that understood?'

'Perfectly, thank you, sir,' said Clay. 'Might I suggest I retire with Captain Donnelly to agree a plan?'

'Good idea,' said Vansittart. 'Can I have a little more of that wine, while we await the fruit of their deliberations?'

'By all means,' said Popham, waving his steward forward as the captains left the cabin.

'Are you sure that was wise?' asked Vansittart, when they were alone.

'I don't give a damn if they succeed or not,' scoffed Popham. 'But Clay is right. Making some attempt to save our shore party will look better in London. And you forget the most important reason to let him go ashore.'

'Which is?'

'That the Dons may play their part, this time, and rid me from Clay's sanctimonious presence.'

*****

Clay and the River of Silver

Benjamin Slater came from the new breed of naval surgeons entering the service. He had completed his seven-year course of medical study, one of the innovations introduced by Sir Gilbert Blane, the reforming Commissioner of the Navy's Sick and Hurt Board. HMS *Diadem* was his first posting, and as soon as he had arrived, he had immediately started a regime of cleanliness and better diet for the crew. Although the sailors had grumbled at the change, few could deny that their health had improved. So when Captain Gillespie, the *Diadem*'s marine commander, had been put in charge of the squadron's landing party, he had naturally requested that the ship's talented naval surgeon should come to look after his men. With the prospect of replacing endlessly patrolling the Rio de la Plata with time visiting a new city, Slater was happy to agree. But now he was starting to regret his decision.

The flow of badly injured sailors and marines being brought to him had long since overwhelmed the little room he had been allocated as a dispensary. Instead, he had moved to one of the barrack rooms. Here he worked feverishly away, leaning over a table that had been dragged across the parade ground from the officers' quarters. 'More light here, Tomlinson,' he demanded of the man standing beside him.

'Like that, sir?' said his assistant, holding the oil lamp close.

'Much better,' said Slater, resuming his stitching. 'I am sorry you have had to wait for attention, Lieutenant, but as you see I have been quite overwhelmed with patients.' He indicated the lines of wounded that filled one end of the room, some sitting on the floor with their backs to the wall, others lying on pallets. 'We shall soon have that gash in your leg closed, and then you will have a scar to show your grandchildren, doubtless with a fine tale to accompany it.'

Macpherson grimaced through clenched teeth in acknowledgement, but was unable to speak as the needle, painful as if molten hot, was pushed through his skin again.

'Try and hold still, sir,' continued Slater, his glasses glittering in the light as he worked. 'I shall not detain you long.' He drew the last suture tight, cut it close with his knife, and lay a reassuring hand on the patient. 'Tomlinson here will swab the wound and then bandage it, after which you should take rest with your leg elevated.'

'Thank you for that, Doctor, but as soon as your man is finished with me, I shall be obliged to return to my post. I fear we may be assaulted at any moment.'

'Well, if you must, at least give me your word you will keep the wound dry and clean,' said Slater. 'I do not want to have to remove your leg because corruption has set in.'

'I will do my bes— ahhh! That's mighty fierce!'

'Yes, spirits of wine does sting a bit,' explained Slater, as Tomlinson continued to clean the wound.

'But 'tis wonderful stuff, sir,' enthused Tomlinson, his hands busy on Macpherson's bandage. 'I reckon Old Lofty used to add it to his grog. Doctor Lofthouse that is, your predecessor, sir, begging your pardon. For I never saw him dispense any, yet we was always in need of more. There you go, sir, all done. Shall I help you into your trousers?'

'Thank you, but I can manage,' said Macpherson, getting to his feet. 'You have more urgent cases to attend to, Doctor.' Macpherson indicated where Evans and O'Malley stood near the door, helping to support Pembleton between them. His arm was black with dried blood.

'Bring him over, men, and lay him on the table,' ordered Slater. 'And stay by to help me. I may need you to hold him

Clay and the River of Silver

down. Tomlinson, a bowl of water and some rags. Let us see what we are dealing with.'

'Aye aye, sir.'

'Come on, Ted,' said Evans. 'The sawbones will have you sorted, brisk enough.'

Slater bathed the arm gently to remove the blood, but his face grew progressively grimmer as his washing revealed the extent of the sailor's injury, the butter-coloured ends of splintered bone and the blood that pulsed out freely the moment his torniquet was loosened. 'What is your name?' he asked.

'P-Pembleton,' croaked his patient. 'Edward Pembleton.'

'Well, Pembleton, I am going to need you to be very brave. A musket ball is an unwelcome visitor, and this one has quite destroyed your arm. I shall have to cut it off, but I will be as swift as I am able. First, drink a few tots. It will serve to dull the pain. Bring grog, Tomlinson. Along with the restraints.'

'M-my arm, sir?' said Pembleton, trying to rise. 'No! No! That can't be!'

'I'm sorry, but it is beyond saving,' said Slater. 'You others, help him to sit up there, so he can drink.'

'I don't want no drink!' protested the patient. 'Doctor! I can't be losing an arm!'

'Don't want no grog?' queried Tomlinson, holding the mug up to his mouth. 'Whoever heard of a sailor refusing drink? You may not fancy it now, but you'll be thanking me in a moment. Come on. Down the hatch and into the hold.'

He made Pembleton choke down some of the fiery spirit, and then he was laid back. He continued to struggle but was too weak from loss of blood. While Slater fetched the equipment he would need, O'Malley leant close. 'Easy there, Ted. Try not to struggle. Your man's only after saving your

Philip K Allan

life.'

The surgeon returned, his sharpest knife in one hand, a fine-tooth saw in the other. 'You seem the strongest,' he said to Evans. 'Take the strap across his shoulder, and see he doesn't move. One of you clap on to his arm, another across his chest. Tomlinson, you have the gag for the preservation of his tongue?'

'Yes, sir.'

'I beg you, Doctor,' moaned Pembleton. 'Please!'

'Come, now,' said Slater. 'You won't be the first sailor to be parted from a limb.'

'But I'm no sailor. I'm a lacemaker! I need my hands! Both of them!'

'That is as may be, but unless your arm is gone, and swiftly, the corruption will kill you for certain. Besides, they have machines to make lace these days, do they not?'

Pembleton's retort was cut short by the leather gag being placed in his mouth. 'Hold him firm!' warned the surgeon, bringing the knife down in a sweeping motion.

Lieutenant Macpherson hurried outside as swiftly as his leg would permit, just as the first choked scream rang out. His wound throbbed painfully, and he had a splitting headache, but the rain wetting his hair and face helped to ease that. Then he remembered Slater's warning about keeping his bandage dry. With the memory of the surgeon's saw glittering in the lamplight still fresh, he hurried across to where Russell stood with Captain Gillespie in the shelter of the barrack gatehouse.

'Ah, good to have you back, Lieutenant,' said Gillespie.

'Patched up and ready for duty, sir, thanks to your Mr Slater.'

'Well met, Tom,' said Russell. 'The captain and I were just discussing our situation.' He pointed to the plumes of gun

Clay and the River of Silver

smoke rising into the evening sky from the city centre. The distant sound of fighting was continuous, and at least one building seemed ablaze, adding its steady glow to the briefer flicker of gunfire.

'Have we had any word of how the Highlanders fair, sir?' asked Macpherson.

'None all day,' said Gillespie. 'And it is not for want of trying. I have sent countless messengers through, some dressed as civilians, but all have returned reporting that the general is quite surrounded by the enemy.'

'Do we need messages, sir?' queried Russell. 'Look at all that. I fear it must be going very ill for them.'

'What should we do, sir?' asked Macpherson.

'The last instructions I received from the general was to clear those barricades, but that was last night,' said Gillespie. 'And I am getting no direction at all from the commodore.'

'Then we must shift for ourselves, sir,' said Macpherson.

'Should we not try and break through to the general?' asked Russell. 'What resources do we have?'

'Not enough to attempt that,' said Gillespie. 'I sent some scouts out earlier. They reported that all the roads towards the centre are strongly held by militia backed up by artillery. And half our men are dead or wounded. In truth I doubt we have means to defend this place against a determined assault.'

'Aye, it could easily become a trap, sir,' said Macpherson, looking around him. 'That perimeter wall is much too long for solid defence, and see how it is overlooked? From the church there, and those buildings away yonder. The enemy made ready use of marksmen placed on high against us this morning.'

'Yet do we have a better place to occupy?' asked

Philip K Allan

Gillespie. 'And we cannot abandon our wounded.'

There was silence for a moment as the officers considered this. The rain continued to fall, dripping from the roof above them, and the last light of day faded from the sky.

'I have it!' exclaimed Russell. 'The very place!'

'You have somewhere in mind, William?' asked Macpherson.

'I do. It lies no great distance from here. Certainly close enough for us to move the wounded there. An exceptionally solid building, with the strongest of doors, surrounded by an iron fence.'

'Easily defendable?' asked Gillespie.

'It has no windows on the ground floor, and those above have iron bars fitted. And I even have the keys in my quarters.'

'The city treasury!' exclaimed Macpherson. 'Why it is perfect! Clever laddie!'

'It is also hard by the port,' said Russell, looking significantly at Macpherson. 'When it is daylight, we may be able to signal to the squadron to take off the wounded.'

'Let us get this done before the enemy perceive what we are about,' decided Gillespie. 'We shall need hand carts for those unable to walk, and we can pair up the walking wounded with able-bodied companions to hurry them along. And we should take as much ammunition as we can manage.'

'Right you are, sir,' said Macpherson. 'Let us call the men together and make our preparations.'

Clay and the River of Silver

Chapter 16
Night

A few hours later the gate of the barracks opened a little. It had stopped raining, but cloud still blanketed much of the night sky overhead, and there were few lights showing in the buildings nearby. Russell peered out into the street, listening intently. The sound of fighting from the city centre continued to rumble away, distant flashes against the clouds caught in the puddles left by the rain. When he was satisfied that no enemy was near, he turned and summoned the first group forward. 'You understand your orders, Mr Todd?' he whispered.

'Yes, sir. I secure the first intersection, and if all is well, signal to you.'

'Good. And you have your shuttered lantern?'

The midshipman held something aloft which gave off a smell of hot brass and whale oil.

'Very well, off you go.'

'Nice and quiet there, men,' hissed Todd, and his party of sailors vanished, shadows in the night.

Russell waited for the signal, the thump of his pulse a counterpoint to the bang of artillery from the Plaza Mayor. Behind him he could hear the rest of the column waiting. The gasps of the wounded, accompanied by the sound of quiet orders. He felt more than heard the presence of Gillespie arriving on his shoulder. 'Has Mr Todd reached his position?' murmured the marine.

'Not as yet, sir, but … hold a moment.' Russell

advanced a little out into the street and saw an orange eye open in the dark, blink three times and then vanish.

'There it is, sir,' he reported. 'We can proceed.'

'Right, you and Macpherson lead with your men. I will follow with the wounded.'

'Aye aye, sir. Griffins, with me.'

The two officers set off down the middle of the street, a dim canyon between silent, forbidding buildings. Russell could tell that most were occupied from the occasional line of gold where light leaked out around an ill-fitting shutter, or from the smell of wood smoke in the air. Fortunately, with the rumble of battle still echoing through the city, those inside were staying put. From somewhere behind him came the sound of the wounded, moaning and cursing in the darkness as if it was the spirits of the dead who followed. Further back again would be Gillespie, with most of the remaining marines to act as a rearguard.

'Who approaches?' demanded a voice ahead.

'Friends,' replied Russell, in a stage whisper. 'Lieutenants Russell and Macpherson with a party from the *Griffin*.'

'Anything to report, Mr Todd?' asked Macpherson.

'Nothing stirring, bar a few stray dogs, sir.'

'Very good,' said Russell. 'We shall wait here for the column to close up on us.'

'Aye aye, sir.'

Russell examined the next section of road while they waited. It ran level at first but then began to go gently downhill, to judge from the gurgle from the gutters on either side. Beyond the roofs of the city he could see the Rio de la Plata, a wide glimmering expanse of grey, stretching to the horizon. Out on the water was a constellation of points of light, where the ships

Clay and the River of Silver

of the squadron lay at anchor. He looked at the *Griffin*, filling out its missing details in his mind between the spots of brightness, and felt a longing to be safely back on board, cocooned by her thick sides. Then he was brought back to the present.

'What was that?' hissed Macpherson, staring down the road that crossed theirs. Russell listened and heard approaching voices. Spanish voices.

'Not a bloody patrol,' muttered Russell. 'I thought all was going too well.'

'Perhaps they'll not come this way,' whispered Macpherson.

Russell stared down the street and saw a lantern appear, carried aloft on a short pole. In its light were five militiamen, all with muskets slung on their shoulders, two of them in animated conversation. They were some way off, but were walking slowly towards him. Meanwhile, from behind him came the sound of the approaching wounded.

'The lantern robs them of proper night vision,' said Macpherson. 'But they will mark our column for certain. They must be killed, with the minimum of fuss.'

'But how?' said Russell. 'Their light means they will see anyone approach them.'

'Not from the rear they won't,' said Macpherson. 'We need to set a wee ambush for them. Cold steel only, mind. A couple of my lads are former poachers who can move like cats in the dark, when they choose.'

'Evans and Black are the best of my men in a fight, although I doubt if they can shift like cats,' said Russell, indicating the largest two sailors in the group.

'No matter,' said the Scotsman. 'We need to get into cover swiftly. I'll take this side of the road, you the other. Wait

Philip K Allan

for them to pass before you strike.'

'Right,' said Russell. 'Evans and Black with me. Mr Todd, run back and ask Captain Gillespie to hold his position.'

'Aye aye, sir.'

'Baker! O'Neal!' hissed Macpherson. 'Leave your equipment and bring just your bayonets. The rest of you, around the corner out of sight.'

'Right you are, sir.'

The patrol was still a hundred yards from the intersection when the two officers hurried forward, keeping to the dark shadows close to the buildings. Russell quickly found a cobbled alleyway, black as the entrance to a mine, running between two houses. But there was no equivalent on Macpherson's side. The best he could manage was to go a little further, where a grand mansion was set back from the road behind railings. Here the marines crouched down in the shade of a tree overhanging the pavement.

The passageway Russell had chosen had a stone channel running down its middle, to judge from the tinkle of rainwater flowing along it. He positioned himself close to the entrance, with the bulky figures of Evans and Black looming over him. Gradually his mind filtered out the sound of the drain, and he heard the patrol approaching. The splosh as they crossed a large puddle, and the sound of coughing. Then one of them made a comment and was rewarded by a burst of laughter, shockingly close. Light from the lantern glimmered off the wet pavement, and he felt the two sailors behind him grow tense.

'Might be for the best if Sam and me go first, sir,' growled Black in his ear.

'Very well,' he whispered. 'But await my signal.'

Suddenly lamplight shone directly down the alleyway, blinding them for a moment, and then it was gone as the patrol

Clay and the River of Silver

moved past. Russell inched forward and looked across towards the far side of the street. He saw two figures running up behind the patrol in a low crouch, silent as panthers, followed by Macpherson, limping along in their wake. 'Go now!' hissed Russell, and the sailors were away.

The marines reached the patrol first. The one called Baker came up behind a militiaman who was trailing in the rear of the group, wrapping a long right arm around him and clamping a hand over his mouth. A bayonet flashed in his left hand as he drove it upwards into the man's chest. The soldier jerked once in his arms, and then was still. He gently lowered him to the ground, reaching out to catch the Spaniard's musket before it slipped from his shoulder. Meanwhile, O'Neal, the second marine, jumped past him, closing with another victim, but before he reached him, everything began to change.

One of the patrol turned to speak to the man carrying the lamp and saw Black and Evans lumbering towards them, with Russell just behind. For a moment his face was frozen with surprise, but then he managed a shout of warning, and they all began to turn around. O'Neal's victim twisted free of his grasp, grabbing the arm holding the bayonet. For a moment the pair danced around each other, until the man with the lamp smashed it down on O'Neal's back, and flaming oil engulfed him. With a scream he let go and threw himself down, rolling this way and that in a desperate attempt to quell the fire.

Then Evans and Black arrived, crashing into the group like a force of nature. One militiaman swung his musket up to protect himself, only to have it wrenched aside by the huge Londoner, who followed it up with a series of smashing punches with his left fist. Meanwhile, Black lunged at his opponent with his bayonet, extracting a howl of pain as the blade sliced into an arm.

Philip K Allan

'Baker! Help O'Neal' ordered Macpherson, still struggling to come up to the fight.

Russell danced past Evans and charged, sword in hand, for the militiaman who had been carrying the lamp. Burning oil had spread across the wet ground, and his opponent retreated behind it, pulling his musket from his shoulder, while Russell skidded to a halt, unsure what to do.

'Don't let him fire, William!' warned Macpherson. 'The noise, man! It will bring the enemy down on us!'

Russell launched himself through the flames, while his opponent continued to back away. He heard the click as the weapon was cocked and sped forward as it began to swing around towards him. He ducked low under the musket and knocked it upwards with his left arm and thrust hard with his right. Driven by his momentum, the sword sank deep into his opponent's body. For a moment he was face to face with the man, the Spaniard's eyes wide with fear, glittering in the light of the flaming oil. Then he was falling forward, down on top of his opponent. His sword hilt was wrenched from his hand as they crashed to the ground, and as the musket hit the road, it went off.

Russell crawled to one side, gasping and retching. The muzzle had been close to his ear, deafening him, and he was winded by the fall. He had badly wrenched his right wrist, which throbbed with pain. From somewhere far away he heard Macpherson, his voice muted and vague. It came as a surprise to feel a hand on his shoulder and to see the Scotsman was just beside him.

'How do you fare, laddie?' said the marine, speaking slow and loud.

'I ... I'm all right, I think,' said Russell, the ringing in his ear starting to fade. 'My wrist hurts like hell, mind.' He

Clay and the River of Silver

looked around and saw his opponent lying dead in the mud beside him. The flaming oil had almost burnt away, and in the last of its light he could see the rest of the patrol, inert on the ground, while his men collected their weapons. 'Sorry, Tom. I did my best to silence him.'

'Och, you did fine. Better than me. Thanks to this damned leg, I took no part in the scrimmage.'

'Is anyone hurt?'

'O'Neal is a wee bit scorched, but he'll live,' said Macpherson. 'The rest are fine. Now on your feet, laddie, and let us make haste to be away, while we yet can.'

*****

It was well past midnight before the fighting in the Plaza Mayor subsided. Beresford pulled out his pocket watch and held it towards the smouldering embers of the burning building, but there was too little light for his tired eyes to read it. The house stood on one corner of the square, and had caught fire after it had partially collapsed under the enemy's artillery fire. He had let it burn at the time, as the thick black smoke had helped conceal his men from the sharpshooters that still plagued them from the rooftops. But by morning it would have gone out, leaving his men exposed once more when the sun rose.

'What time is it, Lieutenant?' he asked.

'Two in the morning, sir,' said Dalrymple.

'And we have been up since before dawn yesterday. No wonder I feel so dashed tired.'

'You could catch a little sleep now, sir. The enemy seems to have stopped their attacks for the present.'

'I fear my bed chamber, along with the rest of the viceroy's palace, is quite full with our wounded,' said the

Philip K Allan

general. 'Besides, I daresay the Dons have only paused to regroup and replenish their powder and shot. They will renew their assault when they are good and ready. Let us walk a little to hold back sleep.'

The centre of the square was full of the bodies of the dead, arranged in long lines. To his surprise, Beresford saw pairs of men moving along the rows, one holding a lantern while the other crouched down to each corpse in turn.

'They are recovering any unused cartridges by my order, sir,' said the voice of Colonel Pack from the darkness. 'My quartermaster opened his last case an hour back.'

'Will we be compelled to yield for want of ammunition, Colonel?'

'We have enough to stand another assault, perhaps two, after which time want of men may be more of a dilemma, sir.'

'How many does the regiment muster?' asked Beresford.

'I'm having the count done now, but most of my companies are at half strength, sir,' said Pack. 'While the enemy, for all the hundreds we have slain, seem undiminished.'

'Let us hope that will suffice to see us to victory,' said Beresford.

'Amen to that, sir.'

Beresford next walked towards the cathedral. It was still in British hands, and marksmen from the Highlanders' light company had been using its superior height to make life difficult for the enemy sharpshooters on the buildings close to. The main door was thrown open, and candlelight shone out illuminating the fountain in front of it. The sound of cascading water made Beresford realise how thirsty he was. He tried to recall when he had last had a drink, but under all the incessant Spanish attacks there had been no time. He hastened forward,

Clay and the River of Silver

but found his way blocked by several Highlanders. They reeked of powder smoke and were festooned with their comrades' water canteens, which they were filling. As they noticed him, they stepped back, saluting smartly. 'No, pray carry on, men,' he said. 'Your need is greater than mine, I am sure.'

There was an awkward pause, and then they resumed their work. In the light from the cathedral Beresford could just make out the "71" painted on each powder-blue cover. When the soldier next to him had finished filling one, he paused for a moment and then handed it across to the general.

Beresford took it, drank deeply and wiped the top with his sleeve before returning it. 'Thank you. Might I know your name?'

'Private Douglas Mackenzie the Sixth, sir,' said the Highlander, refilling the canteen and pushing the stopper home.

'The sixth, you say?' queried Beresford.

'Aye, there's a fair few Mackenzies in the regiment, so we have to be distinguished for the muster book, sir. I have four cousins, just in my company. Had, I should say. Only the two now.'

'I'm sorry for your loss, Private,' said the general, touching the soldier's arm. 'Pray carry on, men.'

Next Beresford walked across to the nearest intersection. From the six-pounder field gun with the broken wheel, he recognised it as where he had witnessed the first Spanish assault, an age ago. The buildings on either side of the street were scarred and battered by round shot and one on the corner had collapsed completely. Rubble and broken beams had been pulled into a rampart to give the defenders some protection. Dotted among the masonry were Highlanders, some sleeping, others talking quietly. As he approached, a voice barked out, ordering them to their feet. 'None of that,' snapped the general. 'Pray let the men rest while they can.'

'Yes, sir. Thank you, sir,' said the man who had spoken. He stood to attention, his already impressive figure made taller by his feather bonnet.

'Where are your officers, Sergeant?' asked Beresford, noticing the soldier carried a half-pike instead of a musket.

'There are none left, sir,' said the man. 'Captain Mackay fell a while back along with Lieutenant Fraser. I'm in command of the company now.'

'What is your name?'

'Sergeant Mackenzie, sir.'

'Of course it is,' smiled Beresford.

'Sir?'

'I was just now speaking with a clansman of yours. And how goes it?'

'The enemy pressed us close in their last assault, but we saw them off, sir. That was when the lieutenant was killed. But in truth, our line grows awful thin, begging your pardon. A few more men, or another wee field gun would be a comfort, sir.'

Beresford nodded at this but gave no answer. 'Show me over your position,' he suggested.

Mackenzie led the way forward, and Beresford found himself picking his way through the blocks of stone and stepping over sleeping Highlanders, until he stood looking down the street they guarded. It was littered with Spanish bodies, clumped into shadowy lines, like weed on a beach, each one indicating the highest point a tide had reached. The nearest corpse was only twenty paces from him, lying across a flag he had been carrying. A corner of the material flapped against the cobbles, the only movement among the dead. He was about to turn away, when he thought he heard a different sound. He stopped, his head on one side. 'What was that?' he asked.

Clay and the River of Silver

Mackenzie paused to listen. 'I hear nothing beyond that wee rag fretting in the breeze, sir. Mind, my hearing is not to be relied upon. I've had a deal of musketry close about me this day.'

'Lieutenant Dalrymple, you have young ears,' said Beresford. 'Pray come and listen. From the bottom of the street, perchance?'

The young officer bent forward to listen, just as a faint grating rumble came whispering up the hill, followed by the hiss of what sounded like an order. 'Might it be guns being wheeled forward, sir. And something beyond?'

Beresford stared down the hill and saw a pool of movement filling the bottom of the street. 'Sergeant, have your men stand to,' he ordered. 'Lieutenant, pray find Colonel Pack. Tell him to arm every man he has and send them to reinforce the line companies. Musicians, cooks, even any of the wounded the surgeon deems have recovered sufficiently to fire a musket, I'll take them all. Make haste now.'

'Yes, sir.'

Beresford had barely made his way back behind the crude barricade when there was the roar of a cannon firing from behind him, the flash from its muzzle lighting up the whole street for an instant. He ducked as the ball struck the road short of the Highlanders' position, throwing a cascade of stone shards over him. 'And so it begins again,' he said to himself, as he stood back up, shaking the dust from his coat.

*****

Clay had been expecting the knock on his door. He was sitting in a comfortable chair, with his feet resting on a locker, reading in the pool of light from one of the oil lamps. He had heard the

Philip K Allan

flow of boats as they passed beneath the cabin's run of windows, each new arrival greeted by a lusty hail from Midshipman Sweeney. 'Come in!' he said, laying his book aside.

'Mr Taylor's respects, and the squadron's boats are all alongside,' said a breathless Midshipman Drake, his dirk by his side and his eyes alight at the prospect of action.

Clay contemplated the thirteen-year-old for a moment, waiting.

'Oh!' exclaimed the youngster, just before the pause became uncomfortable. 'And Lieutenant Hunter of the *Narcissus* has come on board, sir.'

'Thank you, Mr Drake,' said Clay. 'Kindly let Mr Taylor know I will be on deck directly.'

'Aye aye, sir.'

'Here is your sword, sir,' said Harte, bustling in laden with weaponry. 'And your pistols for good measure.'

'I hope it won't come to such close-quarter fighting,' grumbled his captain, putting a pistol into each coat pocket, while Harte knelt down to buckle his sword into place. 'This is to be more of a rescue.'

'Aye, but them wicked Dons may have different ideas, sir,' said Harte, sitting back on his haunches and contemplating his captain's feet. 'I wonder if your boot might have room for a knife?'

'No, just my hat, if you please,' said Clay.

Up on deck, he strode across to join the officers gathered in the light of the ship's binnacle. 'Good evening, gentlemen,' he said.

'Good evening, sir,' said Taylor, and then indicated a tall, spare man standing beside him. 'This is Lieutenant Hunter, second of the *Narcissus*.'

Clay and the River of Silver

'Captain Donnelly sends his compliments, and best wishes for tonight, sir,' said the officer, touching the brim of his hat.

'Just his best wishes, Lieutenant?' queried Clay. 'Nothing from Captain Popham?'

'No, sir. I have not seen the commodore of late.'

'Well, thank Captain Donnelly for me,' said Clay. 'I trust he has also sent the boats he promised?'

'The *Narcissus*'s two launches and longboat, sir.'

'With minimum crews, as agreed? We may well need to accommodate large numbers, and if closely pressed, not have the leisure of a second passage.'

'A coxswain, one man on each oar, and two in the bow to serve the carronade, sir.'

'Excellent,' said Clay. 'And what of the transports? They have all provided their contributions?'

'The launch from the *Willington* has just come alongside, sir,' reported Taylor. 'The other transports sent their boats across earlier, sir.'

'Good, then let me share the plan I agreed earlier with Captain Donnelly,' said Clay. 'I shall press ahead in my barge, and go ashore to ascertain the situation and try and contact our people. Mr Hunter, you will take command of the rest of the boats. You will lay off the shore until I send word it is clear for you to approach, or return to Captain Donnelly for instructions if no signal is received. Is that clear? Are there any questions?'

'Yes, I have one, sir,' said Hunter. 'What will we do if we find we have to bring off the 71st as well as the remaining sailors and marines?'

'I will be delighted to be burdened with that problem, but in truth I see no prospect of us encountering more than a few stragglers,' said Clay. 'There has been no word from

Philip K Allan

General Beresford for a day and a night, and now the guns have fallen silent. I pray all is well, but I fear the worst.'

'May I make a suggestion, sir,' said Taylor. 'Goodness knows what you will encounter on shore. Would it not be wiser if I go in your place?'

'Thank you, George, but it must be me,' said Clay. 'Captain Popham insisted on it, and in truth it makes a deal of sense. Only I have the seniority to issue orders to Captain Gillespie, or any Highlanders we encounter. Besides, I shall need you to command our *Griffin* if I should fall. Now, shall we depart?'

'Aye aye, sir.'

The water over the side reflected what little light there was, making the boats clustered beside the *Griffin* seem like dark lily-pads afloat on a luminous pond. Clay hitched his sword around clear of his feet, and climbed down into the barge. 'Make for the shore, Sedgwick,' he ordered, once he was settled into the stern sheets. 'But none too swift, so Lieutenant Hunter and the others can follow.'

'Aye aye, sir,' said the coxswain. 'Shove off in the bow there. Now give way, rowing easy, lads.'

The surrounding dark, combined with the gentle pace, robbed the barge of any sensation of movement. Only sound told Clay that they were in motion. The creak and dip of the oars. The whisper of wake from the rudder. He glanced behind him, to check the other boats were following, and then pulled out his night glass to concentrate on the city ahead.

It sprawled along the bank, marked by the points of light, a dark fretted roofscape against the paler sky. Faint lines of smoke from fires and the occasional church stood out. At its heart was the squat mass of the cathedral, one face lit by the glow of fiery embers. Closer to, he could see the masts of river

Clay and the River of Silver

boats clustered along the quayside. The whole city was strangely silent, as if the residents had recently fled, abandoning their homes with lamps and fires still lit. Then he heard the crack of a musket from somewhere ahead.

'Did you mark that shot, Sedgwick?' asked Clay.

'I didn't see a flash, sir,' said the coxswain. 'It sounded muffled like. I reckon it came from a fair way back'

Clay continued to search but all seemed quiet again. Now they were entering the port proper, with the black silhouettes of boats all around them. He glanced over his shoulder to see that they were still being followed, and then returned his attention to the inside of the boat. 'Silence,' he cautioned. 'There is a slipway off to larboard, Sedgwick. Bring us in there.'

'Aye aye, sir,' whispered the coxswain, pulling the tiller across. 'Easy now.'

The barge ground to a halt, and the crew tumbled out and ran them further up. In the dark behind them Clay could see the other boats resting on their oars fifty yards out, the frigates' ones to the fore, covering the rest with their carronades. 'Leave two of the crew with the barge, and bring the rest with you,' he ordered.

'Aye aye, sir,' replied Sedgwick. 'Rodgers and Abbot, guard the boat, the rest with me and the captain. Bring yer muskets.'

While Sedgwick organised the boat crew, Clay advanced cautiously up the slipway. He felt in his pocket for the reassurance of a pistol as he reached the level of the quay. Slowly he studied the area around him. To one side was a pile of something, fishing nets to judge from their smell. Ahead of him he could just make out the faint outline of a two-wheel cart, its shafts pointing skyward like the prongs of a pitchfork. He listened carefully for any sign of life, but there was nothing save the slop of water and the whistle of the breeze through the rigging of the moored boats.

Sedgwick appeared by his side, a reassuring presence with the sailors at his back.

'Blimey, it's quiet,' muttered one. 'Is the bleeding plague in town?'

'Hush yer noise, there,' growled Sedgwick. 'What now, sir?'

'I had hoped to find Mr Russell close to the water,' said Clay. 'Perhaps we will be obliged to seek for him ourselves. Let us go over there. That dark building is the treasury. Their barracks lies up a street close by.'

But Clay had not gone very far when he heard the bang of a field gun from somewhere distant. He paused again as other guns joined in, until there was an almost constant sound of bombardment. Orange light flashed off the underside of the clouds and fresh plumes of smoke rose above the heart of the city. 'It seems to be coming from near the cathedral,' he mused.

'Aye, sir,' agreed Sedgwick. 'I reckon them Highlanders are getting it again, poor souls. But stay! What's that?'

From a few streets away came a splutter of shots, followed by the crash of a volley.

'Musket fire!' exclaimed Clay. 'And a deal closer! Someone is in trouble! Come on, men!'

Clay and the River of Silver

Chapter 17
Escape

After the Griffins had dealt with the patrol, the column hurried forward as fast as the wounded could manage, hoping to reach the treasury building before the alarm was raised. But they had not gone very far before Russell heard shouts of anger from where they had left the bodies of the slain militiamen. Then came the sound of running feet from a road parallel to theirs. Finally, from the intersection ahead, he saw flickering light washing across the cobbles. He hurried forward with his party of sailors to investigate. As he came nearer, he heard the crunch of approaching boots and the sound of shouting. When he reached the last building, he slowly peered around the corner.

The light was coming from another lantern on a pole, this time supplemented by two burning torches. They were held by a group of militiamen advancing down the street towards him, with more people, mainly civilians armed with knives and staves, joining them all the time. At their head walked a tonsured man in a monk's habit, who brandished a staff aloft with a cross mounted on the end. Russell ducked back into cover before he was spotted.

'What have you seen, laddie?' asked Macpherson.

Before Russell could answer, a shot banged out behind the Scotsman. Looking that way, he saw a man lean out of an upstairs window and fire down into the wounded. Meanwhile, behind the column more flaming torches and lanterns appeared, carried by a large, jeering crowd who had emerged from a side

Philip K Allan

street.

'Concentrate!' urged the marine, grabbing Russell's arm. 'Captain Gillespie's a good man. He'll hold off that mob. Our task is to clear the way ahead. What's around that corner?'

'A dozen militia and some civilians coming towards us. Being encouraged by a priest, if you'll credit it. How can we be so hated, Tom?'

'Don't worry about such matters,' said Macpherson. 'We're in a tight spot and need to get clear of it. How far back was your cleric?'

'A hundred yards when I looked. Less now, of course.'

'The closer the better for what I have in mind. Did he see you?'

'No, I don't think so,' said Russell.

'Then let us use the advantage we have,' said Macpherson.

'Which is?'

'Surprise!' said the Scotsman. 'I'll draw my marines up on this side of the road, you post your lads to continue my line. When I give the word, we swing around the corner like a door on a hinge, halt when we face the enemy, give them a volley and charge immediately. Have your lads follow my lead.'

'Very well,' agreed Russell.

There were now only fifteen marines from the *Griffin*'s original contingent of forty left unharmed, including O'Neal in his charred tunic. This meant their close-order line barely stretched from the pavement to the middle of the street. Russell had only twenty of his shore party left to supplement them, but at least the small numbers meant that Macpherson's plan could be quickly explained. In their midst stood the Scotsman, his claymore in his hand, waiting quietly. Russell placed himself at the end of the line with Todd beside him. He went to draw his

Clay and the River of Silver

sword, but realised when it was halfway out of its scabbard that his sprained wrist would never control its weight. He considered using it left-handed, but opted for his pistol instead.

The torchlight from the advancing mob was growing all the time, glittering on the wet road. The sound swelled from an indistinct rumble to individual voices. He looked across to where Macpherson stood, wondering when he would give the order. Surely the enemy must be almost upon them? Behind Russell the first of the wounded arrived, gasping and coughing as they came to a halt and leaning heavily on those helping them. Another shot rang out from a window, drawing a cry of pain.

'At the double, marines will advance!' ordered Macpherson at last.

The block of redcoats swung rapidly around the corner, with the sailors struggling to keep pace with the arc of men. Russell at the far end had to run. Barely twenty yards in front was the crowd, who stopped in shocked silence at the apparition in front of them.

'Present!' ordered the Scotsman, and fifteen muskets swung smoothly up, followed rather less tidily by the sailors. A few of the militiamen started to haul their weapons from their shoulders, while those at the rear of the crowd slunk away.

'Fire!'

The volley crashed out, the noise booming back from the walls on either side, filling the street with smoke. Both torches went out as they dropped onto the wet ground, either discarded, or because their bearers had been shot, but the lantern burnt on, an orange sun in the fog. The first of the wounded began to cry out in pain.

'Marines will advance!' ordered Macpherson, and the line swept forward. In a few quick strides they reached the enemy.

The volley had been fired at such close range that almost every bullet had found a mark. The street was thick with huddled bodies, some inert, others crying in pain. Among them was the friar, staring upwards with lifeless eyes. The dazed survivors turned and fled, the militiaman with the lantern in their midst, and darkness returned to the street.

'What a victory!' exulted Russell. 'Not a man hurt, and the enemy running like rabbits.'

'Halt and reload, lads,' ordered the marine, before turning to the younger man. 'Steady, William. It was well done, I grant you, but we did no more than drive off a few shopkeepers. With a ruse that I doubt will work again. Now, what's that fellow with the lamp about?'

Macpherson had been looking down the street after the fleeing enemy, to where the militiaman with the lantern had stopped. He was waving it to and fro on its pole. Russell was suddenly conscious that the sound of firing from around them had intensified.

'That's a signal, or I've never seen one,' said the Scotsman. 'Has everyone reloaded? Good, back to the column. Make haste, men!'

In the main street leading to the port, the situation had deteriorated in the time that the men from the *Griffin* had taken to see off the enemy. The crowd behind them had swelled alarmingly in size, and was now trading musket shots with Gillespie's marines. Closer at hand, many more upper windows in the houses that lined the street had been flung open, letting light stream out. Most of the residents seemed content to hurl abuse at those in the street beneath them, but others were throwing more dangerous objects. Russell saw a chamber pot tumble through the air, spilling its contents, until it exploded

Clay and the River of Silver

into fragments as it struck the cobbles among the wounded. From another window there was a flash as a pistol cracked out. He could see bodies lying on the cobbles where other shots had found their mark.

'Mr Todd, go find Captain Gillespie and tell him the way is now clear,' ordered Russell.

'Aye aye, sir.'

'Come on, men,' said Macpherson. 'Resume the advance! Sanctury is near!'

But while the port area was close, the enemy was closer. Progress was painfully slow as the wounded became exhausted. All hope of secrecy was gone and the column ran the gauntlet from those in the buildings on either side. Shots and missiles from above were supplemented by civilians armed with knives, lurking in the shadowy passageways and alleys that opened on to the street. They would wait until Macpherson's marines had passed, before dashing out from hiding to attack one of the wounded. At each intersection there were parties of militiamen, wary of coming too close to the Griffins in the lead, but happy to shoot at those who followed. The column's route across the city was marked with the bodies of the fallen, and still the crowd following them swelled in size.

The road dropped down a gentle slope towards the river, the port with its treasury just one more city block away. It was with relief that Russell saw the houses on either side, with their hostile residents, had given way to more commercial property – warehouses, offices and a custom's building fronted by a pillared veranda. After this was the port, dark and abandoned. Russell sensed the pull of the Rio de la Plata, as only a sailor could. There was a freshness in the air from the open water, even if it lacked the clean salt tang of the ocean. He turned as a large gun bellowed out somewhere behind him, and saw with relief that it came from far back in the heart of the city. Then he felt contempt as he realised what the renewed bombardment might mean for others.

'The poor 71st are getting it again,' said Macpherson as they waited for the wounded to catch up.

'What will they think of our escape?' asked Russell as he watched the orange light flicker off the low clouds.

'They'll feel ill-served, for sure, but will accept it,' said the marine. 'Defeat comes to all soldiers, in time. But what makes you think we have won through? We have yet to reach this treasury of yours. Look to our front!'

Macpherson's advice was timely. The column was still being attacked from the rear. Now a fresh group of militia appeared to block the end of the road. Russell watched as the men were pushed and shoved into a thick line by a bawling officer, sealing them off from the port beyond.

'Trapped at last,' said Russell, massaging his sprained wrist. 'What did you say? Defeat comes to us all?'

'None of that talk, laddie,' snapped Macpherson. 'Form your sailors up to the right. My lads will take the left. We have not come this far to give up now.'

*****

Clay led his men through the deserted port, picking their way amid various piles of cargo, drawn forward by the sound of firing. Off to his right was the treasury building, dark and forbidding behind its iron railings, but from the road beside it came a flicker of orange light. He stole closer and began to hear more. The bang of muskets and another, stranger sound. It was a low rumble, like that made by a troubled sea beating against a shore. He ordered the barge crew to wait, and then made his

Clay and the River of Silver

way forward with Sedgwick. They advanced in a crouch behind a long stack of dressed stone blocks awaiting delivery to some building project. This brought him close to the entrance of the street from which the light and noise was coming. When the two men were level with it, they cautiously raised their heads.

In contrast to the deserted port, the road was alive with people. Immediately in front of them was a thick line of militiamen blocking any access to the port area. Clay was about to duck back down, but then realised they all had their backs to him, and were concentrating on something further up the way. They had only recently arrived, to judge from the way their officer was pushing them into formation. Once he was sure he hadn't been seen, Clay stood up taller, to try and see beyond the soldiers.

The road sloped gently up away from him. Perhaps a hundred and fifty yards further back, facing the Spanish, was another line composed half of marines and half of sailors. Beside him Sedgwick plucked at his sleeve.

'I reckon all them at the front be our shipmates, sir,' whispered Sedgwick. 'That lofty one on the left can only be Sam Evans.'

'I believe you're right,' muttered Clay. 'I mark Mr Russell with Tom Macpherson by his side. I would recognise those black whiskers anywhere. But what is going on beyond them?'

Clay pulled out his night glass and focused past the Griffins, at what was further up the slope. Stumbling towards him was a pitiful procession of wounded. Some were shuffling along unaided, others leant heavily on able-bodied companions. Among them were men who were barely conscious, sprawled on carts pushed along by teams of sailors. In his eyepiece he recognised Pembleton, one arm draped around the shoulder of

Philip K Allan

a marine, the other a bandaged stump. Then he looked further back, where a solid block of scarlet perhaps a hundred strong was facing off a huge mob. He realised that both the strange noise he had heard and the flickering light he had seen came from the crowd. As he watched, all the torches and lanterns borne by them surged towards the marines, before retreating again, like angry waves running up a beach. Then the collective roar of the crowd reached a new pitch, as they saw that their enemy was cut off. This time they almost reached the glittering hedge of British bayonets. Then came the flash and billowing smoke of a volley, the sound reaching him moments later, and the crowd pulled back, leaving more bodies in their wake.

Clay watched for a moment, and then dropped out of view, pulling his coxswain down with him. He sat with his back to the stone blocks, desperately thinking. His foot tapped the ground and his hands clenched and relaxed. If he was back on the *Griffin*, he would have paced the deck in search of inspiration, finding calm in the rhythmical exercise, no matter what madness was going on around him. Instead, he took a few deep breaths, and forced his mind to think clearly, ignoring the crackle of musket fire. Although the port was in darkness, he could see the ships of the squadron out on the water. The wind had moved around towards the north, swinging them so that they were stern on to him. He looked at the *Narcissus* and wondered if Popham was looking back towards him, or was he now dead drunk, being put to bed by his servant. Then he looked at the *Griffin*, thinking of all the battles he had shared with her, and he knew what he would do.

'Sedgwick,' he said, 'go and rejoin the men. Choose a reliable hand to take word to Mr Hunter. Tell him I wish the boats to be waiting at the slipway, ready to take off the wounded. Then return here with the rest of the men.'

Clay and the River of Silver

'Aye aye, sir,' said the coxswain, vanishing into the night.

Clay returned to watching. A lively exchange of fire had started between the men blocking the road and the advanced guard. Several of the militia were down, but the rest were standing firm. Sedgwick appeared again beside him, this time accompanied by the rest of the barge crew. There were nine of them behind the pile of stones, including himself and Sedgwick.

Not much of a force to take on the fifty or so militia blocking the column, Clay reflected. But they were all hardened fighters and would have something more precious on their side. 'Gather in tight, men,' he urged, 'and let me explain what I need. Over yonder are our shipmates, trapped in that street, with enemies hard about them. Between us and them are some soldiers. Not regulars like our Lobsters but militia. Now, I won't lie. They have greater numbers in their favour. So we shall attack them from behind, like when the old *Griffin* stern-rakes an opponent. No enemy can long endure such an assault, doubly so when they aren't expecting it. We move in silence, act as one, and fight like the very devil. No one is to fire until I do. Understood? Any questions?' He paused to look around the circle of dark figures, trying to detect any reluctance, but sensed only determination. 'Very well. Follow me close.'

*****

Macpherson looked at the wall of militiamen in front of him, and wondered when this night would end. The wound in his leg ached, his eyes stung from powder smoke blowing into his face. The breeze must have changed direction, he decided, as he watched the men exchange shots with the enemy. His marines were firing quickly, their hands a blur as they raced through the

Philip K Allan

stages of reloading. By contrast, Russell's sailors were much more methodical. He watched Evans bite the bullet from a cartridge, then pause, trying to remember what came next.

'Powder, bullet then wad, Evans, and keep a pinch to prime the pan,' he told him.

The marine on his other side fired at that moment, and one of the militiamen crumpled to the ground. 'Good shot, Baker,' enthused Macpherson. The space created in the enemy line was only there for a matter of seconds before it was filled by a soldier from the rank behind. Yet in that moment, the Scotsman felt certain he had seen something through the gap. A thread of light and a shadowy movement. He stood perfectly still, trying to decide what it might have been. A bullet fired from ahead passed by his ear, but he barely flinched. 'Light reflecting from a steel edge, perchance?' he mused, and turned to his fellow officer. 'Mr Russell, we should advance.'

'Advance? Are you sure? My men are exhausted.'

'There is something afoot behind that line,' explained Macpherson. 'I don't know what, but if they are friends, we need to hold the enemy's attention on us.'

'Friends?' queried Russell, gesturing around them. 'Do we have many of those here?'

'Did the captain not tell us to make for the port in need? There it lies, man. Just ahead. Come on!' Macpherson drew out his sword once more and turned to his dwindling band of marines. 'A last push will see us through,' he said. 'Follow me close.'

He began to march towards the enemy, trying his best to supress his limp, with his little band of marines to either side and feeling desperately exposed. Several of the militiamen paused in their reloading to watch him. Another levelled his musket and Macpherson forced himself to stride on, even when

Clay and the River of Silver

the flash came and the man vanished behind a puff of smoke, leaving him surprised he was unharmed.

'Come on, men!' yelled the voice of Russell behind him. 'Are we going to let the Lobsters fight alone? Advance now, at the double!'

He heard the sound of running feet, and after another ten yards the sailors fell into step beside him. Now the enemy line was only eighty yards ahead. More shots rang out, and a marine beside him clattered to the ground with a cry of pain, clasping at his leg. Macpherson ignored him as he carried on, searching past the enemy line for any sign of movement.

Seventy yards, and the anonymous row of soldiers ahead became individuals in the flickering light. A tall, thin man towering over those around him. One with a large paunch that distended the symmetry of his cross belts. A heavily bearded face among plenty of moustaches. An order was given, and the firing died out, while some men along the line continued to reload. 'Clever bastards,' muttered the Scotsman. 'Holding back a volley until none can miss.'

Sixty yards, and the Griffins were marching forward into growing silence. The sound of battle still raged behind them, but ahead, more and more of the enemy had completed their reloading. Macpherson felt a bead of sweat run down the side of his face, and raised a gloved hand to wipe it away. 'On my word, we charge!' he ordered, in what he hoped was a stronger, more commanding voice than he felt. The last few of the enemy were pulling their ramrods free.

Fifty yards, and an order in Spanish echoed down the road. The militiamen's drill lacked the precision of the marines or the Highlanders, but there was no doubting the menace of the row of muskets that eventually settled, pointing at the advancing British. Macpherson sensed the line around him

Philip K Allan

slowing under the threat, but the order to fire never came.

The tall man that Macpherson had noticed collapsed to the ground, his musket clattering away from him, and lay motionless. The figure of Sedgwick appeared in the gap torn in the enemy line, jerking free his bayonet from the fallen man and then plunging it into another dazed militiaman. Suddenly the line bulged in several places, as men staggered forward with cries of pain, while those beside them turned to look behind and all broke up in confusion.

'Griffins!' roared Macpherson. 'Charge!' The men quickly ran ahead of Macpherson's ability to keep up with them, but Russell was able to lead them, his pistol awkward in his left hand. Attacked from two sides, the remaining militia melted away into the night, leaving the ground strewn with bodies and discarded weapons.

'Well met, William,' said Clay, appearing in front of Russell and grasping his empty right hand. 'Oh, my dear sir! Are you hurt?' he added, in response to the lieutenant's cry of pain.

'A sprained wrist, sir. No more than that. And I am pleasantly surprised to see you.'

'Surprised?' queried his captain, with a smile. 'I thought we had an agreement to meet here? But let us not tarry. The squadron's boats are waiting for us in the port. But surely, there must be more than these few left?'

'I am afraid not, sir,' reported Russell, his face grim.

'I knew it was you, sir!' exclaimed Macpherson, arriving at last.

'Well met,' said Clay, quickly embracing him, and then becoming bustling efficiency. 'Enough of this, gentlemen, we must be away, before the whole city descends on us. Mr Russell, take charge of getting these wounded to the boats and

Clay and the River of Silver

away. They are waiting by the slipway over there.'

'Aye aye, sir,' said Russell.

'Mr Macpherson. With my barge crew, and the rest of the shore party, can you hold this end of this street?'

'I can, for a while,' replied the Scotsman.

'Good, I must go speak with Captain Gillespie, if he yet lives. I take it he is in charge of the marines holding off that crowd with torches?'

'Yes, sir.'

The wounded flowed past Clay as he made his way up the street. He smiled reassuringly and touched the occasional shipmate from the *Griffin*. Then he was beyond the last of them, and found himself walking alone towards the marines, stepping over bodies and discarded equipment, the noise from the baying crowd growing all the time. A rock came sailing down the street towards him, and he ducked aside, before hurrying forward once more.

As he approached the rearguard, he realised how well organised it was. The soldiers were divided into two formations. One held the crowd back, while the other retreated twenty yards or so. Here they stopped to reload their muskets, and then formed up. Once they were ready, it was the turn of those holding off the mob to withdraw, passing through their comrades, to create a fresh defensive line further back. The officer in charge turned in surprise as Clay appeared beside him.

'What are you doing here, Sir Alexander?' exclaimed Gillespie. 'It is most unsafe.'

'I have come to help get your men back to the squadron's boats,' said Clay. 'The wounded will shortly be evacuated, with your men to follow.'

'Boats, sir?' queried the marine. 'I thought we were

withdrawing to the treasury?'

'Would you sooner take your chances there?'

'No, of course not, sir. This is most welcome. Does it mean we are abandoning the city?'

'I fear so,' said Clay.

'And what of General Beresford's men, sir?' asked Gillespie. 'Are they to be taken off too?'

'Only if they can fight their way down to the port,' said Clay.

Gillespie was quiet for a moment, looking back towards the Plaza Mayor, where the Spanish bombardment thundered on. 'I believe I understand, sir.'

'We must look to the enemy before us,' said Clay, indicating the crowd who were edging closer.

'Indeed, sir,' said the officer, raising his voice to bellow, 'Lieutenant Adams, are the second rank ready?'

'Yes, sir!'

'First rank! Pull back when you are able!'

The crowd had come within thirty yards of the leading marines. Clay saw knives flashing in the torchlight as they were brandished aloft and the puff of smoke as a musket cracked out. There was a barked order, and the British fired a volley in response, sending the crowd scurrying back once more and leaving a few more dead and wounded lying on the ground. The marines backed away smartly, passing through their comrades to take up a fresh position where they began reloading. The two officers hurried down after them.

'You seem to have matters under control, Captain.'

'For now, sir,' said Gillespie. 'The narrowness of our position prevents the enemy from using their superior numbers, thank goodness. But matters will change when we are obliged to leave the confines of this street.'

Clay and the River of Silver

'From there to the boats is a good three hundred yards,' said Clay.

'Too far for us, sir. This crowd will be upon us long before we reach the water.'

'I have my men waiting to support you. Will that not help?'

Gillespie looked back at where Macpherson had organised the Griffins into a defensive line, and shook his head. 'Look at the size of this crowd, sir. Six, seven hundred strong? With more joining all the time. Once we are in the open, they will be able to come at us from every side. It will be a massacre. I suggest you and your men return to the boats and prepare to pick up any of my lads who somehow make it through to them.'

Clay looked at Gillespie for a long moment, until the marine started to feel uncomfortable, but behind his pale eyes his mind was groping for a way out of the dilemma. The crowd were relatively safe, so long as they were confined to the street, but the moment the marines withdrew, nothing would hold them back. But there was something else he was missing, something Gillespie had said. 'Return to the boats,' he muttered.

'I think it would be for the best, sir.'

Clay looked back down the street. Macpherson had set some of the men to bring stone blocks from the pile he and Sedgwick had sheltered behind to create a defensive barrier across the end of the road. It started in front of the customs building and stretched halfway to the warehouse opposite, but was only a single course high. A barrier. The customs house. The boats. They swirled around in his head for a moment more, and then began to slot into place. 'Captain Gillespie, can you time the retreat of your men such as to give me twenty minutes before they reach Lieutenant Macpherson down there?'

Philip K Allan

'I'll try, sir,' said the officer, pulling out his pocket watch to note the time.

'Pray carry on then, but keep an eye on me. A moment will come when I will signal to you, after which you and your men will need to fly with the utmost speed. Do you understand your orders?'

'Yes sir. Twenty minutes of steady retreat, and then pull back rapidly when you signal. What is it you plan to do?'

'Something to keep that crowd off our backs long enough for us to make good our escape. But I must make haste.'

Clay and the River of Silver

Chapter 18
Dawn

Clay left Gillespie and ran down the road, pausing only to look over the customs building. It had a large studded wooden door with shuttered windows on either side opening out on to a veranda, with stone pillars fronting on to the street. He stepped back to look at the upper stories they supported. The royal arms of Spain had been carved into the stonework and there were more windows, all closely shut. Then he rejoined the men at the end of the street, stepping over the low barrier they had created. 'Have the wounded all gone?' he asked.

'The last few are being taken to the squadron now, sir,' said Macpherson. 'Mr Russell has been sending back the helpers to assist with my wee breastwork, although dressed stone is heavier than I imagined.' He prodded the little wall with his boot. 'This will protect little more than our shins.'

'No matter,' said Clay. 'We shall put it to good use. Sedgwick!'

The coxswain came running over. 'Yes, sir?'

'Do all the frigates' boats have carronades mounted?'

'Yes, sir. Mr Taylor ordered them fitted, as did Mr Hunter for the *Narcissus*.'

'How many rounds does each carry?'

'Six, sir. One up the pipe, canister over ball, an' five reloads in case of need.'

'And a twist of slow match, should the flintlock get wet?'

Philip K Allan

'That's right, sir,' confirmed the coxswain. 'The gunner issued some earlier.'

'Excellent. Take the boat crew and run back to the slipway. My compliments to Mr Hunter, and I want all the spare charges brought back here, along with a length of slow match. Quickly, now.'

'Aye aye, sir.'

Clay turned next to Macpherson.

'Now Tom, you've led a few raids in your time. To destroy coastal batteries, bridges and the like, have you not?'

'Aye, that I have, sir.'

Clay indicated the customs building. 'Could you bring down that frontage, such that it chokes the street with rubble?'

For a moment Macpherson was left speechless at the idea, and then he smiled broadly. 'Now there is a notion, sir.' He stepped up on to the veranda and examined the stone columns. 'Only four of them,' he reported. 'I should judge that if either of the two central ones were removed, this whole overhanging part would fall.' He slapped the nearest one. 'Mind, they seem mighty solid. Heaping powder charges up against the base might not answer, for much of the blast would disperse.'

'Unless it was contained,' suggested Clay. 'By large stone blocks?'

'Aye, that'll work! Mr Todd! Set the men to bringing those stones up here! At the double.'

'Aye aye, sir!'

Clay stepped back to watch the Scotsman directing the men, pointing to where each heavy block should be placed. Gradually a hollow box began to grow, with one side provided by the column, and the other three built by the Griffins. Clay idly wondered which church or civic building the stone had

Clay and the River of Silver

been ordered for.

'That'll do,' decided Macpherson, when the well in the centre was deep enough. 'Now reinforce the sides, and hold back a brace of stones to roof it over.'

'Where do you want these, sir?' asked one of the barge crew, appearing with an armful of powder charges held against his chest.

'Stand clear!' exclaimed Clay. 'Keep them back until we are finished! A dropped slab may cause a spark. I am as keen to be back on board the *Griffin* as the next man, but I would sooner not fly there directly.'

'Aye aye, sir,' said the sailor, retreating to where Sedgwick and the rest of the barge crew where gathered.

'Three more blocks, here … here and on that side,' ordered Macpherson. 'Aye, that should do it.'

Clay stepped out into the street to see how Gillespie's men were doing. Two of his marines were coming towards him, supporting an injured comrade between them. The rest had retreated to within a hundred yards, followed closely by the crowd. 'Sedgwick!' he called. 'Bring up the powder!'

'Aye aye, sir!'

The cloth cylinders were much smaller than the *Griffin*'s eighteen-pounder charges his men were familiar with, but as each sailor came forward, the rows of bags began to fill the space Macpherson had left. When only one powder charge remained, Sedgwick produced a length of slow match and his pocket knife, and turned to Clay. 'How long a fuse, sir?'

Clay gauged the distance the marines still had to come, and calculated swiftly. 'The burn rate is five minutes to the foot, is it not?' he asked. 'That should be about right.'

Sedgwick made a delicate cut in the top of the final charge bag, and then pushed the end of the slow match deep into it. He brushed away some loose powder, estimated the length and cut the fuse. Then he gently pushed the bag into a space among the others. Although the sound of the mob clashing with Gillespie's marines was close and loud, it had gone very quiet by the pillar.

'Good,' said Clay. 'Mr Macpherson, leave two men to handle the last few stones, and take the rest to join those at the end of the street.'

'I could stay ...' began the Scotsman.

'No! I need you to organise a defensive line to hold back the crowd. Captain Gillespie's men will be arriving in some disorder. With the enemy hard on their heels.'

'Yes, sir.'

While the others retreated, Sedgwick crouched over his tinderbox. He struck the flint a few times, and then stooped to blow a tiny flame into life. Then he held the end of another length of slow match to it and it spluttered and caught. He whirled it around in the air until it glowed red, and then looked towards his captain.

Clay glanced back at the crowd. The noise they were making was deafening now, filling the street with echoing fury. As he watched, the front rank of the marines fired a volley into them, and then retreated once more through their comrades. After a pause to pull the dead and wounded clear, the mob surged nearer. He stepped across to join his coxswain. 'Light it,' he ordered.

Sedgwick held the glowing end of the match to the fuse. When Clay was certain it was burning properly, he turned to the two sailors Macpherson had left. 'Bring that stone across, and lay it there. Softly now! Place the other one beside it. Good!'

The smoking fuse vanished under the last slab, the sound of its venomous hiss cut off, although Clay still felt sick

Clay and the River of Silver

with fear as he stood beside it. A slight flaw in the burn rate, or a few grains of powder out of place, and the charge might go off at any moment. 'Get away,' he ordered. 'Back to join Mr Macpherson.' The two sailors made off at speed, Sedgwick with more reluctance.

Clay looked at his pocket watch, estimating when he should order the marines to pull back. Too soon, and there was a risk the pursuing crowd would discover the charge. But then leaving it too long might cut off the marines' retreat, or worse bring the building down on top of them. Fortunately, his watch was an expensive gift from his wife and was one of the few in the squadron to have a second hand. He decided on the right moment, and then stepped out into the middle of the street. Behind him was Macpherson's thick line of marines and sailors, all standing to arms, with more joining them as the last of the wounded were loaded onto the boats. Just beside him was the innocent-looking pile of stones. Ahead was the crowd, a raucous, seething mass still held in check. He could see Gillespie, only fifty yards away now, looking expectantly towards him. He glanced back down at the watch, and realised he was trembling so much he could hardly read it. He forced himself to focus on the sweeping second hand. Was that one minute to go, or two? He grasped his right hand with his left and the face became steady. It was time. He pulled his hat off and waved it furiously.

'Marines will pull back!' yelled Gillespie. 'At the double!'

Clay hurried away, aware of the growing sound of boots on the cobbles behind him and the rising tumult of the crowd. He reached Macpherson's line at the same time as the swiftest marines. Then he turned to see what was happening.

The street was filled with running soldiers, with

Philip K Allan

Gillespie in their midst. Close behind them was the crowd. One marine tripped and fell, and the mob broke over him like a wave. There was an eddy of flashing knives and swinging staves, and then they moved on.

'Present!' ordered Macpherson, and all his men shouldered their muskets, pointing them down the street. The crowd slowed to walking pace, unwilling to face another volley, and the last few marines made good their escape.

Clay glanced at the watch. Still a minute to go, and the crowd had almost reached the customs building. In the torchlight he could see the intriguing pile of stone from where he stood. A moment more and someone might spot it and decide to investigate. 'Mr Macpherson!' he ordered. 'I'll have the men advance ten paces.'

Macpherson glanced across at his captain, and then gave the order. The line marched forward, closer to the deadly charge, but the surprise move brought the mob to a halt. A few rocks were thrown, and a man in the crowd's front rank reloaded his pistol, but otherwise there was a tense stand-off. From behind came the sound of Gillespie and his sergeants ordering their men back into formation.

'Captain Gillespie! Get your men to lie prone on the ground!' Clay ordered.

'Eh ... yes, sir!' came the reply. 'You heard him, men! Everyone down!'

Clay glanced back at his watch again. Any moment now. 'Mr Macpherson!' he yelled. 'Fire a volley and then pull back!'

'Yes sir! Take aim ... Fire!'

It was a ragged volley, but it served to fill the street with smoke and confusion. From ahead came fresh cries from the wounded in the crowd.

Clay and the River of Silver

'Pull back, Griffins!' ordered Macpherson.

Figures appeared from out of the gunsmoke they had created, streaming towards Clay, marines and sailors freely mixed together, the upright figure of Macpherson last of all, limping towards him.

'Down! Get down! All of you!' Clay yelled. 'Now!'

Everyone was throwing themselves to the ground, Clay among them. 'See you cover …'

The end of the order never came. There was a flash, bright as the sun, and a deafening blast shook the ground. A hot wind ripped over Clay, snatching his hat from his head and pulling at his coat. Fragments of stone pattered down all around him, followed by a thunderous roar and a cloud of choking dust rushing out of the street.

Clay shook his head, to try and clear his ears, and rose shakily to his feet. Around him was a thick fog of smoke and dust that was settling on the ground like falling snow. He filled his lungs to shout an order but could only cough and splutter. All around him figures were picking themselves up, dust pouring off them. He pulled a handkerchief from his pocket and held it across his mouth and nose. Then he tried again.

'Back to the boats!' he croaked, but his words sounded vague and distant. He began pushing those around him into motion, gesturing towards the port. 'Back to the boats!' he tried again, his voice coming from far away. Now more of the men were emerging from the smoke. The figure of Captain Gillespie appeared in front of him, his hair powdered white as if he was attending a ball, the blood trickling from a cut somewhere in his scalp brilliant in contrast. 'Back to the boats,' Clay said once more, this time getting a nod of agreement. Near him, Macpherson was hauling marines to their feet by their cross belts and sending them on their way, the Scotsman's sharp orders suddenly audible as the hearing in one of Clay's ears returned. He looked back towards the site of the blast, unrecognisable with shattered stone and broken tiles banked like shingle across the road. He half expected the Spanish mob to come surging over it, but the only movement came from the lines of tiny flames flickering along the top of the broken beams. He turned his back on the city and checked around him to see that no one had been left behind. Then he set off across the port himself.

Ahead of him was a mass of sailors and marines making good their escape: dusty grey figures, some limping, others nursing minor injuries, many with torn clothes like his. Then he realised that he could see them clearly for the first time. He glanced to the east and noticed the sky was flushing pink. He went to check the time, but the glass of his watch was shattered and the second hand lifeless. What will I tell Lydia, he pondered as he reached the crowded slipway. All around him survivors were clambering into the boats clustered there. He looked back towards the city but could see no sign of the enemy. When the last of the shore party had found a place in a boat, he walked down towards his barge, pausing only to scoop up some of the water of the Rio de la Plata to pour over his head. Then he stepped into the boat, picked his way through the dazed marines filling the middle, and took his place in the stern sheets.

'Back to the *Griffin*, sir?' asked his coxswain.

'I would like that above all things, Sedgwick,' he replied.

*****

The 71st Highlanders had survived the night too, but it had been a close-run thing. Once it was clear how few gunners the British

Clay and the River of Silver

had left, the enemy had rolled their cannons closer, pummelling their opponents. The defenders had almost come to welcome the bombardment, knowing that while it went on, they would be spared from the waves of infantry attacks. These only came when the guns fell silent, launched up the various streets leading off the Plaza Mayor. Some had almost broken through, with only the most desperate of hand-to-hand fighting driving the enemy back.

Beresford stood in the centre of the square and let the light of a new day fall on his face. He closed his eyes for a moment against the glare, but then opened them again with a stagger as he felt sleep washing over him. 'Wake up, man,' he urged, forcing his aching legs into motion as he set out on another tour of his men.

The rows of dead Highlanders were much longer now. He stood at one end, not daring to count them. A lazy fly buzzed past him, brought out by the departure of the rain, and drawn by the plentiful corpses. He walked on, towards the fountain by the cathedral. One of the regimental pipers was standing in a triangle of early morning sun, playing to encourage the men. Beresford couldn't place the tune but it was a popular one with his comrades, to judge from the number of voices singing along with it. Then the first shot of the new day rang out from the rooftop above, striking the piper in the back of his head. He fell forward onto his instrument, the drones playing on until the weight of his body had expelled the last air from the bag and they faded into silence.

'Sir!' called Dalrymple.

Beresford tore his gaze from the dead musician and turned towards his aide. The officer was a pale shadow of his usual self. He had yet to replace his lost hat, and his uniform was torn and bloody. 'What is it, Lieutenant?'

Philip K Allan

Dalrymple indicated a Highlander standing beside him. 'This man is one of the detachment posted on the roof of the cathedral. He reports that there is activity among the ships of the squadron.'

'What sort of activity, Private?' asked Beresford.

'Boats in the water and signalling and the like, sir.'

'Perhaps they mean to come to our aid, sir,' suggested Dalrymple.

'Perhaps,' said the general. 'Go find Colonel Pack and bring him to join me on the palace roof. The port is visible from there.'

As Beresford hurried across to the viceroy's palace, more shots began to bang out around the square, from sharpshooters on the roofs or return fire from the Highlanders below. Inside there was no relief from the fighting. He went up the main stairs and along a corridor, but every room he passed was filled with wounded groaning in pain or calling out to those tending them. At the end of the passageway was another, smaller staircase that led up to the servant's bedrooms on the upper floor, and then on up to the roof. He stepped out into the morning sunshine, just as the Spanish artillery began firing again, turning the streets around him into smoke-filled canyons. He could see some more smoke, down by the port, although it was thin and was rapidly dispersing.

'More like dust,' he concluded, pulling out his pocket telescope and focusing on the squadron. The ships looked like models, sat out on the smooth brown water. He could see some of the boats that the soldier had reported next to the two frigates. As he watched, one slowly rose dripping into the air and then was swung on board the larger of the two warships.

'What's all this about a rescue, sir?' asked Pack, emerging out on to the roof. 'By Jove, you get a capital view

Clay and the River of Silver

from up here.'

'In truth, I don't know what is going on,' said the general, passing across his telescope. 'The squadron seem to be taking their boats out of the water, rather than launching them. See, the *Narcissus* is lifting one now.'

'The commodore's ship, sir?' said Pack. 'So she is. And now a flag has been raised on her. A plain blue one. What might that mean?'

'Damned if I know,' said Beresford. 'These navy types are a mystery to me, with their bunting and ropes and whatnot.'

'It's called a Blue Peter, sir,' announced Dalrymple.

The other two looked at him in surprise. 'And what does it signify, pray?' asked Pack.

'I'm afraid it means they're going to leave us to our fate, sir,' said the aide. 'I saw the commodore raise that flag before we left Madeira and again at St Helena, so I asked one of the crew about it. It is their way of warning others to be prepared for immediate departure.'

'Departure!' exclaimed Pack. 'But … but what about my regiment?'

'Not to mention all their folk,' added Beresford. 'The marines and sailors … oh! That must be what the boats were for!'

'So they have rescued their own and that is it?' demanded Pack. 'They're off, and the devil may take us. Did you know about this, sir?'

'No, I did not,' said the general, his knuckles white where they gripped the parapet in front of him.

The officers watched in silence as the last boat was lifted from the water, and a fresh line of signal flags rose up the *Narcissus*'s rigging. Then tiny figures began clambering up the shrouds of the ships and the first scraps of white canvas appeared along some of the yards.

'I can well imagine Commodore Popham cutting and running, but I'm surprised at Sir Alexander going along with it, sir,' fumed Pack.

'I daresay he had no choice but to obey orders, Colonel,' said Beresford. 'The navy is not so very different than the army in that respect. But if there is any blame to be attributed it is mine, for listening to that damned man in the first place. One regiment and a handful of marines! We must have been deranged! I ask you, what force is that to hold a place like this?'

'What do we do now, sir?' asked Pack.

'We give Lieutenant Dalrymple here five minutes to clean himself up and find another tunic and hat. Then we fashion a white flag for him and send him to ask what terms the enemy will offer for our surrender. Your men have fought like lions, Colonel, but I see little point in prolonging their suffering now that there is no prospect of victory.'

*****

It took Popham's little squadron a week to pick their way back through the treacherous waters of the Rio de la Plata. Many of the navigation buoys removed by the Spanish had not been replaced, and even the *Narcissus* with her Scottish river pilot had to grope her way as she led the others forward. But in time they reached deeper water, rejoining the ships of the line still blockading Montevideo. There Popham transferred back to the *Diadem*, to a fresh round of salutes as his commodore's flag appeared on the sixty-four from all his command except the *Griffin*. Then the surviving marines were returned to their original ships and Clay was summoned across for a lengthy meeting with Popham. When he returned, he marched straight

Clay and the River of Silver

across to the binnacle, glanced up at the ship's commissioning pennant, and then turned to his first lieutenant.

'Mr Taylor, I'll have the ship put on the starboard tack, if you please.'

'Aye aye, sir. Pipe all hands, Mr Hutchinson!'

'Mr Todd, kindly signal the *Diadem*. "Proceeding as directed".'

'Aye aye, sir.'

The other officers on deck watched the signal soar up the mizzen halliard, while their captain stood lost in thought. When the midshipman reported it had been acknowledged, he turned on his heel with a nod and went straight down the companionway and into his cabin.

Half an hour later, Vansittart was by the quarterdeck rail speculating about their likely destination with Macpherson and Preston, when the captain's steward came and stood in his eyeline. 'Yes, Harte, what is it?' asked the diplomat.

'Sir Alexander's compliments, an' would you join him in the great cabin, when convenient, sir.'

'Which in the navy means directly, whether convenient or not, what?' said Vansittart with a wink towards his companions.

'Aye, that's so,' confirmed Macpherson. 'We'll make a mariner of you yet, sir.'

'How does the captain seem, Harte?' asked Vansittart, as they approached the cabin door. 'He appeared a trifle vexed when he came on board.'

'He's striding up and down like a fox outside an 'en coop, sir,' said the steward, opening the door and standing aside. 'Best of luck.'

'Good morning,' said Vansittart as he entered the cabin. 'You wished to see me?'

Philip K Allan

'Yes indeed,' said Clay, indicating a chair and thumping down in one himself. 'Would you care for a drink? I know I need one.'

'By all means. That would be most welcome.'

'Light along the madeira, if you please, Harte,' ordered Clay.

'Aye aye, sir.'

'How was Captain Popham?' asked Vansittart, once he had his drink.

'Rather distracted,' said Clay. 'He started by moaning about my continued refusal to salute his flag, although only in a half-hearted sort of way. He then ordered me to convey you and his dispatches back home. All of them, of which he gave me a veritable sack. I have never seen the like.' Clay lifted two enormous bundles of letters from his desk. 'To the Admiralty, of course, but he also seems to have written to every prominent personage in the realm. The king, peers, the prime minister, sundry lord mayors; why even the Archbishop of Canterbury has not been spared! What you see here is but a third of his correspondence, if you'll credit it.'

Vansittart burst out laughing at the sight. 'My dear sir, I suppose you know what he is about?'

'Pray enlighten me.'

'He plans on using this ship's admirable speed to ensure that his version of what has happened here arrives several months before anyone else's. And of course, your *Griffin* has the bulk of the treasure in her hold, to sweeten ill tidings.'

'Hmm, that will explain why the interview went on to become so heated.'

'That sounds interesting,' said Vansittart, settling more comfortably in his chair. 'Pray tell.'

'He began by asking to know what my view was of

Clay and the River of Silver

recent events.'

'Naturally, since you will arrive along with his glowing reports of his own achievements,' said the diplomat. 'He wouldn't want you contradicting them.'

'Well, I took the opportunity to protest about the manner in which this squadron abandoned General Beresford in Buenos Aires,' said Clay. 'I said that I completely failed to understand our haste to depart the moment our people were on board. The ships were not in any danger, and Captain Gillespie had shown that it was possible, at a cost, for those ashore to reach the port. I also told him it was a view I would be obliged to share with our superiors.'

'By Jove, did you now?' said Vansittart. 'He was displeased, naturally?'

'To put it mildly,' confirmed Clay. 'But when he had calmed down, he spoke of the night before we left Buenos Aires, when we were all on the *Narcissus*. You will recall that Captain Donnelly and myself retired to agree our plans to rescue our shore party, leaving you alone with him.'

'I do. I also recall he was beastly drunk.'

'But not so drunk that he doesn't remember you telling him to order the squadron's departure the moment I returned to the *Griffin*.'

'He said that did he? Well, I suppose I might have suggested it,' conceded Vansittart, spreading his hands. 'But I am only a civilian. I am hardly able to issue orders.'

'Except that in these waters you speak for the government,' said Clay. 'You must have known that to someone as concerned as Popham is about his prospects, your suggestion might as well have been an order.'

'If I made the suggestion, I was simply concerned about the treasure not being put in jeopardy, that is all.'

Philip K Allan

'Oh, of course,' said Clay. 'The bloody treasure. So in the end, was it all just about the money? All those who perished, did so in little more than a pirate raid?'

'Alex, it was always about the money,' said Vansittart. 'I can see you are upset, but think for a moment. How do you suppose wars are fought? Armies need weapons, navies need ships and men need feeding and paying.'

'Then why did we not leave when we had secured it, for God's sake? It would have saved countless lives, on both sides.'

'I am of your way of thinking,' said the diplomat. 'Popham and Beresford should never have declared this ridiculous New Arcadia.'

'And will they ever be held accountable for it?'

'Popham will be censured, for certain, as it was his idea,' said Vansittart. 'But with his favour at court, I daresay he will not be punished too severely. And the bullion will go a long way towards softening the cabinet's anger. Might I trouble you for a little more of the madeira?'

Clay picked up the decanter from his desk and refilled the glasses. 'Then who will be held responsible for the loss of a fine regiment of Highlanders? Not Beresford, who may very well be dead. Not Popham, thanks to the excellence of his connections.'

'Can responsibility not lie with an enemy who proved too strong?' suggested Vansittart. 'With the citizenry of Buenos Aires?'

'And what lay behind their determination, I wonder?'

'Alex, I grow weary of this discourse. Pray solve your riddle. Where do you believe blame should lie?'

Vansittart found Clay's pale eyes studying him for a long moment before he spoke. 'Does it not lie with you?'

'With me! Have you quite lost your mind?'

Clay and the River of Silver

'No, I believe I am beginning to see things more clearly.'

'This is preposterous!' protested Vansittart. 'You ask to much of our friendship, sir. Explain yourself!'

'How long have you known *Señor* Pueyrredon and the rest?' asked Clay.

'Pueyrredon?'

'Yes, the gentleman who Macpherson says claimed your acquaintance when we first landed,' said Clay. 'The gunrunner whose activities you ignored, to our ruin.'

'If you must know, I met with him in London last winter with Popham,' said Vansittart. 'He and his associates were revolutionaries, and wanted our help driving off the Spanish. It was Pueyrredon who first spoke of the treasure to be found here. As we were already proposing to send a force into these waters to recover the Cape, it seemed that there was a natural confluence of opportunity. And he and his friends proved useful to assist in our invasion.'

'To be discarded when no longer needed?' asked Clay. 'Now I begin to understand the uncivil fury of their reaction. They were strung along as allies with the prospect of gaining independence, only to find they had swapped one colonial master for another. How did you expect them to react?'

'Alex, I give you my word of honour, I had no knowledge of what Popham was planning with his ridiculous New Arcadia. My intention was always for us to leave the city in good order to the revolutionaries. But once those fools had declared their colony, I had no alternative but to go along with it, for the reasons I made clear at the time. Declarations of that sort cannot be lightly tossed aside. We have an empire held together by the belief that our word has some consequence.'

'So you take no responsibility at all for what happened?'

Philip K Allan

'By no means. You are right to point the finger of blame at me in one regard. If I had my time again, I would have used my influence to block Popham's appointment, and insisted on you commanding the squadron instead.'

Clay looked at him in surprise for a moment, and then shook his head sadly. 'What a calamity. I cannot help but think of those poor soldiers we left.'

'Actually, that is only one of two calamities, my friend. The other may be of more consequence. This much is certain. There will be an independent nation here one day, and it will be born with little love for Britain.'

As Clay considered this, there came a sound from somewhere down on the lower deck.

'Are the men singing?' queried Vansittart. 'I wonder why?'

'I imagine because they are happy to be leaving this godforsaken place,' said Clay. 'Harte, pray open the cabin door a moment.'

'Aye aye, sir.'

'I believe I know this tune,' said Vansittart. 'Not the most loyal of ballads, but a fair summary, in truth. But how do they know the nature of your orders already?'

'That, Nicholas, is one of the mysteries of commanding a king's ship,' said Clay.

The song was well-known, for it was almost as old as the navy itself, and the sound swelled as more voices joined in, until the words rang through the *Griffin*.

Farewell and adieu to you, Spanish ladies,
Farewell and adieu to you, ladies of Spain,
For Pipe's received orders to sail for old England,
So we're heading off sharp, before we're beaten again.

Clay and the River of Silver

Epilogue

In the dining hall of Pueyrredon's hacienda, the same four men who had gathered there months before were taking their ease again. The room had changed little in that time. The same glazed terracotta tiles covered the floor. The same cedar beams supported the lofty ceiling, and the same long table dominated the room. But the men seemed different. Not physically perhaps, but in the way they sat, and the confident way they spoke.

'I hear that General Liniers is to be our new viceroy,' said Pueyrredon.

'You heard correctly,' confirmed Castelli. 'Sobremonte is to return home in disgrace, once safe passage can be agreed with the *Inglés*. It is part of the negotiations over a prisoner exchange; their soldiers for some of our men captured at Trafalgar.'

'I saw the regimental flags of those Scottish devils the other day,' commented Belgrano. 'They at least will stay, and look very fine hanging on the cathedral wall.'

'General Liniers' appointment will be a problem for us,' cautioned Saavedra. 'He is loyal to Spain, and unlike Sobremonte, he is no fool.'

'Neither are we, comrade,' said Pueyrredon. 'We have learned much in these last few months, about both defeat and victory. I, for one, feel twice the man I was, now that I have led men in battle.'

Philip K Allan

'Well said,' agreed Belgrano, banging the table. 'We have learned a salutary lesson, my friends. We thought we could rely on an outside power to win us our freedom, and found we had invited the very devil into our house. If we truly want to be free, we must fight for it ourselves. No one else will do so for us.'

'Agreed,' said Castelli. 'And I believe it will not be so difficult, now that the mystique of Spanish rule has been broken. If so few *Inglés* can conquer Buenos Aires, what might the people not accomplish, with us to led them?'

'Gentlemen,' said Pueyrredon, raising his glass. 'Then let us drink to the future. To the United Provinces of the Rio de la Plata!'

'You know, I have never really liked that name,' said Castelli, once the toast had been drunk. 'The Rio de la Plata is just a small part of our country. We should choose a name that includes everyone, wherever they live.'

'Very well. Does anyone have a better name to suggest?' asked Pueyrredon.

'I was born here, but my family originally came from Genoa,' said Belgrano. 'My father always called this place the land of silver, which sounds well in Italian. Argentina.'

'Argentina,' repeated Castelli. 'It does have a certain ring to it. Why not?'

The End

Historical Note from the author

Those familiar with my work will be aware that my novels are a blend of the truth with the made up, and *Clay and the River of Silver* is no exception. These notes are for readers who would like to understand where the boundary lies between the two.

Alexander Clay, the *Griffin* and her crew are fictional, as are the ships and crews of the *Willemstad* and the *Cape Allerton*. Likewise, Lower Staverton and Polwith are also made up. All other places and ships mentioned are historical, although I have modified some of the detail for the purposes of my story. Popham's squadron did have a thirty-eight-gun frigate, the *Leda*, which I have replaced with the *Griffin*. The two forty-gun French frigates *Valeureuse* and *Volontaire* were based at the Cape, but my battle between the *Volontaire* and the Griffin is fictional. The *Volontaire* was captured after she was chased into Cape Town, having been fooled by the British garrison continuing to fly Dutch flags. She did have a contingent of soldiers from the 54th West Norfolk regiment on board that had been captured some months before. The *Valeureuse*'s career ended when she was so badly damaged in a storm that she had to be broken up as uneconomical to repair.

There were South American revolutionaries in London at the time of my book lobbying the British government to intervene on their side, although Juan Martin de Pueyrredon was not among them. One of the more active was the Venezuelan freedom fighter Francisco Miranda, known as "*El Precursor*", who was supported by his friend, Captain Popham. Although Nicholas Vansittart is a historical character, he is not known to have been involved with South American politics, and did not take part in the events in this book.

My description of the expedition to retake the Cape of Good Hope is largely correct in terms of the regiments, the senior officers and ships involved. I pushed back its departure from Madeira, so that Clay could credibly be both at Trafalgar (see *Clay and the Immortal Memory*) and take part in this campaign. A frigate, the *Narcissus*, was sent ahead to reconnoitre the Cape, and did fight with and defeat the French ship *Napoleon*. It never visited Namibia's Skeleton Coast, to this day, a fascinating graveyard of ancient wrecks. Captain De Bruyn is also fictional, although the attitudes he expresses in my book are typical of many Cape Dutch at the time.

I simplified my account of the invasion of the Cape by omitting various diversions to confuse the Dutch, and several delays caused by the notoriously difficult surf on the Atlantic coast of South Africa. The Battle of Blaauwberg was won by General Baird, but without the assistance of any naval eighteen-pounders. It was some of the general's soldiers that became unwell after eating raw ostrich eggs. The cottage where Lieutenant-Colonel von Prophalow and General Baird negotiated the treaty of surrender has since been demolished, but the tree under which they sat can still be found in the Cape Town suburb of Woodstock. While the *Cape Allerton* is fictitious, an American merchant vessel commanded by a Captain Waine did arrive in Cape Town shortly after the British occupation, with a message for Captain Popham from Buenos Aires.

Captain Home Riggs Popham was one of the Royal Navy's more controversial figures. On the one hand, he was a talented surveyor and chart maker, who gave the navy the signalling system that Nelson used at Trafalgar. On the other hand, he was thoroughly disliked by most of his brother officers. His avaricious love of money saw him prosecuted early in his career for sharp practice, and he almost certainly stole part of the bullion seized at Buenos Aires. He was exceptionally ambitious, and cultivated a friendship with the Duke of York, brother of George III, to clamber up the naval hierarchy over the heads of more deserving officers. This was deeply resented in the navy, not least because Popham had seen very little enemy action in his career. Typical of his behaviour is that during the events in this book, he did indeed insist on his subordinates treating him as a commodore, a rank to which he had no right.

The British invasion of South America in 1806 is one of the stranger events of the Napoleonic Wars. That such a tiny force succeeded in capturing Buenos Aires, with minimal loss of life, makes it even more remarkable. In general terms, the invasion followed the path set out in my book. For simplicity, I have combined two small battles fought between the Spanish and British prior to the capture of Buenos Aires into one action. The city then surrendered with little resistance after Viceroy Rafael de Sobremonte abandoned it. The contents of the treasury had previously been moved to the town of Luján, where it was recovered by a detachment of the 71st Highlanders, although it was never hidden in a monastery.

Things began to go wrong for the invaders when Popham and Beresford issued a proclamation, declaring the city and the surrounding area to be a British territory called New Arcadia. Up until this point the local population had been either supportive or at least indifferent to the invaders. The declaration changed all that, with supporters of an independent Rio de la Plata becoming active opponents. Prominent among these were Pueyrredon, Castelli, Belgrano and Saavedra. Initial resistance used guerilla tactics within the city, including an attempt to tunnel under and blow up a barracks, only discovered when a dropped ramrod vanished through a floor. Meanwhile, in the countryside, landowners like Pueyrredon were raising and training armed militia. Although the British continued to win victories, such as the Battle of Perdiel, each success left them weaker than before. When General Liniers arrived with a force of regular Spanish troops to take charge, the writing was on the wall. Surrounded in the Plaza Mayor, Beresford's men fought heroically for several days until forced to surrender. No rescue attempt of the kind Clay organised took place, and two hundred Royal Marines and a hundred and fifty Royal Navy sailors were captured along with their army colleagues. After the loss of Buenos Aires, Popham sailed away to rejoin the rest of his squadron blockading Montevideo. The British occupation had lasted for less than two months.

There is some controversy as to why the attack on the Rio de la Plata took place. The official position at the time was that Popham was a rogue commander who was acting without orders. After New Arcadia failed, Popham was removed from his command and sent home to be tried by court-martial for abandoning his mission at the Cape of Good Hope. But history is seldom so straight forward.

There were certainly some in the government who were sympathetic to a British intervention, including the prime minister. And if Popham was really acting on his own initiative, how did he manage to persuade the cautious General Baird to support the attempt? In the interests of simplicity, I omitted that Popham's squadron stopped at St Helena on the way to the Rio de la Plata, where the governor also agreed to contribute some of his garrison. Would two such senior men have weakened their commands if they thought that Popham was acting without orders? Furthermore, if London was really against any British invasion, then Popham was an unwise choice as naval commander. He was a known supporter of South American revolutionaries, and had written several letters to the government calling for British intervention. But Popham was an excellent choice if a scapegoat might be required to take the blame for failure, since his unpopularity in the navy meant that few of his colleagues would come to his defence.

A more plausible scenario is that he was encouraged, probably unofficially, by a government interested, at the very least, in securing the bullion in Buenos Aires. It is this more ambiguous political background that I have sought to show in *Clay and the River of Silver*. All might have been well if Popham and Beresford had not assumed that a lack of local enthusiasm for Spanish rule meant the same as support for rule by Britain.

Although my story ends with Clay and the crew of the *Griffin* returning home, some readers may be interested in what became of the historical characters I feature. Popham's court-martial resulted in him being "severely reprimanded" (the military equivalent of a slap on the wrist and a suspiciously lenient result that did little harm to his future career). The City of London later bestowed upon him a sword of honour for his efforts to "open up new markets for Britain."

Beresford and Pack spent a short while in Spanish captivity, before escaping the following year to join a second British expedition to the Rio de la Plata that was besieging Montevideo. Both men went on to have distinguished military careers. Pack fought throughout the Peninsular War under Wellington, and was a brigade commander at Waterloo. Beresford was appointed as commander in chief of the Portuguese army. In this role he oversaw the retraining and re-equipping of its regiments along British lines, providing an invaluable part of the army Wellington used to drive the French out of the Iberian Peninsula.

The soldiers and sailors that were left behind in Buenos Aires spent rather longer as prisoners, but were ultimately returned to Britain. In 1810 the 71st Highlanders were reconstituted as the 71st Highland Light Infantry, and fought throughout the rest of the Napoleonic Wars with distinction.

The relative ease with which the British captured Buenos Aires exposed the fragility of Spanish colonial control. In May 1810, the United Provinces of the Rio de la Plata declared independence from Spain, with Pueyrredon, Castelli, Belgrano and Saavedra prominent among the leaders of the revolution. It was to be a short-lived entity, thanks to tensions between Buenos Aires and Montevideo. After further bouts of fighting, the north bank of the Rio de la Plata became Uruguay, while the rest became a new state called Argentina.

Books by Philip K Allan

The Alexander Clay Series

The Captain's Nephew

A Sloop of War

On the Lee Shore

A Man of No Country

The Distant Ocean

The Turn of the Tide

In Northern Seas

Larcum Mudge

Upon the Malabar Coast

Clay and the Immortal Memory

Clay and the River of Silver

World War 2

Sea of Wolves

The Wolves in Winter

About the Author

Philip K Allan comes from Hertfordshire in the United Kingdom where he lives with his wife and daughters. He has an excellent knowledge of the 18th century navy. He studied it as part of his history degree at London University, which awoke a lifelong passion for the period. A longstanding member of the Society for Nautical Research, he also writes for the US Naval Institute's magazine *Naval History*.

He is author of the Alexander Clay series of naval fiction. The first book in the series, *The Captain's Nephew*, was published in January 2018, and immediately went into the Amazon top 100 bestseller list for Sea Adventures. The sequel, *A Sloop of War*, was similarly well received, winning the Discovered Diamonds Book of the Month Award. He has now published thirteen novels, including two set in the Second World War.

If you want to find out more about him or his books, the links below may be helpful.

Website: www.philipkallan.com

Facebook & Twitter: @philipkallan

Instagram: @philipkallanauthor

About the Cover

The cover artwork for this book was commissioned from the talented marine artist Colin M Baxter. If you would like to acquire a signed reproduction of this picture or to see any of his other work, please contact Colin direct.

Colin M Baxter Marine Artist

Telephone: +44 (0)2392 525014

Email: colinmbaxter@hotmail.co.uk

Website: www.colinmbaxter.co.uk

Printed in Great Britain
by Amazon